D0540429

SHRINES OF GAIETY

SHRINES OF GAIETY

Kate Atkinson

doubleday

TRANSWORLD PUBLISHERS
Penguin Random House, One Embassy Gardens,
8 Viaduct Gardens, London SW11 7BW
www.penguin.co.uk

Transworld is part of the Penguin Random House group of companies
whose addresses can be found at global.penguinrandomhouse.com

Penguin
Random House
UK

First published in Great Britain in 2022 by Doubleday
an imprint of Transworld Publishers

A CIP catalogue record for this book
is available from the British Library.

ISBNs 9780857526557 (hb)
9780857526564 (tpb)

Typeset in 11.5/15pt Goudy by Jouve (UK), Milton Keynes
Printed and bound in Great Britain by Clays Ltd, Elcograf S.p.A.

The authorized representative in the EEA is Penguin Random House Ireland,
Morrison Chambers, 32 Nassau Street, Dublin D02 YH68.

Penguin Random House is committed to a sustainable future
for our business, our readers and our planet. This book is made
from Forest Stewardship Council® certified paper.

MIX
Paper from
responsible sources
FSC® C018179

For Peter Straus

Every morning, every evening,
Ain't we got fun?
Not much money, oh, but honey!
Ain't we got fun?

1926

Holloway

'Is it a hanging?' an eager newspaper delivery boy asked no one in particular. He was short, just thirteen years old, and was jumping up and down in an effort to obtain a better view of whatever it was that had created the vaudeville atmosphere. It wasn't much past dawn and there was still hardly any light in the sky, but that had not failed to deter a party crowd of motley provenance from gathering outside the gates of Holloway prison. Half of the throng were up early, the other half seemed not to have been to bed yet.

Many of the congregation were in evening dress – the men in dinner jackets or white tie and tails, the women shivering in flimsy backless silk beneath their furs. The boy could smell the tired miasma of alcohol, perfume and tobacco that drifted around them. Toffs, he thought. He was surprised that they were happily rubbing shoulders with lamplighters and milkmen and early shift-workers, not to mention the usual riff-raff and rubber-neckers who were always attracted by the idea of a show, even if they had no idea what it might be. The boy did not count himself amongst the latter number. He was merely a curious bystander to the follies of the world.

'Is it? A hanging?' he persisted, tugging at the sleeve of the nearest toff – a big, flushed man with an acrid cigar plugged in his mouth and an open bottle of champagne in his hand. The boy supposed that the man must have begun the evening in pristine condition, but now the stiff white front of his waistcoat was stained with little dots and splashes of food and the shiny patent of his shoes had a smattering of vomit. A red carnation, wilted by the night's excesses, drooped from his buttonhole.

'Not at all,' the toff said, swaying affably. 'It's a cause for festivities. Old Ma Coker is being released.'

The boy thought that Old Ma Coker sounded like someone in a nursery rhyme.

A woman in a drab gaberdine on his other side was carrying a piece of cardboard that she held in front of her like a shield. The boy had to crane his neck to read what was written on it. A furious pencil hand had scored into the cardboard, *The labour of the righteous tendeth to life: the fruit of the wicked to sin. Proverbs 10:16.* The boy mouthed the words silently as he read them, but he made no attempt to decipher the meaning. He had been press-ganged into Sunday School attendance every week for ten years and had managed to pay only cursory attention to the subject of sin.

'Your very good health, madam,' the toff said, cheerfully raising the champagne bottle towards the drab woman and taking a swig. She glowered at him and muttered something about Sodom and Gomorrah.

The boy wormed his way forward to the front of the crowd, where he had a good view of the imposing gates – wooden with iron studs, more suited to a medieval fortress than a women's prison. If there had been three of the boy, each standing on the shoulders of the one below, like the Chinese acrobats he had seen at the Hippodrome, then the one at the peak might have just reached the arched apex of the doors. Holloway had an air of romance for the boy. He imagined beautiful, helpless girls trapped inside its thick stone walls, waiting to be saved, primarily by himself.

On hand to document the excitement was a photographer from the *Empire News*, identified by a card stuck jauntily in his hatband. The boy felt a kinship – they were both in the news business, after all. The photographer was taking a group portrait of a bevy of 'beauties'. The boy knew about such young women because he was not above leafing through the *Tatlers* and *Bystanders* that he pushed through letterboxes once a week.

The beauties – unlikely in this neighbourhood – were posing in front of the prison gates. Three looked to be in their twenties and sported plush fur against the early-morning cold, the fourth – too young to be a beauty – was in a worsted school coat. All four were striking elegant poses as if for a fashion plate. None of them seemed a stranger to the admiring lens. The boy was smitten. He was easily smitten by the female form.

The photographer transcribed the beauties' names into a notebook he excavated from a pocket somewhere so that they could be identified faithfully in the paper the next day. Nellie Coker had a hold on the pictures editor. An indiscretion of some kind on his part, the photographer presumed.

'Ho there!' he shouted to someone unseen. 'Ramsay, come on! Join your sisters!'

A young man appeared and was brought into the huddle. He seemed reluctant but gave a rictus grin on cue for the camera flash.

Then, with no fanfare, a small door set into the great gates of the prison was opened and a short, owlish woman emerged, blinking at the oncoming light of freedom. The crowd cheered, mainly the toffs, shouting things like, 'Well done, old girl!' and 'Welcome back, Nellie!' although the boy also heard the cry 'Jezebel!' go up from somewhere in the middle of the crowd. He suspected the drab gaberdine.

Nellie Coker seemed lacklustre and the boy could see no likeness to what he had heard of Jezebels. She was almost dwarfed by the enormous bouquet of white lilies and pink roses that was thrust into her arms. One of the beauties was carrying a large fur coat which she threw around the released prisoner as if she were trying to smother a fire. The boy's mother had done much the same thing when his baby sister had fallen in the grate, her loose smock catching the flames. They had both survived, with only a little scarring as a reminder.

The beauties crowded around, hugging and kissing the

woman – their mother, the boy surmised. The younger one clung to her in what in the boy's opinion was a rather hammy fashion. He was a connoisseur of the theatrical, his round took him to all the stage doors of the West End. At the Palace Theatre, the stage doorman, a cheerful veteran of the Somme, let him slip into the gods for free during matinée performances. The boy had seen *No, No, Nanette* five times and was quite in love with Binnie Hale, the luminous star of the show. He knew all the words to 'Tea for Two' and 'I Want to Be Happy' and would happily sing them, if requested. There was one scene in the show where the chorus and Binnie (the boy felt that he had seen her enough times for this familiarity) came on the stage in bathing costumes. It was thrillingly scandalous and the boy's eyes nearly popped out of his head every time he witnessed it.

As a drawback, in order to gain free entry he had to listen to the long-winded wartime reminiscences of the doorman, as well as admiring his collection of Blighty wounds. The boy had been one when the war began and, like sin, it meant nothing to him yet.

Ramsay, Nellie's second son, was made to relieve his mother of the burden of the bouquet and was caught by the photographer holding the flowers like a blushing bride. To the annoyance of his sisters (and himself too), this would turn out to be the photograph that graced the newspaper the next morning, beneath the heading SON OF NOTORIOUS SOHO NIGHTCLUB PROPRIETOR NELLIE COKER GREETS HIS MOTHER ON HER RELEASE FROM PRISON. Ramsay hoped for fame for himself, not as an adjunct of his mother's celebrity. He started to sneeze in response to the flowers, a rapid volley of *atishoo-atishoo-atishoo*, and the newspaper delivery boy heard Nellie say, 'Oh, for heaven's sake, Ramsay, pull yourself together,' which was the kind of thing the boy's own mother said.

'Come along, Ma,' one of the bevy said. 'Let's go home.'

'No,' Nellie Coker said resolutely. 'We shall go to the Amethyst. And celebrate.' The pilot was taking the helm.

*

The crowd began to melt and the newspaper boy continued on his way, his spirits lifted by having been a witness to something historic. He suddenly remembered an apple, old and wrinkled, that he had squirrelled away first thing that morning. He retrieved it from his pocket and chomped on it like a horse. It was wonderfully sweet.

The toff with the cigar spotted him and said, 'Good show, eh?' as if he valued his opinion, and then cuffed him amiably on the side of his head and rewarded him with a sixpence. The boy danced happily away.

As he left, he heard someone in the crowd yelling, 'Thief!' It was a term that could have applied to any of them really, except perhaps the man who had been watching the proceedings from a discreet distance, in the back of an unmarked car. Detective Chief Inspector John Frobisher – 'Frobisher of the Yard' as *John Bull* magazine had styled him, although somewhat inaccurately as he was currently on loan to Bow Street station in Covent Garden, where he had been sent to 'shake things up a bit'. Corruption was acknowledged to be rife there and he had been tasked with seeking out the bad apples in the barrel.

John Bull had recently asked Frobisher to write a series of articles based on his experiences in the force, with a view to making them into a book. Frobisher was not a narcissist – far from it – but he had been enlivened by the proposition. He had always been a books man and a literary challenge was something that took his fancy. Now, however, he was not so sure. He had suggested it be called *London After Dark*, but the magazine said they preferred the title *Night in the Square Mile of Vice*. He didn't know why he had been surprised by this when every cheap rag howled with lurid tales of foreign men seducing women into venality of one kind or another, when in reality they were more at risk of having their handbags torn from their arms in broad daylight.

Nothing had yet been published, but every time he submitted something to *John Bull* they asked him to make it racier, more 'sensational'. Racy and sensational were not part of Frobisher's character. He was sober-minded, although not without depth or humour, neither of which was often called on by the Metropolitan Police.

He was idly following the progress of a couple of women who were stealthily working their way through the crowd, skilfully picking pockets. Frobisher recognized them as subalterns in the female Forty Thieves gang, but they were comparatively small fry and of no interest to him at the moment.

A pair of cream-and-black Bentleys – one owned, one rented for effect – drew up and the Coker clan divided themselves between them and drove away, waving as if they were royalty. Crime paid, fighting it didn't. Frobisher felt his law-abiding bile rising while he had to quash a pang of envy for the Bentleys. He was in the process of purchasing his own modest motor, an unshowy Austin Seven, the Everyman of cars.

The delinquent Coker empire was a house of cards that Frobisher aimed to topple. The filthy, glittering underbelly of London was concentrated in its nightclubs, and particularly the Amethyst, the gaudy jewel at the heart of Soho's nightlife. It was not the moral delinquency – the dancing, the drinking, not even the drugs – that dismayed Frobisher. It was the girls. Girls were disappearing in London. At least five he knew about had vanished over the last few weeks. Where did they go? He suspected that they went in through the doors of the Soho clubs and never came out again.

He turned to the woman sitting next to him on the back seat of the unmarked car and said, 'Have you had a good look at them, Miss Kelling? And do you think that you can do what I'm asking of you?'

'Absolutely, Chief Inspector,' Gwendolen said.

The Queen of Clubs

At the Amethyst, Freddie Bassett, the head barman, presented another oversized floral offering to Nellie. 'Welcome home, Mrs Coker,' he said. No 'Nellie' for him, he never cheapened himself by being anything less than formal with the family. He had his standards. He had trained at the Ritz before losing his post there due to an unfortunate incident involving two chambermaids and a linen cupboard. 'You can imagine the rest,' he said to Nellie when he applied for the job at the Amethyst. 'I'd rather not,' she said.

Nellie disliked flowers, considering them to be too needy. They should be reserved for weddings and funerals in her opinion, and not her own, thank you very much. Nellie wished to leave the world unadorned, as she had entered it, with not so much as a daisy.

Instead of flowers, she would rather be given a box of cakes from Maison Bertaux around the corner in Greek Street – chocolate éclairs or rum babas, preferably both. She had a terrific sweet tooth, acquired from the soor plooms and Hawick balls of her Scottish childhood. The food had been the worst thing about prison. Her daughters had brought boiled sweets for her on visiting days in Holloway. Nellie had acquired many thoughts on prison reform during the course of her sentence and top of the list would be a tuppence worth weekly allowance of sweets – marshmallows and coconut ice, for preference.

When she entered Holloway six months ago, the staff of the

9

Amethyst had sent her a cornucopia befitting a harvest festival –
a large bouquet of flowers and a basket of fancy fruits that had
been composed by a Covent Garden trader who was a regular
patron of the club. The staff had badged it with the words *Good
Luck*, the letters cut out from fancy embossed silver card that
had been rummaged from the obscure cupboard that housed the
club's New Year decorations.

This extravagance had been removed by a wardress as soon as
Nellie stepped inside the forbidding walls, and the exotica of
pineapple, peaches and figs had been divvied out between the
staff while Nellie dined on meagre prison fare – a regular round
of pea soup, suet pudding and beef stew, a rancid dish that had
never met the cow it claimed to be acquainted with.

Before Nellie went to sleep that first night, a flower – a rose, a
red one plucked from the bouquet – was poked through the
hatch in her cell door. It was unclear to Nellie what spirit it had
been given in – contemptuous or consoling. Her cellmate, a Belgian woman who had shot her lover, was less confused. She
snatched the rose and stamped it beneath her boots until the
petals stained the cold stones of their cell floor.

The club had only just closed and most of the staff had stayed
on to pipe their captain back on board, although the band had
packed up and gone (they clung stubbornly to their autonomy).
They had played 'God Save the King' over an hour ago, the final
heroic survivors of the night swaying to attention. Nellie was
strict (her rules were adhered to even more strictly when she
was *in absentia*) – no one sat for the King, not even the most
inebriated. Now only a couple of regulars lingered, amiably dipso-
maniac boulevardiers, adding to the chorus of pages, porters,
waiters and the breakfast chef who all echoed Freddie: 'Welcome back, Mrs Coker.'

They had just endured an unusually heated midweek evening
when every second person seemed fresh from a rugger match or
a Varsity drinking club. A clutch of weary dance hostesses fussed

around Nellie. Close up they smelt stale, a cheap infusion of face powder, perfume and sweat, but nonetheless it was a welcome, familiar scent after the noxious air of Holloway and Nellie let them embrace her before shooing them on their way to their beds. The Amethyst deflated with the dawn. It needed the night to come alive, its open maw demanding to be fed with an endless parade of people.

The chef put the burners back on in the kitchen to make breakfast for Nellie. The hens of Norfolk were kept busy supplying the Amethyst with eggs, which came up by the dozen on the milk train overnight. The chef was eager to know about the prison breakfast. 'A lump of bread and margarine and a mug of cocoa,' Nellie informed him. 'I'll add a couple of sausages to your plate, I expect you need feeding up,' he said solicitously. 'I expect I do,' Nellie said.

The family retired to one of the private rooms, where a waiter set a table with fresh linen and silver cutlery and Freddie opened a bottle of champagne for them. Dom Perignon for the family, a lesser brand for the club, bought for seven shillings and sixpence and sold for three guineas. Eight for a magnum. Was there a happier sound, Nellie said, than the pop of a champagne cork?

'As long as it doesn't come out of the profits,' Edith said, in whose veins Coker blood ran in a fast and furious torrent.

Nellie Coker's progeny in the order in which they entered on to the world's stage. First of all, Niven – unsurprisingly absent from Holloway this morning – followed soon after by Edith. There had followed a hiatus while Nellie attempted to refute further motherhood and then, having failed, she produced in quick succession Betty, Shirley and Ramsay, and bringing up the rear, the runt of the litter, eleven-year-old Kitty, or *le bébé* as Nellie sometimes referred to her, when searching and failing to find the right name amongst so many. Nellie had received a French education, something which could be interpreted in several ways.

There was a father on Kitty's birth certificate, although Edith

11

said she knew for a fact that it was the name of a major who had died at the first battle of the Marne a year before Kitty was born. ('A miracle,' Nellie said, unruffled.)

The three eldest girls were the crack troops of the family. Betty and Shirley had both gone to Cambridge. 'Wear their learning lightly,' Nellie said proudly to prospective suitors. ('Hardly wear it at all,' Niven said.) Sometimes, Nellie was more like a theatrical promoter than a mother.

Edith had eschewed both university and marriage in favour of a course in bookkeeping and accounting. While Nellie was *hors de combat* in Holloway, the Coker ship had been steered by Edith. The Amethyst had been closed down, although Edith reopened it, of course, the day after Nellie was sentenced, under another name – 'the Deck of Cards' – but to everyone it was still, and always would be, the Amethyst.

Edith was Nellie's second in command, her *chef d'affaires*, and made of the same stern stuff as her mother. She understood business and had the Borgia stomach necessary for it. Money was the thing. They had all known what it was like to have some and then to have none and now to have a lot, and none of them wanted to fall off the precipice into penury again. Perhaps not Ramsay, so much. He wanted to be a writer. 'I despair,' Nellie said.

Ramsay, at just twenty-one, was continually beset by the feeling that he had just missed something. 'As if,' he struggled to explain to Shirley, his usual confidante, 'I've walked into a room but everyone else has just left it.' Niven had gone to war, Betty and Shirley to Cambridge, but Ramsay had been too young for the war and didn't last more than a term at Oxford before being condemned to an Alpine sanatorium for lungs that resembled 'a pair of squeezeboxes', according to his consultant at Bart's. It had been a relief, if he was honest. He was cowed by his fellow students. There were still men at Merton finishing degrees that had been interrupted by the war. They had been through the fire. They were older than the date on their birth certificates suggested, while Ramsay knew that he was younger.

Ramsay seemed transparent to his family; Niven, on the other hand, was an enigma to them all. He had a share in a car dealership in Piccadilly, was a partner in a wine-importing firm, raced a dog at White City, and owned a half-share in a horse that popped up occasionally at a racetrack, unfancied by everyone, before stealing first place. ('Funny that,' Nellie said.) He knew criminals, he knew dukes. ('No difference,' Nellie said.) He hardly drank at all, yet he went to a lot of parties. He had no time for people who went to parties. He had no time for people in general and didn't suffer fools at all. He never indulged in drugs, as far as they knew, but he used to be in with all the Chinese who sold them and was known to visit Limehouse and could have been found sitting in the notorious Brilliant Chang's restaurant in Regent Street, sharing a pot of chrysanthemum tea with him before he was deported. He would have made a good Wesleyan but he had no time for the church.

Nellie's own ancestral origins were lost in the mists of time – or, in her case, Irish bog fog – but what was known – or claimed – was that her maternal grandmother had been thrown out of Ireland for vagrancy, thereby having the good fortune to miss the Great Famine and establish the beginnings of the dynasty. This woman had washed up in Glasgow, where she peddled 'soft goods' from door to door before migrating eastwards and being taken up – who knew how? – by a well-off laird from the Kingdom of Fife, a second son, elevated to first by the death of his brother in mysterious circumstances. There were some ignorant rumours that he had been cursed.

There was a hasty wedding. Nellie's grandmother was already carrying the secret of Nellie's mother inside her, after whose birth the new laird enthusiastically set about gambling away the family money at the same time as drinking himself to death.

By the time Nellie came along there was little of the family fortune left. When she was still quite young she had been packed off to France to be educated, at a convent school in Lyons, before being 'finished' (in more ways than one) in Paris. Fresh from the French capital and possibly already *enceinte* with Niven, she returned to Edinburgh and married a medical man from Inverness. They set up a lavish home that they couldn't afford in Edinburgh's New Town and Nellie discovered that her new husband was not only a drinker but a gambler to boot, and when all the money and goodwill had eventually drained away, Nellie took matters into her own hands and yanked her children into a third-class carriage at Waverley and hauled them back out at King's Cross.

All except Niven, her eldest, who had already been conscripted into the Scots Guards in Edinburgh and was serving at the Front. Not volunteered. Niven would not have volunteered for the Army. Or, indeed, for anything. He had been conscripted into the ranks, having refused the officer's commission for which he was eligible, thanks to his attendance at Fettes. The public schools of Great Britain had helpfully provided fodder for the notoriously short-lived junior officer ranks. Niven had harboured no wish to be preferred in this way. He would take his chances in the other ranks, he said. He did, and lived.

Nellie left the rest of them sitting on their trunks on the platform while she went looking for lodgings. One pound a week for first-floor rooms in Great Percy Street, just round the corner from the station. Lacking even the money for the first week's rent, Nellie handed over her wedding ring as a deposit. It wasn't her own wedding ring – that had been lost some time ago (carelessly, some might say) and she had bought a cheap nine-carat one from a pawn shop. A war widow, Nellie told the landlady in Great Percy Street, her husband killed at Ypres. The children regarded their mother with interest. Betty and Shirley had seen their father only the previous week, spotting him rolling drunkenly around St Andrew Square as they walked home from school.

Nellie expanded on her misfortunes – six children, one (more or less) still a babe-in-arms and one of them fighting on the Front. The landlady's defences crumbled easily and she welcomed them warmly over the threshold. She refused the wedding ring. She was a kindly old soul, still dressed in the fashion of the previous century.

There were four floors to the house. The landlady herself lived below them on the ground floor and above them was a noisy family of Belgian refugees, and in the attic a pair of Russian 'Bolshevists' – very nice men, if rather dirty, who did odd jobs around the house and taught the young Ramsay a little of their language as well as how to play a card game called Preferans. They could play all night, drinking potato vodka they bought in Holborn from an illicit still. Nellie was furious when she found out. Gambling had been the downfall of her family in the past, she said, and she would not let it be their downfall in the future.

The girls were delighted with their new lodgings because the landlady had a big dark-furred cat called Moppet and they spent a good deal of time fussing over him – dressing him up in Kitty's smocks and bonnets and brushing his splendid coat until poor Ramsay thought his lungs would implode. Nellie herself brought in a little money from taking in sewing; she was an excellent plain needlewoman, having been taught by nuns in her alma mater in Lyons. The landlady had a Singer treadle that she no longer used. The Bolshevists heaved it up from her quarters to the Cokers'.

Nellie's purse strings were tightly drawn. The soles of their shoes were mended with liquid rubber solution, their white collars were rubbed with lumps of bread to clean them, and they dined on liver soup and eel pie. Nellie was an excellent economist. All the while that she was saving, pennies here, pennies there, she was hatching a plan.

The children would have been happy to remain in Great Percy Street, but the landlady died a few months later and her son, who lived in Birmingham and never visited, wrote to say he had decided to 'sell up' and move to America on the proceeds. Nellie had grown fond of the landlady in the course of the time they had lived there, sometimes taking tea with her in the afternoon. The woman was a keen baker, her repertoire based on the Be-Ro recipe book – rock buns, drop scones, queen cakes, all much appreciated by Nellie.

Nellie was accustomed to hearing the little sounds of everyday life from the landlady's domain – water running, doors closing and so on. It had dawned on her slowly during the course of the day that all was silence below and she went down to investigate. She had read the landlady's cards the night before and had seen 'a great change' coming, but nothing about death.

When there was no answer to her knock, she had opened the landlady's door, knowing it to be always unlocked. The rooms felt empty, the dust of silence sat heavily. Nellie was saddened but not surprised to find that the landlady had never risen that morning and was still in her bed, sleeping the eternal rest.

Nellie tidied the place up a little. Shelves and drawers: putting things away, taking things out. There was cash, she knew, in a caddy, a commemorative one for the Coronation of Edward VII. The money was truffled out and slipped into the pocket of her apron. Beneath the high brass bed on which the corpse was serenely reposed, Nellie spotted a rather rusty metal box, like a large cash box. Nellie hooked it out from beneath the bed with the old lady's walking stick. It was locked; it took a good deal more rummaging to come up with the key that was hiding in a little pot-pourri vase.

Nellie had been expecting dry, dusty papers. A lease, a will. She had not been expecting a treasure trove. A queen's ransom. Diamonds, rubies, sapphires, opals and garnets. Rings and brooches, bracelets and bangles. Cuffs and chokers, an emerald tiara in the Russian style, a five-strand pearl necklace. Cameos, corals, a pair of fine aquamarine chandelier earrings, a many-stranded opal bracelet set with rubies and diamonds.

What kind of a secret life had the unassuming landlady lived to have garnered such prizes? Nellie chose not to speculate. It was only later that she learnt that the kindly old landlady had in fact been a fence for the London gangs and the jewellery had already been stolen several times. Nellie couldn't help but be impressed by the landlady's quiet duplicity. It was a lesson in disguise.

As far as her own guilt was concerned, Nellie reasoned to her inner judge that the landlady might have given her the jewellery freely if she had known she was about to die. An unlikely but comforting narrative. Nellie's tread on the stair was remorseful as she made her way back up to her own floor, where she sent Edith to fetch a doctor for the landlady. 'Is she ill?' Edith asked. 'Very,' Nellie said.

Later, Nellie wondered if she had been reading her own cards, not the landlady's, for a great change did come to their lives. They said goodbye to the Bolshevists, who set off back across Europe to their revolution, and left Great Percy Street before they were turned out by the son and before the landlady's criminal friends could come looking for their looted goods. For many years, perhaps even now, Nellie would look over her shoulder in the street, wondering if the thieves had found out that she had stolen their booty and were about to wreak vengeance on her.

They proceeded to rent a mildewed, mice-infested basement in Tottenham Court Road. They took Moppet with them and he turned out to be an excellent mouser, more than earning his keep. Penitentially, Nellie chose to sell her favourite piece – a magnificent early-eighteenth-century amethyst necklace – to a pawnbroker she was acquainted with, beating him up to the grand sum of fifty pounds. Nellie was an expert haggler. The rest she put away to be sold, piece by piece, as necessary. Nellie was parsimonious where business was concerned. One endeavour, she believed, should finance the next. Business begat business.

Nellie had spotted an advertisement in the *Gazette*, from someone called Jaeger. He was a coarse, weaselly little man but he seemed to have some idea of what he was doing. He had been holding 'tango teas' during the war in a basement in Fitzrovia, but the fashion for the tango had passed and he was looking for

someone to go into partnership with him, to hold *thés dansants*.
Together, Nellie and Jaeger found a basement – a cellar, really –
in Little Newport Street, near Leicester Square, and spent a fair
amount of money doing it out, after which they sold subscriptions for two shillings a night for dancing and refreshments.
'Jaeger's Dance Hall,' they called it.

The Savoy – the champagne and orchids trade – charged five
shillings and Nellie supposed they served dainty food. Jaeger's
Dance Hall provided a more robust *thé* – iced cakes, sandwiches,
lemonade and something called 'Turk's Blood' which was bright
pink: lemonade, Angostura bitters and some extra cochineal. No
liquor licence, of course. At first, they abided by the law, but if
they didn't serve drink someone else would. So they did.

As a help in this move into illegality, Jaeger acquired the services
of the law, in the shape of a policeman – a certain Detective Sergeant Arthur Maddox, who worked at Bow Street police station.
Maddox was a helpful sort of policeman who, for a sum of money
every week, would turn a blind eye to the licensing laws and tip
Jaeger and Nellie off if he heard that a raid was imminent.

Jaeger's Dance Hall took off like a rocket, people jazzing and
foxtrotting to a ragtime band until they dropped. It seemed that
people wanted nothing more than to enjoy themselves during
the convulsion of war. It was the spring of 1918 and people everywhere were sick of attrition.

It was an eye-opener for Nellie. She couldn't fail to notice that
many of the men went home at the end of the night with a dance
hostess who had been a complete stranger to them a handful of
hours earlier. 'The young ladies get very good tips for that,' Jaeger said phlegmatically. 'Can't blame 'em, can you?'

On Armistice night there had been couples – again strangers
to each other – actually fornicating in the shadows in the dance
hall. Outside in the streets an orgy was taking place. 'Copulation,' Jaeger said, even more phlegmatically. 'Makes the world go
round, don't it? And better than killing each other. Fucking's
natural, innit?'

Nellie recoiled from the word, but she had to agree, if reluctantly. So many had been lost in the war, she wondered – attempting to put a veneer of refinement on the base vulgarity of the proceedings – if they weren't following some instinctive compulsion to restock the human race. Like frogs.

She supposed she should come to terms with the concept of 'fun'. She didn't want any for herself but she was more than happy to provide it for others, for a sum. There was nothing wrong with having a good time as long as she didn't have to have one herself.

One of the dance hostesses – Maud, an Irish girl – had died that night of an opium overdose. It was Nellie who had found her, slumped behind the bar in the hour before dawn.

Jaeger was nowhere to be seen, so Nellie mobilized a couple of rough Army privates on furlough to carry the girl out, paying them with a bottle of whisky each to get rid of her. 'Where?' one of them asked. 'I don't know,' Nellie said. 'Use your brain. Try the river.' With any luck, the girl would meander through the Essex marshes and eventually be washed out to sea. Nellie never saw the soldiers again and had no idea if they followed her suggestion. 'Out of sight, out of mind' was one of the useful epithets that had guided her life.

Jaeger was merely a stepping-stone to Nellie's future, an apprenticeship. She was hatching a grander plan. After the Armistice, she sold her share in the dance hall to him for five hundred pounds. Afterwards, he was raided on several occasions, found guilty of 'selling intoxicating liquors' and allowing the dance hall to be the 'habitual resort of women of ill-repute', with a three-hundred-and-twenty-five-pound fine on each occasion. After the fourth raid in a row, he admitted defeat and left the nightclub business.

With her profits from Jaeger's Dance Hall, Nellie started a cabaret club ('*Cabaret intime,*' as she referred to it) called 'the Moulin Vert' (or 'the Moolinvurt', as those with no French called it), inspired by nostalgia for the Paris of her younger years.

19

Taking the lease on a filthy cellar in Brewer Street, Nellie transformed it into a palace – gilded fittings and a sprung dance floor, little café tables *à la Montparnasse* around the edge of the room. A vision – 'A *mise en scène*,' she said to the veteran of the Artists Rifles she engaged to paint the place. He obliged with murals in the style of Renoir. You could imagine you were on a Parisian street, Nellie said, and in an out-of-character gesture she gave him an extra five pounds in gratitude.

The Twenties roared in and the Moulin Vert opened with a bang. There was dancing between the cabaret acts – culled from all the West End theatres – and nearly the entire chorus from the Gaiety pitched up after midnight. Nellie hired a Tzigane orchestra – not French, it was true, but foreign enough for the crowd that inhabited 'the Moolinvurt'. Liquor flowed freely and so did the money. They were rarely raided; Sergeant Maddox had continued to work for Nellie.

A few months after they opened, Nellie heard that the artist who had painted her murals had shot himself. He wasn't the first soldier unable to cope with the peace. Nellie and Edith raised a glass to his memory after hours.

After a couple of years, Nellie had an offer that was too good to refuse and she sold the club. She marked the occasion by buying each of the girls a single strand of the new Ciro pearls with little diamanté clasps.

With the money from the Moulin Vert, Nellie bought the premises for her new club. Looking for a name, she thought of the hoard of glittering jewels that she had taken from Great Percy Street. She considered 'the Diamond'. 'The Sapphire'? Or perhaps 'the Ruby'? And then she thought of the necklace that had given her a start in London. And, like Goldilocks, she found the name that was just right. The Amethyst.

Currently, Nellie's empire comprised five nightclubs – the Pixie, the Foxhole, the Sphinx, and the Crystal Cup were the others. But the jewel in the crown had always been and always would be the Amethyst.

Before Holloway, Nellie could be found most nights in the little draught-proof cashier's box at the entrance to the club. She ruled her kingdom from there – settling bills and accounts at the end of the evening, handing change to the waiters, taking entrance fees. One-pound entry. Members only. Paying the pound made you a member. The club took a thousand pounds a week. It was better than a goldmine.

No one got in for free, not even the Prince of Wales. Last week, Rudolph Valentino had been here, the week before it was the young Prince George. He had no money on him, of course – these people never had cash and his companions had to scrabble in their own pockets for the fee. Nellie had a way of making people feel she was doing them a favour by giving them entry to the Amethyst. That was just the beginning of the fleecing. You couldn't even leave without handing over a shilling to the cloakroom girl if you wanted to retrieve your coat at the end of the night. Plus a tip, of course. The Amethyst ran on tips. The dance hostesses were paid three pounds a week, but on a good Saturday – the Boat Race or the Derby – they could go home with as much as eighty pounds in their purses. No one ever asked for a raise. No one dared.

The Amethyst did not have pretensions to the *haut monde* like the Embassy club, nor was it scraping the gutter for custom like some of the flea-ridden dives of Curzon Street.

The London gangs who all streamed into the club from time to time treated it like a battlefield. The Elephant and Castle mob, Derby Sabini's roughs, Monty Abrahams and his followers, the Hoxton gang, the Hackney Huns, the Frazzinis. Luca Frazzini, the Frazzinis' chieftain, was a neat, dapper man who was often to be found sitting quietly at a table in the corner of the Amethyst, a glass of (free) champagne sitting on the table in front of him, barely touched. He could have passed for a stockbroker. There was an *entente cordiale* between himself and Nellie. They went back a long way, to the days of Jaeger's Dance Hall. They trusted each other. Almost.

'Ordinary' members of the public and gang roughs rubbed shoulders with royalty, both those in exile and those still in possession of their thrones, Americans rich beyond measure, Indian and African princes, officers of the Guards, writers, artists, opera singers, orchestra conductors, stars of the West End stage, as well as the chorus boys and girls – there was nowhere else in England, possibly in the world, where so many different estates could be found together at one time, not even in Epsom on Derby Day. Unlike many – indeed, most – Nellie harboured few prejudices. She did not discriminate by colour or rank or race. If you had the money for the entrance fee, you were allowed ingress to her kingdom. In Nellie's view, money was the measure of a man – or woman.

Once you had negotiated the Cerberus-like presence of Nellie at the entrance, you passed through a bamboo curtain and progressed down a dimly lit, narrow flight of stairs as unprepossessing as coal-cellar steps. It added to the 'drama' of it all, Nellie said. Everyone wanted drama. At the bottom of the stairs, you were greeted by another doorman, this one liveried with frogging, epaulettes and so on, a costume that would not have looked out of place on a rear admiral in an operetta. This individual, Linwood, who was much given to bowing and scraping (he made an astonishing amount in tips), was a disgraced butler from one of the royal households. Nellie believed in second chances, she herself had benefited from several. It was amusing to see the startled expressions on the faces of some of the club's more regal patrons if they recognized Linwood (as was the way with butlers, he had no other name), for he was the keeper of many of their more *outré* secrets. Of course, although most servants will recognize their masters, few masters will remember the faces of their servants. Then Linwood would draw back the heavy black bombazine curtain that shrouded the entrance and you were finally granted entry. A *coup de théâtre*.

Ta-dah – welcome to the Amethyst!

*

The bacon and eggs arrived, along with the promised sausages for Nellie and sweet milky coffee, and Keeper, Niven's German shepherd, nosed open the dining-room door, heralding the arrival of Niven himself.

The dog was the only creature on earth that Niven seemed to have respect for. He still referred to him as a 'German shepherd', not an 'Alsatian', immune – or indifferent – to the enemy connotations of the name. Like many men in the trenches, Niven had known dogs like Keeper, working dogs, but that was one of the few pieces of information about his time in the Scots Guards that he was prepared to share with anyone. At no point in the war or after, including the Armistice and the Peace, did Niven ever think anyone had won.

He no longer had the patience for people's foibles. No patience for people at all. No time for religion, no time for scruples, no time for feelings. Niven's heart appeared adamantine, fired in the crucible of the war.

He had been a sharpshooter, picking off Germans in their trenches with his Pattern 1914 Enfield. To level things up, the Germans did the same. One morning during the battle of Passchendaele, a corporal spotting for Niven had his head blown off next to him. In the afternoon, the same thing happened to another spotter. Understandably there was a reluctance to spot for Niven a third time. Snipers and spotters generally took it in turns and the next time Niven was on duty he chose to spot, to demonstrate, if nothing else, the laws of chance. He wasn't killed. Perhaps he had been lucky or perhaps he was simply good at knowing when to put his head above the parapet and when it was better to stay down.

He had been closer to the dining room than they thought, in one of the club's storerooms, listening to a tale of woe from one of the dance hostesses amongst the crates of beer and champagne and the boxes of kippers that came down by train from Fortune's in Whitby every week to fuel the Amethyst's breakfasts. He'd put an end to the tale of woe by giving the girl enough cash to make her 'problem' disappear. There was a woman in Covent Garden whom the girls all seemed to know about. The solution was often worse than the problem, but 'you take your chances', the girl in the storeroom said. Her problem was not of Niven's making. He was careful to leave no trace of himself in this world.

He sauntered into the room now and, kissing Nellie lightly on the cheek in the continental fashion, said, 'So, Mother, the jail-bird has been set free from her cage, has she?' He pinched a rasher off Betty's plate and tossed it to a surprised Keeper.

The kiss disturbed Nellie. It felt more like Gethsemane than filial affection. 'Time we were all in our beds,' she said sharply.

Niven saluted his mother, managing to make the gesture appear both impeccable and subversive at the same time, a talent honed in the war. '*Sofort, mein Kapitän,*' he said. Nellie frowned at him. She may not have known German but she recognized the language of the enemy when she heard it.

Bow Street

'It's your day off, sir,' the desk sergeant on the early-morning shift said, alarmed at the sight of Frobisher steaming through the doors of Bow Street station.

'I know that, sergeant, I'm not in my dotage yet.'

'Never thought you were, sir.'

The desk sergeant was still easing into the day with an enamel mug of strong, well-sugared tea and was unprepared for action. It was his custom to be sensitive to the new Detective Chief Inspector's state of mind. Frobisher had been in Bow Street not much more than a week now and the desk sergeant was still getting acquainted with his daily character. This morning he cautiously gauged optimism and said, 'Make you a brew, sir?'

'No, thank you, sergeant,' Frobisher said briskly.

Frobisher had omitted to tell Miss Kelling that today was his day off. Nor had he told his wife, but then Lottie took little interest in his comings and goings. He was here to do a job, to clean a mired house. Dirt never slept, so neither would Frobisher until he had swept it away. He was a man inclined to a metaphor.

Bow Street was not a quiet place. Frobisher could hear the metallic clanging and banging of the cell doors and the overnight prisoners' voluble protests at their incarceration. The cries of the damned rising from Hades, Frobisher thought, although the cells in Bow Street were not below but on ground level. He caught a high keening from the women's cells up on the floor above – grief or madness, it was hard to say. A fine line divided them. He thought of his wife.

He had been up at an unearthly hour to go to Holloway and his empty stomach felt sour. It needed to be lined with a good breakfast. Frobisher's thoughts turned to porridge, with honey carved from the comb and cream straight from the cow, and perhaps an egg fresh from beneath a fat-feathered hen. Unlikely on all fronts. Frobisher had enjoyed a rural childhood. He was into his forties now but he had never exorcized Shropshire from his soul. They had had chickens when he was young, free to roam, and it had been his job when he came home from school at the end of the day to search out the eggs, each discovery a small triumph, the pleasure of which had never palled. No egg had ever tasted as good since.

'What's the night's tally, sergeant?' he asked.

'Full house, sir. It'll take all day for the Magistrates' Court to get through them.'

'The usual?'

''Fraid so. Run-of-the-mill stuff – solicitation, thieving, intoxication, assaults. A full tank of drunks stewing in their own misery. A murder in Greek Street—'

'Oh?' There had been a spate of baffling murders across London over the past few months. Unexplained random attacks on innocent passers-by. Of course, there were some superstitious fools, encouraged by the scandal sheets, who blamed the curse of Tutankhamun. Frobisher had been working with the murder squad in Scotland Yard and knew at first-hand how vexing these killings were, as there seemed to be no rhyme or reason to them. He could only conclude that they were the work of a madman.

'Nothing special, sir,' the sergeant said. 'Just a pair of intoxicated gentlemen trying to batter the living daylights out of each other. The Laughing Policeman's on it.'

'Sergeant Oakes? I wish people would use his real name.' God, how Frobisher hated that stupid Charles Penrose song.

'Yes, sir. Oakes is a cheerful sod though, you have to admit. Always sees the funny side of things.'

Oakes was experienced and, if nothing else, he seemed to Frobisher to be a safe pair of hands, although his constant jocundity was already beginning to grate. 'Is Inspector Maddox on duty today?' he asked.

'Still on sick leave, sir.'

'Still?' Maddox had been on leave from the day that Frobisher had started at Bow Street. Frobisher was convinced that the canker at the heart of the station, the most rotten of all the apples in the barrel, was Arthur Maddox. 'What in God's name is wrong with the man? Is he a malingerer?'

'He has a bad back, I believe, sir.'

A bad back didn't stop a man doing his job, Frobisher thought irritably. 'Well, if by any chance he comes in this morning, tell him that I'm looking for him.'

Maddox, promoted to inspector after the war, was thought to be in the pay of the very people he should be pursuing. He lived above his salary – a large semi-detached house in Crouch End, a wife, five children. (Five! Frobisher couldn't imagine having even one.) A car, too, a Wolseley Open Tourer, the kind of car a well-off man owned, the kind of car a man negotiating for an Austin Seven felt envious of. Not to mention a summer holiday for the whole family in Bournemouth or Broadstairs, not in cheap boarding houses but in good hotels. Frobisher was certain that Maddox was in collusion with Nellie Coker, that he protected her from the law, but what else did he benefit from? Maddox was as sly as a fox and Nellie kept a henhouse, the queen of the coop. Did she also give Maddox free access to her chickens? (Yes, prone to extended metaphors.)

At the mention of Maddox's name, the desk sergeant inhaled and stood up straighter, actions that caught Frobisher's attention. He had become interested lately in what could be referred to as body language or 'sub-vocal thinking', whereby a man betrays himself with the slightest of indications. Of course, he was willing to concede, the desk sergeant may just have been straightening out a twinge in his back. He would concede the occasional twinge, but not a whole week off work, for heaven's sake.

Frobisher sniffed the air. The ambrosial scent of frying bacon wafted towards him from somewhere. His stomach growled with envy. He frowned. Did they *eat* when he wasn't here? Bacon *sandwiches?* What else did they get up to in his absence? He experienced an odd sense of disappointment, as he had done when he was younger and had been left out of the other boys' pursuits. He had been an awkward, reticent child. Now he was an awkward, reticent man, but better at disguising it with a stiff carapace.

He frowned at the desk sergeant and the desk sergeant, sensing that his bacon was at risk, saved it literally with a swift change of subject, saying, 'I heard Ma Coker got out this morning.' The desk sergeant was only too well aware – the whole station was – of Frobisher's fixation on the Cokers, particularly Nellie.

'She did,' Frobisher said.

'Did you go, sir?'

'I did.'

Frobisher didn't elaborate and the desk sergeant didn't push his luck by asking him to. Frobisher had no small talk, he never had done. It meant that he was a much misunderstood man, presumed to be stand-offish, arrogant even. He had tried, God help him, to chat and prattle about the weather or horse-racing, even films, but he ended up sounding like a poor amateur actor. (*Well, constable, how's that allotment of yours coming on?*) His real passions were esoteric, of little interest to the common man or his colleagues in Bow Street, certainly not to his wife – the Berlin Treaty between Germany and the Soviets (how could that end well?) or a demonstration of a 'televisor' to the Royal Society by a chap called Baird (like something from an H. G. Wells novel). He had an enquiring mind. It was a curse. Even sometimes for a detective.

At home in Ealing, he was saved from the rigours of small talk by mutual incomprehension. His wife was called Charlotte – Lottie – although she had no birth certificate to prove that and Frobisher had his doubts. The detective in him would like to have investigated further, the husband in him thought it wise to leave the subject alone. She was French, or Belgian, she seemed unsure, certainly borderline, plucked from the blighted remains of Ypres at the end of the war with nothing but a bulb of garlic in her pocket, and had no papers to elucidate, and did not care to remember on account of what the doctors called 'hysterical amnesia'.

When younger, Frobisher had imagined many qualities in his future wife, but he had not anticipated hysterical amnesia. Lottie's story was tragic and complicated – again, something he had not predicted in his future wife.

A woman, screeching her innocence, was hauled in through the door by two constables, saving Frobisher from further thought.

'Dolly Pargeter, accused of pickpocketing on the Strand,' one of the uniformed constables who was trying to control her said to the desk sergeant.

'You're out and about early, Dolly,' the desk sergeant said amiably. 'Let's get you checked into the Ritz, shall we?' His nose twitched, he was being kept from his bacon, but to tend to it would be admitting its existence to Frobisher.

'I'll be off, then,' Frobisher said reluctantly. He preferred the police station to his Ealing terrace, which said much about the Ealing terrace. As he turned to go, the desk sergeant said, 'Sir, I forgot – a girl washed up, fished out from the pier at Tower Bridge. She's probably still in the Dead Man's Hole. Thought you'd want to know.' Frobisher took an almost unhealthy interest in dead girls, in the opinion of Bow Street.

'Thank you, sergeant,' Frobisher said, grateful to be reprieved from Ealing. 'I'll take a look.'

'It's your day off, sir,' the desk sergeant reminded him.

'Crime never sleeps,' Frobisher said testily. He sounded priggish, he knew. 'By the way, sergeant—'

'Yes, sir?'

'I think your bacon's burning.'

Frobisher couldn't help smiling to himself as he made his way out of the station. That would serve them right for not including him, he thought.

As he crossed the road, he was forced to do a neat quickstep to avoid an approaching motorcycle. An Enfield, the rider anonymous behind goggles and leather helmet. How easy it would be to be killed on the streets of London. By accident or design.

An Awkward Age

Even before the Cokers were piling into their Bentleys outside Holloway, fourteen-year-old Freda was awake, roused by the shouts and tuneless singing of the night porters in Covent Garden market as they unloaded the lorries that started rumbling in at midnight from all over the country – apples from Evesham, mushrooms from Suffolk, exotica from all over the world.

Since running away from home, Freda – Alfreda Murgatroyd – had been renting an attic room in a dingy boarding house in Henrietta Street, so close to the market that she could swear she could smell the rotting cabbage leaves trodden underfoot. Freda had come to London to find her fortune, to become a star of the West End stage. She had not yet been discovered, but her courage had held and this Saturday she was to have an audition. Her life, she was sure, was about to change.

Although small, Freda looked older than her years. For a pretty girl, she was surprisingly lacking in vanity about her looks, which she considered to be more a matter of chance than anything else. Or God-given, if you believed that God gave beauty as a gift, which seemed unlikely. It was more like the kind of trick that the Greek gods played on people – a curse rather than a gift. One of the few books Freda had read was an illustrated anthology of Greek myths (*A Child's Guide*) that she had found abandoned on the seat in a train carriage when she was ten years old. It was hardly a helpful primer for life.

Freda had been on display since she was able to sit up unaided and had a battery of photographs that catalogued her progression, from appearing in Bonny Baby competitions to playing the locally sourced Clara in a professional touring *Nutcracker* the previous Christmas. Her mother, Gladys, once the chronicler of her daughter's looks, had recently lost interest and transferred her energy into finding a new husband to sponsor her indolent lifestyle. Gladys had, in the past, exploited Freda's looks for an income, but the investment was no longer paying off. 'You've lost your bloom,' she said to Freda. Freda frowned. She felt she still had a lot of blooming ahead of her.

It was her talent rather than her looks that gave Freda cause for pride. The hours she had put in spinning, turning, tapping, pointing and *chassé*-ing. Since the age of three she had attended a dance school from which, every year, the Theatre Royal harvested the best pupils to swell its pantomime chorus, as did the touring ballet and opera productions that came to York, hence her Clara (*Girl from the Groves charms in role*). The Groves was a district of York, but Freda liked the way that (to her mind) it made her sound like a wood nymph, rather than someone who lived in a shabby end-of-terrace in the hinterland behind Rowntree's factory. They used to live in a much better house on Wigginton Road, right opposite the factory where Freda's father had worked when he was alive, but they had been bundled out by the bailiffs three years ago.

In the short span of her years, Freda had acquired an extensive repertoire playing cats, dogs, baby bears, snowflakes, fairies and an assortment of 'village children' (yet somehow always the same), who danced and sang and skipped around maypoles. No Christmas pantomime, it seemed, was complete without a scene in a village square. Freda was a dainty child and took instruction well; it made her popular with adults.

Freda believed that there was nothing in the whole wide world that was better than standing on a stage. There was a grandeur to it that transcended the otherwise humdrum world. Her heart soared in her chest at the very thought of it.

Between the ages of seven and thirteen, Freda had modelled hand-knitted garments for a yarn manufacturer. And not just for the photographs on their paper patterns – posed in a chilly attic studio in Manchester – but also in mannequin parades that toured parts of the north, hosted by local wool shops, who sold the patterns and needles and balls of wool with which to make the garments on display.

These sporadic little cavalcades took place mostly in dispiriting church halls, and mostly to an audience of women still worn out and raw from the bereavements of war. And always in winter, for some reason. 'That's the nature of wool, I suppose,' Vanda said.

They were a team, Vanda said. There were three of them, Duncan, Vanda and Freda, plus Adele, who 'worked for the company' and was responsible for their travel and accommodation, clutching her Bradshaw's in one hand and with the other lugging a suitcase full of 'the Knits' as she called them (indisputably a capital letter) from one smoky third-class train carriage to the next. None of them, not even Adele, knew how to knit anything beyond plain and purl, although Duncan claimed he could do French knitting. Vanda laughed and said, 'Don't be filthy.' He had been a sailor in the war. Sailors were fond of knitting, apparently.

They were always being asked questions when they were demonstrating the wares – *What kind of a selvedge is that?* Or *Is that a wishbone stitch?* Vanda had a way of turning these questions into flattery. *Oh, you noticed that, clever you! What kind of stitch do you think it is? I expect you're the expert.* And so on.

Their 'costume changes', as Adele referred to the swapping of one knitted garment for another, took place invariably in a dimly lit annexe at the back of the hall that was used as a storage area for hymn books and crumbling Nativity mangers and other neglected church paraphernalia.

In the hall, they did not walk on a stage, if there was a stage, which there often wasn't, but proceeded individually down the aisle between the lines of rackety old chairs occupied by their audience. When they reached the back of the room, they did a measured twirl and then returned to the front. 'The slower the better,' Adele counselled. 'They haven't come out on a wet Wednesday evening for the knitting, they've come for the occasion.'

Freda modelled a variety of intricately patterned cardigans and sweaters and three-piece outfits with pleated skirts and Shetland tammies. Pom-poms abounded. 'You look very covetable,' Vanda said.

Freda had quickly grown accustomed to gazing straight ahead and smiling serenely while members of the audience reached out and plucked a sleeve or pinched a rib-stitch hem or, occasionally, Freda herself – nipping the back of her hand or patting the calf that rose firm and inviting above her white socks and black patent shoes, shoes that were removed immediately afterwards, in case they got scratched, and replaced with her plain brown leather Oxfords.

Freda often received a smattering of applause which had nothing to do with the Knits but rather was on account of the way that she shone with the promise of a future, a future that would surely be better than the past. It sanctified her in the eyes of the audience. If they could have kept a piece of her as a relic – a finger bone, a lock of hair, even a pom-pom – they would have done.

Vanda was tall and raw-boned, with hair the colour of ginger nuts. Glamorous in a rather seedy way, she was always doused in Molinard's Habanita, which could knock your socks off if you got too close. She even dabbed the perfume on the Sarony cigarettes that she smoked continually and that made her Teesdale accent as 'hoarse as a crow', as Duncan liked to say. Vanda was always offering Freda one ('Go on, treat yourself, pet'), her hacking, phlegmy cough announcing her presence long before she became visible.

Duncan, who before the war had 'trod the boards', had once shared a stage with an ingenue Edith Evans at the Haymarket – 'spear-carrying stuff', he said dismissively. This entire sentence had been incomprehensible to Freda, but she learnt by a kind of osmosis and often things said one day made more sense the next. She thought 'spear-carrying' sounded rather noble.

It was Duncan's job to sport the pullovers, cardigans and waistcoats, many in complex Fair Isle patterns and often with the accessory of an unlit pipe to make him seem more manly. Even at her young age, Freda had been able to discern that manliness was not necessarily a quality Duncan strove for. He had a funny accent that was 'posh Liverpool', according to Vanda, which Freda rather liked and spent a good deal of time trying to imitate.

Vanda was a seasoned performer, too, having been on the stage herself once, in the music halls, as a magician's assistant, levitated on a nightly basis.

'It's not real, pet,' she said to Freda when she expressed admiration. 'It's a trick.' But that was even better than real!

Vanda paraded 'women's fashion items', words, she said, that covered 'a multitude of sins' from boleros to sweater dresses to matronly cardigans. Babies and toddlers were short-changed, although Vanda occasionally carried a large doll in full matinée fig. The doll appeared mysteriously from nowhere – too big, surely, for Adele's suitcase. It was called Dorothy. 'Nearest I'll ever get to being a mother,' Vanda said, in triumph rather than sorrow, as she adjusted the ribbons on the inanimate Dorothy's bonnet.

Unlike her mother, more ramshackle by the month, Freda was an exceptionally neat and tidy child. ('Fastidious,' Duncan said.) Every night before bed she tied her hair in rags and rubbed bicarb on her freckles as someone had told her once that it would make them fade. Before getting into bed, a bed often shared with Vanda, she would fold all her clothes and place them pyramidically on a chair – skirt at the bottom up to knickers at the top, coped by her socks, all ready for the next day when the pyramid was dismantled in reverse. 'Aren't you good!' Vanda said admiringly. They shared a bedroom in a variety of boarding houses. Vanda, like Freda's mother, was slovenly, clothes dropped where they were

removed, face powder spilt everywhere. Freda made no judge-
ments. She was learning about womanhood. You take it where
you can, as Duncan would say.

Freda was very good at packing, too, she could get twice as
much in her little suitcase as Vanda did in her big one. Sometimes she took over Vanda's packing for her. It was all in the
folding. Like geometry, Duncan said. Freda's understanding of
geometry, or any branch of mathematics, was lamentable. Sometimes she wondered if she shouldn't be in school more often.

'Don't worry, pet, you only need to be able to count to eight
if you're going to be a dancer,' Vanda said.

Vanda owned a coat that she claimed had been given to her by
an admirer and was stitched from the pelts of thirty-six ermine.
It was like a great snowy cloud and Freda often found herself
asleep on Vanda's fur-clad shoulder in one train carriage or
another. It was made from rabbits, not ermines, Duncan said.
Freda had no idea what an ermine was. An animal, she knew that
much, although her acquaintance with any kind of animal was
limited. She had never owned a pet, never visited a farm or a zoo.
Cows and sheep were merely ornaments that dotted the land-
scape of the north as it rolled past the train window. Although
embarrassed by her ignorance now, she had been astonished
when Vanda explained that sheep were the origin of the Knits.

In the evenings, in the boarding houses, Duncan would take a
bottle out from his suitcase. He was never without one. He
always offered Freda a 'tipple'. She always refused. She had tried
it once and it had made her insides heave. 'Old Navy rum,' Duncan said. 'Strip the paint off a battleship. That's where I got a
taste for it – in the rum old Royal Navy.'

Sometimes on these occasions, Vanda (who preferred port)
said, 'Tell us some of your war stories, then, Duncan,' with a
strangely vulgar leer on her face, and Duncan would laugh and
say, 'Oo, will I buggery, love?' but then would proceed to regale
them with the tale of how he'd gone down on HMS *Formidable*
in 1915 in the English Channel before 'popping back up again

like a cork'. What was vulgar about that, Freda wondered? She presumed that the cork story was a joke of some kind, or a magic trick. Duncan rarely mentioned the five hundred or so sailors who didn't pop back up with him. The war was history, and history didn't interest Freda, she'd had no part in it. She was vibrant with the present and hungry for the future.

Vanda had 'lost her man' early in the war. Freda thought he must have been killed in battle, but Duncan said he'd run off to Barnsley with a barmaid. 'Alliterative adultery,' he said.

'Big word,' Vanda said.

'Which one?' Duncan said.

On these companionable boarding-house evenings, sometimes in 'the public lounge' in front of a hissing gas fire, but more often than not in the bedroom that Vanda and Freda shared, Duncan taught Freda to play cards, the pack laid out on the bedspread. He taught her how to cheat as well, which was even better – 'cold stacking' and the 'third card deal' as well as many other 'tricks', as he called them. She was a natural, apparently.

'Nimble little fingers,' Duncan said appreciatively. Freda was precocious, he told Vanda. Freda thought he meant 'precious'. They played for matches. By the time they all parted company for the last time Duncan was heavily in debt to Freda. He would need to raid one of Kreuger's warehouses to pay her back, he said. Kreuger was the Match King, he said. If she married the Match King, Freda wondered, would she become the Match Queen?

Vanda was skilled with cards, too, having learnt all kinds of tricks from her time as the magician's assistant. She was willing to explain to Freda how you went about sawing someone in half (usually a woman) and also how you made someone disappear (also usually a woman). Very useful knowledge, in Freda's opinion. 'Misdirection,' Vanda said. 'That's the key.'

Vanda was happy to be a traitor to the secrets of the Magic Circle – 'Punishable by death, probably,' she said cheerfully – but wild horses could not have made her divulge her age. ('A lady's prerogative.') Twenty-five, Freda guessed, although not to her face. 'Double that and take away ten,' Duncan said.

And where was Freda's mother in all this? More often than not, she could be seen teetering out to the Co-op with a jug and coming back with it filled with sherry 'from the wood', which makes it sound refined, when it was just a barrel with a spigot at the back of the shop.

Freda's father, much older than her mother, died ('keeled over') one day at work. He'd managed to sidestep the war because of his eyesight but was caught out by his heart when Freda was only five. 'He was an old fuddy-duddy,' Gladys said, 'all pipes and slippers, I don't know what I was thinking,' although in fact she knew very well that she had been thinking about not having to trudge to work every day in Rowntree's offices, which was where she had met Freda's father, a widower 'in management'. 'Management' sounded rather grand to Freda's ears. When she thought about her father, she smelt chocolate and tweed and tobacco. He used to bring home a bag of mis-shapen chocolates every week, a supply that was tragically cut off with his death.

Freda's father was rarely awarded a name by Gladys now that he was in the afterlife. He was simply 'your father' when Gladys spoke about him to Freda, or quite often 'a pig', awarding him in Freda's eyes a mythic quality, as if he had come down from Mount Olympus especially to impregnate Gladys before absconding back to the divine regions. In Freda's book of Greek myths, girls seemed to be in almost continual danger from being taken unaware by an over-eager Zeus in the form of a swan or a bull. Even an ant. Why not a pig?

In the real world, Freda's father had simply been foolishly flat-tered by the attentions of a younger woman. At first, Gladys had made him feel young, and then within a short time she made him feel old. A story as ancient as the Greek gods themselves.

Why did Zeus need to put on a disguise? Vanda mused, leafing through the pages of Freda's book in a railway carriage in the no man's land between Rotherham and Sheffield. 'Surely you'd rather be tupped by the king of the gods than an ant? And how on earth would it work with an ant anyway? The size difference would be ridiculous.'

'Tupped?' Duncan snorted. 'What are you? Little Bo-Peep? Call a fuck a fuck, Vanda, dear heart.'

This entire conversation was, fortunately, held in Freda's absence, as she was in the corridor, hanging out of the window, getting smuts in her eye from the engine and putting herself in danger of decapitation. She was not averse to the thrill of danger.

In the face of parental dereliction of duty, both voluntary and involuntary, Vanda and Duncan were the nearest thing to a chaperone for Freda. Not Adele. Adele was all timetables.

'We're a funny little family, aren't we?' Vanda said.

'You take it where you can,' Duncan said.

And then Adele had taken Freda to one side and told her she had grown 'too womanly' for the kiddies' Knits and her service was no longer required.

'I'm sorry?' a confounded Freda said. How could she not be wanted? She considered herself to be very wanted.

'You're demobbed, dear,' Adele said, with more sympathy than usual. (She rarely roused herself to emotion.) But it was true that, despite her elfin features and sprite-like demeanour, Freda had developed a highly visible bust and had embarked upon her 'monthlies' some time ago, a disconcerting journey overseen by Vanda in lieu of Freda's own mother. She had 'growing pains', Vanda said. What on earth were they, Freda wondered? She had an image of being stretched on the rack.

'You're advanced for your age, dear,' Adele said. 'In every way.'

'We'll miss you,' Vanda said, hugging Freda to her tobacco and Habanita-infused mohair. Searching in her handbag for some kind of parting gift, Vanda could only come up with a handkerchief, embroidered with a 'V'. It was creased but 'not used', she reassured Freda. Duncan gave her his pack of (marked) cards. That was nearly a year ago now and Freda had felt grief at the thought of her companions going on without her in the drizzle of Darlington or Doncaster, but then learnt from a chance encounter with Adele in the Shambles a few weeks ago that the Knits were no more and Vanda had unexpectedly married a man called Walter who owned a building firm in Grantham, 'of all the places', Adele said, making it seem as unlikely as Timbuctoo. Even more unlikely, she had heard that Vanda was expecting a baby. (In triumph or sorrow, Freda wondered?)

Freda had no idea where Grantham was, but she had a good idea of where London was on the map. She was already dreaming about living amongst its pleasure palaces. 'Dens of iniquity,' Adele said. Freda had no idea what that meant but she thought that it sounded entrancing.

Duncan, too, it seemed, had abandoned wool, having taken a job as an assistant restaurant manager at the Scarborough Grand, but the odds must have turned against him because he was currently serving two years' hard labour in Armley Gaol for gross indecency. 'You don't want to know what that is,' Adele said and then told her anyway. Freda had the great gift of rarely being surprised.

Freda's school attendance at Park Grove, always sporadic, came to an end when she reached her fourteenth birthday, and Gladys announced that now she was no longer at school Freda was obviously going to have to get a job. Freda didn't feel the imperative, she was happy to wait until she found an opportunity for stardom. Unfortunately, other than a couple of indifferent amateur dramatic groups, no one seemed to want Freda to model or dance or act (she was at an 'awkward age', apparently), and certainly not for money. Pantomime season was a long way off and anyway Freda felt unsure that the Theatre Royal would be ready for her transition from village child to village maiden.

Gladys prompted her to apply for a job in a milliner's in Coney Street. Freda thought it would entail nothing more than graciously assisting women to choose their next hat and was horrified to learn that she was to be confined to a basement, where she was expected to steam felty cloches into shape on a faceless, bald wooden bust. She lasted half a day before walking off in her lunch hour. The railway offices on Station Rise, then, Gladys said. Or behind the counter in the new Woolworth's. Or Terry's. Or Rowntree's – surely they would take her on with her family connections?

Freda was not going to work in Rowntree's! She was going to be a star! She was going to be famous! She was going to go to London! She would rather die of a surfeit of exclamation marks before she worked in an office or a factory!

What she needed was a kick up the bum, Gladys said. Full stop.

The night porters in Covent Garden had given way to the day-time barrow boys and stallholders. The world was waking up. Freda's feet were already practising steps beneath her thin coverlet. Florence, sharing the lumpy horsehair mattress, moaned a protest in her sleep.

The Grand Tableau

Nellie's flock still nestled in their beds, all apart from Niven, whose whereabouts were an eternal mystery to the rest of his family. The Cokers were, of necessity, nocturnal, the dawn chorus their lullaby, although it was already fading by the time they arrived home after celebrating Nellie's release. They roosted in Hanover Terrace, where Regent's Park was literally on their doorstep. Their grand white stucco house was a world away from the seediness of the Soho that paid for it.

Nellie, however, had grown accustomed to the harsh prison clock, being woken at six by the wardens banging and crashing on cell doors as if sleep itself were a sin. Sore-eyed with insomnia, she rose now from her sleepless bed after barely an hour, made herself a pot of tea and took her cup out to the garden just for the pleasure of opening a door and breathing her own air.

While she drank her tea, Nellie watched a freckled thrush tugging a worm out of a bed of red tulips. The worms would have their vengeance, for one day they would eat the thrush. They would eat Nellie, too. She feared it would not be long before she was worm food. She must prepare. She needed a plan.

When she had finished her tea she threw the residue into the flowerbed, surprising both tulips and thrush equally, and scrutinized the tea leaves that remained in the bottom of the cup. They confirmed her suspicions. Change was coming. It was time to do a Lenormand Grand Tableau.

Nellie went back inside the house and laid out the full pack of cards on the huge dining-room table. (Early Georgian, Cuban mahogany, a bargain obtained from the estate sale of an ancient lineage destroyed by the war. Nellie loved a bargain.)

'Hmm,' she said when she scrutinized the cards. A more expressive sound than it appears when written down. There was nothing mystifying about the cards. You might have said their message was Ozymandian. The serpent, the scythe, a coffin and a bouquet. The end of the party.

Nellie was tired. For perhaps the first time in her life she was wearying of the relentless drive required to keep their lives thrusting forward. The anchor of the Amethyst, the drag of the whole empire, was tugging her down. She knew that her health would not survive incarceration a second time and while in Holloway had begun to wonder about retiring – Deauville possibly, or even Torquay (a residential suite in the Imperial Hotel perhaps) – handing the keys to the kingdom to her children, with the crown going to the ever-reliable Edith.

Maddox had failed her in his role as protector. There had been no warning of the unexpected raid, of the sudden arrival of the uncouth troupe of uniforms who had lumbered into the club that night and arrested her. It had been humiliatingly public – the night of the Lord Mayor's Show – and the club had been packed to the rafters. She had been led away in handcuffs, bolstered a little by the supportive jeering aimed at the police by the Amethyst's regulars.

Maddox had visited her in jail, vigorously defending himself. He had not been on duty on the night of the raid, he said, and she must surely understand that, despite his best attentions, he was unable to divert the entirety of the Metropolitan Police all of the time. 'Methinks he doth protest too much,' Nellie said to her new cellmate.

The Belgian woman who had murdered her lover had been moved to a long-term wing. Nellie's new cellmate, Agnes, was from a family of cockney crooks and thieves; she and her sister were members of the notorious Forty Thieves gang. All women. ('Good idea,' Nellie said.)

There was a grapevine telegraph in Holloway that buzzed with a heady mixture of rumour and fact. Agnes herself was well acquainted with Maddox. 'He's after you, Nellie,' she warned. 'He's watched you all these years, seen how well you've done and now he wants it for himself.' It seemed that Maddox was no longer content to be the knave, he wanted to overthrow the Queen of Clubs and make himself the King.

'Over his dead body,' Nellie said.

She was puzzled. Why wasn't he making his move while she was in jail?

'Had to recruit,' Agnes said. 'He can't take over all on his own.' Maddox, she said, had trawled the streets for ne'er-do-wells – tramps, homeless men, toe-rags of the first water and disaffected war veterans press-ganged on street corners. Not to mention some of his own colleagues from Bow Street, who fancied a slice of the pie that Maddox was planning to feast on. 'Going to take your clubs by force,' Agnes said.

Furthermore, just to add to Nellie's woes, Agnes said a new broom was about to arrive in Bow Street, a Detective Chief Inspector John Frobisher, who intended to sweep the Cokers and their ilk out of the door.

Disturbed by her own soothsaying, Nellie collected her Lenormand cards from the dining table and returned them to the silk square that they were always wrapped in. She would go for a walk, she thought. A stroll, a leisurely one, merely for enjoyment. Walking was usually a practical activity for Nellie, it got her from one place to another and had little to do with enjoyment. Enjoyment was something that other people paid Nellie for. Nowadays, of course, she had the Bentley and her chauffeur, Hawker, and hardly walked anywhere. She had a bad hip, exacerbated by a thin prison mattress on an iron bed. In the Amethyst earlier, Edith had given her the present of a silver-topped cane, 'to mark your coming out', Edith said, as if Nellie were a debutante.

'I'm going for a walk,' she said to the cook, who raised an eyebrow at Phyllis, the new little scullery maid, once Nellie was out of sight. The cook had been with the Cokers so long that she had acquired their expressions for her own. The Cokers all had very eloquent eyebrows. They could conduct entire conversations with them, without saying a word. Phyllis had not yet mastered this skill and said, 'What?' to the cook, but the cook had turned her attention to the pair of eggs she was boiling for Shirley. Breakfast, which rarely took place before lunchtime, was a moveable feast in Hanover Terrace. The cook was driven to distraction by the Cokers' irregular eating habits and had been threatening to hand in her notice for years now but knew that Nellie would call her bluff.

'By the way,' Nellie said, reappearing so suddenly that the cook gave a little scream. Phyllis, who came from a disorderly home, was less prone to be unnerved by Nellie's well-practised gift of stealth.

'Yes, Mrs Coker?' the cook said.

'Keep an eye on Edith for me while I'm out.'

'Edith?'

'Yes, Edith. She's not herself.'

She disappeared again and both the cook and Phyllis held their breath until they were sure that she had gone this time.

It was Phyllis's turn to raise an eyebrow. She was a quick study.

Nellie had walked too far, almost as far as the zoo, and felt quite weak. She stopped to rest on a bench. Something very troubling had happened to her in prison. Startled awake in the middle of the night, she had watched as a woman glided out of the wall and approached her bed, where she floated a few inches above the floor, staring silently at Nellie.

Nellie did not cry out in horror at the sight of this spirit. She did not wake her cellmate, Agnes, or call for a wardress. There was no point, because she knew the identity of her ghost. It was Maud, the hostess who had died of an overdose on Armistice night in Jaeger's Dance Hall.

The spectral Maud was covered in river mud, her hair embellished with dripping weed. Water streamed off her clothes on to the stone flags of the cell floor. Nellie even recognized the dress she was wearing – oyster satin and lace, now stained dark with water. She remembered the girl's cards, how they had bewildered her. The robber mice, a coffin, a ship. A fearful journey by water. Did Maud drown? Had the girl been alive when she went into the river? And now she had dredged herself up to haunt Nellie?

The phantom had faded back into the stone wall of the cell and did not return to Nellie during the rest of her time in Holloway, but she knew that it was not the last time she would be visited by her. Maud was an account demanding to be settled. There was a reckoning coming for Nellie. Could she outrun it? That was the question. Not even Deauville seemed far enough.

Everything Nellie had done had been done for her children, not so much from love as from biology, the maternal imperative to foster and protect the generations, enabling the Cokers to go on and on until the crack of doom and the Last Judgement, a day that Nellie preferred not to think about. It couldn't all be thrown away, whether through death or retirement or general fecklessness on the part of her children. She must safeguard that legacy for the future, even if sacrifice was necessary, her own or someone else's. Someone else's, for preference. Frobisher must not be allowed to destroy it, and Maddox – or anyone else, for that matter – must not be allowed just to waltz in and swallow it whole. Deauville was shelved, it seemed.

Nellie flinched, as if an icy hand had touched her nape. Looking around Regent's Park, she could see only the tardy workers rushing to their offices and the early nannies with their perambulators. She suspected Maud, no living person would have such a cold touch. Although there *was* someone – flesh and blood, not a ghost – a man who was lurking behind a large beech tree, half hidden by its wide girth. When he saw that Nellie had spotted him he stepped further out of view, although his shoes remained comically visible.

Of course, in Nellie's (quite wide) experience, a man lurking behind a tree could be up to any number of things, most of them unpleasant. Especially one who was wearing two-tone shoes. Co-respondent shoes may be good enough for the Prince of Wales, but it was Nellie's belief that they gave a man a vulgar air (although few people would have taken fashion advice from Nellie Coker). But this man belonged to her.

He was making himself very obvious. Shouldn't a spy try to fade into the background a bit more? And why was he watching Nellie at this moment in time? He was supposed to be keeping an eye on Hanover Terrace, for heaven's sake.

She got up from her bench and waddled towards the beech tree, lifting her new cane as if it were a bayonet with which she was intending to stab the owner of the shoes.

Landor, unshakeable in the face of most violent assaults, took a step back in alarm.

'Stop lurking,' Nellie said.

A Shropshire Lad

On his way to the Dead Man's Hole, Frobisher took a detour through the Floral Hall opposite the police station. He could smell lilac. The scent drew him inside like a thread, to a stall that had a row of galvanized buckets full of great-headed blooms that must have come up from the country somewhere.

He should buy Lottie some flowers. She disliked lilacs. And lilies, of course, the French reserved lilies for funerals. Freesias, perhaps, something that indicated spring. Or tulips. You couldn't go wrong with tulips. He would stop in on the way home.

He was keeping knowledge of Lottie away from Bow Street. His colleagues would have been intrigued to know he had a French wife, even more intrigued to know that she was often not in her right mind. He preferred that they imagine his wife was called Hilda or Mabel and that she scurried around him when he came home, hanging up his overcoat, frying him a pork chop, soothing his troubled brow. They would have been baffled by the erratic Lottie, who would sometimes spend an entire evening crooning to a little cloth doll she had made.

He drank in the perfume of the lilacs. There had been lilacs growing wild along the lane leading to the farm cottage where he lived when he was a boy. And hawthorn, its sour scent the herald of summer. God, he missed the smell of the hedgerow.

'Help you, guv'nor?' the stallholder said, but Frobisher shied away, overcome by reminiscence of the past, for the innocent hopes of boyhood. It was unexpected, where was it coming from? It could hardly have been aroused by the Cokers. And not by Miss Kelling, surely? He had only met her for the first time yesterday, not long enough for her to have pierced his shell (he imagined a needle rather than a sword).

Had he done the right thing in engaging Miss Kelling? He was not about to put her in any danger, was he? She seemed the spirited type ('Absolutely, Chief Inspector'). It was a relief to come across that in a woman. She was not mad, nor French, nor particularly beautiful. She was a librarian.

He left thoughts of Gwendolen Kelling behind, along with the lilacs. There was a dead girl waiting for him. Perhaps she was the one he should be taking flowers to.

Après la Guerre

'Have you had a good look at them, Miss Kelling?' Detective Chief Inspector Frobisher asked Gwendolen as they watched the Cokers swagger away in their Bentleys. 'And do you think that you can do what I'm asking of you?'

'Absolutely, Chief Inspector.'

Gwendolen believed that it was always best to sound confident, even if you were not. It helped to prevent those around you from faltering. It was something that had served her well during the war, of course, but it had also proved a useful trait to have in the Library afterwards. Her fellow assistant librarians – the Misses Tate, Rogerson and Shaw – often seemed to need a steadying hand on the tiller. It had never ceased to surprise Gwendolen how much panic could be engendered by a misplaced book or an index card wrongly filed. Miss Tate, Miss Rogerson, Miss Shaw and even their Head in Clifford Street, Mr Pollock (yes, a man – a man, it seemed, must always be the Head), could get all a-twitter over the smallest thing. York was planning a new Carnegie Library in Museum Street and Gwendolen worried that the delicate hearts would not be able to stand the excitement of the move, let alone the reshelving of all those books.

One of the many casualties Gwendolen had nursed during the war had been a man – a boy – who had taken hours to choke to death on his own brains after a sniper shot to the head, and he had certainly not been worrying about where Sir Arthur Conan

Doyle's new book on spirit photography should land in the Dewey Decimal System.

'You are so sensible, Miss Kelling,' Mr Pollock often said to her. 'Sensible' was a very uninspiring adjective in Gwendolen's opinion, possibly bordering on insult.

The genteel and rather elderly coven of the Misses Tate, Roger-son and Shaw had exasperated her, but they meant well and so Gwendolen had suffered them sublimely, every morning don-ning a mask of docility, along with the librarian habit of lisle stockings, tweed skirt, woollen cardigan and one of her increas-ingly worn-out lawn blouses. She ~~may~~ as well have joined a holy *might* order, so cloistered did her life grow between the Library and Mother.

Gwendolen was staying at the Warrender, a modest establish-ment near the Victoria and Albert Museum that advertised itself as 'For Ladies Only' and was owned and run by a Mrs Bodley, who was as stringent as an Army matron and, as with Army matrons, left Gwendolen feeling rather rebellious.

When she had booked the room, Gwendolen had hoped that her fellow guests would be independent, professional women with whom she would have stimulating conversations over the pre-dinner sherry. Or, at the other end of the spectrum of pos-sibilities, perhaps she would be entertained by the sight of glamorous types being collected by their beaux every night to go dancing or to dinner. The reality was somewhat different. Apart from a straggle of tourists, the Warrender seemed to be pri-marily a permanent home for elderly residents or 'Distressed Gentlewomen' as Mrs Bodley referred to them, affording them capital letters.

Gwendolen had been pounced on that first night by the Dis-tressed (she was 'fresh meat', she thought) and had already made up a fourth at Bridge and been the unwitting prey in a cut-throat game of Euchre. The Misses Tate, Rogerson and Shaw were lambs compared to Mrs Bodley's so-called Gentlewomen.

The Library had not been a career choice (after all, who would choose to be a librarian?) but a financial necessity after the family money was lost. No, not lost – stolen. Many things were lost – wars and keys and hearts and boys at sea – but family fortunes, even modest ones, were stolen.

Gwendolen couldn't deny that at first there had been balm for her war-weary soul in the hushed oak of the bookshelves, but it was balm that sadly dissipated the moment she returned home at the end of the day for another endless evening of skirmishes with Mother and her list of complaints. She had lost her two sons to the war – Gwendolen's two younger brothers – and wore her bereavement with triumph rather than sorrow. For a woman who reported herself to be at constant risk of fainting and who spent her fragile afternoons lying on a chaise-longue, picking her way through one of Terry's expensive 'fancy boxes' of chocolates, she remained remarkably bellicose even after the end of the war. (As a family, they were loyal to Terry's, not Rowntree's, a fealty based on their house's proximity to Terry's factory on Bishopthorpe Road.) Gwendolen's mother had been a foolish woman, inclined to believe any passing nonsense. Of such people were patriots made, in Gwendolen's opinion. More's the pity.

Before the war, the Kellings were well off. There had been five of them: Mother, Father, Gwendolen and her brothers, Harry and Dickie. They lived in a lovely house close to the Knavesmire and employed a cook, a scullery maid, a parlour maid and a gardener. There was a croquet lawn and a pond, an orchard of apples, pears and plums. The Kellings had been rooted firmly to the ground beneath them – it would have to be a great wind that could blow away such a life. And so it was. The war had been an awfully great wind.

The money came from the family business – a small wireworks that had been started by Father's own father the previous century. It had prospered even before the war. 'People will always want wire,' their father said. He could have had no idea just how much wire a world at war would want.

The wireworks had been in a grimy side street, more a snicket, really, in the centre of town. It was surrounded by medieval streets and buildings and was an unusual industry in a town that, if the breeze was right, carried the comforting scent of cocoa on the air from Rowntree's factory or the uplifting perfume of sugar and strawberries being boiled down into their jellies.

Gwendolen often stopped by the wireworks on her way home from school. Their father had a glass-walled office that over-looked the busy, noisy workshop from a mezzanine. On one or two occasions in the recent past, Gwendolen would be scrub-bing a pan with steel wool – she was extraordinarily skilled at burning sauces – and the metallic tang in the air would transport her back in an instant to the wireworks, to her father, to the past.

'I've profited from death,' her father had said sadly to Gwen-dolen when she was home on leave in 1917. They had watched together as bale after bale of barbed wire was brought out from the workshop and loaded on to a wagon, destined for the Front. 'Crowns of thorns,' he said, sounding unusually poetic. He was a dutiful churchgoer, more to placate Mother than anything, but there were depths to his soul that were unplumbed by that same woman.

Her father died not long after, leaving a considerable sum, but the probate was in her mother's hands. Gwendolen was not dis-charged until 1919. It was all influenza cases in the Army by then, of course – one last savaging from the Furies – and when she finally set foot on Yorkshire soil again it was to find the money had all gone. At first, her mother had tried to blame her father, saying he had squandered it on the stock market, but eventually she had to admit that she had transferred it all to a man whom she had met – of all places – at her church. A man called Thomas Noble, who had enticed money from her mother on the pretext that he would 'handle her investments'.

'How could I have known?' her mother wailed. How could she *not* have known!

She was not the first foolish woman to be hoodwinked by a

cheat, but that was hardly a comfort. The ignoble Mr Noble was, of course, long gone, never to be heard of again. 'Lost,' her feeble mother said. 'Everything lost.' (No! Not lost! Stolen!)

They should have sold the lovely house, it would have released much-needed money if they had moved somewhere more modest, but Mother had refused to sell it and so time had limped on. The wireworks were sold for a cheap price, the world no longer wanted their never-ending bales of barbed wire, indeed it preferred to forget it had ever wanted them. They shut off half the rooms in the house and retreated, scrimping off Gwendolen's meagre salary from the job she took in the Library. She realized now that she should have found a way to take matters into her own hands, but one grief after another – her brothers, Father, the money, not to mention the war itself – had taken its toll on her and she had allowed herself to be worn down on the grindstone of Mother.

When war broke out Harry was just eighteen, at Oxford. In the middle of the Michaelmas term he came home and said he was going to join up. It was only later that Gwendolen discovered that he had been bombarded by letters from their jingoistic mother urging him to volunteer. The next day Mother accompanied him to the Green Howards recruiting office, as triumphant as if Harry were already a victor.

'Don't worry, Gwennie,' Harry said. 'It will be over in months and it will keep Mother quiet for once.'

Harry was their mother's favourite, Gwendolen was her father's. Dickie fell between the cracks, so Gwendolen took him on. He was a terrible prankster, always getting on everyone's nerves, always trying to attract attention. She could have happily boxed his ears on a daily basis for some joke or other he had played. He was given a 'Magic Set' for Christmas and never stopped pestering them with rope tricks, card tricks, coin tricks ('See this coin in my hand? I shall make it disappear before your eyes. Prepare to be surprised!') until they shouted at him to go away.

And so he did. Dickie had no need of dragooning. When he was fifteen he conjured his best disappearing trick of all, running away from home and lying about his age to join the Navy as a Signal Boy on HMS *Indefatigable*. 'Are you surprised?' he wrote in his appalling hand on a postcard from Portsmouth. 'I am having fun and japes. I expect you all miss me hugely. Here is a special kiss just for Gwennie. x'

Harry had been devoured by the amnesiac mud of Flanders fields with nothing to mark where he fell. And, like Dickie soon after him, no grave for them to mourn beside. The same month that Harry disappeared into the mud, HMS *Indefatigable* went down at Jutland and the deep took Dickie, along with a thousand of his fellow sailors.

When they had come to London six years ago to participate in that harrowing pageant, the funeral of the Unknown Warrior, Mother convinced herself that it was Harry who was destined for the tomb. Although she knew it couldn't be, Gwendolen liked to think that it was Dickie. He had had such a short little life and to be the one who 'was buried amongst kings' might be some compensation. But, of course, if it had been Dickie, he would have pushed away the coffin lid and sprung out like a jack-in-the-box. ('Are you surprised?')

All the missing, all the lost. Forever haunting the dogwatch that Gwendolen took alone every night.

Just when it had begun to seem to Gwendolen that the drudgery of her life might go on for ever, Mother had surprised her by beginning to fail. The Library service gave Gwendolen an unpaid leave of absence. Gwendolen had nursed many men near to their end, but she did not think that any of them had clung to life as stubbornly as Mother. The dull days of her dying seemed to stretch ahead with no end, just as the dull days of her living had. The Misses Tate, Rogerson and Shaw sent a little card, forget-me-nots, the kind you would send to a sweetheart, writing, 'We are thinking of you, dear, from your friends at the Library.' (Not

Mr Pollock, she noted.) Gwendolen was so touched that she wept, but quietly, for her mother would have been monstrously jealous of such emotion. She had claimed grief for her own long ago.

Gwendolen had missed the gentle, April-violet-scented presence of the Misses Tate, Rogerson and Shaw. Missed the quiet talks about nothing that threaded through the Library days. 'Gossip,' Mr Pollock called it dismissively, but Gwendolen thought that was the word men gave to women's conversation. Men talked in order to convey information or to ruminate on cricket scores and campaign statistics. Women, on the other hand, talked in an effort to understand the foibles of human behaviour. If men were to 'gossip', the world might be a better place. There would certainly be fewer wars.

'Goodness, Miss Kelling, you are quite the radical,' Mr Pollock said when Gwendolen voiced this opinion. It had been during a rather heated discussion on acquisitions. There had already been a long-running battle over *The Green Hat*, by Michael Arlen, Mr Pollock fearing its ability 'to corrupt the provinces' with its immorality. There were topics in it, he declared, that he couldn't even name in decent company. 'Venereal disease? Homosexuality? Promiscuity?' Gwendolen offered, unable to stop herself. Mr Pollock looked quite apoplectic. It was so very easy to light Mr Pollock's fuse and then watch him go off.

The battle over *The Green Hat* was won by Gwendolen mostly by dint of the fact that she was the only one in the Library who had read the novel. She disliked Arlen's writing, disliked his narrator, disliked his green-hatted *femme fatale*, Iris Storm, and her abstracted, irritating character. They said she was based on Nancy Cunard, that the whole thing was a kind of *roman à clef*, and Gwendolen wondered what it would be like to find yourself in a novel. Infuriating, she suspected. Nonetheless, she was willing to go into combat for it, arguing that it was important for the Library not to be out of step with modern times, and also, was it really their job to decide what people could or could not read? ('Yes,' Mr Pollock said.) Of course, part of her didn't really care, but she had rather enjoyed these sorties with Mr Pollock.

There was a constant stream of requests from female readers for the 'racier' writers of the day – Elinor Glyn, Ruby M. Ayres, Ethel M. Dell. 'The hot stuff,' Miss Shaw giggled. Lately there had been a positive deluge of calls for the new E. M. Hull novel, *The Sons of the Sheik*, something Mr Pollock, in particular, objected to.

But why shouldn't they stock the popular novels of the day? Gwendolen argued. What was so wrong with a little harmless pleasure, for heaven's sake, especially after so much that had been endured. Must everyone read Scott or Smollett? Even Austen was heavy-going for some readers. Mr Pollock himself lauded Addison and Carlyle. Gwendolen could think of nothing worse. The sequel to *The Sheik* would be acquired over his dead body, he said, causing the benevolent coven to turn their grey heads and regard him speculatively, as if he had just spelled away the remainder of his grey and dusty life. Gwendolen couldn't help but laugh.

As the deathbed vigil finally neared its end, Gwendolen vowed to herself that if she returned to the Library, she would tolerate Mr Pollock in a saintly manner. A counsel of perfection that, she knew, was bound to fail. But she didn't have to go back. She didn't have to categorize books and stamp tickets. Nor did she have to scrub saucepans and darn stockings. Gwendolen was finally discharged from a daughter's duty, for even malingerers die eventually. The winds had picked up, she was out of the doldrums.

In the Library she had been, naturally, the subject of many sympathetic condolences on her mother's death from the Misses Tate, Rogerson and Shaw and had accepted them with due sobriety. Her colleagues had sent a small wreath to her mother's funeral, *From your friends at the Library*, and Gwendolen thanked them, saying, 'Mother would have been touched.' In fact, her mother would probably have complained at the paucity of flowers or that they made her sneeze or were the wrong colour. She had been overly fond of purple shades – it was a dreadfully suffocating colour to put up with. Gwendolen would be happy if she never saw mauve again.

Although she had told Frobisher that she was on leave from the Library, she had already made her farewells before embarking on her trip to London. She wanted him to think her anchored, she intuited he would respect that more than her current circumstances.

'We shall miss you so much, Miss Kelling,' Miss Shaw said. Gwendolen was kissed affectionately on the cheek by them all, except Mr Pollock, of course, who gave her a lifeless handshake and said he wished her well.

She had been picked up from the Warrender at an unearthly hour this morning by Detective Chief Inspector Frobisher in a car driven by a police constable – a fact that did not go unnoticed by Mrs Bodley.

Detective Chief Inspector Frobisher – what an unwieldy moniker. Gwendolen decided she would call him Frobisher in future, although perhaps not to his face. He had a very solemn face. He was the taciturn sort – she had known a few – and seemed pained by her attempts at conversation.

It was still barely eight o'clock when he returned her to the Warrender and Gwendolen said, 'So shall you go home now?'

'Home?' he repeated with a perplexed frown, as if he wasn't sure what the word meant. (Surely he had a home?) 'No,' he replied after a pause. 'Duty calls, I'm afraid. I shall go to work, to Bow Street.'

'And that's where I shall come to give you my "report"?' She laughed at the word, at the enterprise ahead of her. (She was feeling a little giddy.) When he frowned at her again – and he did frown rather a lot – she said, 'Don't worry. I will be sensible, I promise. I am known for it, unfortunately.'

'You must not attract attention to yourself.'

'I am a librarian,' she had reassured him. 'We are accustomed to moving through the world unnoticed.'

The constable who was driving them opened the car door for her and Gwendolen ran up the steps of the Warrender, turning at the top to salute Frobisher. How full of vigour she was. It felt as if a great weight had been removed from her, which it had, of course, because her mother was dead. Alleluia!

Mrs Bodley – rarely absent from reception, Gwendolen had discovered – glanced inquisitively at her outdoor clothes. 'Out early, Miss Kelling?' she enquired, when what she meant, Gwendolen presumed, was 'Back late, Miss Kelling?'

'I barely saw my bed last night, Mrs Bodley,' Gwendolen said breezily. She was rewarded with a pruny look. 'I do hope I haven't missed breakfast.'

Breakfast, like all the meals in the Warrender, was a hefty affair. A large silver pot of coffee circulated round the dining room continually, a thin young waitress called Violet staggering beneath its weight. Poor Violet was cowed by both coffee pot and Mrs Bodley.

Porridge, fat back bacon, fried egg and black pudding, followed by toast and marmalade. You could say what you liked about Mrs Bodley but the Distressed were never knowingly underfed by her. Gwendolen ate it all with relish. How full of rude health she was. She was not yet thirty-two, she reminded herself. She had lived beneath the shadow of the war for long enough. She could be free of it now. The Relief of Gwendolen, like the lifting of a siege. She signalled for more coffee and exchanged smiles with Violet. They were almost like conspirators, Mrs Bodley their joint foe.

Could she do what Frobisher had asked? She had no idea, but she would give it a go. It would be an adventure. With any luck it would *not* be sensible.

Frobisher Deskbound

It was only by chance that Gwendolen Kelling had caught him yesterday, brooding at his desk in Bow Street. Frobisher spent as little time as possible in an office, preferring to be out and about. A man in an office saw nothing, a man on the street saw much, especially a suspicious man. The happiest time in Frobisher's career had been when he was a young constable in uniform, patrolling the streets, wearing out the leather of his big boots. He had been on crowd duty for the old Queen's funeral and for the new King's coronation, and for the one that followed, too.

He had seen the best of London, but since the war the capital had gone into decline. *O tempora! O mores!* he thought. Everyone had gone quite mad in the peace, he sometimes wondered if they were not approaching the death of Western civilization. But then he supposed people had been talking about the end of civilization since Babylonian days, or, indeed, Tutankhamun. Those inclined to superstition talked a great deal about the curse that had come with the opening of the Pharoah's tomb. It was deemed to be manifesting itself across the capital. Frobisher was dismissive of such irrationality, although of course he had been as thrilled as everyone else by the discovery of the tomb. (*Wonderful things!*) He had taken out a subscription to *National Geographic* just so that—

There had been an efficient knock on his door and then—

'Chief Inspector?'

'Yes. Miss . . . ?'

'Gwendolen. Gwendolen Kelling. Your name was given to me,' she said, 'by a Mr Ingram. He was told by someone to contact you at Scotland Yard, but he couldn't find you there.'

'That's because I'm not there. I'm here.' Was it really beyond Scotland Yard's capabilities to have redirected this Mr Ingram to Bow Street? (Yes, was probably the answer to that question.)

'Well, I have found you now. I'll get straight to the point, shall I?'

'Please. Take a seat first, won't you, Miss Kelling?'

'Well, the thing is,' she said, sitting on the chair opposite him, 'I'm looking for two girls, Freda Murgatroyd and Florence Ingram. They're fourteen – barely out of childhood, Florence in particular – she's rather immature, apparently, convent-educated, and I'm afraid Freda persuaded Florence to run away with her to London.'

'And you are an . . . aunt?' Frobisher had asked, adding hastily, 'Or sister?' in case 'aunt' implied age. She was in her early thirties, he guessed, old enough to be an aunt, he supposed, although he was more skilled at judging the age of a horse than a woman. He still occasionally went hacking in Epping Forest. He would rather be on horseback than in an Austin Seven. Horses were on their way out, they would not be coming back.

'No,' she said, breaking into his wandering thoughts. 'I'm a friend of Freda's sister. Freda has no father and her mother is useless, I'm afraid, and Cissy – the sister, half-sister really – has small children, whereas I have no dependents and have taken a leave of absence from my employment – in a library – and am fancy-free, so I volunteered to come down to London to look for her.'

Frobisher found himself having trouble keeping up with all this information. She had a very rapid style of conversation. She seemed full of energy and amusement, it was an unusual thing to encounter in his own office. It threw him rather. 'Do you perhaps have a photograph of either girl?' he asked.

'Of course,' she said, hitting her forehead with the palm of her hand. (She was quite expressive for a librarian. Almost Italian. The word 'librarian' had previously conjured up an image of a vinegary spinster, not the animated creature before him.)

61

'What an idiot I am not to think of that!' she said. 'I'll ask Cissy to send me one of Freda in the morning's post. I'm sure she'll be able to get hold of a photograph of Florence as well. Her parents are desperate, but I'm afraid Freda's mother was rather glad to be rid of her.'

'Are these girls capable of fending for themselves?'

'As I said, Florence is rather young for her age.'

'And Freda?'

'Quite the opposite, I'm afraid. I do have a note that Freda left behind for her mother but I don't think you'll find it much use.' She took a piece of creased pink notepaper from her bag and passed it over his desk.

'*Dear Mother,*' Frobisher read aloud. '*I have run away to London to seek my –* what's that word, Miss Kelling?'

'Fortune.'

'*To seek my fortune. I am going to dance on the stage. The next time you hear from me I will be – ?*'

'Famous. Her handwriting is atrocious. There's an exclamation mark after "famous",' she added. 'You've made fame sound very pedestrian, Chief Inspector. It's a word that seems to demand a sparkle.'

Frobisher ignored this remark. It seemed safest. He was never sure how to respond to mockery, even the mildest kind, and certainly not from a woman. Nor was he sure how to put a sparkle on a word. Or indeed on anything. Instead he continued to read doggedly from the pink notepaper. It was impregnated with something rather unpleasant.

('Scented geranium, I think,' Miss Kelling said.)

'*I will be famous. You don't need to worry about me. Sincerely, your daughter, Freda.*'

A note was better than no note, Frobisher supposed. Girls who left no note walked through a door and disappeared into thin air. Girls who wrote notes left some evidence behind. A note had purpose behind it.

'*Seek my fortune,*' he murmured thoughtfully, handing the pink notepaper back. He supposed he could send a constable round the dance schools – they were likely places to find girls who were 'seeking their fortune' on the stage.

In London, he told Miss Kelling, dancing girls were an indus-try, 'churned out like steel or coal, I'm afraid'. There was an enormous number of dance schools on Frobisher's patch. The majority of girls who 'graduated' had no hope of making it into a theatre and finding the fame they craved so badly. Instead, they were siphoned off into the nightclubs or sent abroad to dance and were often never heard from again. Some ended up on the street, of course. Or washed up on the banks of the Thames, fished out at Wapping and Deptford. Or Tower Bridge. He didn't mention those ones to Miss Kelling.

'And what do the girls do in the nightclubs?' she asked. 'I'm from York – I'm not sure we have nightclubs.'

'The girls are paid to dance with the customers,' Frobisher said. 'They're called "hostesses".'

'That sounds rather like . . .'

'Exactly. The worst are Nellie Coker's clubs. They seem to eat girls. Mrs Coker's "Merry Maids", as they're known. Interpret that as you will.'

And that was when Frobisher was struck by an idea.

'Miss Kelling? I have a proposition for you.'

'Infiltration, Chief Inspector?'

'Well, I don't know if that's the word I would use. It seems a little dramatic – perhaps "reconnoitring" would be more accur-ate. Just for one evening, Miss Kelling. In the Amethyst, Nellie Coker's biggest club. Her command post, you might say. I've no female constables in Bow Street at the moment. I need someone who wouldn't look entirely out of place.'

'Entirely?'

'Be my eyes and ears for the night. Tell me if you see anything untoward. And, who knows, perhaps you'll spot one of your missing girls.'

She barely wavered. 'Very well, why not? With you?'

'Me?' He was alarmed by the idea and said hastily, 'No, no, not me. I'll arrange for someone to escort you. I must warn you, Miss Kelling, the club is a den of iniquity, you may come across behaviour that might shock you.'

'I nursed throughout the war, Chief Inspector, I doubt there is anything left on earth that could shock me any more. Shall I assume a false name, an alias?'

He had not expected her to be quite so eager. 'That won't be necessary, Miss Kelling. You must exercise caution, it is very easy to be seduced by these people.' He hesitated and then said, 'If you are willing, the matriarch, Nellie Coker, the so-called Queen of Clubs, is being released from Holloway prison tomorrow morning. Why not accompany me to watch the spectacle?'

'Will it be a spectacle?'

'Almost certainly.'

'Excellent. I am keen on spectacles, I have not had enough lately. And now I should go,' she said. 'I have taken up enough of your valuable time. I am off to do some shopping and sightseeing.'

'Sightseeing? Do you have a Bartholomew's? You will need one. Oh, and . . .' – a thought struck him – 'you will need an evening gown for the Amethyst, Miss Kelling. Do you have one with you?'

'Absolutely, Chief Inspector.'

'Just Inspector will do, Miss Kelling.' He imagined her calling him John. It distracted him so much that he stood up abruptly and said, 'I shall make arrangements, then. I shall send word to . . . ?'

'The Warrender. In Knightsbridge. I am all anticipation, Inspector.'

Nightbirds

'Where's Ma?' Shirley asked, joining Betty and Kitty at the dining table.

'Search me,' Betty said. 'Am I my mother's keeper?' Niven's dog pricked up his ears, in vain. His thoughts were always on Niven.

Hanover Terrace had no Bradshaw's timetable to keep them on track, there was no pull or push to their days, they simply drifted into them. Edith alone was propelled, although not today. They rose at their leisure in the late morning or early afternoon and ate a meal that meant something different for each of them. Shirley, for example, was contemplating the boiled eggs that had just been delivered by the cook, while Betty was tackling some kind of salad in aspic ('Shrimp, I think, but it could be anything, really'). Salads were not the cook's speciality; this one looked as if it would have been more at home in an aquarium.

'I heard Ma go out earlier,' a jam-smeared Kitty said. She was sitting on the window-seat entertaining herself by reading out loud from the gossip columns in the papers. She had recently been expelled from boarding school (arson, vehemently denied) and no one seemed to know what to do with her, so Nellie had tasked her with being the one who kept an eye on the papers for useful snippets of information – *Lady Melchior has departed from Durban on the* Windsor Castle *and is homeward bound to Southampton*, for example. Then a head waiter in one of the clubs could murmur, 'Welcome home from South Africa, Lady Melchior, good to have you back,' as he presented her with a bottle of champagne that would appear to be free but would be cunningly rolled into the bill at the end of the night. Nothing was free in Nellie's world, not even love. Perhaps especially not love.

The uncharacteristically tardy Edith, frowzy with sleep, joined the gathering flock and said, 'I'm feeling peaky.'

'You do look green around the gills,' Betty said, summoning sympathy from somewhere. Sometimes she surprised herself. Betty was very hard-nosed yet occasionally mawkishly senti-mental, a combination shared with her mother and many dictators both before and since.

Ramsay yawned his way to the table and mumbled something that could have been a greeting or an insult. They rarely resorted to good manners with each other.

An ashen Edith pinched out a piece of toast from the rack but then put it to one side as if it were crawling with spiders.

'Have some rum,' Shirley suggested. 'That always does the trick for me.' Edith shuddered at the idea.

'Try an eggnog,' Shirley suggested. Edith gagged.

'Is Ma all right? Betty asked no one in particular. 'Not ill or anything?'

'Ill?' Edith queried. 'Why do you say that?'

'I don't know. She just doesn't seem to be quite herself.'

'I think prison gave Ma too much time for thinking,' Shirley said.

Neither Betty nor Shirley had much time for thinking. The 'life of the mind' was a waste of both life and mind as far as they were concerned, despite Cambridge. Or perhaps because of it.

'*What is the hour at which nightlife begins? At Buckingham Pal-ace I am told it is nine o'clock; Maida Vale, which likes a "nice long evening", plumps for seven thirty; Mayfair (Mr Michael Arlen will correct me if I am wrong) for half past eight; South Kensington tucks its legs under the solid mahogany a quarter of an hour earlier; and Wimbledon wants the aspidistra removed and the hire-purchase masterpiece ready for action by eight sharp.*'

'Oh, do shut up, Kitty,' Betty said.

'What *is* that drivel?' Shirley asked.

'Vivian Quinn, in his Society Paragraphist column,' Ramsay said wearily.

'Can't Kitty read *Children of the New Forest* or something?' Edith asked irritably.

Kitty daydreamed of being mentioned in the newspapers herself. *The fashionable youngest daughter of wealthy West End worthy Mrs Coker was seen last night at the Grafton Galleries . . .* and so on. The rest of them were disdainful of the so-called 'journalists' who wrote these social diaries. 'Fleet Street hacks,' Edith said dismissively. Patrick Balfour, Horace Wyndham, Vivian Quinn, of course – they were waspish men of a certain type, acerbic and snobbish and what Nellie termed 'quietly flamboyant'. 'An oxymoron,' Betty said. 'Exactly,' Nellie said.

Despite her own instinctive distrust for the society gossip columns, Nellie recognized the value of publicity in places like the *Express* or the *Sketch* and the Diary in the *Evening Standard*. Their readers loved to feast on tales of celebrities, and if those same celebrities were parading themselves in the Amethyst or one of her other clubs then so much the better. The clubs were hungry and they had to be fed. The bread and butter of the trade wasn't the Tallulah Bankheads of this world, but the couples who came up to town on the Metropolitan line from Pinner for the evening, hoping for a bit of fun.

Since his return from Switzerland, the burden of nurturing the columnists had fallen on Ramsay's unwilling shoulders. He was buttering a slice of toast very slowly, as if delaying the moment when he would have to bite into it. Ramsay was not feeling in great form either this morning (too much dope last night), but he wasn't going to incite Edith's wrath by saying as much. Edith enjoyed a fight. He sighed in a way that made her raise a threatening eyebrow at him.

'Are you ill as well?' she asked sharply, ready for a contest.

'Not at all,' he said, taking an enormous bite out of the toast to prove his health and almost choking on it. Sometimes it felt to Ramsay as if his life were just one long struggle to be real. (He was inclined to melodrama.) He must have unconsciously voiced something to that effect because Shirley startled him by saying, 'Oh, sweet, darling Ramsay, of course you're real!' (She was much the nicest of them all.) 'You suffer because you're creative. Artists *have* to suffer, it's how they arrive at the truth of the thing.'

In the Alps there had been nothing to do but lie on a veranda and stare at Swiss snow that was as blank and blindingly white as new paper until he thought he was going to go mad. No one travelled to visit him, although that didn't really surprise him. His mother could easily have taken the Orient Express to Zurich but claimed she was too busy. With each child she had produced, Nellie's interest had waned, so that Ramsay and Kitty at the tail end were dreadfully neglected.

Ramsay had begged Nellie to send him reading material but it was Niven who obliged, sending out crates of books for him, everything from the Mabinogion to Virginia Woolf. When he returned to English shores a few months ago, Ramsay's brain was so infected with words that he was almost overcome by the insistent need to purge them. A novel, he decided, he would write a novel! (A great one, obviously.) Unfortunately, the actual act of putting anything on paper (paper as blank and blindingly white as Swiss snow) had proved less easy than it looked.

Shirley and Betty had bought him a little Remington portable for his recent twenty-first birthday. (*The machine for the man who travels* – not true unless you counted Switzerland, which Ramsay didn't.) What to write?

'Don't they say "write what you know"?' Betty said. 'But you don't know anything, do you?'

'Thanks.'

If he wrote what he knew, it would be a sparse novel about a man in a Swiss sanatorium in the grip of hopelessness and existential dread. Who on earth would want to read that? Ramsay certainly wouldn't.

'All you have to do,' Shirley advised, 'is write one sentence after another and – *voilà!* A novel.'

It would be easier if he had a title. If he had the right title then the rest of his novel would start to flow naturally from it. Could you be a writer if you hadn't actually written anything? An artist if you hadn't actually produced any art?

'Of course you can,' Shirley said. 'You have the *soul* of an artist, you don't necessarily need to *do* anything.' Edith snorted contemptuously but Shirley continued blithely, 'You know, how's this for an idea, Ram? You and I could run off together – to the Riviera or Paris – and live in the traditional garret, and I'll paint, and you'll write the great *roman du jour*, you know, like *The Green Hat*.'

Oh, not that book again, Ramsay thought. Ramsay was sick of hearing about it. Anyone could write a provocative but ultimately quite tedious contemporary novel.

'*You* could!' Shirley said, without irony.

Ramsay didn't know that Shirley painted. 'I don't,' she said airily, 'but I'm sure I could.'

From her seat at the window, Kitty had a good view of the man who was standing in the private gardens that separated Hanover Terrace from the street. The man was staring fixedly up at the house, as if he were waiting for something to begin. He was olive-skinned with a foreign look about him. Smoking a cigarette, he had the brazen air of someone who didn't care about whether he was seen or not. He was wearing two-tone brogues that Kitty knew were called co-respondent shoes, although she didn't know why and no one would tell her when she asked.

Her being there didn't put him off, in fact he seemed amused by Kitty's presence. She raised an enquiring Coker eyebrow and he touched his hat in a small gesture of acknowledgement and ambled away. Kitty chewed thoughtfully on a piece of toast. She said nothing. The man was too interesting to share.

*

Niven came in with the post that they had all been too lazy to collect from the doormat and distributed it around the table by tossing it in the direction of its recipients. He poured himself a cup of coffee and drank it standing up, his overcoat still on, a lovely tweed ulster from Huntsman. It had a deep beaver collar that Kitty had a sudden urge to stroke; she reached out a hand to touch the fur but Niven batted her away as if she were a fly. The collar reminded her of Moppet, their cat from Great Percy Street. He had been run over by a dustcart the previous year and Kitty wished that they had had him stuffed or made into a collar. Or even mummified, like the Egyptian cat that decorated the bar of the Sphinx. She was not allowed in the Sphinx – the most rackety of the Coker clubs – but that didn't stop her going there.

'Ma's deserted,' Shirley told Niven, callously decapitating her second boiled egg. 'Absent without leave.'

'She'll have to go in front of the firing squad, then,' he said. 'That's the penalty.'

'Poor old Ma,' Betty laughed.

'What's that?' Kitty asked, hanging round Ramsay's neck like a boa constrictor as he opened an envelope addressed to him.

'Get off, you're strangling me.'

She read aloud. '*You are invited to Romps. The Honourable Pamela Berowne requests your company at a Baby Party.*'

'What the heck is that?' Shirley asked. 'Do you have to bring a baby with you? That would be a nightmare.'

'She's a Bright Young Thing,' Ramsay said gloomily, unwinding Kitty from his neck. 'She's in pursuit of me,' he added. 'God knows why.'

'I know Pamela,' Betty said. 'She's not in the least bit bright.'

All of the Cokers poured scorn on the so-called Bright Young Things.

'She's not even that young,' Shirley said.

'Just a thing, then,' Betty said.

They cackled, delighted with themselves. They often were.

'Are you going to go?' Kitty asked Ramsay.

'Maybe. Something interesting might happen, I suppose.'

'Something you could write about,' Shirley said encouragingly.

'Ma will want you to show your face,' Betty said. 'Fly the Amethyst flag.'

'We have a flag?' Kitty asked.

'Your friend Vivian Quinn will go, I expect,' Betty said.

'He's not my friend,' Ramsay said. 'His column's moronic. *He*'s moronic.'

'Vivian Quinn?' an eager Kitty said to Ramsay. 'I didn't know he was your friend.'

'He's *not* my friend,' Ramsay said. 'Why does everyone say he is? I just happen to know him, that's all. I don't even like him.'

'You see him all the time,' Betty said.

'I see *you* all the time, that doesn't make you my friend.'

'Apparently,' Betty said, unflustered by this slight, 'he's writing a *roman à clef*. I wonder if you'll be in it, Ramsay,' she laughed. 'Are you all right, Edith? You look like you're going to be sick.'

Edith did look green but remained stoically at the table.

'Why on earth should I be in it?' Ramsay said. 'I'll have Quinn killed if I am.'

'By whom?' Kitty asked.

'Niven, of course,' Shirley said.

'You can do your own dirty work,' Niven said. 'I've done enough killing.'

'Have you? Killed people?' Kitty asked, seeing Niven in a new, interesting light.

'What do you think war is, you idiot?'

Betty had moved on from her salad to a peach that she was flaying meticulously with a little solid-silver penknife that was engraved with her initials and had been given to her by an admirer. Nellie was in two minds about this gift – more useful than flowers, certainly, but to what end would you give a woman a knife, she puzzled? It was an invitation to a stabbing, in Nellie's

71

opinion. Chekhov had his gun, Betty has her knife. Caution seems to be required in her narrative.

'I saw you yesterday,' Betty said accusingly to Niven.

Niven had still not sat down or removed his coat. He was someone who was always either coming or going, they found it disconcerting when he lingered like this between the two states.

'Near St James's,' Betty persisted. 'You were stopped at those new "traffic light" things and there was a woman in the car.'

'Who was she?' Shirley asked.

'No one,' Niven said.

'She must have been someone. Were you taking her for a spin?'

Betty guffawed in a very unladylike way and said, 'Oh, is that what they call it now?'

'Did you, Niven?' Kitty asked with commendable innocence. 'Take her for a spin?' He ignored the question.

'Are you going out again?' Betty asked him. He ignored that question, too. 'Give us a lift, won't you? Shirley and I are going to Selfridges.'

'Can I come with you?' Kitty asked.

'No.'

Niven had the best car, they were all agreed – a Hispano-Suiza so magnificent that people stopped in the street and gazed in awe at its beauty. ('Divine,' Kitty drawled, fluttering her hands in an inexplicable gesture. She always had some star or celebrity that she was emulating. She tended towards iconolatry.)

'Well, *will* you give us a lift, Niven?' Betty said. The now naked peach on her plate was a perfect ripe globe that could have under-studied for one of the golden apples that distracted Atalanta.

In answer, Niven reached for the peach and took a great bite out of it, at which outrage Betty jumped like a scalded cat, yelling at him that he was a dark-hearted bastard who deserved to die, and Edith said, 'There's a child present' (Where? Kitty asked), adding, 'Do put the knife down, Betty.'

Niven clicked his fingers and Keeper jumped to attention. The pair of them left swiftly before anyone could claim a seat in the Hispano-Suiza.

The rest of them parted as smoothly and instinctively as a flock of crows will suddenly break apart and scatter, each to its own destination. Edith went to 'have a lie down' in her room, but only got as far as the downstairs cloakroom, where they all heard her being sick.

'I hope whatever it is isn't catching,' Betty said.

'She was drinking gin last night,' Shirley said.

'She really shouldn't, doesn't have the stomach for it.'

Betty and Shirley had to cram themselves into Betty's little Sunbeam while Ramsay, bolstered by Shirley's faith in him, disappeared to his room to think about his novel. Writers needed to think a great deal, in fact they almost needed to do more thinking than writing.

A discarded Kitty returned to the window-seat and finished the equally abandoned peach. She was hoping that the mysterious man might have returned to his watch, but the gardens were empty so she ran herself a bath and emptied an entire jar of Betty's Mermaid bath salts into it. Afterwards, feeling rather shrivelled, she asked the cook to make her *chocolat chaud* ('Eh?' the disgruntled cook said) and then pilfered several large slices of ham from the larder and ate them, until she felt almost as sick as Edith.

When Nellie eventually returned home to Hanover Terrace from her enchantment in the park she took Kitty by surprise, appearing suddenly at the French windows. She was locked out and Kitty let her in, although it crossed her mind not to.

'Shouldn't you be in bed?' Nellie said.

'I've only just got up,' Kitty said reasonably.

The Dardanelles

Niven took up his usual post in the barber's chair, where he was muffled in a steaming towel by a mournful man called Emin who seemed to carry the weight of the Ottoman Empire on his back. He was a fierce type, too, wielding his cut-throat razor with a dramatic flourish. They were in largely mute agreement over many things, particularly both Churchill and the disastrous folly of Gallipoli, but even so Niven restrained himself from voicing his thoughts on the subject as no man wants to discuss politics with someone holding an open blade in their hand.

Emin meant 'trustworthy' in Turkish, he had told Niven on more than one occasion, as if he needed to prove his honourable credentials. Niven, on the other hand, liked to keep his virtues well hidden from the world. The woman, for example, spied by Betty in his car in St James's yesterday had indeed existed, but she was not the sort of woman that Betty presumed. Betty was both long-sighted and short-sighted at the same time – a considerable feat (or 'blind as a bat', according to Nellie). If she had been wearing her spectacles, she might have recognized the woman as one of the cleaners from the Amethyst. (Or perhaps not. Betty wasn't the sort to remember cleaners.)

The cleaner had broken an ankle falling down the stairs in the club and Niven had carried her all the way back up to the top – and she was the hefty sort – and then driven her to St Thomas's hospital, where he counted off five pound notes from his wallet and gave them to her, because he knew Nellie would give her the sack when she found out. Absenteeism was not tolerated at the Amethyst, no matter the cause. It ensured the staff stayed hale and hearty, Nellie said. '*Pour encourager les autres*, and so on.' Niven could have done with his mother by his side in the trenches during the war. The peace was a different matter.

'*Efendim?*'

'Nothing, Emin. Carry on.'

'I met a man yesterday,' Emin said casually.

'Oh?'

Emin met many men in the course of his day, he said. He heard many things, too. A man will often let fall his secrets when swaddled in the barber's chair. Niven waited patiently for whatever was to come next.

'A man called Azzopardi. Was sitting right here where you are now.'

'Turkish?'

'Maltese. A bad man. Do you know him?'

'Never heard of him.' Emin slapped cologne on his face. 'Is there something I should know?' Niven coaxed when nothing more was forthcoming from the Turk.

'He is inviting your mother to meet him tomorrow. For afternoon tea.'

Niven barked with laughter. 'Afternoon tea? He certainly does sound bad, Emin.'

'She should watch her back, *effendim*.'

'My mother is nothing *but* back, Emin.'

Niven clicked his fingers and Keeper stood to attention. Emin was duly paid and tipped. So, Niven thought, Azzopardi had set the wheels in motion. The man wanted something from Nellie, but just what was unclear.

Last week, when Nellie was still tucked away inside Holloway, Azzopardi had sidled up to Niven on the rails at the dog track

75

and introduced himself. A prelude followed when flattery was purred in Niven's ear, not something he responded well to, before Azzopardi eventually got to the point.

He was a large bull walrus of a man with affected mannerisms and silky speech and came across more like a pantomime villain than a threat. Niven wouldn't have been surprised if he was not in fact from Malta but Ramsgate or Southend and had adopted this theatrical persona for effect. A clown, Niven concluded. His English was surprisingly fluent. His life of crime, he said, had begun when he was a boy with stealing a goat. And now, Niven suspected, he wanted to steal an empire. Nellie's empire.

'Not theft,' he said. 'Compensation.'

'Compensation? For what?'

The dogs came out of the traps.

Azzopardi offered a cigar. Niven refused and they watched in silence as the dog that Niven owned came in first.

'Yours?' Azzopardi asked.

'No,' Niven said. He sensed that this man didn't like dogs, and it made him reluctant to confess to owning one. Keeper had been returned home, the dog track was problematic for him. 'Not my dog,' he said. Lying came easily to Niven, he thought of it as a means of protecting the truth.

Nellie was an old woman, Azzopardi said. She was growing weak. Wasn't it time for her to leave the field, to enjoy the fruits of her labours?

'She's only in her fifties,' Niven said, amused by the man's arrogance, 'and if you're after her clubs she'll send you away with your tail between your legs.'

'You're your mother's natural heir.'

Niven laughed. 'I think you'll find that's my sister Edith. And, trust me, we're not about to inherit.'

Niven was a pragmatist, Azzopardi said, he could see the writing on the wall. Nellie was no longer hungry. 'And the world today, Mr Coker, belongs to those with the appetite for change. For new ways of thinking. The victor will take the spoils.'

'You sound like an anarchist,' Niven said. 'Or an Italian fascist.'

'No, Mr Coker, I sound like a businessman.'

The Sights of London

'You will need an evening gown for the Amethyst, Miss Kelling. Do you have one with you?' Frobisher had asked her, casting a doubtful eye over her old coat and worn shoes.

'Absolutely, Chief Inspector.' Best to sound confident, et cetera. The only evening wear that Gwendolen had brought in her luggage was an ancient velvet frock, probably more suited to a vicarage tea party than a London nightclub, not that she had ever been to either. Something more glamorous was clearly called for, something more *à la mode*. The sightseeing she had mentioned to Frobisher could wait. Liberty's here I come, she thought.

'Going out again, Miss Kelling?' Mrs Bodley said as Gwendolen passed beneath her sentry eye. She considered replying with something worthy – the British Museum or the National Gallery – but instead she enjoyed ruffling Mrs Bodley's starched feathers further by saying gaily, 'To Liberty's in Regent Street, Mrs Bodley. I am on a mission to buy a new wardrobe.'

Mrs Bodley rewarded this frivolity with an almost imperceptible moue of disapproval.

Too bad, Gwendolen thought. She had had her fill of rectitude.

In the York that Gwendolen had left behind two days ago, the daffodils were still lingering on the slopes of the city walls, but here in the public spaces of the capital they had long gone over. Gwendolen had not been to London since the funeral of the Unknown Warrior, when she and Mother had been part of the sombre crowds lining the route to Westminster Abbey. Like so many others they had been sternly armoured in the breastplate of grief. Barely a sob could be heard, just a rustling sound as if a great flock of black birds had descended silently on London. Then, the whole enshrouded city had been in muffled mourning, and to see it now, dressed for spring, was something of a shock.

Invigorating, too, and she swung her arms as she strode through Hyde Park. The 'Cock o' the North', the regimental march of the Gordon Highlanders, had crept into her head uninvited and refused to be dislodged. She would have preferred some sprightly Mozart – the Clarinet or the Horn – but the martial music swept her onwards.

She had once formed a pleasant, short-lived attachment to an officer in the Gordon Highlanders. There had been a little sedate flirting between them, nothing more. (No opportunity for more, she remembered ruefully.) He had passed through her hands, literally, at a field hospital at Wimereux – shrapnel in his leg, not too bad – and was evacuated back to England. When he returned to the Front, she looked for him in the daily reports, but his name never appeared amongst the dead. He didn't write, but then neither did she.

Everyone she worked alongside in France had been insatiable letter-writers and resolute diary-keepers, but Gwendolen had felt no urge to chronicle, no desire for an *aide-mémoire*. Life was for absorbing, not recording. And in the end, it was all just paper that someone would have to dispose of after you were gone. Perhaps, after all, one's purpose in this world was to be forgotten, not remembered.

'How practical you are, Miss Kelling,' Mr Pollock said. 'How ruthless,' her mother said.

Would ruthlessness have recommended her to Frobisher, she wondered? Or was he the kind of man who regarded women as delicate flowers to be nurtured and protected. He was a man of sighs, frequent and doleful, like a dissatisfied dog, and yet she was sorry he wouldn't be accompanying her on Saturday night. *I am going to dance on the stage*, he had read awkwardly from the scented notepaper, and Gwendolen had had to stifle a laugh.

She made a small detour to inspect the new memorial to the Royal Artillery Corps at Hyde Park Corner, out of curiosity more than any reverence. She disliked memorials. The truth of the battlefield was absent – the mud, the globs of bloody flesh, the scattered bodiless limbs and limbless bodies. The rendering of suffering into cold stone could not convey the horror. In York, Mother had insisted on attending the unveiling, by the Duke of York, of the City Memorial, a project that had been mired in controversy. Like many others, Gwendolen had considered that it would be better to do something for the living of York – a maternity hospital or a park like the one that Rowntree's had donated to commemorate the men of the Cocoa Works who had died. *Their name liveth for ever more* was carved into the York memorial. Another lie. Who remembered Dickie now?

No use speaking to her mother about such things. The war itself was of no interest to her, only the aftermath of her bereavement.

There was an attractive neo-gothic monument to the South African War in Duncombe Place, near the Theatre Royal. Gwendolen passed it often. How far in the past the Boer War seemed – the stuff of dreary history books now – a dried-up beetle on a pin compared to the raw, raging behemoth of Gwendolen's own war. (She was possessive of it, it had changed everything.) Impossible to believe that one day it, too, would be the forgotten past, remembered only in indifferent stone.

At least, she thought, the new Royal Artillery memorial had the guts to show a dead soldier. For that, if nothing else, she gave it respect. She refused to worship at these shrines to the dead and yet Gwendolen's heart was moved by the sight of a small posy of withered flowers that had been laid on the memorial. A faded note declared simply *For Daddy*. What a wicked, wicked world it was that had allowed such a war.

Her destination beckoned, the 'Cock o' the North' finally exorcized from her brain. She paused for a moment on the pavement to appreciate the splendid exterior of Liberty's new Tudor-style building and then experienced a quiet thrill when she enquired of the doorman, 'Ladies' Fashions?' and was silently directed towards the lift. Was he mute, she wondered? Not a very handy thing in a doorman. She had known men have their throats destroyed by gas.

She ignored the lift and sped up the magnificent staircase. The war was vanquished now. Here was all beauty.

Gwendolen was beginning to regret that she had not gone shopping for at least one decent outfit before leaving for London. It wasn't as if there weren't any dress shops in York. She was embarrassed by how shabbily provincial she must seem in the eyes of the assistant in Liberty's who swooped on her like a hawk, sensing prey.

The assistant was only too well acquainted with thieves and knew that they prowled the shop floor in good clothes in order to blend in with the better class of customers who shopped there. Gwendolen sensed her calculating that someone as pitifully dressed as madam must be in possession of a new husband or a sudden windfall, rather than being intent on shoplifting. 'Of course,' the assistant concluded, 'let me see what I can do for you.' Was madam looking for something in particular?

'Well,' Gwendolen replied, 'I think I'm looking for everything.' What a gift she was to commerce!

Where did this new-found wealth come from, you ask? A few days after her mother's funeral, Gwendolen had visited the family solicitor, a Mr Jenkinson, whose offices were in Stonegate, opposite the old wireworks – now a wool shop. 'Like swords into ploughshares,' she said to Mr Jenkinson, who welcomed her warmly, offering tea 'or a small glass of port?' She declined both.

It was, as she suspected, a case of a few signatures and some small paperwork. No hidden secrets, no coins that reappeared like magic. Gwendolen couldn't help but give voice to a lament over the loss (theft!) of everything her father had strived to build, and Mr Jenkinson said, 'Well, then perhaps, Miss Kelling, this would be a good time to access the trust.'

Trust?

'The trust your father put in place. I have been curious why you have left it on deposit for so long.'

Trust? *Prepare to be surprised!*

He explained it patiently, as to a child. Her father had set up a discretionary trust for his children. After his death, they were each to inherit an equal amount on reaching the age of twenty-one. Five thousand pounds.

Five thousand pounds?

'Each.'

Each?

He frowned at her. 'You really didn't know? Your mother didn't tell you? I did write letters to you.'

Mother knew? She had stolen (there was no other word for it) letters addressed to Gwendolen?

'Naturally. She wasn't able to touch it, but she knew of its existence. And, of course,' the solicitor continued, 'the way the trust is set up, on the death of one, the money is shared between the others. Harry and Dickie died long before their twenty-first birthdays (my sincere condolences, by the way, Miss Kelling), so their share remained intact. When Harry died his share was inherited by you and Dickie, and then when Dickie died you inherited *his* share. So you have, in total, fifteen thousand pounds.'

Fifteen thousand pounds?

'Your father was making a great deal of money before his death.'

Fifteen thousand pounds? Mother knew that there were fifteen thousand pounds sitting in a bank somewhere – no, not 'somewhere', in a deposit account in the Yorkshire Penny Bank in Coney Street, to be exact. Had their father been prescient? Did he know that his foolish wife couldn't be counted on with even a farthing, let alone his entire estate?

'I do wonder why your mother said nothing,' Mr Jenkinson said.

'Yes, I wonder,' Gwendolen said, but in fact she knew. Gwendolen with money would be independent. Gwendolen with money – despite her promise to her father – might abandon her mother and strike out to live life on her own terms. Gwendolen with money would not be shackled to her mother by frugality. Gwendolen with money would be free. Mother preferred to live in woefully reduced circumstances than risk losing her slave companion.

'And the house, if I sell the house?'

'I would expect it to sell for three thousand pounds at the very least. It's a very fine house.'

'And there are fifteen thousand pounds in the bank?' (In the next street!) 'Are you sure?'

'Plus interest accrued, of course.'

'If you don't mind, Mr Jenkinson, I think I will have that port now.'

She further celebrated by walking the short distance to Terry's restaurant in St Helen's Square and lunching in solitary splendour – feasting on oxtail soup, chicken in a white sauce, and sherry trifle. She was a woman of substance now. From riches to rags to riches again. She was almost ashamed at how happy it made her.

She wished to be neither frugal nor profligate, but she would like to make her money work. She would reinvest it in something solid, or perhaps in another manufacturing venture, not a wireworks. Or a little shop. In London she had passed several enterprises owned by women. There was a hat shop called Audrey's, a dress shop called Barbara's, a florist called Jean's. She could set up Gwendolen's, she thought, in York, or Harrogate, although for the life of her she couldn't think of anything she would want to sell. The one thing that it would not be would be dreary. The time of dreariness was over.

Gwendolen left Liberty's and joined the crowds of shoppers. She had purchased a fine new wardrobe in Ladies' Fashions but she was still sporting her old librarian tweed and wool. Her purchases were to be boxed up and delivered this afternoon to the Warrender, leaving her free to ramble along Regent Street with no encumbrance apart from her handbag. It, too, was her old one – shabby and well used.

She had missed luncheon at the Warrender, which was no great loss as it was a cold collation of sandwiches that the Distressed fell on like wolves in an effort to secure the better ones – egg and cress, boiled ham – leaving the fish-paste ones as poor consolation prizes for latecomers.

Further along Regent Street, she passed a man who was playing the cornet – 'busking' – on the pavement outside Hamley's. He was wearing impenetrable dark glasses and propped against his case was a sign that said simply 'War blind'. He was no amateur – he was wonderfully talented, in fact, quite up to orchestra standard. The instrument's case, upturned in front of him like a begging bowl, contained only a paltry handful of halfpennies.

Gwendolen slowed her pace and then finally stopped so that she could listen better. The cornetist was playing 'Blow the Wind Southerly', very beautifully, and Gwendolen didn't think she had ever heard anything sadder – the 'Last Post' perhaps, but that, by its very nature, was the embodiment of grief and melancholy.

The tune was doing him little good as no one was tossing any coins his way, and he changed tack, towards the English hymnal. 'What a Friend We Have in Jesus'. Again, he played it in a terrifically mournful manner. Gwendolen hadn't previously thought of the cornet as such a wretched instrument. She was tempted to request 'I Want to Be Happy' – the poor man would make more money.

What a friend we have in Jesus. (Do we, Gwendolen wondered?

past tense

might/

She had lost any religion she ~~may~~ have once had.) It was the hymn
the men sang their own lyrics to, you heard it everywhere. *When
this bloody war is over.* She had heard a rousing chorus once, from
a mixed bag of walking wounded and stretcher cases being evacuated home, a job lot of Blighty wounds on an ambulance train
that she was accompanying to Boulogne.

They were words one didn't hear in mixed company – not just
'bloody' but 'arse' and 'fucking' – and when they spotted Gwendolen, they all grinned ruefully and gave apologetic little salutes,
murmuring down the line *Sorry, Sister . . . Sorry, Sister . . . Sorry,
Sister.* As if – years into the war by then – she could still be dis-
comfited by words alone. (She was not a sister, but they were all
sisters to the men.) She had bed-bathed some of those men, you
would think that might be more awkward for them than her
hearing an 'arse' or a 'bloody' on their lips. Or indeed a 'fucking', come to that – a word she had certainly never heard before
she went to France but which she heard plenty of times once
there. Patients *in extremis* were inclined to obscenities and men
close to death were not always as polite as people liked to think.

In the rose-tinted accounts of her fellow nurses in those endless diaries, the men were all pukka and cheery, even the most
broken, even those nearest to death. Suffering in silence was for
saints, not soldiers, in Gwendolen's opinion. Where was the virtue in a quiet death – slipping below the waves, sinking into the
mud? Or living on, limbless after gas gangrene or with a body
flensed of flesh or ripped to ribbons by artillery fire?

Sorry, Sister . . . Sorry, Sister . . . Sorry, Sister . . . Sorry, Sister. She
had laughed and said, 'Good luck, boys.' Some – most – would
be back in a few weeks. Some – many – would be dead or badly
injured by the end of the year. She could have wept for them,
but what good did weeping do?

The veteran moved on to 'Abide with Me', which was tricky
on a cornet. It had been played on the wheezing church organ
at her mother's funeral. The cornetist's sombre repertoire had
made her spirits drop. She no longer felt elated by her spree – her

purchases had been paid for with those never-ending bales of barbed wire, no different really from profiteering from armaments and munitions. Her father knew he had blood on his hands, it had been unkind of him to pass on the poisoned chalice to her, tainting her new-found sense of release. She had been wrong, the war would never be vanquished. And, even if it was, another one would come along and overlay the memory of this one.

One must be cheerful, she determined. And she must give the poor man some money. Fumbling in her handbag for her purse, she was suddenly rushed at by someone – a woman – and knocked to the ground. Gwendolen gave a cry, more of shock than pain, as she lay sprawled full-length on the pavement. Quite stupefied by the collision, it took her a moment to understand that it had been deliberate – she had been robbed! Her handbag had been stolen. Only this morning, in the car outside Holloway, Frobisher had warned her that there had been a spate of women being robbed of their handbags. What a fool she was not to have been more vigilant.

As she lay prone, momentarily stunned, she watched as her battered old cloche hat rolled into the road and was squashed beneath the wheels of a butcher boy's bike. Several people stepped around her. So this is what London is like, she thought.

'Goodness, Miss Kelling,' Mrs Bodley said when Gwendolen returned to the Warrender after her encounter in Regent Street. 'What on earth happened to you?'

Gwendolen supposed she looked a sight. Her cheekbone had hit the pavement and must already be bruising, a black eye seemed inevitable. There was an ugly tear in one of her stockings, she had a badly scuffed shoe and her skirt was smeared with something unpleasant. Thank goodness it was her shoddy old clothes.

A man had helped her to her feet – or rather, he hauled her up efficiently – and asked her, quite brusquely, if she was all right. Was she injured?

'Just my dignity, I'm afraid,' she said.

'They took your handbag, and your money with it, I presume.'

'They?'

'There were two of them, women. Allow me to give you a lift somewhere,' he said. 'My car's parked just around the corner in Conduit Street.' He had a supercilious eyebrow that managed to make this simple offer sound cynical.

Ordinarily, Gwendolen would have resisted – accepting a lift from a strange man in a strange city might be regarded as the height of folly – but now that she was on her feet, she had begun to feel woozy – the shock, obviously. And he was right, she had no money for a cab, although her thieves might be disappointed by how little remained in her purse.

The man offering her a lift was smartly dressed, just this side of being a 'swank', although he had one of those moody manners that some – nay, many – women (and particularly the Brontë sisters) seemed to find attractive. Still, it seemed unlikely that a handsome man in a smart car (the adjectives were interchangeable) was planning to shanghai her, so she said, 'Thank you, that's very kind of you.'

His car had indeed been just around the corner. There was a dog on the back seat, a big wolfish Alsatian that regarded her indifferently. Exactly the kind of dog you would expect a man like that to have.

The car itself was a magnificent beast. Gwendolen knew nothing about cars, but she knew a thing of beauty when she saw one and she recognized the stork in flight on the bonnet from the car in *The Green Hat*. In the novel, Iris Storm's car was yellow, but this one was the colour of clotted cream. 'Hispano-Suiza,' she said, and he said, 'I'm impressed. Most women don't know one make of car from another.' The way he said 'most women' bordered on the dismissive.

'My apologies,' she said after a few minutes of driving in silence. 'In all the drama I forgot to introduce myself. My name is Gwendolen. Gwendolen Kelling.'

He didn't reciprocate and she wondered if he wanted to

remain anonymous for some reason – was he a famous film star trying to be incognito? Or a criminal, avoiding identification? Or was he just displaying the gruff reticence of the Heathcliff type. She had known a few of those in her time. Gwendolen liked an open-faced, optimistic manner in the opposite sex.

Eventually he answered. 'Niven. My name's Niven.'

'Pleased to meet you, Mr Niven.'

Her rescuer spoke with a light Scottish burr. A Celtic accent was another attribute that some women were persuaded by. Her friend Cissy used to say she was in danger of marrying any Irishman who spoke to her. Luckily none had. It would take a good deal more than an accent to capture Gwendolen.

Her rescuer took her straight to the Warrender, no shanghai-ing, and helped her out of the car. She caught his swift assessment of her, her faded clothes, her poor coiffure. Her hair had been cut off (some might say hacked) by herself with a pair of surgical scissors during the war and she had never really learnt to deal with it since. At least she had not been alone in tiring of the impracticalities involved in being a woman during wartime.

'The Warrender,' he said, reading the name above the door.

He seemed to find amusement in the plaque that announced the hotel to be 'For Ladies Only'. 'You're in a convent,' he said, with no little sarcasm.

'Better than a brothel,' she bristled. He gave her a long look. She refused to be discountenanced by him.

'Will you be all right?' he asked.

'A cup of hot sweet tea and I'll be as right as rain.' God, she sounded like one of those cheery, diary-writing nurses she had derided. She was grateful when she was allowed to escape. She was embarrassed – he had witnessed her weak and undignified, it was not how she liked to be seen.

'Well, thank you very much, Mr Niven, for all your help,' she said, and turned on her heel and entered the Warrender.

*

'I tripped on a kerb,' Gwendolen said, unwilling to tell Mrs Bodley about her misfortunes. Mrs Bodley was the kind who would censure you for the faults of others.

She settled in the hotel lounge with a tea tray in front of her – she really did need the hot, sweet tea. What an extraordinary few hours – from Holloway first thing, to being assaulted and robbed on Regent Street, not to mention being recruited to spy on the notorious Cokers by Frobisher the previous day. The Library could not compete.

She must have fallen asleep over the tea tray as she was roused by Mrs Bodley approaching. 'A gentleman,' she said, giving the word the full weight of her displeasure, 'has left something for you at reception.'

Following Mrs Bodley to the front desk, Gwendolen discovered, to her astonishment, that the 'something' left there was her stolen handbag. How on earth had it found its way back to the Warrender?

'It wasn't a Mr Niven who left it by any chance, was it?' she asked.

'Gave no name,' Mrs Bodley said. 'Good-looking sort. It might not be my place to say it, Miss Kelling, but you shouldn't be running around London consorting with types like that.'

'I will do my best not to meet good-looking men in future, Mrs Bodley,' Gwendolen said solemnly.

The mystery deepened, for on further investigation, Gwendolen discovered that there was nothing missing from her bag, not so much as a farthing or a handkerchief. It must have been Mr Niven, no one else knew about the theft, but there was no note, no explanation at all as to how the bag had been returned intact. Of course, a note would have necessitated a response, an expression of gratitude. A correspondence might have propelled further acquaintance, which was clearly not desired by him. She would not flatter herself to think he had an interest in her. All he had seen was the tired tweed and dreadful hair and all he had felt was pity, most likely. She was annoyed with herself for the little pang of disappointment she felt.

Iced Fancies

A few months before Freda ran away to London, her feckless mother, Gladys, acquired a suitor, or a 'fancy-man' as Freda had heard a neighbour refer to him. There was, in fact, nothing fancy about Mr Birdwhistle (a ridiculous name!) except for his cakes. He owned a small chain of bakeries and courted Gladys with what he referred to as his 'specialities': gluey vanilla puffs and sickeningly sweet French fancies. He was always saying to Freda, 'Call me Uncle Lenny.' Freda would not.

Mr Birdwhistle made many rash promises – an engagement ring, a house on the Mount and so on – but nothing had as yet materialized. Gladys blamed Freda's cheek. 'Be nice to him,' she warned. 'With any luck he's going to be your new father.'

Freda felt that the last thing she needed was a father, new or otherwise.

She wasn't completely *au fait*, as Duncan would say, with how a father should behave, but she was pretty sure it was not like Mr Birdwhistle. He contrived to pull and pinch and pat Freda even more than she had been pulled and pinched and patted when she had been modelling the Knits. He was always inviting her to perch on his hammy thigh or give him a kiss on his tobacco-flecked moustache. She was used to being pawed, of course. The previous year she had been Peaseblossom in a Rowntree Players' production of *A Midsummer Night's Dream* and the Mechanicals could hardly leave her alone, but it was just teasing really and they were easy to distract. Mr Birdwhistle, on the other hand, was relentless.

He had begun to 'stay over' at the weekends, Gladys going through the charade of making up the 'guest room' – an airless, windowless box-room at the back of the house – as if Freda had no idea what was going on beneath her nose. As soon as they were all in their respective beds, she could hear Mr Birdwhistle slithering across the landing to her mother's room, which, after an indecent interval, was followed by Mr Birdwhistle's porcine snoring.

Not counting Vanda and Duncan – now both lost to her – Florence Ingram was Freda's only friend. She was a veteran of the same dance school as Freda, but sadly had little in the way of either looks or talent and was usually consigned to the clodhopping back row in the end-of-term concerts. This neglect had not made her envious of Freda's star turns. On the contrary, she spurred Freda on to shine and basked in her friend's reflected light. Nonetheless, Florence understood feelings. She had many, some quite dramatic.

She was a robust, kind girl, almost unnaturally clumsy, and the pantomime village never mustered her lumbering limbs to dance in its square or around its maypole, although both girls had been in a production of *Dick Whittington and His Cat* last Christmas at the Theatre Royal.

They had played cats. Not *the* Cat, just one of several who were friends of *the* Cat. They got billing in the programme notes, though. Freda was 'A Pretty Cat'. They performed a routine called 'The Cat Dance', although Freda doubted that any cat had ever been taught to tap. They also did a great deal of washing of their ears with their paws. Florence had made it on to the stage playing 'A Comedy Cat', a plump, ponderous feline who garnered much audience laughter with its bumbling antics. 'Not much acting needed,' Freda overheard the pantomime's director say to the costume mistress. Poor Florence!

Freda had spent many hours of their friendship coaching Florence in improvements – to stand up straight and learn to

91

carry books on her head (near impossible), to discard her thick, pebble-glass spectacles whenever possible (which led to not infrequent bruising, unfortunately), and to close her mouth when breathing and eating (which occasionally led to choking). Florence really should have her adenoids out, in Freda's opinion. Florence's mother had a friend who knew someone whose daughter supposedly had bled to death on the operating table while having her adenoids removed, which was why Florence was still in possession of hers. 'Bleeding to death' sounded gloriously operatic to Freda's ears. She was, of course, a connoisseur of the opera, having had all kinds of walk-on (and skip-on) parts when children were deemed a necessary addition to the scenery by the touring companies that came to York.

Florence's parents, Mr and Mrs Ingram, were well off and Florence lived in a big, detached house out on Tadcaster Road that Freda spent a lot of time cycling to. Mrs Ingram had a 'daily' – which meant a woman – and the house always smelt of cleaning products – Brasso and ammonia and wax polish, scents that were never present in Freda's home in the Groves. The downstairs rooms were half-panelled in oak and the floors were something called 'parquet', which was solid and polished and a contrast to the torn lino in Freda's house.

The Ingrams had a prodigiously prolific garden. 'The garden of unearthly delights,' Mr Ingram called it and laughed. Freda guessed he was referring to something. He did that a lot. Shakespeare, Dickens, Wordsworth, recited in a special performance voice – *Now is the winter of our discontent made glorious summer*, or *It is a far, far better thing that I do, than I have ever done*. He would pause for a few seconds, waiting to see if Freda had caught the reference, and when it was clear that (inevitably) she had not, he would then explain it. He was a teacher in a private boys' school, where Freda supposed he must do this kind of thing all day long. It was incredibly boring, but it was the price that Freda had to pay in order to be included in Florence's well-ordered home life.

Florence attended the Bar Convent school for girls because the Ingrams were Catholics. She had been adopted by Mr and Mrs Ingram when she was a baby. Freda had spent many years trying to make herself look equally adoptable in the Ingrams' eyes, but they never took the bait.

The Ingrams had used a religious agency to find a baby and Florence had been delivered to them late one night, by a nun. She had been left on the doorstep of a Catholic convent in a snowstorm when she was just a few hours old. 'It reminds one a little of *Oliver Twist*, does it not?' Mr Ingram said. ('Mm-hm,' Freda said non-committally. She had heard of Oliver Twist but thought it was a kind of biscuit.)

'At least Florence's mother might have been a Catholic,' Mrs Ingram said, as if that mitigated the sin of abandonment. (Catholicism was 'mumbo-jumbo', according to Duncan, who said he was 'lapsed', which made Vanda snort with laughter and say, 'Is that what you call it?')

Florence found her mysterious nativity fascinating. Where had she come from? She liked to imagine that she was being kept safe in secret by the Ingrams until she could claim her rightful birthright. 'A throne somewhere, perhaps,' she speculated. Freda didn't like to dash Florence's hopes by pointing out that it was more likely that she was simply an unfortunate mistake on the part of her real mother. ('Born out of wedlock,' Vanda said when Freda told them about her friend. 'A bastard,' Duncan said more straightforwardly.)

Freda even taught Florence how to ride a bike. Florence's parents had bought a really good Raleigh loop-frame for her birthday that Freda coveted, but they had never managed to get her up in the saddle. Florence took for ever to get the hang of it, wobbling and weaving all over the place, and she and Freda had to lie to her parents about how many times she fell off, but eventually they were able to go on long bike rides together, to Elvington and Bolton Percy and on one heroic occasion (there were hills, Florence wasn't good at hills) all the way to Brandsby and back.

As the daughter of a Rowntree's employee, even a dead one, Freda was able to enjoy all manner of advantages provided by his beneficent employers – Christmas parties, the Yearsley swimming baths, sports days, summer fêtes, amateur dramatics. Freda always managed to include Florence in these perks. You would think the Ingrams would be grateful, but 'They think you lead me astray,' Florence said, contentedly sucking on a liquorice bootlace as they took a promenade around the city walls. Freda liked the view of York from the walls, it was as if they were backstage or behind the scenes of the city, quite different from being at ground level in the tightly knotted ancient streets.

Despite the Ingrams' reservations about Freda, they nonetheless tolerated the companionship because, without her, Florence would have had no friends at all. 'She's a little slow, I'm afraid,' Freda had overheard Mrs Ingram say to someone. It was true, Florence wasn't the speediest of girls and she was pretty tardy at catching on to some things – playing cards, for example. Freda had tried to teach her Rummy, but to no avail. She enjoyed Snap because Freda always let her win, although sometimes the wait for Florence to recognize a pair and excitedly yell 'Snap!' was tortubus.

'Cards?' Mr Ingram said. 'You're not gambling, are you?' Of course they weren't! Freda would have emptied Florence's blue-glass piggy-bank a long time ago if they had been playing for money.

'Hm,' Mr Ingram said. He never seemed to believe anything Freda said, even though she made every attempt to be truthful with the Ingrams.

I am damned by the court of public opinion, Freda thought, which was one of Duncan's sayings.

One day, Mr Birdwhistle caught Freda off-guard, sneaking up behind her in the scullery when Gladys had popped to the butcher's to comply with her paramour's request for polony sausage to fill his lunchtime sandwich. Freda sensed a *double entendre*

at work but was unclear on the details. Despite her appearance –
the womanly bosom, the 'cheek', the aplomb – if you drilled
deeply into Freda's heart you would find only innocence.

This particular day, Freda had been charged with the task of
washing the breakfast pots and, in an attempt to mitigate the
dreariness of the task, was trying to do it while *en pointe*. She
was concentrating so hard on staying on her toes while wielding
the dishcloth on the porridge pot that she didn't realize Mr Birdwhistle was there until his bristly moustache was prickling her
neck and his plump little hands were everywhere on her body, so
that it felt as though he had taken a leaf from Zeus's book and an
octopus was sizing her up.

'Come on now, Freda, be a good girl for Uncle Lenny,' he
panted, his breath hot against her ear.

He gave a gruff little gasp of ecstasy when one of his tentacles
found the womanly bosom and then a less ecstatic gasp when
Freda's sharp little elbow found his ribs. She pirouetted professionally and brought a nimble knee up into his 'dangles', as
Vanda called them. Vanda had explained the male anatomy to
Freda when she was still a tender age but the words she used
were more of a hindrance than a help to Freda's understanding,
already muddled by swans and ants. Duncan's preferred
term – 'fishing-tackle' – was even less helpful.

Mr Birdwhistle, jack-knifed with pain, hissed 'You little bitch'
at Freda, just as Gladys made a timely entrance, announcing the
arrival of the polony, like someone walking on stage in a poorly
written farce. The octopus gave his side of the story – Freda had
attacked him for no reason, like a mad cat with all claws out.
Freda was not surprised when Gladys showed no interest in her
own daughter's version of events, but instead scolded her and
told her to go to her room and think very hard about her 'future
in this house'.

As Freda lay on her bed, as tidily as one of the recumbent
statues on tombs in the Minster that she had seen, gazing at the
peeling whitewash on the ceiling, she wondered why her mother,

usually so indolent, had not sent *her* to the butcher's for the much discussed polony. Why had she left her alone with Mr Birdwhistle? Had she been a lure, a temptation for his flagging appetite? Like a sweetmeat or a trifle, a misshapen orange cream plucked off Rowntree's production line. A slow tear rolled from her eye. She dabbed at it with Vanda's handkerchief. It smelt of Habanita and conjured the spirit of Vanda.

Freda sighed and sat up and took out Duncan's cards from the drawer in her bedside table. Riffling the pack soothingly, she did, as instructed, consider her future in this house. She dealt from the bottom, a cheat's trick Duncan had taught her. The Queen of Clubs flipped out of the pack and Freda slipped it back in. She didn't regard it as a fortune-telling card. Cards were nothing beyond their face value.

As to her 'future in this house', Freda decided that perhaps she didn't have one.

Running away to London was not the first idea that Freda had when considering her future. Her first idea actually had been to join a circus. She had no circus skills, but could it really be so difficult to hang from a trapeze or walk a tightrope or even stand on the back of a horse while it ran around the ring? After all, she had excellent balance. It was, perhaps, the sparkling, glittering costumes that attracted her more than the acts themselves, but it didn't matter as, alas, there was no circus in town and nor did Freda have any idea how to go about finding one. Failing the circus, she had to fall back into the unsatisfactory safety net of family.

There had been a half-sister for Freda from her father's first marriage – a resentful daughter called Cissy, already in her teens when Gladys ensnared her father. It wasn't too long before Cissy went to France to nurse in the war and she never returned to their house. 'Glad to see the back of her,' Gladys said. Cissy was married now with several children and lived on the other side of town. Cissy had 'ideas above her station', according to Gladys.

Freda thought that seemed like a good thing – how else did you elevate yourself out of a lowly little life?

Freda had overheard Cissy telling Gladys that Freda was 'a show-off brat'. She had been wounded by her sister's judgement of her character. I am not a brat, merely unusually confident, she thought, observing herself practising *port de bras* in the narrow cheval mirror in her bedroom. She could also see the reflection of her dressing-table, on which were proudly displayed her many little trophies won in dance competitions. Swimming, too – she always won the breaststroke in the Rowntree's swimming galas in Yearsley baths. She took pride in her achievements, particularly as no one else seemed to – apart from Florence, who was always to be found on any sideline, cheering her on.

'Move in with us?' Cissy said doubtfully. 'Well, you know, Freda, our house isn't exactly roomy – it's just three bedrooms and there's six of us living here already.' Freda's sister's home was a new semi-detached house in Acomb. It seemed plenty roomy enough to Freda.

Freda perched on the edge of a chair at the kitchen table, ankles politely crossed, back straight. She was minding her manners and working hard to keep a smile on her face and not appear as a 'show-off brat' (the remark still stung). Freda was playing a desperate part – that of the charming younger sister.

'I could help you with the children. As payment, you know.' Freda couldn't even remember all of Cissy's children's names. The first one was Barbara, she was fairly sure of that. Barbara was currently at school. Two more – twins – were playing on the linoleum of the kitchen with wooden bricks. If they had been kittens she would have adored them, but sadly they bore no resemblance to kittens.

'I am their aunt, after all,' Freda said, smiling benevolently at the twins in an effort to be aunt-like, although, in truth, she didn't think she had ever come across an aunt. 'And I can bed down anywhere. On the settee in the lounge, for example?' She cocked her head to one side, attempting winsomeness.

Cissy had been performing an awkward little ballet, pouring boiling water from the heavy kettle on to the tea leaves in the pot while holding the struggling baby on one hip. ('Bobby,' Cissy reminded Freda.) Both tea and baby seemed to be in peril.

'Can you take him?' Cissy asked. A reluctant Freda held out her arms to an equally reluctant Bobby, who made a great show of refusing the invitation. What a fusspot! Freda took a firm hold of him and after a quick tug-of-war secured his release from his mother.

'I'd be like a lodger,' Freda said, jiggling a mewling, fidgeting Bobby around. She thought of Dorothy, the doll that Vanda carried for the Knits. Much easier. Freda wondered where Dorothy was now, and, perhaps more pertinently, how Vanda was coping with motherhood. Grantham. If she knew where that was Freda would consider going there right now and throwing herself on Vanda's soft, rabbit-furred mercy, baby or no baby.

'Just for a bit, Cissy,' Freda had persisted, 'while I work out what to do.' She could hear the pleading note in her voice. She hated herself for it.

'I don't really need help,' Cissy said placidly. She was one of those women, Freda thought, who took to motherhood like sainthood. How different from her own mother.

'And even if you stayed here for a bit . . .' Cissy seemed to be puzzling as to whether there was a cupboard or trunk somewhere that she could stuff Freda into, like a doll being put in a box or a suitcase, Freda thought. She felt an unexpected kinship with Dorothy.

She watched Cissy hefting the kettle back on to the hob and thought, the same blood runs in both our veins, isn't that supposed to count for something? Was it too late to start being a family? Freda felt suddenly and unaccustomedly feeble.

'Well, let's have tea, just now,' Cissy said. 'You can put Bobby down.'

A grateful Freda abandoned Bobby on the rug, where he lay on his back, waving his arms and legs around like a struggling beetle while Cissy poured the tea and laid out scones. Gladys never baked. Mr Birdwhistle kept her in constant provision of cakes, which Freda refused to eat on principle. The thought of Mr Birdwhistle and his specialities made her wince. Of course, Freda knew that she could tell Cissy about Mr Birdwhistle's lewd approaches, but she was used to being blamed for the bad behaviour of others and suspected it would be no different in the case of the octopus's wandering tentacles.

'And you will still need to find yourself a job,' Cissy said. 'Earn a living,' she added, as though Freda might not know what a job was. 'I'm surprised you didn't take to the millinery. I would have thought that it was quite artistic. Perhaps my friend Gwen could get you a job in the Library.'

'The Library?' Freda echoed, unable to keep the horror out of her voice. A library – the deathliest place on earth.

'Yes, the Library, stacking shelves or something.'

'I'm not really a reader,' Freda said.

'Well, you don't have to be a reader to put a book on a shelf,' Cissy chided. 'You *can* read, can't you?'

'Yes, of course I can.' What a cheek! She had read the entire book of Greek myths, cover to cover.

The twins started throwing their wooden bricks at each other. One caught Bobby on the head and he started to shriek, an unearthly, piercing sound that could have been used as a weapon of war. The enemy would have given in immediately. Cissy merely laughed and, scooping Bobby up, said, 'No rest for the wicked,' which was exactly the kind of thing that people like Cissy said. And it was a stupid saying, in Freda's opinion. The wicked were undoubtedly getting a great deal of rest, idling about drinking sherry from the wood and eating éclairs and iced fancies.

'Come on,' her sister said, 'you can help me fetch Barbara from school.'

A tribe of Bedouins preparing to cross the desert with a

caravan of camels probably took less time to get underway than Cissy and her brood.

'You know what,' Freda said, halfway through these interminable preparations, 'I should be getting home, Mother will be wondering where I am.'

'Will she?' Cissy said dubiously. She dithered for a moment and then said (without any conviction, in Freda's opinion), 'You know, if you really wanted to come and live here, Freda, I suppose you could always share a room with Bobby.'

The Fisher King

Strangely, in all his time in the force, Frobisher had never had the need to visit the Dead Man's Hole, as the morgue beneath Tower Bridge was known. The way the currents ran in this stretch of the Thames meant that the piers of the bridge snagged the dead on their way downriver and the Dead Man's Hole was where the bodies were grappled out and temporarily stored. Some drownings hooked out of the water were accidental, usually drunks, occasionally murders, but many were suicides. Frobisher was not unacquainted with would-be suicides – his wife had been one.

The river this morning was brown and sluggish with a never-ending flotilla of barges and boats, the commerce of the city. No lilacs here. No scent of a hay meadow or of a stand of lime trees, only the stink of a noxious city. Frobisher felt his soul shrivel.

The morgue, he found, was a particularly bleak place, infected with the unhealthy air of the river. Stone steps led up from the Thames to a small concrete platform on to which the bodies were hauled. The open tunnel beyond, into which the bodies were moved, echoed with damp despair, the glazed white tiles redolent of a gentlemen's convenience and lacking all sympathy. A small door in the wall led to steps that took him down inside the pier into a dank, fetid room where the dead were stored before being sent on their way. Bad enough to be dead, but to be dead and end up here . . . Frobisher shuddered.

There was no girl, drowned or otherwise. An attendant was

winkled out of whatever hidey hole he occupied when he had no
guests and said, 'She's gone to Southwark.'

Frobisher crossed the river, joining the trudging crowds on Tower
Bridge. He sensed the misery coming off them like a miasma, the
war had undone them – but perhaps it was his own gloom he was
feeling. Sometimes he thought he could feel the weight of history
in London pressing down on the top of his head. He yearned for
the open fields and airy woods of his childhood. He had been
brought up amongst horses. His uncle had been the local farrier
and his father a ploughman. Recently, Frobisher had caught himself wondering what his life would have been like if he had
followed in his father's footsteps, plodding silently in the steady
furrow behind the great yoked horses, their breath steaming in the
cold air. Instead he had been given an education – a scholarship to
the grammar school in the nearest town. He had to walk five miles
there and five miles back, whatever the weather.

He would trade in his books now for the clink of the head
brasses on the huge Suffolks and the mist rising off the land in
the early morning. This had to stop. He was drowning in nostalgia. It was worrying how fanciful he had suddenly become. Like
a disease, almost.

'Chief Inspector?'

'Yes.'

There were plenty of corpses in Southwark mortuary but no
washed-up young girls. Unlike the Dead Man's Hole, Frobisher
had been here many times in the course of his career. The morgue
occupied the site of the old Marshalsea prison, known to Dickens. 'Little Dorrit,' he said to the morgue attendant, who replied,
with not a trace of wit, 'No one by that name here, guv'nor.'
Frobisher sighed.

No Amy Dorrit. No drowned girl. 'Try Snow Hill,' the morgue
assistant said with little conviction. 'Or Kew,' with even less
conviction.

He set off again. Much as he disliked being chained to his desk – Frobisher bound, his liver pecked at by bureaucracy – this pointless trailing around was time-wasting. He wished someone – that Baird chap, for example – would invent a portable telephone. Much more useful than a televisor.

Not at Snow Hill. Not anywhere. The end was his beginning – he found her in the small Bow Street police mortuary.

His walk back along the Embankment had left him feeling low. He couldn't help the odd sense that Gwendolen Kelling's missing girls were the harbinger of something. There was evil in the air of London.

Frobisher took an inventory of the girl laid out on the marble. A skinny little thing, stranded for ever somewhere in her teens, never to grow old, her life snuffed out like a candle. She was as naked and exposed as the day she was born. Brownish hair, still damp. Small breasts like moulds, a veil of freckles across her body not bleached away by the river water. Frobisher winced at the lack of modesty. Gingerly, he lifted an eyelid. No matter how lifeless the dead appeared to be, Frobisher always felt unease that a corpse might suddenly flinch back into life if he touched it. A milky hazel eye gazed back at him. Definitely dead.

Her clothes had been removed and neatly piled at her feet. A frock, underwear and one shoe, silver. The kind of shoe that girls went dancing in. The frock was a flimsy, shiny thing, as if she'd been to a party, but that meant nothing – London was one long party. Traces of lipstick on her mouth indicated she hadn't been in the water long. Given the tide, she might not have travelled far on her river journey. No identification, of course. A big bruise on her cheek like a lilac in full bloom. A small silver locket still on a thin chain around her neck.

The police doctor, Webb, appeared, pipe in hand. 'Wondered where you were, Frobisher,' he said. 'She's been on the slab for hours.'

'You sound like a fishmonger,' Frobisher said, not bothering with the niceties. He disliked Webb. He was glib and 'full of himself', as Frobisher's long-dead mother would have said.

'Well, then that makes you the fisherman, Frobisher.'

'Found drowned?' Frobisher asked curtly. *Found Drowned* – it was the title of a painting he had seen somewhere, he couldn't remember the artist – Millais or Watts, someone like that. Another fallen woman. And, yes, he went to art galleries, they were a healthy reprieve from the more loathsome aspects of his job. He dabbled himself in watercolours. Amateurish stuff that he showed to no one. His taste was for neither the classical nor avant-garde but for the Romantic, maudlin even. Something else that was not to be shared with Bow Street.

'Yes and no,' Webb said. He pointed to a small wound in the girl's neck. 'Carotid artery,' he said. 'A knife. A small one.'

'Big enough,' Frobisher said.

'Unconscious before she went in the water, I would think, but there's water in her lungs. So she drowned before she bled to death. The water is too cold for anyone to survive very long in it. Their body temperature drops rapidly and they succumb to what we term "hypothermia". The cold alone would have been enough to kill her. Whichever way you look at it, she had no chance.'

Frobisher felt nauseous. It was long past lunchtime and he still hadn't eaten. There would be nothing waiting for him in Ealing tonight. Lottie was in one of her blue moods. An inadequate word for the nearly catatonic state she fell into regularly.

'Third female this month, so far,' Webb said.

'Fourth,' Frobisher said. 'A woman washed up at Richmond last week. Suicide, I think.' He picked up the shoe and examined it. 'Just the one?'

'Yes.'

With Webb's assistance, Frobisher removed the locket from the girl's neck. When it was opened it revealed a photograph of a woman, undamaged by immersion. The girl's mother, he supposed. You might expect the photograph of a father on the other side of the diptych but instead there was a slightly out-of-focus picture of a dog, a terrier by the look of it. For some reason the dog made him sadder than the mother did. Perhaps he should get a dog for Lottie? A little spaniel or a Yorkshire terrier – would that cheer her up? Did she even like dogs? Frobisher had no idea. He hardly knew his wife at all, she had a fugitive nature, unwilling to be *present*. He'd had a dog all through his boyhood, a collie, a farm dog called Jenny. He tried never to think about her. The manner of her death (poison, meant for crows) had marred his Arcadian childhood.

The thinking had led him back to Shropshire. What he wouldn't give to be walking through a meadow at the height of summer or listening to the dawn chorus rising from the wood. He sighed. This had to stop. He was drowning again in nostalgia. An unfortunate phrase.

He slipped the dead girl's locket into his pocket. 'I'll get someone to ask around the London jewellers, you never know.'

'Needle in a haystack,' Webb said dismissively. '*Virgo intacta*, by the way,' he added. 'In case you were wondering.'

Frobisher took one last look at the girl. *Cover her face. Mine eyes dazzle. She died young.*

'Put a sheet over her, for God's sake, man,' he said brusquely to Webb.

'Back again, sir?' the desk sergeant said affably. Ah, thought Frobisher, he has had his revenge on me for the burnt bacon by sending me on a wild goose chase. Frobisher did not give the sergeant the satisfaction of seeing his frustration at the morning's futility; instead he said, rather sharply, 'Get someone to fetch me Constable Cobb, will you, sergeant? I have a special task for him.'

In Haste

'A note came for you,' Mrs Bodley said, approaching Gwendolen in full sail as she took her seat for dinner.

'A note? Delivered by a good-looking man?' she hazarded.

'No. A policeman, in uniform,' Mrs Bodley said disapprovingly as she handed it over. 'Miss G. Kelling' was written on it in a bold hand on the envelope. Gwendolen waited until a lingering Mrs Bodley, overcome with intrigue, left before opening the envelope. *Dear Miss Kelling, could you please ask your friend to find out if either of your girls wore a locket? Thank you. Yours sincerely, John Frobisher.*

So his name was John.

She knew nothing of his circumstances. Perhaps he was married, although he didn't seem the uxorious sort, he seemed so very wifeless. Of course, he knew nothing about her circumstances either, nothing of her unexpected wealth. She hadn't disabused him of the Library. It seemed to be a source of comfort for him. She supposed librarians rarely disturbed the status quo of a man's heart.

It took a moment or two to digest Frobisher's request, she had been waylaid by the revelation of the 'John'. Her heart sank when she realized the implication. She knew what it meant. He had found a body. A soldier from the battlefield could be identified by his dog tags. A girl found in London could be identified by a locket.

She had, of course, presumed that Freda and Florence were

alive and well somewhere. It had never even crossed her mind that it might be otherwise, but Frobisher's query about the locket hinted at a dreadful fate. And if not for Freda and Florence, then for some other poor girl. She felt horribly contrite, she had been treating London as a jaunt while the sober-minded Frobisher had his mind on corpses. How dreadful it would be if either Freda or Florence turned up dead. She could not imagine passing that news on to Freda's sister.

Cissy Murgatroyd had been Gwendolen's closest friend, they had travelled through their girlhood together and volunteered to nurse at the Front together, signing up for Red Cross training when they were barely out of school uniform and shipped out to the Front in 1915. The Armistice had parted them. Cissy returned home when peace was declared, but Gwendolen carried on the fight until she was discharged in 1919. When Gwendolen came home, it was to find Cissy married to a civil engineer and already embarked on her first baby.

The man she married was called Wilfred and he was a good sort, with a cheerful, affectionate disposition. If a woman must wed, then she could do worse than Wilfred. ('Oh, Gwen, do marry him yourself if I die before my time!' Cissy said, absurdly delighted by this idea.) But Gwendolen was looking for neither husband nor child, and the one seemed to be the inevitable consequence of the other. (Must loving a man necessitate motherhood? Could you not have one without the other? 'Tricky,' Cissy laughed.) It was hardly a problem anyway as there were no men to be found, even if she wanted one – the war had seen to that. If she wished to be loved, she could get a dog. If she craved a child, she could adopt an orphan, Lord knows, there were plenty of them to be had, although she doubted that she had the nerve for motherhood.

'I think you have the nerve for anything, Gwen,' Cissy said. 'Even love.'

'Pah,' Gwendolen said eloquently. She would not be beguiled by romantic notions, no matter how well intentioned. Nor would she be constrained by marriage, no matter how cheerful and affectionate the man by her side.

An image of Frobisher, sober and upright at his desk, came into Gwendolen's mind. What kind of husband would *he* make? She couldn't imagine him mucking in with nappy-changing and potato-peeling the way that Wilfred did. The idea made her laugh. He was on a mission, of course, and men on missions had little time for fripperies. He had been sent to Bow Street to 'clean the house'. Corruption. It was everywhere, even Miss Shaw at the Library could be bribed out of issuing a fine for an overdue book with a boiled sweet.

At Cissy's suggestion, she had gone to see Florence's parents before leaving for London. Mrs Ingram had fussed about, laying out coffee and biscuits in the drawing room. She was the tremulous sort, the cups and saucers rattled, the coffee pot wobbled in her hand until Mr Ingram said gently, 'Sit down, Ruthie, let me do that.'

'We tried,' Mr Ingram told Gwendolen. 'We contacted Scotland Yard, they gave us the name of a detective – Frobisher – they said he was the person to talk to – but he never got in touch with us. We've tried many times.'

'She was led astray by that minx,' Mrs Ingram interjected.

'Freda?'

'Her mother's a slattern.' It was an unexpected word on the lips of someone so genteel. Mrs Ingram kept putting her hand to her throat as if feeling for an invisible rope of pearls. 'And a thief, too.'

'Freda?'

'We welcomed a serpent into the bosom of our family and now Florence is probably lying dead in an alleyway somewhere,' she moaned.

'Now, now, Ruthie, we know that she's alive,' Mr Ingram said.

How was he so sure, Gwendolen wondered? In answer, Mr Ingram had pulled open a drawer in the dresser and taken out a little stack of picture postcards that he passed to Gwendolen. 'She writes,' he said, 'as if she was on her holidays.' Mrs Ingram groaned and was afforded another 'Now, now, Ruthie.'

Gwendolen studied the postcards. None of them had a helpful return address written on the back. The postcards looked as though they had been torn off a larger strip and indeed they were all marked 'The Sights of London' – St Paul's, Big Ben, and so on. '*Dear Mummy and Daddy,*' Gwendolen read aloud, '*I'm having a lovely time in London. Miss you!*' Mrs Ingram looked as though she was going to be sick.

'You see,' Mr Ingram said, 'the last postmark is only two days ago. She's fine.'

'She's *backward*, Alistair,' Mrs Ingram wailed. 'Retarded! She can't look after herself.' Mr Ingram heaved a great sigh and said, 'Just "slow", Ruthie, that's all. Florrie's a little slow.' He sighed heavily again. 'The policeman I spoke to in Scotland Yard said that girls go missing all the time in London.' Mrs Ingram howled. 'I would have gone down to look for her myself,' Mr Ingram said, 'but I couldn't leave poor Ruthie – her nerves have always been very frayed, you know.'

Gwendolen had known men in the war whose nerves had not just been frayed but shredded by the abominations they had witnessed. Mrs Ingram could not compete in those stakes, yet her sobs were awful and Gwendolen berated herself for the flint in her soul; the woman deserved compassion.

'We thought about perhaps employing a private detective,' Mr Ingram said.

'Gladys Murgatroyd is useless,' Mrs Ingram said bitterly. 'I do believe she doesn't care if she never sees her daughter again.'

'I'm going to London,' Gwendolen reassured Mrs Ingram. 'I'm going to look for them. I'm going to find them.' A shepherdess, she thought, looking for the lost lambs. Although you wouldn't really call Freda a lamb, more of a black sheep if anything.

As she walked back down the drive of the Ingrams' house,

Gwendolen thought she could hear Mrs Ingram's lamentations still ululating in the air.

'I promise,' she had said, 'that I'll bring Florence home to you.' She had created a hostage to fortune, hadn't she? Beware of promises, she thought. What if the daughter she returned to the Ingrams was no longer living? It didn't bear thinking about.

There was notepaper and writing material on a desk in the residents' lounge and after dinner Gwendolen sidestepped a game of Bridge with the Distressed, took up the pen provided and wrote a short note for Cissy, saying, 'Did Freda wear a locket? Can you ask the Ingrams if Florence did?' Perhaps it was best not to elucidate further, although Cissy must also have read those red and green tags around the necks of the war dead.

'Dratted child,' Cissy had said when she showed Gwendolen Freda's farewell letter (*Dear Mother* . . .), but Gwendolen felt sorry for Freda. She had never been given much of a path in life to follow beyond showing off and now no one, not even Cissy, seemed terribly concerned that she had run away; but then Cissy regarded Freda as the cuckoo that had turned her out of her nest.

She added a postscript – 'I hope you have sent the photos of Florence and Freda.'

The Hellespont

Niven was a member of a club in Piccadilly. It was useful in many ways, particularly if he needed to be left alone to brood. He had barely sat down in one of the masculine leather chairs in the library when a waiter approached and, in the discreet murmur perfected by such men, said, 'There's a lady downstairs asking for you, sir.' There was the slightest nuance given to 'lady'. 'Shall I dispose of her for you, sir?'

'Not necessary,' Niven said. Women were not, of course, allowed in the club, the very presence of the woman downstairs would constitute a dangerous invasion as far as the club members were concerned. Niven had arranged a meeting with the 'lady' in question and, to the waiter's relief, he swiftly escorted her out of the building and into his car, and from there into the snug of the Lamb and Flag, a more suitable venue for the business they had with each other.

She was not his type, although he didn't really have a type. On the whole, Niven preferred the kind of woman he could forget about the moment she was out of his sight. That was why Gwendolen Kelling annoyed him so much. He still remembered her. And she was definitely, categorically, not his type.

The woman he was with in the Lamb and Flag was a member of the Forty Thieves. He placed a ten-pound note on the table in front of her and she finessed it discreetly into her bag. In exchange for the money, Niven found himself in possession of a handbag that was barely fit for rag and bone, let alone a ten-pound ransom.

He threw the offending item into his car and set off along the Mall. He sensed the journey he was on wasn't as simple as crossing the straits of Hyde Park Corner to reach Knightsbridge and the Warrender on the other side. He was swimming the Hellespont. That was not a story that ended well.

The Home Front

Over time, Frobisher's stomach had accustomed itself to his foreign wife's cuisine. He doubted that even the French in France used as much garlic as Lottie did. It had a talismanic quality for her. Something to do with Ypres, he supposed, where she had lost a daughter. Frobisher kept a constant supply of peppermints in his pocket to counter the garlic on his breath. It would have appalled Bow Street.

The bulb of garlic that had been in Lottie's pocket when she was found in Ypres had been conserved and cherished. The garlic was old and dry by the time Frobisher met her, on the eve of the Armistice, standing on the parapet of Waterloo Bridge preparing to jump, but she had later brought it back to life, planting each individual clove in a little pot of earth, watering and tending them as keenly as Isabella did her pot of basil. They had studied Keats at school. Scraps often came back to Frobisher, uninvited.

The lineage of the original bulb lived on in their back garden, where Lottie also grew a foreign array of *herbes*. ('Airb,' Frobisher had thought she was saying for a long time.) Before he married her, Frobisher's only encounter with herbs had been in the form of a mint sauce with lamb or a parsley one with cod. No one in England referred to mint and parsley as 'herbs'.

When his wife was on form, Frobisher feasted like a French peasant. He worked with men who thought eel pie and mash was a gourmet dish. They would have been impolite towards Lottie's

113

cassoulets and *coq au vins*. There was no feasting today, however, for Frobisher. In the cold Ealing kitchen, he made himself a corned beef sandwich and ate it standing up by the sink.

Lottie had barely looked up when he came in. 'I'm home!' he always shouted as he came through the front door, followed swiftly by a cheery '*Bonjour!*' so as not to appear too partisan. He had some French, remembered from school, but Lottie preferred him to speak English. His indifferent attempts at her language insulted her ears.

He had congratulated himself for remembering to stop by the Floral Hall on the way home. As the end of the day approached, the flowers were sold off cheaply and Frobisher had bought a fine bunch of mixed tulips – pink, red, yellow – at a bargain price. It was the time of day when the flower-sellers descended to pick up the contents of their *boutonnières* and posies and nose-gays. Not Eliza Doolittles, just old women who would stand on cold street corners for hours to scrape a living. Frobisher some-times bought a little nosegay of violets from them, more out of charity than anything, but he loved to plunge his nose into them and drink in the sweetness, the plague of London vanquished for a moment.

The tulips had seemed gay and cheerful in their paper wrapper as he had made his way home. He had taken the train back to Ealing. He was picking up his car from the showroom next week and it struck him how much he would miss the hustle and bustle of public transport. It made him feel as though he was part of something and not stranded in solitude. There was an *Evening Standard* discarded on one of the seats in the carriage. The head-line read OLD MA COKER RELEASED FROM JAIL. Frobisher disliked that soubriquet. It made Nellie Coker seem like a benign charac-ter in a fairy tale, when in fact she was, if anything, the witch.

A woman in his carriage – rather downtrodden-looking, he thought – smiled at him and said, 'I wish my old man would buy me flowers.' He'd had no answer to that, but now he regretted not saying, 'Here, please have these,' and presenting her with the whole bunch, for his own wife had scowled at them as if they reminded her of something she would rather forget.

Lottie was in retreat, in her customary place in the back parlour. When she was in one of her moods, she would sit in her chair by the window and gaze listlessly at the garden for hours.

Lottie was a good needlewoman and from an antique shop in New Conduit Street Frobisher had bought her a pretty little rosewood sewing-table, lined inside with pleated pale-blue silk. She was working on a tapestry cushion cover of brightly coloured parrots, but more often than not she picked it up and then put it down again without working a stitch.

Frobisher had also put up a bird table in the garden so she would have something to look at, but she seemed to take no notice of the flock of greedy finches who preyed like vultures on Frobisher's charitable offerings. It was dusk now, the birds all roosted, but Lottie stared into the darkness as if she were waiting anxiously for someone to emerge from the gloom. Her daughter, he supposed. A tiny casualty of war.

She gave him a bleak look, almost as if it were he who was responsible for her state of mind. The glacial chill of neglect was on the house, too. There were only cold ashes in the hearth, so Frobisher set about the satisfying task of laying a fire. The warm spring day had turned cold as twilight encroached.

The marital bed would be frosty tonight, too, as it was on many nights. When she was in a good mood ('up', he thought) she would fling her thin arms around his neck and smother him with so many kisses (Mon amour, mon amour, je suis désolée) that he almost wished she would stop. Her abandonment could be disturbing. There would be no disturbance tonight. Lottie, dressed in the thick cotton nightdress that reminded Frobisher of a shroud, would turn her back on him and he would lie awake and think about how different his life would be now if he had come along five minutes later and Lottie had already plunged into the Thames and been on her way to the Dead Man's Hole.

He put the tulips in a jug because he couldn't find a vase and placed it on the sideboard where she would see it. Then Frobisher sat in his armchair and watched the fire catch. He supposed he could make another start on his piece for *John Bull*. A few days ago he had begun soberly enough –

> The district of London known as the West End, and described by His Majesty's Post Office as 'London W1', is roughly one mile square. It includes Piccadilly Circus and Leicester Square, and all the little restaurants and clubs that form Soho, which is not so much an area as an atmosphere that pervades that part of the West End.

'Jazz it up,' the editor of *John Bull* told him. 'It's not a street gazette. Our readers know where the West End is. They want things that they don't know about or what's the point? You know, little titbits.'

He laid down pen and paper without having written a word.

He would have liked to tell Constable Cobb to keep an eye out for Maddox in the Amethyst, but what if Cobb was in league with Maddox? It was unlikely but not impossible. What if they were *all* in league with Maddox? What if the whole barrel was rotten? He mustn't become delusional, suspecting everyone and everything, like a paranoiac. Oakes, the so-called Laughing Policeman, seemed like he might be a man he could trust. Perhaps he should enlist him in his mission.

It was no good, he was too restless to unwind. He threw his half-smoked cigarette into the flames and put the fireguard in place. Shrugging on his overcoat, he took his hat from the hallstand. 'I'm popping out to get some fresh air, I won't be long,' he shouted, but received no answer.

He walked around the streets of Ealing. Not a policeman's purposeful beat walk but the meanderings of a man who found no comfort at home. It was late and he received one or two suspicious looks. Perhaps he should get a dog, after all. No one felt at risk from a man with a dog.

When Frobisher arrived home, it was to find that the fire he had made had gone out. He raked through the ashes and patiently brought it back to life with kindling and small pieces of coal until the flames were bright and lively once more. He dropped off to sleep in his armchair and when he woke he found the fire had gone out again. It was like his history with Lottie, he thought, but he was too tired for the challenge of making a metaphor from his marriage. Instead he made his weary way up the stairs to bed.

Afternoon Tea at the Goring

The following morning, the first post brought something for Nellie, yet the envelope with her name on it remained unopened on the dining table in front of her. It was unusual for Nellie to receive post in Hanover Terrace, she preferred everything to go to the Amethyst, away from prying eyes. ('Ma loves to keep secrets,' Shirley said. 'Even when she doesn't have any,' Betty said. 'Especially then,' Shirley said.)

Nellie was sitting at the table with Betty, trying to teach her the principles of accounting. With the exception of Kitty, Nellie found Betty to be the most frivolous of her children, but also, with the exception of Edith, the most amenable to tuition.

'Money in, money out, that's all you really need to know, isn't it?' Betty said.

'Well, not quite,' Nellie said, drawing on her always limited reserves of patience. 'Balancing the books isn't just about balancing the books. It's more subtle than that.'

'Subtle? How can *accounts* be subtle? – Oh, I get it! It's about fraud, isn't it? *Légerdemain* with numbers. Avoiding the tax inspector and all that stuff. Why didn't you say? But Edith does all that, why do I have to learn it?'

Because I'm not always going to be around, Nellie thought. There was no point in saying that to Betty, Nellie knew that her children thought her incapable of dying. She was too monumental. But if she handed over the reins to Edith, then Edith would need a lieutenant of her own, a Coker who was willing to do

118

anything necessary to preserve the legacy of the business. Betty might be shallow but she had depths of ruthlessness not shared by Shirley and Ramsay.

'If you look at the left-hand column of the ledger,' Nellie persisted, 'you'll see—'

'Are you going to open that?'

Nellie regarded the envelope suspiciously.

'It's not a bomb,' Betty said.

'Might be,' Nellie said.

In lieu of a letter-opener, Betty offered her little penknife and Nellie sighed her resignation and slit open the envelope, gingerly removing the contents – one sheet of heavy-weave paper on which someone had written in black ink in a spiky, foreign hand.

'Is it a billet-doux?' an amused Betty asked.

'No,' Nellie said. But it was.

An invitation. Nellie feathered up for the occasion – draping her plum-pudding figure in a matinée coat borrowed from Shirley that was trimmed with ostrich plumage ('Taken, not borrowed,' Shirley complained) and wearing a strange little hat made by a milliner Nellie knew in Ingestre Place. It gave the impression that a blackbird had landed on her head and died there. It would do very well for a funeral, Nellie thought. Not that there were any coming up that she knew about. But there would be, as sure as autumn follows summer.

'Mr Azzopardi is already here,' the manager murmured, as if he were imparting a precious secret. He led her to the table.

'You look charming,' Azzopardi said, standing up to greet her.

As the waitress poured the tea into their cups, he said, 'I love hotels. In fact, I *adore* them.'

Nellie had never taken afternoon tea at the Goring before. Very nice china, everything elegant. 'I have a sweet tooth,' she said, ignoring the sandwiches and going straight to an éclair.

'So I've heard,' Azzopardi said. 'And yet you are sweet enough as it is.'

Buttering her up, she thought. Nellie was strangely disappointed, she had expected more villainy and less cliché from this courtship. The éclair was excellent though.

He used to live in London, he said, but left during the war, moving abroad for a while. Nellie guessed that meant prison. It usually did. Yes, he freely admitted – a prison hulk anchored off Gibraltar. When he returned, he said, it was to Scotland. 'Your country, I believe?'

'Just a small part of it,' Nellie said, unwilling to claim the whole of Scotland for herself. 'It's very uplifting. The scenery and so on.'

'Ah, yes, the scenery,' he agreed. Who *was* this man, Nellie wondered? His English was surprisingly fluent, better than Kitty's certainly.

'Are you staying here?' she asked.

'The Goring? No, I've taken a house in Eaton Square. I thought I would return for old times' sake. I once had an unfortunate experience here.'

'And yet you wanted to return?'

'To lay the ghosts to rest. And,' he chuckled to himself, 'to see if anyone recognized me. I have changed a good deal since I lived in London.' His eyes moved to the back of his hand, where Nellie had already noticed an ugly star-shaped scar, a wound that didn't look as if it had been stitched properly, if at all. She refrained from commenting. 'It's always amusing to reinvent oneself, don't you think?' he said, looking pointedly at Nellie.

'I wouldn't know,' she said, raising an eyebrow over a second éclair.

Even Azzopardi found it necessary to answer the demands of a Coker eyebrow. 'The law exists to be broken, you of all people must know that.'

Nellie frowned at the fag-end of the éclair in her hand and placed it back on her plate.

'Something the matter, Nellie – may I call you Nellie?'

'I'd prefer it if you didn't, if you don't mind.' Was he trying to *flirt* with her? Better men than Azzopardi had tried and failed. The man was oily. She supposed he was after the clubs. Probably heard that Maddox was going to make a move on her and decided to pre-empt him. Why didn't he just get down to business and make her an offer, instead of all this flim-flam? She calmed herself down with a scone.

'I would like to offer you fifty thousand pounds,' he said, sensing her impatience.

'For what?' she said innocently, the butter knife her only weapon of defence.

'Your nightclubs. What do you say?' He blinked slowly, like a tortoise.

The clubs were worth twice that, at least. Another testudinal blink from Azzopardi. 'More tea?' he said, signalling to a hovering waiter.

'Don't mind if I do,' Nellie said.

Azzopardi asked for the bill. 'May I offer you a lift somewhere?' he asked Nellie.

'No, thank you. I shall go to the powder room before I leave.'

'And you will consider my offer?'

'Of course.'

'And give me your answer next week?'

'Of course.'

They both rose from the tea-table. Azzopardi proffered his hand, but when Nellie reached out to shake it he alarmed her by grabbing her hand and pulling her closer – close enough for her to smell his eau de cologne. Rather disconcertingly it was the same one that Niven wore. He alarmed her further by kissing her on the cheek, *one-two*. Not usually xenophobic – she would have had no business if she had been – nonetheless Nellie couldn't help thinking *bloody foreigner*.

*

In the Ladies' (very pleasant), Nellie frowned at herself in the mirror. She felt breathless, as if she'd been running (an unlikely occurrence). I am not for sale, she thought grimly. She had the strange feeling that Azzopardi was toying with her. A cat with a mouse. He didn't want to pay money for the clubs. Did he even want them? She suspected he was after something else altogether, but she couldn't imagine what. Whatever it was, she sensed he would be relentless and what he couldn't acquire through persuasion he would take by piracy. First Maddox, now Azzopardi. The barbarians were at the gate. Nellie sighed. Deauville was clearly going to have to wait until after the dénouement of this affair. She fluffed up her feathers and left the powder room.

The doorman at the Goring helped Nellie into the Bentley. Hawker, the chauffeur, glanced at her in the rear-view mirror when she huffed on to the leather. He worried that there was a crack in her shell since prison. A strong Nellie was predictable, but a weak Nellie might do anything.

Hawker lived in a small flat above the garage in the mews behind the house in Hanover Terrace. He was keen to retire – he fancied an allotment – but had nowhere else to live. He'd be fit only for the knacker's yard by the time he found somewhere, he said to his daughter. He'd been with Nellie for five years now. Sometimes he worried that he knew too many of her secrets for her ever to let him go. In a series of tortuous negotiations with Nellie, Hawker had managed to secure one day off every fortnight. 'It's like being a medieval serf,' he said to his daughter.

'Where to, Mrs Coker?' he asked.

'The Crystal Cup,' Nellie said.

Voilà!

It was peaceful in Hanover Terrace, even Kitty was quiet, although that was often a bad sign. These were ideal conditions for the creation of his magnum opus and Ramsay was hammering on the Remington's keys and shuttling its carriage with abandon, fuelled by nothing more than Lipton's tea and a tin of cocaine throat pastilles that he'd cadged off one of the dancers at the Sphinx. He was no longer thinking – he was writing! It had come to him in a kind of *coup de foudre* – he should write a crime novel – a 'murder mystery' – they were all the rage, after all. He had just finished reading the new Christie, *The Murder of Roger Ackroyd*, and, yes, yes, it was very clever in its twisty-turny way, but Ramsay was aiming for something more real, more gritty.

A corpse was necessary to set the ball rolling, he thought. Someone pushed out of a window, perhaps. Defenestration, he had noticed, was popular in the crime novels of the day. A body lying mysteriously on a pavement. But whose body? And why?

And for a crime novel he would need a detective, one who would take his place in the pantheon of celebrated sleuths – Poe's Dupin, Sherlock Holmes, even Christie's Poirot. Ramsay did not want someone elegant or clever or well mannered – no, he wanted a Scotland Yard detective, someone who was jaded and well acquainted with the seamy side of life.

Write what you know. Betty had said that he didn't know anything, but she was wrong, he did know something – he knew the Saturnalia that was London after dark, didn't he? The streetwalkers, the dope, the gangs, the mad parties, the fancy dress, the night-clubs, the gambling, even the awful Bright Young Things – from the sordid to the glittering and everything in between. Given his profession, his detective would move unhindered between these worlds. And in a further lightning-stroke of genius, Ramsay had finally found his title – *The Age of Glitter*. The whole fictional enterprise was spread out ahead of him like a shimmering woven tapestry!

Down to business. First of all, his detective should have some-thing that marked him out as different, unique even. Perhaps one of those memorable characteristics or tics that they all seemed to have – a violin, a moustache and so on. Welsh! Ram-say couldn't think of any Welsh detectives, couldn't even think of anyone Welsh, for that matter, apart from Lloyd George, and even he hadn't been born in that benighted country, had he?

And as God created Adam, so Ramsay created Jones.

Detective Chief Inspector George Jones – or 'Jones the Police-man' as he was known back home in the Valleys where he came from (from whence he came?) **was waiting on a platform in Paddington Station for the 5.05 from Taunton. He checked his pocket-watch. Police-issue pocket-watch.** (Did the police issue pocket-watches? Did it matter if they didn't? It sounded right.) **He checked his police-issue pocket-watch – his trusty police-issue pocket-watch.** (Better.) **The 5.05 was on time,** (NB – find out if there *is* a 5.05 from Taunton) **steaming slowly towards the platform. Jones smiled to himself**

Why? Why is he smiling? And why, for that matter, would a master criminal have been in Taunton? Ramsay had chosen Taunton at random. Perhaps somewhere like Bristol or even Manchester would have more credibility as a hotbed of lawless-ness? Birmingham certainly, the city's gangs came down for the Derby and treated the Amethyst like Liberty Hall. He supposed he could decide later. He wondered if there was a Bradshaw's anywhere in Hanover Terrace. It seemed unlikely. No one ever caught a train.

Jones smiled to himself because he was looking forward to confronting Reggie Dunn. As if on cue, the doors of the train opened and the passengers began to alight on to the platform. First-class carriage, Jones noted. Dunn, the reprobate head of a Soho crime racket, walked nonchalantly along the platform without a care in the world – strolled nonchalantly along the platform, unaware that his nemesis was waiting to greet him. 'Hello, Reggie,' Jones said. 'Been to the races?' (That sounded rather flat. Been up to mischief? Been up to no good?)

'Been up to your old tricks, Reggie?' (Better.) 'How about we take a little walk and discuss – Discuss what? Creativity was surprisingly tiring. Ramsay yawned and lit a cigarette.

'Hello, Reggie,' Jones said. 'Been up to your old tricks? How about we take a little walk and you can tell me all about what you did with Lady Lorchan's diamonds?'

Excellent stuff! He lit a cigarette from the stub of the old one. He could hear the grandfather clock in the downstairs hall chiming. It was getting late, he should be setting off for the Sphinx soon, but really the place ran itself.

Ever onwards. Next chapter.

He lit another cigarette.

Jones kept to the shadows, he was

The peace was suddenly rent by a tremendous scream coming from the nether regions of the house. Ramsay hoped for something hair-raising but found only the little scullery maid, enthusiastically thrashing an enormous rat with a frying pan.

'There,' she said, breathless and flushed with success, when her victim finally lay vanquished and bloody on the stone of the scullery floor.

They were alone – the cook had gone home – and Ramsay poured them a glass of brandy each to celebrate her triumph. It was only the cooking brandy, but nonetheless Nellie would probably have had a fit if she had found them sitting companionably around the scrubbed deal of the kitchen table drinking her alcohol.

'What she don't know can't hurt her,' the scullery maid said, sipping the brandy. What a sensible person she was, Ramsay thought. And bold, too. Why had he not noticed her before? He hadn't even known that they had a scullery maid. Her name was Phyllis, she said, and in the course of their illicit conversation he discovered that she was the white sheep (or lamb, perhaps) in a family of East End thieves, so he spent a useful half-hour researching his novel by questioning her about housebreaking, pickpocketing and 'smash and grab'.

'Well, thank you for telling me about your people,' he said, when they had finished their (second) brandy.

'My people?' Her eyebrows shot up, reminding him of Edith. 'Like we're a different breed?' She seemed to be in high dudgeon all of a sudden. 'We're all people, we're all equal!' (Was she a communist?) 'And "my people", as you put it, may be thieves, but at least they're honest thieves. *Your* people are the rotten ones!' She stalked off, leaving Ramsay feeling hurt. And he had thought they were getting on so well. Never mind, she might make an interesting character in his novel.

His Prepar'd Prey

'Run away? To London? Really, Freda?' Florence had been nasal with excitement. She really should get her adenoids fixed. 'Like Dick Whittington!'

'Well, not quite like him but, yes, London,' Freda said. 'We'll catch the train and go. It's that simple, if you think about it.'

They had just left the Picture House in Coney Street and were eating chips, hot and greasy from the paper, as they wandered around St Helen's Square when Freda first proposed this audacious venture.

'But what shall we do in London?' Florence puzzled.

'Why, dance, of course,' Freda said. 'And sing, too, I expect. On the stage. Become stars!'

Florence did a cumbersome little jig in the porch of the church that gave the square its name. Freda was reminded of the Comedy Cat Florence had played in *Dick Whittington*.

'Oh, Freda,' Florence said, clutching her breast in a melodramatic fashion. 'How marvellous! Do you really think *I* could be a star?'

The Comedy Cat was going to go to London with Dick Whittington. 'Of course,' the Pretty Cat said brightly. It was clear that the odds were stacked against Florence, but Freda was sure she had enough optimism for both of them.

'Do you really think the streets are paved with gold, Freda?' Florence asked as they shivered on the wind-whipped platform at York station, waiting for the train to take them to London. Oh, that dratted pantomime, Freda thought. It had given Florence unrealistic ideas about fame and fortune. Success required hard work and discipline – not to mention talent – and truthfully she knew that Florence was inclined to none of those things.

'No, that's just a fairy tale,' Freda said, but her answer was drowned out by the arrival of the train.

They were not penniless like Dick Whittington. Freda had deemed that Mr Birdwhistle's own lack of morals made him fair game and when she saw his jacket left unattended, hanging on the back of a chair in the kitchen, she had slipped her hand into the inside pocket. She had been wary, half expecting something – a rat or a ferret – to bite her hand off. She remained unmolested, however, and managed to trawl out her catch – a wallet, fat with Saturday shop takings.

Mr Birdwhistle himself was otherwise engaged with Gladys in the front room ('the parlour' as Gladys insisted on calling it). He had recently bought Freda's mother a gramophone and a pile of popular records that were currently pumping out loud music. There were other noises emanating from the so-called parlour, but Freda doubted that they indicated dancing, certainly not on the obnoxious octopus's part. Freda had seen them grappling with each other, their lips clamped together as if they were trying to suck the air out of each other's lungs. Disgusting!

Under cover of Billy Murray singing 'Clap Hands! Here Comes Charley!' Freda filleted several notes out of Mr Birdwhistle's wallet before replacing it carefully in his jacket. Altogether it amounted to four pounds and ten shillings – a small fortune.

Mr Birdwhistle's money was safely transferred into Freda's own little purse and from there into the somewhat larger handbag, an old one of Vanda's that she had given her. Freda planned to be on the train to London before Gladys and Mr Birdwhistle had even truffled their way out of their stale bedding. She took some pleasure in imagining how furious the octopus would be when he realized that she had robbed him. Propped up on the mantelpiece, she left a farewell note written in pencil on her best pink notepaper.

Dear Mother, I have run away to London to seek my fortune. I am going to dance on the stage. The next time you hear from me I will be famous! You don't need to worry about me. Sincerely, your daughter, Freda.

Florence made her own contribution to their escape trove – nearly two pounds in small coins from the blue-glass piggy bank that she smashed open.

When they had settled on to the benches of their third-class carriage, the engine champing at the bit to get away, Florence took Freda by surprise by slyly sliding a string of pearls out of her coat pocket and displaying them, wide-eyed and mute with triumph, to Freda, sitting opposite. Freda recognized them only too well, she had seen them many times around Mrs Ingram's rather plump neck. Duncan had once told her about the pearl fishers in Ceylon, how they could hold their breath longer than anyone so that they could dive down into the deeps to retrieve the oysters' hidden treasure, and she had wondered how many times they had to dive to make Mrs Ingram's lovely necklace.

In the manner of Vanda's magician taking a rabbit from a hat, the pearls were followed by a turquoise cuff (Mrs Ingram's birthstone) and an enamel and gold brooch in the shape of a blue-bird that Freda knew Mr Ingram had given Mrs Ingram for her fiftieth birthday. There had been a small tea party to celebrate this milestone, at which Freda had been present, as she was at many of the Ingrams' unassuming family celebrations. Mrs Ingram's eyes had filled with tears when she unwrapped the little blue brooch. 'Oh, how thoughtful, Alistair,' she said. 'I'm so touched. Thank you, dear,' and Mr Ingram said, 'Dearest Ruthie, you have put up with so much.' What had Mrs Ingram put up with, Freda wondered? Mr Ingram himself, she supposed. He was a dreadfully dry old stick. They had kissed, modestly, which was how adults should kiss, in Freda's opinion.

'Put them away,' Freda hissed at Florence, under cover of the engine letting off steam prior to departure. They were not alone in the carriage. An elderly man in a seat at the window was absorbed in the *Times* obituaries and a crotchety-looking woman had already stared at them with displeasure for no greater crime than their youth and sex.

Rather reluctantly, Florence returned her treasure to its cache. It would be bad enough when the Ingrams discovered that their precious Florence had run away, without finding that Mrs Ingram's jewellery had disappeared along with her. Freda suspected she would be blamed for both absences. In the end, she supposed, she would be blamed for everything.

They had barely clambered out of the train at King's Cross when Freda began to feel the burden of Florence's naivety. A woman had approached them while they were still on the platform retrieving their suitcases and asked if they were looking for lodgings, and Florence, who was like an affectionate but neglected dog, eager to make friends with anyone, said, 'Yes, we are, how kind of you,' before Freda dragged her away by her coat sleeve. 'Don't talk to anyone who approaches you like that. In fact, don't talk to anyone.'

'Why not? She was just being helpful,' Florence protested.

She was a lamb inviting slaughter! Had she never heard of the white slave trade? Of the yellow peril? Of Arab sheiks holding Western women captive in desert tents?

'That's all just in films, silly,' Florence said. (And this from the most gullible person Freda knew!) 'And we do have to find somewhere to sleep tonight, Freda.' It was nearly five o'clock. 'Nearly tea time,' Florence added, betraying the anxiety of someone used to regular meals. Oh, Lord, Freda thought. Florence was not accustomed to fending for herself, whereas Freda felt as though she had done nothing else for her whole short life. 'Don't be such a grouch, Freda. We're on holiday, after all.'

No, they weren't! It had been a mistake to propose to the guileless Florence that she come to London with her.

They left the station and walked out into the crowded, overwhelming streets of London. Freda, although she couldn't admit it, felt her stomach clench with sudden fear, but Florence, despite the weight of her suitcase, wasn't in the least disconcerted and trotted happily along the pavement.

They found lodgings in a boarding house in Henrietta Street. The boarding house itself was as unfriendly as its keeper. There was neither name nor number on the door, only an iron knocker, fashioned with a demonic face that gave Freda a sense of foreboding when she first saw it, and as she lifted it she felt a little frisson of fear, like electricity, go through her body.

The door had opened quite suddenly, releasing the scent of cheap stewing meat, followed by a woman in a filthy, greasy apron who fired the discouraging opening salvo of 'What?'

Her name, it transpired, was Mrs Darling – rarely had a woman been so badly named – and she glanced quickly up and down the street before saying, 'Get inside,' as if she wanted no one to see them enter. Freda had hesitated on the threshold and it was only her fond memories of playing Tinker Bell in an amateur Christmas production of *Peter Pan* that allowed Mrs Darling to grasp her sharply by her forearm and pull her into the dark hallway. Florence, already inside, looked over her shoulder and said, 'Come on, Freda, don't be such a slowcoach,' which was, ironically, something that Freda usually said to Florence. Freda sighed and followed.

Mrs Darling offered them tea in her dismal front room. The cups were filthy and Freda only pretended to sip at the weak liquid made with leaves that she recognized as having already been brewed several times.

There followed some confusion about the purpose of their visit. Mrs Darling, surveying Freda, offered to 'solve' her 'problem', and it took some time before their new landlady understood that the 'problem' was the difficulty of finding lodgings. She laughed – a grating, humourless kind of sound – and said, 'Well, as it happens, you're in luck. A room in the attic's just been vacated.'

Freda was always up long before Florence and had to shake her awake most mornings. Only the promise of breakfast was enough of a lure to rouse her from her bed. They ate breakfast out every day – Covent Garden was full of cheap cafés catering for the workers in the market. There were no cooking facilities in the boarding house, although Mrs Darling put on a meal every evening, food so awful that even Florence, who had an heroic appetite, occasionally blanched at what was on offer. She wanted to eat in a restaurant every night and Freda, the keeper of their treasury, was growing weary of continual denial.

'Come on,' she said to Florence, pulling the bedclothes off her. 'You can sleep when you're dead,' which was something Vanda used to say to Duncan.

After breakfast they made their way to the West End and trailed up and down Regent Street and Oxford Street, as well as most of the smaller streets in between, to pass the time. Occasionally (rather often, in fact) Florence saw something in a shop window that took her fancy and she dived in and came out triumphantly with a trifle she didn't need – a pencil set, a Kewpie doll, a powder puff. Freda supposed Florence had never wanted for anything and so hadn't developed a concept of thrift. And Florence was like a magpie where anything shiny was concerned, her eye caught by the cheapest of baubles. You could have laid a trail of glitter and Florence would have unthinkingly followed it.

She had to be restrained outside Hamley's. She was always wanting to go in the toy shop and look at the dolls, although she was obviously far too old for dolls. 'No one's too old for dolls,' she said staunchly. The dead-eyed dolls gave Freda the shivers. Florence was still a child, Freda thought ruefully, she believed in angels and fairies and the goodness of mankind, all rejected some time ago by Freda.

At Freda's insistence, when they first arrived in London they had enrolled in a dance school – the grandly titled Vanbrugh Academy of Dance. It was important, Freda told Florence, that they keep their practice up, and the London dance schools would put you forward to the theatres if you were any good. It was run by a Miss Ada Sherbourne, who was as thin as a board and straight as a poker, wore only black and white, and carried a whip-like cane that was employed in an animated fashion when she was drilling a chorus troupe. Occasionally, she used it to smack the back of their legs if they got out of time. 'Crikey,' Florence said.

They bought copies of the latest editions of *The Stage* and scrutinized them for open auditions, turning up early at the stage doors of the West End theatres to become a part of the snaking queue of eager girls, dance shoes in hand, waiting to be let in. Once inside, they joined another serpentine line of hopefuls, before taking to the empty, echoing boards to the accompaniment of a lone, spiritless pianist. The first time, at the Palace, Freda had been so overawed by standing on an actual West End stage that she could barely croak out her name when asked.

Poor old Florence, of course, stood no chance. The Muse Terpsichore had not favoured her, Miss Sherbourne said. It was true, Florence had no ear for either music or timing and her feet may as well have been encased in deep-sea diver's boots. Freda, at least, usually managed to tap out a few nervous bars before someone unseen in the front row yelled, 'Thank you, next!'

'I'm afraid the standards in the metropolis are very different from those in the provinces,' Miss Sherbourne told Freda. 'You might be the star of your local provincial school, but here you're just another girl, I'm afraid. I'm sure I'll find you something eventually, though. And if the worst comes to the very worst,' she added rather darkly, 'then the nightclubs always need girls who can dance.' The Nellie Cokers of this world were ravenous for them, she said.

Although Freda didn't like to admit it, Florence had changed since they arrived in London. Of course, she had lost interest in the stage almost immediately, but that was no great surprise. Instead she had wanted to go to cafés and cinemas and mooch around the West End department stores. She wanted to 'see the sights' and bought an expensive pack of tear-off postcards that was indeed called 'The Sights of London'. The pack folded out like a concertina to show photographs of Buckingham Palace, the Houses of Parliament, the Tower of London and so on, and after each sight had been ticked off, Florence sent a postcard to her parents on which she wrote the same message every time. *Dear Mummy and Daddy, I'm having a lovely time in London. Miss you!* – a sentiment somewhat undercut by the carelessly cheerful exclamation mark and the absence of a return address. The Ingrams had a telephone in their house, but Florence made no attempt to contact them. Freda supposed she had never had freedom before. Freda, who had had nothing but freedom, considered it to be an overrated concept.

As week followed week, Freda had continued the arduous grind around the open auditions in theatres and left Florence to her Sights. Perhaps that was a mistake, because the once reliably sunny nature had often become eclipsed recently by a new querulousness. If Florence wasn't out visiting the Sights (surely she had seen them all several times by now), she was often to be found lounging around with uncharacteristic petulance on their uncomfortable horsehair mattress, picking at a bag of sweets while reading lurid, dust-jacketed thrillers that she bought from a stall in Berwick Street market.

She was seized too, of course, by the idea of Tutankhamun and his curse.

Freda hadn't heard of Tutankhamun – she had never read a newspaper in her life, they were good for stringing up in the outside privy or for wrapping fish and chips, but that was their limit as far as she was concerned. She didn't understand why a big modern city like London – surely the most important city in the whole world – should be convulsed by the idea of someone who died in Egypt thousands of years ago.

'He's haunting the streets, looking for victims,' Florence said, 'because we dug him up and disturbed his eternal rest.'

'No *we* about it,' Freda said crossly. 'I didn't dig him up. I don't even know where Egypt is.'

In York, you couldn't lay a gas pipe or a new drain without digging up a Roman skeleton. If they didn't like their 'eternal rest' being disturbed, then surely the streets of the girls' home town would be full of legions of the dead roaming about. ('They are,' Florence said.) Freda's next-door neighbour in the Groves had a Roman skeleton in his coal cellar, people paid tuppence to come and gawp at it. Freda would rather spend the money on a bag of pear drops.

And visions! The day before they left for London, they had climbed the spiral staircase that led to the roof of the Minster. Freda wanted to say goodbye to York, she intended never to return. Florence huffed and puffed and claimed dizziness at every turn, while Freda – an adept at the pirouette, lest we forget – skipped up the helical steps full of encouragement for her friend. It was a clear day and when they reached the top they could see the Vale of York laid out before them. 'It's like look-ing at the whole world,' Florence said.

'Well, not quite the whole world,' Freda said. 'Just a tiny bit of it, really.'

'Do you think,' Florence said, 'that if we jumped, we would fly?'

'No,' Freda said. What a clot Florence could be sometimes! 'We wouldn't fly,' she said sternly. 'We would fall.'

'I think the angels would catch us. I think I can see them wait-ing,' Florence said, pointing vaguely in the direction of the hills in the distance. (Sometimes, Freda really worried for Florence.) 'Harrogate's over there,' she said with confidence. Apparently, at Florence's school they spent a great deal of time in Geography class drawing and colouring in maps of Yorkshire. Florence and her mother often went to Harrogate on the train, Mrs Ingram preferred the shops there, she said. Harrogate was 'full of angels', according to Florence. What a booby. Freda had accompanied them once and despite afternoon tea in Bettys the interminable round of shops had bored her silly, angels or not.

Once, they had accompanied Mrs Ingram into Hannon's the fruiterers in Stonegate – Mrs Ingram had heard that they had 'wet walnuts' and was eager to surprise Mr Ingram with them. Freda couldn't imagine why you would want to eat a walnut, wet or otherwise. They tasted bitter and stuck in your teeth. The only nuts that Freda liked were the sugared almonds from Terry's, pretty in their pastel colours, that Mrs Ingram kept in a silver dish on the sideboard. 'Filigree,' Mrs Ingram said mysteriously when Freda admired the scrolling cut-out pattern that bordered the little dish. To Freda's ears it sounded like something to do with horses, or perhaps a pretty name for a girl.

In Hannon's, Florence had suddenly grown excited, claiming that she could see the face of the Virgin Mary on a large melon. 'A honeydew,' the brown-coated assistant said, as if that might explain the apparition. Freda had never seen a melon before, with or without the Mother of God embossed on its froggy yellow surface. Now, of course, thanks to living so close to Covent Garden market, she considered herself quite the expert on the world's fruit and vegetables.

Freda had grown increasingly remorseful about the anxiety she was causing the Ingrams and yet Florence herself seemed unusually immune to guilt. *Dearest Ruthie, you have put up with so much.* Mrs Ingram was putting up with a lot more now, Freda thought.

Florence did, however, attend Mass regularly in Corpus Christi, the Catholic church on Maiden Lane, and Freda wondered if she professed her contrition and was absolved (Florence had taught her the word). How handy it must be to have one's slate wiped clean on a regular basis.

Corpus Christi meant 'the body of Christ', Florence explained when a mystified Freda asked. There was a large crucifix hanging above the altar of the church. It was an execution really, wasn't it? It may as well have been a man hanging from a gibbet, in Freda's opinion. Gruesome. Still, the Corpus Christi church was a splendid affair, like a particularly glamorous theatre. Freda had peeked inside, rather cautiously, in case she suddenly succumbed to conversion and found herself wishing that she had a god, any god, if it would entitle her to this magnificence. When younger, Freda had occasionally attended Sunday School – two words that should not belong in the same sentence, in her opinion – but it had disappointed with its lack of decoration.

When she was still quite small, Freda had played the lame boy who was left behind by the Pied Piper in a Settlement Players' production of *The Pied Piper of Hamelin*. It was a non-speaking role, so as well as lame she was also directed to be deaf and dumb. She played for, and received, much sympathy from the audience, indeed she had her own little ovation at the curtain call. Instead of changing the role to that of a girl, they asked her if she would cut her hair. Freda had lovely long plaits at the time, but of course she chopped them off. She would have done anything for a part. And now, she realized, it was she who was the Pied Piper, enticing Florence away and leading her who knew where.

Freda's heart was heavy. It would never have crossed her friend's mind to run away from home without Freda suggesting it. Freda had a feeling it was going to end badly. One way or another.

Bartholomew

Frobisher had sent another note to the Warrender. True to his word, he had sent a constable around the dance schools and he had eventually come up trumps with the name of the establishment that Freda and Florence attended. 'My constable has already asked questions,' Frobisher wrote, 'so there is no necessity for you to go there.'

'But, of course, I shall,' Gwendolen said, addressing the note.

The grandly named Vanbrugh Academy of Dance was located in Frith Street and Gwendolen elected to walk there, which, it was becoming clear to her, had been a mistake. For one thing, it was a long walk, and now that she was here in Soho, she was hopelessly lost in its warren of streets. The people she asked for directions all seemed to be as ignorant of the capital's topography as she was. She must have spent a good half-hour wandering the maze before happening by chance on Frith Street. A map seemed a necessity.

'Well, there is always something for a girl while she's got her looks,' Ada Sherbourne said. The Vanbrugh was the domain of a 'Miss Ada Sherbourne – Dance Instructress'. She had a striking, etiolated figure, wore a tailored black dress – elegant rather than funereal – and she had such good posture that Gwendolen felt a complete slouch in contrast. Miss Sherbourne had also retained her unbobbed locks, twisted up in a neat but complicated style that would have taken Gwendolen hours to achieve (if indeed she ever could). Gwendolen discovered an immediate antipathy towards her.

'Yes, I believe they were enrolled here,' Miss Sherbourne said. One of her eyes had twitched at the mention of the girls' names. Perhaps she simply had a nervous tic.

'When were they last here?'

'Goodness, I can't remember,' she said vaguely. 'A few weeks ago, perhaps. I'm afraid Freda's talents were middling, she was rather gauche. I mean she had reasonable tap and could keep a tune, but I know fifty girls more talented than her. And as for poor Florence . . . Perhaps they moved on to somewhere less reputable.'

What did that mean?

'Tell me, Miss Kelling, what are they to you? These girls?'

'They are girls who are missing, Miss Sherbourne, that is what they are to me.'

'I would try some of the nightclubs, if I were you. Girls like Freda are meat for the Nellie Cokers of this world. She devours them. Although I presumed that they had gone home to whatever northern town they came from.' Ada Sherbourne made 'northern' sound like an insult.

'York,' Gwendolen supplied defensively. 'It's a very attractive town, actually. A lot of history.'

The telephone rang, interrupting this rather scratchy exchange. Ada Sherbourne said, 'Do you mind if I answer this?' and without waiting for Gwendolen to say anything she picked up the phone and placed her hand over the receiver, saying to Gwendolen, 'I'm *so* sorry I can't help you further,' before removing her hand and proceeding to conduct a conversation in syrupy tones with someone clearly in the theatrical profession. Gwendolen had been dismissed, it seemed.

On the way out, she passed a gaggle of girls coming into a class, in their rehearsal clothes, dance shoes in hand. They smiled and murmured polite greetings to Gwendolen.

'Excuse me,' she said, 'but do any of you know a Freda Murgatroyd or a Florence Ingram who attended here?'

A girl at the back of the gaggle piped up, 'I know Freda. She's nice.'

The other girls drifted off.

'When did you last see her?'

'A couple of days ago. At rehearsal.'

A couple of *days* ago? Ada Sherbourne had implied that she hadn't seen Freda and Florence for weeks. Were they so unmemorable, or was there some reason she wanted to forget them?

'And Florence?'

'Not for ages. She only lasted a few days. Why, miss? Has something happened?'

'Well,' Gwendolen said, 'I'm afraid nobody seems to know where they are. I'm a friend of Freda's sister, I've come to London to look for them. Perhaps you can think where they might be?'

The girl cocked her head to one side in order to think. A little bird. She was charming, her dark hair in a sharp bob, a small retroussé nose, Gwendolen could imagine her on the stage – a musical comedy, perhaps. She spoke well, already well versed in enunciation.

'Well, I don't know where they live,' she said, 'but I know Freda has an audition.'

'An audition?'

'Yes, Miss Sherbourne got her an audition at the Adelphi, for *Betty in Mayfair*. It's a revue,' she explained when Gwendolen looked blank. Ada Sherbourne had made no mention of any audition. Why not?

Gwendolen could hear her shouting crossly, 'Cherry! Cherry Ames, are you coming? *Cherry!*'

The girl made a face and said, 'That's me, I've got to practise, I'm going for a solo, I've got an audition tomorrow as well, at the Palace.' She ran off down a corridor and then ran back halfway and said, 'Miss Sherbourne has all our addresses, you know. In her office.'

*

Gwendolen slipped as quietly as she could into Ada Sherbourne's office. Ada Sherbourne herself was now fully occupied with her class, Gwendolen could hear her counting out the beats, 'five-six-seven-*eight*', with remarkable ferocity. The woman was a dragon and Gwendolen was trespassing in the dragon's lair.

The orderly arrangement of things in the office made the task of searching easier than it might have been. Against one wall there was a four-drawer oak filing cabinet, each drawer labelled in copperplate handwriting, with the third one down helpfully announcing itself to be 'Students'. Inside the filing cabinet everything was neatly alphabetical – Ada Sherbourne would have made an excellent librarian, she could have given Mr Pollock a run for his money.

And there she was, in a hanging folder tabbed 'L–M' – 'Freda Murgatroyd' and an address – Henrietta Street, number four.

The counting had stopped and Gwendolen was convinced that she would be accosted by Ada Sherbourne before she could make a successful escape. The idea made the hairs on the back of her neck prickle. She would like to see Ada Sherbourne locked in a room with Mrs Bodley in a draconian contest. Her money would be on Mrs Bodley (her resentments had more flair), but it would be a close-run thing.

'One-two-three-four!' The relentless counting started up again. Gwendolen breathed a sigh of relief when she reached the front door. She closed it quietly behind her.

Cissy had always castigated her sister for being an undisciplined child, but really Freda must have nerves of steel to subject herself to the rigours of dance.

'Ten minutes from here,' a man behind the counter of a tobacconist in Greek Street said when Gwendolen ducked in to ask for directions. She had been going round in circles for some time since leaving the Vanbrugh Academy of Dance. A London 'ten minutes' was beginning to seem a good deal longer than a Yorkshire one.

Long Acre again! She had already walked along Bow Street and was on the verge of giving in to frustration and seeking out Frobisher to ask him to reorientate her when happily she chanced upon Stanford's bookshop and a helpful young man sold her the mysterious Bartholomew's. Of course – a map. She remembered now being asked for one in the Library. 'I'm an idiot,' she said to the helpful young man, who said, 'Not at all, madam,' and, what was more, he unfolded the virgin creases of the map and pointed out the route she should take. 'Five minutes away,' he promised and, thankfully, he was right.

There was no sign of *Betty in Mayfair* at the Adelphi. Instead, the front of the theatre was plastered with posters advertising *The Green Hat*, alongside large photographs of the leading lady, Tallulah Bankhead. (Gwendolen imagined Mr Pollock's wrath.) She would buy a ticket, she thought. Perhaps she should buy two and invite Frobisher, although it was difficult to image that *The Green Hat* would be to his taste. What *would* be to his taste, she wondered? Rigorous opera, perhaps, or exhausting choral music (she liked neither). But surely the man must be in possession of some lightness of being? If he was, she determined she would find it.

The theatre was closed and she eventually found her way round to the stage door in Maiden Lane. Bartholomew had been no help, he seemed to have no interest in mapping the stage doors of London.

The stage door was open, the doorman visible. 'I'm looking for someone – a Freda Murgatroyd – she had an audition here,' she said. A callow youth, rather jaundiced-looking, was sent for. The callow youth gave her a pitying look. 'Do you have any idea how many girls come through this door?'

And did they all also come back out of that door, Gwendolen wondered? 'No, I don't actually,' she said.

'Hundreds, that's how many,' he said indignantly. 'And I couldn't tell you the name of a single one of them.' Gwendolen wished she had Freda's photograph with her, it might have helped to jog this strange boy's memory.

'I shall ask Management,' he said grandly and disappeared for so long that Gwendolen supposed he must have forgotten, but eventually he resurfaced and said, 'No, no one knows anyone by the name of Freda Murgatroyd.' He lit a cigarette, rather ostentatiously, as if proud of being a smoker. Gwendolen doubted that he was much older than Freda. 'Was there something else?' he asked.

As the callow youth turned to go, Gwendolen said, 'Did she get the part?' but the boy just laughed (a joke shared by the doorman, apparently) and said, 'What part?'

In the face of so much intransigence, retreat seemed the only option, and Gwendolen retired to a café and ordered sardines on toast and ate them while studying her precious Bartholomew's. She would soon be quite *au fait* with the streets of London, she thought with some satisfaction.

In Henrietta Street there was no response to Gwendolen's polite knock, so she banged harder. The doorknocker was in the shape of a leering, devilish face, not very welcoming, Gwendolen thought. Perhaps that was the idea. From the outside, the building had an air of abandonment, but a flutter of grimy lace at an upper-floor window hinted at someone on the premises.

She knocked again loudly, but the door sullenly refused to open. There was something untoward about the place. Gwendolen was not usually given to fancy, but something about the house in Henrietta Street gave her a chill. Perhaps that inhospitable door required a policeman's more official knock before it would open. She sighed; retreat was once more the order of the day. Being a detective was frustrating. No wonder Frobisher sighed so much.

A newsagent's kiosk on the Strand was festooned with postcards, including a conjoined strip, advertising itself as 'The Sights of London'. Gwendolen paused. Those were the same cards that Florence had sent her parents, weren't they? She felt strangely impelled to buy a set. The postcards hanging in the kiosk were for display. When they were sold to her, they were folded up and enclosed in a greaseproof envelope. She paid and slipped them in her bag. She must spend a day sightseeing – they might come in useful. And she must send one to the Misses Tate, Rogerson and Shaw. She could only imagine the excitement when they received it.

The Crystal Cup

You might be forgiven for thinking that the Amethyst – by far and away the most famous and lucrative of her clubs – would be the one that would be closest to Nellie's heart, but this was not in fact the case, it was the Crystal Cup for which she had a particular affection. It was here that she was often to be found sequestered in the late afternoons, relishing the quiet before the evening's revels began.

The club's (mostly) exalted clientele was composed of many members of the Lords, as well as several who had taken the silk or indeed sat on the High Court bench, which might explain why it had never been raided. Its location was convenient for neither the Inns of Court nor Westminster, which, Nellie said, explained its discreet attraction for members of the Establishment as no one expected to find them straying this far from their native habitat.

It was the most refined of all the clubs. Nellie had spent eight thousand pounds on the Ritzy blue and gold décor of the Crystal Cup – satin-quilted walls, pleated and gathered artificial silk on the ceiling and a maple herring-bone parquet floor, pretty glass chandeliers, tables with pink-shaded electric lamps – it was like a little gilded chocolate box. Gunter's in Berkeley Square did the catering. It was the only one of Nellie's clubs where caviar was served. She charged seven shillings and sixpence a portion and barely made a profit by her standards. The head waiter was Russian and rumoured to be a minor Romanov, but Nellie had never asked because she didn't want to be disappointed by denial.

The liquor licence was always up to date and the curfew for alcohol, although broken on a regular basis, was never investigated. The dance hostesses were of a superior calibre, nicely brought-up girls only a few shades short of debutantes. They cost two guineas a dance, twice the price of the Amethyst girls.

The restaurant of the Crystal Cup was on the ground floor, and Nellie liked to sit there and watch the last rays of the day seep through the harlequin lozenges of glass in the windows while breathing in the soothing scent of stale alcohol and cigarettes. Sometimes she took a small glass of Mariani coca wine, reckoning that if it was good enough for a pope it was good enough for her, even though she had shunned religion after an unfortunate incident in her girlhood, long before her convent education had finished.

Narcotics in themselves did not put the fear of God in Nellie. In fact, when Niven had set off for the Front in 1916, she had slipped into his kitbag a 'Welcome Present for Friends' bought from Harrods that contained cocaine, morphine, syringes and needles. He had thrown it overboard on the Channel crossing, doubting that drugs would aid his survival.

Usually, however, it was a pot of tea that sat in front of Nellie on the table at the Crystal Cup. If she was still there when the dance hostesses started coming in, they would beg her to read their fortunes and she would fan her cards out on the table in front of her, offering them like promises to the girls. Or threats. Depending on how you looked at it. In Nellie's world, everything depended on how you looked at it.

There was a flat on the floor above, fitted out with every convenience and decorated in shades of pink. No one lived there and Nellie found it extraordinarily soothing to go upstairs and sit in its untouched atmosphere. It was perhaps the only unsullied corner of her life.

The head barman, a smooth Spaniard, assiduously polishing glasses, said, 'Welcome back, Mrs Coker.' Could he get her anything? To his surprise, Nellie said, 'A whisky. A malt. A good one, mind. Neat.'

A Macallan was poured generously and served with great courtesy. She must be celebrating her release, he thought. 'Is she all right?' the manager, a man named Templeton, asked. He had arrived quietly and they observed Nellie together unseen.

'She's drinking whisky.'

'What does that mean?'

'No idea.'

Templeton's days were numbered at the Crystal Cup. Edith had told Nellie that he was suspected of having his hand in the till.

Nellie took a cautious sip from her glass. It was a long time since she had drunk whisky and she was not sure what memories would surface with the taste. Just a faint, peaty one of her wedding night, when she had been tutored in the meaning of the word 'conjugation', which previously she had thought only applied to Latin verbs.

The Crystal Cup ought to be deserted at this hour, that was its charm for Nellie, but when she glanced up she saw that there was someone sitting at one of the tables, over by the far wall.

It was Maud, of course, who else? She was dripping water on to the lovely herring-bone maple of the floor. Nellie had to stop herself calling for a mop; the floor had cost a fortune.

There was a glass of absinthe in Maud's hand and she raised it in a toast. Nellie raised her own glass in silent acknowledgement.

'She's definitely not herself,' Templeton murmured to the barman as they watched Nellie toasting the empty air.

When the band started to trickle in and unpack their instruments and the dance hostesses began to primp themselves in the cloakroom, Nellie heaved herself up from her table and signalled for her coat. Templeton rushed to comply.

'Welcome back, Mrs Coker,' he said as he helped her on with her matinée coat. Jail, he noticed, seemed to have shrunk her.

He noticed, too, that she had acquired a cane, topped with the handsome head of a silver fox. It didn't seem to indicate weakness,

147

as rather than using it as a support she wielded it like a drum major's mace. He half expected to be whacked on the head with it.

'On to the Amethyst now?' he asked, more for the sake of conversation than curiosity.

'Where else?' Nellie said. It seemed like a genuine question. The manager had no idea how to answer.

The Amethyst was still quiet when Nellie's Bentley drew up outside. Hawker helped her out. That new cane, he thought, was more like a theatrical prop.

Rather than entering the Amethyst straight away, Nellie took a little promenade along the street, an animal reclaiming her territory. The club was surrounded by a variety of establishments – restaurants, cafés and all manner of shops, from a ship's chandler to a knife supplier, a barber, a cobbler, a tea importer, and so on. Several of these proprietors came out to greet her. She was a character. She gave the street notoriety. They appreciated that.

Nellie paused for a moment outside the Amethyst. It was disguised by soot-encrusted brickwork and peeling paintwork. The windows on the ground floor were blacked out and the façade gave no clue as to the vastness inside. The building had once housed a Huguenot family, not the silk workers who settled in Spitalfields, but the precious-metal-workers who had made Soho their refuge. Their workshop had been on the upper floor, where there was the most light, and when magpie Nellie first moved in she had spotted a tiny nugget of gold, wedged between two of the broad oak floorboards. It had seemed like a good omen. A promise of greater treasure. Nellie kept it in a silk drawstring bag, where it nestled alongside other charms acquired over the years – the tooth of a Scottish wildcat, a piece of rock crystal, a hare's foot and a lock of hair cut from the corpse of a hanged man, although she would be the first to acknowledge that there was no proof he had been hanged, let alone that he was dead, when the hair was removed from his head. If Nellie had a soul – and there was no verdict as yet – then it was a pagan one.

The bag was kept beneath the mattress of the small brass bed in her bedroom in Hanover Terrace. She had felt the lack of it in Holloway. When she had looked for it on her first night back in her own bed, she was disturbed to find that the bag was no longer there.

To gain entrance to the Amethyst you first had to negotiate the twin granite obelisks that were the doormen, a couple of former bare-knuckle street fighters who were proud to be Nellie's guard dogs.

'Boys,' she said, acknowledging them with a nod of her head.

They barely moved their impassive features to greet her, although they were stirred by a sense of companionship. They had both been to prison on many occasions. Nellie was one of them now.

At the bottom of the stairs, Linwood greeted Nellie fawningly. 'Mrs Coker,' he said, 'good to see you.' Nellie unnerved him with her gaze. Linwood had not been one of those who had stayed behind in the club yesterday morning to welcome Nellie. His absenteeism had been noted by Edith and Nellie in a mute exchange of bobbing eyebrows. He was, unfortunately, the keeper of several secrets, both Nellie's and those of the guests of the club. It made him safe. For now, at any rate. He registered her cane. It seemed to threaten.

He drew back the black bombazine and bowed as if before minor royalty.

'Welcome home, Mrs Coker.'

For it *is* my home, Nellie thought, forgiving Linwood his obsequiousness. The house in Hanover Terrace was where she lived, but the Amethyst was where she existed in all her glory.

'After you,' she said generously to Maud. 'Try not to drip everywhere.'

The Spoils of Egypt

It was a pleasant evening, if rather chill, and the dying minutes of the spring sunset kissed the Portland stone of the capital's buildings. Or perhaps 'caressed'? Ramsay dismissed this as too romantic, along with 'kissed'. 'Gleamed'? No, pots and pans gleamed – in good households, anyway. By the time he had reached a word that satisfied ('brushed'), the sun had long since gone to bed. He was perfectly capable of writing in his head, just not on paper, it seemed. He should carry a notebook with him to capture these moments. (Why didn't he?) He should put the image in his novel.

Ramsay liked to think of himself as a *flâneur*. Like Baudelaire. He could perhaps become a *poète maudit*, drowning in decadence and absinthe. He didn't want to write the actual poetry, though. There was no money in poetry, it was the waste land of literature. Yes, he had read *The Waste Land* and didn't see what the fuss was about. He considered it to be pretentious stuff, just a ragbag of quotes and fragments of history, really.

Two women passed him, giggling and clutching on to each other as if everything were a great joke. They were dressed in varying shades of green from top to toe, including the obligatory green hats. Everything was green. Why was it so popular? Surely nothing to do with Michael Arlen's dratted *Green Hat*? Perhaps it was absinthe, Ramsay loved absinthe. *La fée verte*. The green fairy. Or was it the colour of hope? The healing grass growing back over the mud and the dead in Flanders Fields. It was a good image. *The Healing Grass.* That would have made a good title if he hadn't already found one. Didn't sound like the title of a crime novel though, too Zola-esque. He had struggled reluctantly through Zola in translation in the Swiss sanatorium.

In Soho Square a small group of men – working men, Ramsay thought, excited by the idea – were holding some kind of demonstration. There was much talk in the air of a General Strike and Ramsay amused himself with notions of manning the barricades in Oxford Street. He still harboured fond memories of the Bolshevists in Great Percy Street. Perhaps his next novel ought to be about working men.

The ones ahead of him seemed rough and sounded northern, and occasionally the ragged chorus shouted their familiar cry – '*Not a minute off the day, not a penny off the pay!*' Miners! Ramsay thought. But what were miners doing in Soho? Not much point in trying to make their case here, why weren't they protesting in Westminster? Were they in need of direction? Perhaps if he talked to them they could provide authentic detail for his working-class novel. *Men of Coal* – he rather liked that title. It sounded noble.

Ramsay approached the men, open-faced and open-handed but unsure how to address them. (Men? Comrades?) Before he could choose, one of them turned a weary, grimy face to him and said, 'Why don't you fuck off, you fucking posh fucker.'

Ramsay slunk away, his tail between his legs. So much for the working man.

He reached the Sphinx still licking his wounds. Inside, a large plaster of Paris reproduction of the mask of Tutankhamun greeted him above an inner entrance. Were they inviting the curse by having it hanging there? He passed uneasily beneath the boy king's sightless gaze and entered the long, narrow corridor that sloped down to the basement. Nellie had consulted an Egyptologist from the Ashmolean (her reach was far and spidery) and the corridor was meant to reproduce the tunnelled entry to a pharaonic tomb, although Ramsay thought it was more like entering a drift mine. Not that he had entered either a pyramid or a mine, but he had read about both. Ramsay was not comfortable with the Egyptian dead; when younger he had visited the British Museum and its gallery full of mummies. For weeks afterwards he had suffered a nightmare that he was locked in that room at night and the mummies had come back to life. Surely the dead should be buried, not put on display?

He always experienced a chill in this corridor in the Sphinx, as if he were walking to his own embalmed afterlife, and he was relieved when he finally reached the end and the (relative) safety of the glimmering interior of the club. Nothing was entirely safe, of course, certainly not in the Sphinx.

Each of the Cokers, apart from Niven, was nominally in charge of one of Nellie's nightclubs, and Ramsay, on his return from abroad, had been afforded the Sphinx, the most questionable of them all. Nellie said it would be the making of him, but Ramsay thought it might prove to be the unmaking.

As its name suggested, the Sphinx had been inspired by the Egyptomania that descended on London after Carter and Carnarvon's discoveries on the Nile four years previously and it was tricked out with the mock spoils of Egypt – wall paintings, hieroglyphs, oriental lamps and so on – as well as quite a few genuine artefacts that Niven had procured for Nellie from someone he knew who had been in the Egyptian Expeditionary Force and had managed to bring home several trunks' worth of looted goods.

Nellie had entertained a fancy for a sarcophagus for the Sphinx, preferably with its occupant still inside – Dalton, who ran the Morgue Club in Ham Yard, had coffins for tables – but she had been dissuaded from the macabre, mainly because there was a dearth of such novelties and even Niven was unable to source an Ancient Egyptian mummy in the West End. Shame, Nellie said. She knew that the denizens of the Sphinx would have been unfazed (if not delighted) by drinking their Rum Daisies and Queens of the Night in the company of the dead. It was that kind of crowd.

The best that could be managed was a mummified cat, bought for a shilling in the Museum Tavern opposite the British Museum from a man who was a janitor there and who said that in the basement there was a storeroom that was 'full of the bloody things'. Another nightmare image to keep Ramsay awake at night.

Ramsay was early, only Gerrit, the head barman, was there. The Sphinx's manager, an unnecessarily argumentative Glaswegian, wasn't due for another half an hour, followed in short order by the rest of the staff.

Gerrit was a pugilistic Dutchman who was made to wear a fez by Nellie when working behind the bar, an item that looked comical on top of his large, bland features, although Ramsay would never have voiced this observation as he was nervous of Gerrit. He was a big man with sailor's tattoos on his arms – he had once been a merchant seaman but now claimed to be an artist, only bending his knee to capitalism (by which he appeared to mean Nellie) in order to subsist. He seemed an odd choice on Nellie's part, although the Sphinx was the most disorderly of her clubs. Nonetheless, Ramsay wondered why she hadn't employed someone who looked a little more Byzantine, if not, indeed, an actual Egyptian. Every nationality beneath the sun was available to his mother from the buffet that was London.

Gerrit was behind the bar, sans fez, polishing the countertop – copper with little lapis lazuli lozenge inserts that would have satisfied even Cleopatra's pampered taste. She might not have been so pleased by the cat mummy, which had begun to develop some kind of mould. It had painted-on eyes that seemed to stare at you wherever you were in the room.

'For atmosphere,' Gerrit said when he caught sight of Ramsay's nostrils twitching at the sickly odour in the club. 'Your mother,' he added, by way of further explanation. Ramsay vaguely remembered a conversation when Nellie had voiced a desire for the 'scents of the Alhambra' in the club, whatever that meant. The Alhambra was quite different to Ancient Egypt, he had pointed out, but Nellie said that anything east of Dover counted as foreign to most people. 'We must pander to their ignorance,' she said.

The incense was making the Sphinx smell like . . .

'A whore's boudoir?' Gerrit offered.

'I wouldn't know,' Ramsay said primly.

'No, of course you wouldn't,' Gerrit said. He always seemed to be leering at Ramsay, but perhaps it was just his accent or the arrangement of features on his big pale face.

Gerrit was a communist, muzzled at work by Nellie, who did not allow politics, particularly Russian politics, in the club, not wanting a red flag raised over grenadine and gin, although the fast crowd that generally populated the Sphinx, despite their Russian cocktail cigarettes, had an eye-rolling antipathy to politics.

Women were drawn to Gerrit, as they seemed always to be drawn to brutes. Gerrit, Ramsay noticed, did not reciprocate. Women, he sneered, what are they good for? Laundry and fucking. Ramsay wondered if Gerrit had actually *met* Nellie. His mother seemed good for neither of those activities, but then Nellie wasn't really a woman, she was an element, like iron. Or metonymic – as the King was to the Crown, so Nellie was to the Coker empire.

To Ramsay's ears, Gerrit's throaty accent made him sound as if he were speaking through a mouthful of sponge. It made 'fucking' sound like even more of a debased activity than it was.

'Can I do something for you, Ramsay?' Gerrit asked, looking at him through heavy-lidded eyes. He always called him Ramsay, not Mr Coker. Ramsay suspected that it marked him as a boy rather than a man, in Gerrit's opinion.

Ramsay didn't reply, but Gerrit moved from behind the bar, a languorous movement for such a big man, and made his way to the back of the club, where a red velvet curtain screened an alcoved doorway. A little sign said 'Private' and Gerrit pushed his way through the curtain's heavy folds. He didn't need to glance behind him to know that a lamb-like Ramsay was following his big rolling buttocks.

Those patrons of the Sphinx enticed to peer behind the red velvet curtain beyond which Gerrit and Ramsay had disappeared might have imagined that an alluring domain – a harem or, indeed, the inner chamber of a pyramid – was to be found there. And indeed the antechambers in Tutankhamun's tomb, with their haphazard piling of grave goods – Ramsay had seen the photographs – were not dissimilar to the back room of the Sphinx, except in the Sphinx the jumble was not composed of gilded couches and fans and the decayed remnants of royal chariots, but rather wooden beer crates and packing cases and the cleaning paraphernalia of mops, buckets, soaps and detergents, as well as their stock of tea and sugar for the staff. Food was not provided for the clientele – they consumed such vast amounts of alcohol and dope that they had no interest in eating.

Ramsay took a seat on an upturned empty wooden box with 'Louis Roederer' stencilled on the side, his evening jacket slung carelessly on the handle of a mop. He rolled up the sleeve of his dress shirt to allow easy access to his vein for Gerrit's silver syringe.

'Relax, Ramsay,' Gerrit said as the needle pierced his skin. Ramsay always felt vulnerable at this moment, but Gerrit tended to him gently as if he were a patient, wielding the needle carefully as he penetrated the skin. 'Just a little prick,' he said, much amused by himself. Ramsay flinched nonetheless and Gerrit said, 'You're such a girl, Ramsay.' He was so close that Ramsay could smell his breath on his slobber lips – onions and fish – and hear the flutter of his breath in his nostrils. Ramsay felt both uncomfortable and excited at this proximity. He never felt certain what Gerrit's intentions towards him were.

Ramsay closed his eyes and imagined he was in an exotic opium den somewhere – not Limehouse, he had been to Limehouse, it had terrified him. Singapore, perhaps. Or Shanghai.

155

Ramsay longed for travel and adventure. The romance of the Orient and the Levant – Baghdad, Marrakesh, Beirut, Aleppo. Cairo! Not the tawdry pastiche of the Sphinx, but the real city, ripe with stinking noise and colour.

Where did Gerrit live, Ramsay wondered? He imagined something sordid – an attic room where Gerrit's underclothes were drying on a clothes-horse around a gas fire while a pot of acrid coffee brewed on the stove. An easel was set up in the room, holding an ugly, unfinished Cubist daub. Try as he might, Ramsay could see nothing in abstract art, although, if asked, he was enthusiastic about it, could mumble for hours about 'the necessary truth of the self' and so on. He mostly kept his philistine thoughts to himself. He wished to be regarded as *au courant* by the world at large.

In Gerrit's room, too, there would be the rumpled, soiled sheets of an unmade bed, perhaps Gerrit's lover of the night still entwined in those sheets – a woman. Or perhaps a man. Ramsay started to have palpitations.

'There you go, my man,' Gerrit said suddenly, as briskly as a nurse who had finished her task and was no longer interested in it.

By the time Ramsay managed to prise his eyelids apart again Gerrit had disappeared, back to the world on the other side of the red velvet curtain.

Ramsay stood up – too quickly – and had to drop down again on to the crate to wait for the room to stop revolving.

Ramsay knew that Gerrit bought drugs in a Chinese restaurant on Regent Street, but when he went there to try to do the same, the waiters just smiled at him serenely as if they were deaf and brought out pork chop suey and 'duck de Chine' and something gelatinous that Ramsay wasn't even sure was food. He felt obliged to eat it all and hoped that when the bill was presented it might include at least a little paper packet of dope, but no, just a hefty reckoning and a stomach ache. 'That place is not for you, Ramsay,' Gerrit said afterwards, as if he were a child.

Before Gerrit, before Tutankhamun's tomb was opened, before even Ramsay's lungs were exiled to Switzerland – when he was still at school, in fact – he used to visit Madame Nicolaides in her cellar café in Bateman Street, where she offered cocaine injections at ten shillings a time. For an extra two shillings she would teach you how to inject yourself, but Ramsay was too squeamish to take charge of the needle. Later, Madame Nicolaides moved to the other side of the park from their home in Hanover Terrace and started up her business again from her house. It was mainly nicely brought-up girls who slipped in and out of her Regent's Park Road drawing room.

Ramsay had much preferred the safety of Madame Nicolaides' drawing room with its rugs and lamps and deep sofas to being here in the storeroom of the Sphinx. It had been like dutifully visiting a rather curmudgeonly aunt. Once, she had served him tea and cake – something called *bougatsa* which was really a custard tart with a foreign name.

Ramsay remained sitting with his eyes closed, head in hands, waiting for his heartbeat to slow. When he eventually opened his eyes again, he spotted something that looked like the heel of a shoe, lodged between two beer crates. He stood up slowly and shifted the crate. It *was* a shoe, the silver-sandal type that most of the dance hostesses wore. What had one of the girls been doing back here that had resulted in the loss of a shoe? He couldn't help but imagine Gerrit pumping his stoker's body against one of the sylph-like girls, up against a wall of beer crates.

Ramsay left the storeroom, shoe in hand, looking for its owner, and found the band already taking their seats and tuning up and the dance hostesses trailing in, chatting nineteen to the dozen, their carmined lips still fresh, their face powder not yet caked into the tired lines of their faces. They were like new blooms that would be drooping, their colours faded, by the end of the evening. (Excellent image, Ramsay thought. He would probably forget it, though.) 'Evening, Mr Coker . . . Evening Mr Coker,' they chirped. Ramsay murmured something in reply. He held up the shoe and one of them said, 'Oh, look, it's Prince Charming.'

'I thought perhaps one of you ladies dropped it,' he said, but none of them claimed it.

The Glaswegian manager appeared out of nowhere and said, 'Is there something else, Mr Coker? We're all set up here.'

They were all eager to be rid of him. *Why don't you fuck off, you fucking posh fucker* still echoed painfully in his brain.

A thump on his shoulders indicated Gerrit, fez in place, ready for the evening's festivities. 'Drink this, my man,' he said, handing Ramsay a glass of water. 'And I'll take that,' he said, removing the shoe still clutched in Ramsay's hand.

Pinoli's

Edith, under the weather though she was, had a tryst with her lover. They were possibly the least romantic pair ever to grace the inside of Pinoli's restaurant in Wardour Street.

It was still early, but Pinoli's was bustling as usual. You would think he would prefer to keep to the shadows, but he liked crowded, busy places. He was brazen that way. Edith presumed it would be his downfall one day. And yet it was often the brazen who survived and the meek who went under, wasn't it? Edith was not meek but she was in danger of going under.

'You've done something to your hair,' he said. Was that a compliment? Flattery was always oblique with him. Edith was rarely eulogized by any member of the male sex. 'Betty and Shirley got the looks,' Nellie said, 'you got the brains. You take after me in that respect. You should be thankful.' Betty and Shirley had got scholarships to Cambridge, Edith reminded her mother. 'And look how stupid it made them,' Nellie said.

Edith's appetite was 'in her boots', she had reported to him when she joined him at the table. He was currently eating his way through the three-shilling *table d'hôte*. He had just finished a plate of *filets de hareng à la meunière*, while Edith had sipped briefly on a *crème chasseur* soup that had only increased her desire to retch. She regarded his herrings with distaste – all those tiny bones waiting to catch you out. She had choked on a fish-bone as a child when they were still living in Edinburgh. She had no idea what kind of fish it was, but a herring seemed like a prime suspect to her. Nellie had turned her upside down and shaken her like a piggy bank. To no avail. The bone was eventually dislodged by a nurse in the Hospital for Sick Children. It was the shaking that Edith remembered, not the fishbone. Her lover had moved on to dessert, demolishing a *bombe pralinée*.

'What's up with you?'

'Touch of stomach 'flu, I expect,' said Edith, striking an off-hand note, although her stomach was heaving from the lingering smell of herring. She would never tell him the truth. She would solve her problem without him ever knowing about it. If she didn't, she would never be free of him.

'Do you think I'm attractive?' she asked after an interval of watching him shovel in the *bombe*. He was a surprisingly inelegant eater. Lately she had begun to notice nothing but flaws. She supposed that was how love died, although was 'love' the right word for what they had shared? The question was not posed in the simpering manner that some women might adopt. Edith had never simpered in her life. It was more a case of simple curiosity. She knew her worth to him and it was not founded on vanity.

'Do I think you're attractive?' he said. He considered the question a little too long. (Just say yes, she thought irritably.) 'I would say handsome.'

Wrong answer, she thought bitterly. 'Handsome is as handsome does,' her mother was wont to say. Nellie was full of empty phrases. 'I have to go,' Edith said abruptly.

'So do I,' he said, from which we might presume a family waiting at home, and although this was true, he was usually on one nefarious quest or another in the evenings. He was a Catholic, he would never leave his wife. Edith took some comfort from that.

'Well, I expect I'll see you soon,' she said as he called for the bill.

'I expect so,' he said.

Lately she had been trying to keep him at arm's length. It amused him. She wondered if this was the last time that she would see him. Even if she broke it off, she feared he would still pursue her. He couldn't afford to let her go, she knew too much.

There had been a time, not so very long ago, when Edith had been in thrall to him. He was good-looking, complicated and devious, all three adjectives had made him interesting in her eyes, especially compared to the pleasure-seeking buffoons who populated her working life. Even the clever ones seemed to succumb to idiocy once they were inside a nightclub. Now, however, she understood that 'interesting' was the last thing one should look for in a lover. He wielded a lot of power, more than she could, but nonetheless Edith was strong. I must be on my mettle, she thought. If they were to go into battle with each other it would not be an easy victory for him.

'You should go home,' he said. 'You're not at all yourself.'

'Tell me about it,' Edith said. She had a plan. (She was her mother's daughter.) It was time to execute it.

Edith left Pinoli's quickly and hailed a cab while he was still inside paying the bill. She didn't want him to know where she was going. It certainly wasn't home.

'Bedford Street,' she said to the cab driver, unwilling to share her actual destination. On Bedford Street she alighted, paid the fare and walked the rest of the way.

From what she had managed to glean beforehand, the whole thing would be over pretty quickly. With any luck, all would be done and dusted and she would be back in Hanover Terrace in time for supper.

She walked along Henrietta Street, checking the street numbers, looking for number four. There was no number on the door, but as the house was shouldered by two and six she presumed she had found it. There was an ugly iron knocker on the door, wrought in the image of a demon, or maybe the devil himself. Well, that was fitting, she thought as she lifted it and rapped firmly. The door flew open, seemingly into a void, and Edith said, 'Mrs Darling?' In answer, a bony arm shot out, grabbed Edith by the wrist and pulled her inside.

A Kidnap, a Raid and a Small Fire

Kitty had been abandoned as usual, leaving her free to wander through her sisters' bedrooms in Hanover Terrace. When Nellie had been away in prison Kitty had already thoroughly investigated her room several times, but, disappointingly, the only thing she had been able to find had been a tatty little bag beneath her mother's mattress. It held a tooth, a lock of hair, the mouldy old foot of some animal and other bits and pieces. Kitty recognized witchcraft when she saw it. She had thrown the bag in the canal in case it was used against her and claimed blank ignorance when questioned later by Nellie.

She appropriated a fox-fur tippet from Betty's wardrobe and wound it round her neck and then applied Shirley's blood-red Molinard lipstick. In Edith's room she 'borrowed' two shillings from a little porcupine-quill box that Edith kept on her dressing-table. Kitty was rarely encouraged to come into this room and so it was interesting to investigate Edith's things. There was a bottle of Shalimar on the dressing-table. Kitty sprayed her wrists with it, intrigued. Edith was not known for wearing perfume.

An envelope propped up against the mirror had 'Edith' written on it. It had already been opened, so it was fair game as far as Kitty was concerned, although she would probably have steamed it open anyway. It was dated today and a bold, masculine hand had penned, *Dear Edith, just a note to confirm I will be able to see you tonight. Pinoli's at seven. Yours, A x.* Not just 'A' but 'A' followed by a cross – a kiss! Without the kiss it might have been a

162

note from the brewer who supplied the beer – but a kiss transformed it into something else. Unlikely as it seemed, Edith had an admirer.

Kitty had to make her own way to the Amethyst as no one had seen fit to arrange a cab. Nor had anyone left her any money, so taking Edith's two shillings seemed quite justified to her mind. She left the house and, clutching her two shillings, was waiting on the pavement in the vain hope of a taxi – there were never any on the Outer Circle – when a car drew up against the kerb.

The driver leant across and rolled down the window of the car. He opened the passenger door and smiled at her. He looked foreign, like a portly version of Valentino. 'Hello, little girl,' he said.

'Hello,' Kitty replied politely.

'Hop in and I'll give you a lift. I can take you for a spin, if you like. What do you say?'

Shirley and Betty were in the habit of travelling to the Foxhole and the Pixie together. They did most things together – they were 'Irish twins', born in the same year, and although very different were also very alike, both possessing a preference for style over substance. ('Substance,' Shirley said, 'led to the battlefield, style rarely so.' 'Perhaps a killing look,' Betty said, pleased with herself. They considered themselves to be wits.)

Nellie had insisted on educating them to within an inch of their lives. After their expensive private school they had gone up to Cambridge together, cutting a powerful swathe through Girton College. They had both been icons – for their sporty little cars, their couture clothing, their coiffed hair. Shirley singlehandedly pioneered the raven-wing shingle that every girl in her year then copied, with varying degrees of failure. Their fellow students begged to do them favours, run errands, sit at their feet in front of their coal fire, toasting crumpets on a brass fork for them. And that was just the girls. Young men from the male colleges threatened suicide, offered Herculean labours, wrote poetry. ('Ghastly stuff,' Betty said.)

Although they had been fond of Girton, they had left their alma mater without a backward glance. Orpheus could have sent them in to rescue Eurydice from Hades.

Edith was too useful to Nellie for marriage and Kitty had already been abandoned to chance, so buccaneering Nellie's ambitions for an entrée into the upper echelons of English society rested on Betty and Shirley. She would not be satisfied until they married someone who had climbed to the highest rung on Debrett's ladder. Not her sons, she would just be relieved if they married at all. Particularly Ramsay.

Shirley was currently often in the company of the second son of a duke, a young man called Rollo, whom Nellie had been assiduously courting on her daughter's behalf. To no avail. Shirley said she was fond of Rollo but had met more manly men in the chorus at the Palace. She was resistant to her mother's matrimonial ambitions. She wanted to 'be someone'. ('But you're someone already,' Nellie said.)

Betty's current admirer, he of the silver penknife, was not in Debrett's. He was a Canadian railroad millionaire, which gave him a certain credibility in Nellie's eyes. But perhaps not quite enough. To Nellie, money without a title was almost as bad as a title without money. The war had, disappointingly for Nellie, cut the bloodlines of the aristocracy. Their sons, sacrificed to the greater good, were no longer available to marry Shirley and Betty, and their wealth had been swallowed by the upkeep on their houses.

The Foxhole in Wardour Street was Betty's favourite club. It was a jazzy place with an American bar and a Jamaican band and a glass floor, beneath which there were lights that changed colour all the time. The place got frantic after midnight. It drew its clientele from a mixture of bohemian men and women of the demi-monde and people of every colour and creed in a friendly stew, like Babel before the tower. Chorus boys, still in full stage make-up, often came straight from their encores and poured Brandy Fancies down their throats as if they were dying of thirst.

Betty was popular with this crowd. On some nights she could spend every minute from opening to closing on the kaleidoscopic dance floor. Both Betty and Shirley were excellent dancers, almost professionally spry, unlike Edith, who had two left feet. ('Even possibly three,' Betty said.) They had talked about setting up a dance academy within one of the clubs, where members would pay extra to learn the latest dances or polish up the old ones. Nellie was ruminating on the idea. They doubted she would ever digest it.

Nellie tended to stay away from the Foxhole. It made her feel old. She felt more comfortable paying an occasional visit to the Pixie, just around the corner from the Foxhole. The Pixie was a little bijou affair with aspirations to sophistication. Dancing was the most important thing, the hostesses were all enlisted from the better dance schools, some even from the stage, and there was an entirely female band, as well as a female manager who wore masculine evening dress, tailored to her splendid figure. Men were not unwelcome, but women often partnered each other – something that was not unusual in the wider world either, as the war had taken so many men from the dance floor and never returned them.

There were clubs, Betty and Shirley knew, perhaps more secretive, where women went purposely for this kind of thing (they had no objection – women should stick together in their opinion), but the Pixie attracted a more decorous crowd – rather stiff quicksteps and lots of amused apologizing when the dancers grew confused over who was the man and who was the woman.

There was a cold snacks counter that was very popular – two shillings and sixpence for a sandwich, butter not margarine. The sandwiches were made in the back all night long by a woman called Bertha who was deaf and dumb, and who always had a tea towel draped somewhere about her person, even when she went home.

Shirley had a talent for charades that came in handy with Bertha. Shirley had always hankered for the stage. Nellie was baffled. 'You don't need to go on the stage to act,' she told her. 'Life is just one long play.' Comedy or tragedy, it depended how you looked at it, didn't it? Shirley plumped for nuance. She would learn, Nellie said darkly.

It was their job to establish that all was as it should be every evening, that everyone was in place, that there was a sufficient float in the coffers, and then all they had to do was to wind the clubs up and let them go. Like automata.

Not tonight. There was the most tremendous fuss happening at the Pixie when Betty and Shirley arrived. Most of the guests were standing on the pavement outside, as if they were a promenading audience. A wispy column of smoke was rising into the sky from somewhere at the back of the club and indeed a fire engine arrived at the same time, noisily clanging its way from the station on Shaftesbury Avenue, a late entrant on the stage.

The curtain was soon brought down on the drama with only slight casualties being sustained – a corner of the kitchen out of action and Bertha, too, who had burnt her hand when she had thrown the contents of a large container of baking soda on to the flames.

'Sensible woman,' a fireman said admiringly to Shirley. 'Water would have set it right off.' The fireman seemed to be the senior officer in charge and Shirley was hanging on his every word, as well as clinging to his steadying elbow, claiming she was unstable from shock. Shirley had been too young during the war to value the aesthetic of a man in uniform. She was old enough now.

Bertha was sitting on the pavement being treated by a nurse from St Thomas's who was one of the Pixie's regulars. Had Bertha caused the fire? Perhaps one of her tea towels had flapped carelessly and caught on the gas burners of the stove? Bertha dumbly but vigorously denied this possibility.

It took a lengthy pantomime between Bertha and Shirley to acquire the details of what had happened. The back door had been opened by an unseen hand when Bertha was in the middle of smashing up boiled eggs with salad cream for the sandwiches (it was a detailed account). Obviously she had been unable to hear the door, but she had been alerted to danger by the egregious scent of paraffin. She had an excellent sense of smell. 'One sense will compensate for the loss of another,' Shirley explained to her fireman, who had already grown tired of the histrionic air around the Pixie. Some idiot had started a fire, his men had made sure it was out. That was all he needed to know. He prised Shirley off his elbow.

Bertha persisted, however, with her drama, through the medium of Shirley. She had turned around, she said, and had seen a flaming rag being tossed towards the gas burners and had, by instinct more than design, helped to douse the fire by flinging the bicarb on it. And no, she had not seen the face of whoever had thrown the rag.

'Arson?' the fireman said, his interest revived slightly. 'You'd better get in touch with the police.'

They would, Betty and Shirley promised in unison. They wouldn't. There was more chance of Tutankhamun being resuscitated than there was of Nellie wanting the police involved.

'She'll hold us responsible,' Betty said to Shirley as the clearing-up started.

'I know, but we had nothing to do with it.'

'Doesn't mean she won't hold us responsible.'

The fire engine departed, the guests went back inside, undaunted by the soot and the smell of charring. Bertha was sent home with five pounds from the till by Shirley. In her absence, several guests volunteered to continue making the sandwiches. It never ceased to surprise the Cokers how willing nightclub patrons were to pitch in behind the scenes. For the novelty of it, rather than altruism. They loved a disaster.

'Everything all right?' Nellie asked when Shirley and Betty arrived at the Amethyst. She was referring to the Pixie and the Foxhole, not their state of health or heart or mind. Those things were rarely enquired after by Nellie. She had a little glass dish of cream toffees in front of her and chewed one thoughtfully while scrutinizing her daughters. Nellie had a way of making you feel as though you were lying, even when you were telling the truth.

'A small fire in the kitchen at the Pixie,' Betty said stoutly, resilient in the face of the nightly maternal audit.

'Extinguished straight away,' Shirley added hastily. 'Although . . .'

'Although?'

'It seems it was started deliberately.'

'Well, well,' Nelly said and popped another toffee in her mouth. 'Give me the details.'

Nellie was not a stranger to fire. She had owned a club – the Lucky Cat, acquired not long after the Amethyst – that had burnt down to the ground shortly after it had closed for the night, several years ago now. The Lucky Cat was indeed lucky, because only a few weeks before its destruction Nellie had taken out an insurance policy against just such an eventuality. The fire was ruled an accident, Maddox had been an instrumental witness. ('I noticed faulty wiring.') There had been no loss of life, except, ironically, the cat that lived on the premises to keep the rodent population in check. A few spindly bones were raked out of the ash. Nellie told her concerned girls that the cat had escaped and gone to live elsewhere. 'What you don't know can't hurt you,' she said to Maddox. She did not believe that. What you didn't know was almost bound to hurt you. Nellie liked to know everything.

Nellie continued to brood on the news from the Pixie in her cashier's booth. It had been a clumsy assault, but nonetheless without Bertha's quick wits everyone in the club could have been burnt to a cinder and Nellie would probably have been found guilty of negligence, if not manslaughter, even murder, and put out of business. Which was the whole point presumably. It was Maddox, wasn't it?

Ramsay was about to leave the Sphinx for the night when there was a tremendous commotion. It was heralded by a klaxon, like a clown horn, from up the stairs (later he realized it was a signal from the doormen), followed by the floor juddering and shaking as if an earthquake were in progress. There was a grinding of gears and then the bar and all its bottles – along with Gerrit, who was still standing behind it – began to disappear.

It took Ramsay a good few seconds of readjusting his baffled brain to realize that the bar had in fact revolved, like a train engine on a turntable, or a theatre flat changing. It reminded him of a play he had recently seen where the whole stage had spun round to reveal a completely different set. The 'earthquake' was the hidden engine that drove the mechanism. Now, where the bar once was, there was only a painted wall, and the bar – and Gerrit along with it – had disappeared. Ramsay felt an odd disappointment that the barman hadn't waved farewell as he passed out of sight. Where had he gone? Would he come back?

While Ramsay was being transfixed by this cunning vanishing act, the girls and porters and waiters, not to mention the Sphinx's own patrons, had been conducting a well-drilled performance, sweeping up glasses and bottles and any other signs of transgression against the licensing laws. By the time the police plodded clumsily into the club there was nothing illicit in sight, only a bogus air of virtue.

The red velvet curtain was pushed aside and Gerrit sauntered in from the storeroom like a bad actor coming on stage and said, 'Is there a problem here, officers?' Ramsay stared at him, speechless. There was a secret door into the store cupboard? And no one had seen fit to tell him about the trick with the bar? What else didn't he know? He was supposed to be in charge, for heaven's sake.

'All right, my man?' Gerrit said, slapping him again (rather forcefully) between the shoulder blades. 'Clever, eh?'

Within the space of an hour the disgruntled police had left, the bar had been wheeled back into position and the place was roistering once more. With a slight movement of his head, Gerrit indicated the red velvet curtain to Ramsay. Gerrit was right, Ramsay thought, he definitely needed something to steady his nerves.

*

The downward climb into the Sphinx must of necessity turn into an upward slog to exit it. The rake of the passageway was the wrong way around, surely? One should have to put some effort in at the beginning of an evening but be allowed to slip away easily at the end.

Ramsay moved slowly. The passageway was lit by yet more oriental-style lamps – these were gas with open flames, masquerading as torches. For Nellie's 'atmosphere', no doubt. Ramsay was sure they must be dangerous. Would he be held responsible if the Sphinx caught fire, if all the wayward crowd inside were burnt alive or trampled each other to death while the band played 'Ain't We Got Fun'?

The quivering, ghastly flames illuminated the hieroglyphs. The gas from the lamps was making him feel nauseous again. He felt as if he were turning into a figment of himself. (Was that possible? Did that even make sense? Did anything make sense?)

A rush of cold air indicated that the doormen had let people in, and within seconds Ramsay was engulfed by a glittering tide of people and then left high and dry as they swept into the club. He must get some air. He passed beneath the mask of Tutankhamun again. He almost expected it to say something to him.

He had so much dope in his veins that he was beginning to separate into several Ramsays, different notes on a scale where he had been one harmonious chord. He must stop reaching for an image, it was making him want to vomit.

'Mr Coker?' one of the doormen said. 'Mr Coker – are you all right?'

The two doormen, burly fellows with oxen shoulders that could have pulled a plough, were still in their bulky winter over-coats. Twenty-seven shillings for a winter one, twenty-five for summer, Ramsay heard Nellie say in his head. His mother was a living ledger. Everything had a price. If she could have pawned her children, she would have done. (No, only Kitty, she said.)

'Yes, quite all right, thank you,' Ramsay said stiffly, making a supreme effort to prevent himself from fragmenting completely and disappearing for ever. 'I'm off to the Amethyst now. Good night.'

As he walked through the dimly lit back streets, Ramsay began to develop the uncomfortable feeling that he was being followed by someone. Or something. Something evil. What was the Shakespeare quote? *Something wicked this way comes.* Yes, that was what it felt like. *By the pricking of my thumbs* – rather a good title for a novel.

His agitation grew as he began to see shadows like smoke everywhere. A black cat crossed his path on its nightly rounds. Was that lucky or unlucky? He couldn't remember. For some reason he thought of the mummified cat in the Sphinx, a thought that led to Egyptian mummies in general and from there very quickly back to Tutankhamun and his curse.

What had been in Gerrit's syringe tonight, for heaven's sake? He had presumed it was cocaine – Gerrit called it 'joy dust' (pronouncing it 'yoy dust', which made it sound less happy) – it usually was, although sometimes Gerrit gave him morphine, which was lovely but impractical, and once heroin, which made him swoon with desire for more, but Gerrit refused. Cocaine didn't make him feel jittery like this, it usually made him feel bright and alert, an improved version of himself, ready to be a willing adjutant in the Coker corps.

Niven had warned him that there was some 'funny stuff' being sold and he should be careful what he took and who gave it to him. Ramsay had stoutly denied taking anything. His heart was pulsing very hard in his chest, an overwrought mechanism about to fail. Perhaps Niven had been right about the funny stuff.

He was quite sure now that he was being dogged, every step seemed to be echoed by another's, yet whenever he turned to look there was no one in sight. The streets were deserted, even the nightly gauntlet of streetwalkers he usually had to run was absent. It felt unnatural, like something out of a story by Poe.

And then, dear God – a mummy! An actual Egyptian mummy, lurching towards him, the loose ends of its embalming bandages flapping. His nightmares had come to life. The mummy seemed to be unravelling as it jerked along the pavement. Nearer and nearer. Ramsay was paralysed by the sight. He wondered if he might be going mad. Most artists were probably mad, one way or another. It was almost a badge of honour.

And then he heard the hoots and shouts of drunken laughter and saw that the mummy was being followed by Bo-Peep, then a large, paunchy bear, and, bringing up the rear, a masked harlequin carrying the threat of a wooden bat.

Not the boy king come back to haunt him but a harmless troupe of drunken partygoers in fancy dress.

Relatively harmless. He was suddenly surrounded by them, laughing and jostling as they circled him, not quite as convivial as they seemed at first sight. They reminded Ramsay of the bullies who used to lark around him at school. Close up, the bear smelt rank – it was a costume, of course (he certainly hoped so) – and Bo-Peep, he could see now that he was nearer her, was actually a man. Beneath their costumes people could be anyone, their intentions anything. It was a frightening idea.

Ramsay managed to break free of their dubious embrace and run off.

'Everything all right at the Sphinx?' Nellie greeted him.

'Yes.'

'And the Flying Dutchman – how is he?'

'Same as ever.'

'And you?'

'Me?'

'Yes, you.' Nellie's gimlet gaze bored into him. It was like being the guilty suspect in a courtroom, prosecuting barrister, judge and jury all wrapped in the unholy trinity of his mother. 'Have you been up to something, Ramsay?'

'No!'

'Nothing has happened?'

'Well, yes, a police raid, but it came to nothing. I do think someone might have told me about the trick with the bar.'

'Don't be peevish,' Nellie said. 'It suits you too well.'

'Did you know about it? Did you have a tip-off from Maddox? I thought he wasn't our friend any more.'

'He isn't,' Nellie said. 'We have another friend now.'

A wild-eyed Kitty was the last to arrive, the Molinard lipstick smeared and the fox-fur tippet in a bedraggled state.

'What happened to you?' Nellie asked sharply.

'Nothing much,' Kitty said. She was reluctant to mention her recent misadventure as she would undoubtedly be blamed for it herself.

'Try again.' Nellie stared at Kitty, Kitty stared back. A war of attrition. Kitty finally capitulated.

Despite her inherently reckless nature, Kitty had politely declined the man's offer as she knew from her sisters' conversation that there was something vaguely disgusting about this 'spinning' thing. Therefore, when he had reached out and grabbed her arm and tried to pull her into the car, Kitty had struggled like a fish on a line, roaring, 'Murder!' at the top of her lungs until the man released his catch. He laughed and told her that she was 'more trouble than she was worth', a by-line that would, unfortunately, follow Kitty for the rest of her life.

'What sort of man?' Nellie asked.

'Dunno.'

'Maddox?'

'No, I know what *he* looks like. It wasn't his car.'

'What sort of car was it?'

'A Mercedes-Benz, yellow. The Sports Phaeton model.' Kitty knew cars, she studied Niven's motoring magazines, intending to own a Rolls-Royce when she was older.

'Was it indeed,' Nellie said thoughtfully. It didn't seem to be a question.

173

'Tried to persuade me to go for a spin with him.'

'Did he indeed.'

It was possible, of course, Kitty thought now, that he would not have done something horrible to her but would simply have imprisoned her somewhere (she imagined a bed of straw, a kindly jailer) and delivered plates of hot buttered toast at regular intervals until the ransom demanded off her mother was paid. Would Nellie pay, and if so, how much? There was another scenario, of course, where the man might well have done unspeakable things to her but rewarded her with an endless supply of iced buns and lemonade and many other diversions and she would have got to ride around like a queen in the back of his yellow car. She felt a pang of regret now that she might have missed out. The next time the man – or any man – offered to take her for a spin, she might very well go along just to see what happened.

'Curiosity killed the cat,' Nellie said, as if she could read her thoughts. 'The kittens, too.'

And so it begins, Nellie thought. Opening salvos from the enemy – arson, abduction and a raid. All attempted, all failed. Maddox's signature was all over the raid and the fire. Not the kidnap, though. A yellow Mercedes-Benz had been parked outside the Goring when she arrived there this afternoon. There couldn't be that many in London.

'Mr Azzopardi's?' she had said to the doorman.

'Couldn't possibly say, madam.' The doorman grinned, pocketing her pound note.

Azzopardi was trying to her frighten her, whereas Maddox was trying to destroy her – or rather he was trying to destroy her business, which was much the same thing as far as Nellie was concerned. Maddox wanted the clubs, but Azzopardi seemed to be playing some kind of game with her. Nellie didn't like games, there was always the chance that you could lose.

Nellie turned inward. She was thinking.

Morning Tea

Unlike most men, Frobisher was always relieved when he could go to work. At work he could repair himself. In Ealing he unravelled.

Miss Kelling had been his first thought this morning when he woke, even though his wife lay in bed next to him. He was struck painfully by guilt. Sometimes he wished he was Catholic, absolution must be a great comfort.

Lottie was snoring gently, not an entirely unpleasant thing in a beautiful woman. There were translucent pearls of sweat on her damp forehead and a stray lock of her dark hair was sticking to her cheek. On some (many) days, the house in Ealing seemed more like a sanatorium, their relationship resembling that of doctor and patient rather than man and wife. He was always trying to devise little pick-me-ups for Lottie – wouldn't she like to go for a walk in the park with him? Should he pull her chair out into the garden, where she could sit in the sunshine and watch the birds? How about they take a boat out at Richmond on his day off? And so on and so on.

Frobisher had married comparatively late in life, not knowing what to expect. It had seemed noble, saving a woman, the way he had saved Lottie, but later he had to question – hadn't it simply been weakness when confronted with beauty? Lottie *was* beautiful. If she had been plain, would he have been drawn to her? It was an awkward question, but asked only of himself. She was as opaque as opal and they remained hopelessly unknowable to each other.

Lottie had already been rescued once before. It was not Frobisher who had raised her from the ruins of Ypres, he had been
kept busy fighting the losing battle against crime on the home
front – one war that never ended. It had been an English major
in the Royal Hampshires who had brought her back to England
and then abandoned her.

He had first encountered Lottie balancing on the parapet of
Waterloo Bridge, reminding him of the Winged Victory of
Samothrace, except, unlike the statue, Lottie had still been in
possession of her head, if not her mind. He had grabbed her
around the waist and pulled her back down to earth. He had
saved her, and in doing so he had lost himself.

Frobisher should perhaps have realized that Lottie was a
woman who was resistant to salvage. She had risen and fallen like
the tide, but she seemed to favour the ebb rather than the flow.

Perhaps when he retired they should move back to the countryside for her health (his, too). She had no love for the suburbs,
perhaps the fields and woods would revive her. He gently brushed
the lock of hair from her cheek and she muttered something in
French. Frobisher sighed.

He brought her a cup of tea, the first and last resource of an
English husband.

'Is Maddox back?' Frobisher said, shrugging off his overcoat.

'No, sir. They seek him here, they seek him there,' the desk
sergeant laughed.

'He's not the ruddy Scarlet Pimpernel, sergeant.'

Maddox couldn't play hide-and-seek for ever. Frobisher wondered if he shouldn't pay Maddox a surprise home visit in
Crouch End, catch him red-handed digging his garden or fixing
his roof or whatever it was that husbands with time on their
hands got up to in Crouch End.

'If he comes in, tell him I'm looking for him.'

'Will do, sir. Tea, sir? A brew?'

Frobisher almost relented, but the acceptance of the tea would seem to indicate a weakness on his part somehow. Shouldn't they have a woman about the place? An older one, he imagined, plain and tightly wrapped in an apron, pushing a tea trolley. A cockney accent perhaps and a warm, damp aura of reassurance about her person. 'No, thank you, sergeant,' he said eventually, when the sergeant started tapping an impatient tattoo with his pencil on the countertop. He must be careful, Frobisher reminded himself, not to get lost in his own mind.

Simpson's in the Strand

'May I introduce the beef, sir?' the waiter in Simpson's asked, raising the dome on the great silver serving trolley with a ponderous flourish, as if diners in the Grand Divan lived all their lives waiting for this revelation. The slab of beef took centre stage, oozing thin, pink juices that puddled around it on the salver. Introductions over, the waiter carved two succulent slices, which he laid delicately on the plate like overlapping leaves before saying, 'Horseradish, sir?'

'Yes, please. And the roast potatoes, the creamed leeks, the boiled cabbage, the buttered carrots. And fill the wine glass with a good Bordeaux – Chateau Talbot, 1913? – excellent – and leave the gravy boat on the table, please.' The glass was filled, the claret moving like liquid rubies in the light cast from the huge chandeliers.

God, Azzopardi loved England! He loved the pompous buildings, the scurfy streets. He loved the bitter, bankrupt duke from whom he was renting a house in Eaton Square, and he loved equally the ragamuffin children who followed him in the street, shouting insults about his race. (For some reason, they presumed he was Turkish.) He loved the food in places like this – the bloody beef with its cope of thick yellow fat that he could barely wait to sink his teeth into. And he loved the stodge of a pudding that would follow the joint of beef. Steamed marmalade today, sir. And leave the jug of custard on the table. Please. Thank you.

'The beef for you as well, sir?' the waiter said, turning to

Azzopardi's luncheon companion, his carving knife, like a scimitar, at the ready.

'I'll have the fish, thank you,' Niven said, to the waiter's evident displeasure.

Turbot in green sauce was delivered with considerably less pomp than the beef and Niven's glass was filled with a Vouvray. Azzopardi raised his own glass and caught Niven looking at the scar on the back of his hand.

'Old war wound,' he laughed.

'You weren't in the war.'

'There's more than one type of war, Mr Coker. Anyway, cheers!'

Niven raised his glass in turn. 'Cheers.' The heavy crystal chinked.

'To the future,' Azzopardi said.

Niven raised an eyebrow and murmured, 'The future,' although he had little faith in it. He was content to go along with Azzopardi's belief that they were going to take over Nellie's empire. The Maltese talked of this venture in terms of 'reparations', as if, like Germany, he was smarting under an injustice. If Niven stepped away now he would not be privy to Azzopardi's intentions. He could save his mother or he could betray her. He liked to think that he was undecided, but in his heart he knew that blood would win. It always did for the Cokers.

Azzopardi drained his glass greedily and signalled to the waiter for more wine. 'I think that we are going to be great friends,' he said to Niven.

'Let's just stick to business partners for the time being,' Niven said.

'Better still,' Azzopardi said.

Niven declined the offer of the steamed marmalade pudding. 'You're quite the monk,' Azzopardi said, already eyeing the cheeseboard. Stilton! A truly magnificent cheese.

'Saving myself,' Niven said.

Niven requested coffee – black – from the waiter. 'Nothing else.'

'Not even cream?' Azzopardi asked, looking bereft on the part of the cow. 'You are not one of these "vegetarians", are you?' he asked, stabbing a slice of cheese with his fork. 'Divine,' he murmured. For a moment, Niven was reminded of Kitty. The same strange affectations.

'No, I'm not,' Niven said, without elaborating, although he did sometimes harbour doubts about butchery. He had seen too much of it in the war. Better for a man to hunt down a deer with a bow and arrow, he thought, but he was hopelessly trapped by civilization.

'A man needs meat,' Azzopardi said bullishly. 'Red meat to make red blood.' He was all performance – an effeminate man pretending he wasn't. It hardly mattered to Niven. His own brother was in that particular camp and he loved him no less for it. Did he love Ramsay? 'Love' seemed an odd word in the context of his family. It was a savage emotion amongst the Cokers. He loved Keeper, of that Niven was sure. If it came to a life-or-death choice between his brother and his dog, which would he choose? The balance of his heart lurched towards the dog.

'My commiserations,' Azzopardi said. 'I heard you had a fire in one of your mother's clubs.'

'A small one,' Niven said.

'She's growing weaker. Are you ready for a *coup d'état*? A new regime. Will you join me?' He was a hawk waiting to swoop on his prey, Niven thought. He didn't seem to understand that Nellie was no one's prey. 'If she doesn't return to me what is owed to me then I will take her business off her, one way or the other.'

'What *is* it that she owes you?' Niven puzzled.

'Why don't you ask her?'

Niven laughed. 'It's against my mother's religion to give straight answers.' His, too, of course. 'I have to go.'

Azzopardi patted the great girth of his belly with satisfaction and called for more port. It was the deprivation of prison that had made him greedy. The betrayal, too, that he had suffered when he realized his fortune had been lost. He had remade it, exporting whisky to Prohibition America from Scotland – Leith to New York, via Montreal, he may as well have had his own shipping line – but that only gave him money, it didn't give him vengeance.

He didn't really want Nellie's clubs, they were simply a forfeit. For what was owed to him, for what she had taken from him. 'More port!' he said jovially to the waiter. God, he loved England.

The Audition

Freda had rehearsed and rehearsed for her audition until the City clerk who rented the room beneath them threatened to 'drown her like a kitten' if she didn't stop it. She had a new audition piece – 'Tea for Two' – which she sang while executing a snappy tap dance. She had a nice voice, thin and high.

She had chosen her outfit carefully. After much consideration, she had settled on a tartan skirt and a broderie anglaise blouse beneath her favourite cardigan, cherry-red, hand-knitted in a complicated stitch, with tiny shell buttons in the shape of daisies. It was a tight fit nowadays but had a sentimental value that she hoped would bring luck. It had been the last thing that she had modelled for the Knits, an appearance in Grimsby, and Freda thought of it as a farewell gift from Adele, even though Adele knew nothing about its pilfering. To Freda it felt like a gift, whether it was or not.

Freda had taken an extra bath this week in preparation for the audition. She went with Florence once a week to the public baths on Marshall Street, where they splashed out sixpence for a first-class warm bath, taking it in turns as to who should go in the water first. In honour of her audition, Freda had paid tuppence yesterday for a second-class bath and had the luxury of having it all to herself. The washing facilities in Henrietta Street were limited – they shared a cold-water sink on the landing and a water closet that was always stained and smelling of urine. Mrs Darling was a stranger to cleanliness. She also seemed to have an intense dislike for people and yet, even far away in the attic, they could hear, day and night, the *rat-a-tat-tat* of the demonic doorknocker.

Miss Sherbourne had finally managed to secure a proper audition for Freda, at the Adelphi Theatre in the Strand, for the chorus of a show called *Betty in Mayfair*. 'I pulled a lot of strings to get you this audition,' she said, 'so mind you do your best to impress them.' I always do, Freda thought.

Since running away from home, the bright light of success that Freda thought of as her follow-spot had slowly begun to fade. But now everything was about to change, the light was burning brightly – Freda Murgatroyd was on the road to stardom! At last!

Her cardigan stretched tightly as Freda struggled to fasten the little shell daisy buttons. 'You look nice,' Florence said, still lying lazily in bed, even though the day was in full swing around them in the boarding house. 'They'll be impressed at the Adelphi.'

'Thank you,' Freda said, doing a twirl and dipping a little curtsey. Florence insisted that she pin Mrs Ingram's little bluebird brooch to the red cardigan. 'For luck,' she said. Freda didn't see how it could be lucky to wear stolen goods, but she complied as it seemed to make Florence happy.

'What will you do while I'm at the Adelphi?' she asked Florence. (What *did* Florence do with her time?)

'Oh, this and that,' Florence said. 'I'll meet you afterwards in the Lyons on Coventry Street and you can tell me all about the audition.'

Freda felt a sudden chill. She imagined this was how people must feel on the morning of their execution. The moment of reckoning was upon her. There was a fork in the road ahead. On one side was a path that glimmered with the gold it was paved with, leading to fame and success. On the other side was a soot-smirched alleyway that led to despair. What if that was the path she was forced to take? What then?

'Don't be such a dramatic cuckoo,' Florence said, untangling herself from the bedsheets. 'Come on, let's go and get some breakfast.'

After they had eaten, they wandered around for a bit until it began to rain. They parted on the Strand, near the Adelphi. 'Fingers and toes crossed,' Florence said, giving Freda a hug. She smelt of the mint humbugs that she ate all day long. Florence would turn into a mint humbug if she wasn't careful.

Freda watched Florence crossing the road in the rain. She was expecting her to go back to Henrietta Street or, more likely, find shelter from the weather in a café somewhere (Florence should have had shares in Lyons Corner Houses). She did neither, but hovered uncertainly on the pavement outside the Coal Hole pub. A car drew up and Florence stepped forward and seemed to be in conversation with the driver. He was older, but not as old as Mr Birdwhistle. Freda didn't see what happened next because an omnibus stopped in front of her, blocking her view. By the time the omnibus had loaded itself with passengers and moved on, both the car and Florence had disappeared. Surely Florence knew not to step into a stranger's car? But then Freda thought of Florence's trusting bovine face and knew that it would probably take little more than the offer of a humbug to seduce her.

Two or three girls – the beginning of an early snake of hopefuls – were already queueing at the stage door, waiting for an open audition. Clearly, they had no Miss Sherbourne to recommend them and they cast envious looks in Freda's direction as she walked straight past them and into the holy sepulchre. They probably mistook her for a cast member, Freda thought, preening. The Adelphi's stage door was almost next door to Corpus Christi, perhaps she should have asked Florence to light a candle for her for luck. 'You don't light them for luck,' Florence said. 'You light them for someone else, not yourself.'

Freda was so excited that she failed to notice that there were no playbills for *Betty in Mayfair* adorning the front of the theatre.

At the stage door, Freda found the doorman, who was squeezed into a small booth at the entrance. 'It's off,' he said when she interrupted his solemn perusal of racing tips in the *Daily Mail* to enquire about *Betty in Mayfair*.

'Off?'

'Yes, off. Transferred to Shaftesbury Avenue. We've got *The Green Hat* on now, didn't you see the playbills outside?'

Apparently not. Still, Freda supposed, one show was as good as another.

'I've got a letter, inviting me for an audition,' she said. She didn't, Miss Sherbourne had arranged the audition over the telephone, but it was the same thing really. The doorman seemed the indolent sort and, indeed, he returned to his newspaper and, without looking up, reached out his hand to a telephone on the wall and asked whoever was on the other end to send Mr Lionel. 'There's a girl here,' he added.

After rather a long wait, Mr Lionel appeared. He didn't seem to be much older than Freda herself. He was quite yellow-looking, as if he needed a good dose of liver salts (something Vanda swore by). Was Lionel his Christian name or his surname, she wondered? He said impatiently to the doorman, 'What now, Alfred?' Mr Lionel and the doorman appeared to be at loggerheads over something. A series of barbed comments was exchanged, the subject of which seemed to be a key that had gone missing. The more operatic Mr Lionel grew on the subject, the more taciturn the doorman became. They seemed to have forgotten all about Freda until she gave a little cough to remind them. 'I have an audition,' she said, and Mr Lionel gave a long-suffering sigh as if he couldn't think of anything more tiresome.

'The management, I suppose?' he said to her.

'Yes, the management,' Freda agreed, not entirely sure what that meant in the context of the Adelphi. Her father had been in management, but the Adelphi wasn't a chocolate factory.

The doorman gave a little snort of contempt at the word 'management'.

'Follow me, then,' Mr Lionel said to Freda, with magnificent indifference.

'The belly of the beast,' he said as he led her into this mysterious realm, a place that was cavernous and cramped by turns. York's Theatre Royal was much better organized. The Adelphi was dark and dusty, not to mention chaotic, and Mr Lionel was continually warning her about obstacles that they had to negotiate – coils of rope, enormous costume baskets, a large toolbox, even a small dog that regarded her with disinterest. 'It's a ratter,' was said by way of explanation.

Eventually they fought their way through to an office, where he handed her over to a woman wearing pince-nez who was sitting at a desk amongst a jumble of paperwork. Freda quashed her instinct to tidy. She was Miss Young, she said (she wasn't, she was very old, at least forty by Freda's reckoning). She was also extremely cross. Had something happened to make everyone bad-tempered, Freda wondered, or was this just what the West End was like?

'There's no chorus in *The Green Hat*,' Miss Young said. 'No dancing at all.'

'But I *was* invited for an audition,' Freda persisted. 'For a waiting list, maybe? You audition girls all the time.'

Miss Young rummaged around on her desk until she found a piece of paper and, after giving it the most cursory of glances, said that she had no record of any Freda Murgatroyd being on the call list. 'There's no such person.'

'But there *is* such a person,' Freda protested. 'It's me.' A wave of desperation began to engulf her. She would go under. She would disappear without trace. 'From the Vanbrugh Academy of Dance,' she urged. 'Miss Sherbourne sent me. To see the management,' she added, suddenly inspired.

The word did indeed prove to be an Open Sesame and Miss Young said sarcastically, 'Oh, well, then, if it's the *management* that wants to see you . . .' More wearied sighing on her part. If the Adelphi had been a sailing ship it would be halfway round the Cape by now, fanned by the amount of sighing that went on within its walls.

Miss Young led Freda along another series of confusing passages and then said, 'On the left, second door. Mr Varley,' before abandoning her and retreating.

'Owen Varley', a small nameplate on the door announced. Freda's heart beat fast with anticipation. She stood up straight, took a deep breath and knocked firmly on the door.

From within, an angry voice bellowed, 'Enter if you must!'

Yes, I must, Freda thought grandly to herself. I am opening the door to my future. 'We must gird our loins,' Duncan used to say before they went on with the Knits. Freda girded her loins.

A very large man was seated at a rather small desk. Like everyone else in the building he appeared to be irritated and Freda anticipated more excessive sighing, but his expression changed when he looked up and saw her. 'Ah, my dear child,' he said. 'Won't you come in?'

'Oh, hello, there you are,' Florence said when Freda dropped on to the chair opposite her in the Lyons Corner House on Coventry Street. 'How did it go at the Adelphi? Did you get the part?' Florence was working her way through a plate of rock buns. She was a slow, methodical eater, rather like a cow chewing her cud.

'No, I didn't,' Freda said. Her mouth was so dry she could barely speak. She could taste the iron tang of blood on her tongue. Her heart was pounding because she had run nearly the whole way from the Strand as if the devil were on her heels. She shed her coat and handbag on to the chair next to her and fanned herself with a napkin.

The ruminant Florence was oblivious to the state Freda was in. 'Oh, bad luck,' she said. 'I expect you'll get offered another audition soon. Have a rock bun.'

Freda felt her stomach heave. 'Got to go to the Ladies',' she mumbled before making a quick exit towards the lavatories.

The Ladies' in the Coventry Street Lyons were particularly magnificent, with big marble sinks and crystal-clear mirrors and lovely mahogany woodwork. The soap smelt nice as well, not like the carbolic in their boarding house, and usually when they came here Freda made the most of the facilities.

Not this time. This time she rushed into a toilet cubicle and retched up the contents of her stomach into the bowl.

Hot tears pricked her eyes, but she would not give Owen Varley the precious gift of them. Freda had never felt more sorry for herself than she did at this moment, kneeling on the cold, hard tiles of the Lyons Ladies'. Her soul had been hollowed out of her, along with the contents of her stomach.

Had there ever really been an audition, she wondered? If there had, it certainly had not been for a play. She was so stupid! No mouse ever scampered into a baited trap more blithely.

'Shut the door behind you, dear,' Owen Varley had said. He asked her name and her age, to which she replied 'sixteen', which was something she had been claiming since she was twelve. She had decided to adopt the veneer of a jaded metropolitan girl. 'Metropolitan' was a word she had learnt from Miss Sherbourne. It was the opposite of the accursed 'provincial', apparently. He seemed not to notice her attempt at sophistication.

'Well, Flora,' he said, 'so you want to be an actress?'

'It's Freda actually, Mr Varley, although my stage name is Fay le Mont.' (Miss Sherbourne said that everyone should have a stage name.) 'Actually, I'm a dancer. Miss Sherbourne set up an audition for me.'

'Miss Sherbourne?'

'The Vanbrugh Academy of Dance.'

'Yes, of course, I know her well. So . . . a dancer, eh?' he said. Then he quizzed her about what experience she had and she said, 'Oh, quite a lot, Mr Varley. In the provinces, of course,' she added nonchalantly. It seemed a good idea to get that particular drawback out of the way.

She removed a folder from her handbag – a handbag that was soon to play a part in Freda's downfall. In her role as treasurer, Freda kept both their money and Mrs Ingram's jewellery in Vanda's old bag as there was no safe hiding place in the boarding house in Henrietta Street. The bag had a long strap and Freda wore it, bandolier-style, across her body. Anyone trying to snatch it in the street would have had to fight her to the death for it.

The folder that she removed from this precious bag also contained the portfolio of her most recent stage photographs. She passed it to Owen Varley, who laid it down on his desk without looking at it. Freda began to recite a list of some of the productions she had been in, but she didn't even get as far as a *Babes in the Wood* three years ago, when she had played the usual maypole-dancing village child. Freda would have made a much better job of Gretel than the actress they chose. (She was twenty-five!) She was stopped by Owen Varley saying, 'You're a chirpy little thing, aren't you?'

'Am I?'

'If you could just lift your skirt for me, Flora.'

'I'm sorry?'

'Your legs, Flora. Let me see your legs, dear.'

Well, Freda reasoned, perhaps it wasn't so odd to want to see a dancer's legs. Dancers were all about legs, without them you couldn't dance, could you? And things were probably different in the West End. So, somewhat tentatively, she raised her skirt to her knee. Plenty of women in London were wearing their skirts as short as this, she thought.

'Higher, dear. A bit of thigh, please.'

Freda didn't really think of herself as having thighs. They were just legs, top to bottom.

'That's it, Flora. A bit higher. Don't be shy, we're all friends here, aren't we?'

And as a frog will remain passively in the pot as the water

around it grows hotter, so Freda's skirt gradually crept uncomfortably higher, like a slow-moving theatre curtain. At least no tentacle was touching her, she thought.

'Splendid,' Owen Varley muttered. He was growing red in the face. 'Now your blouse, dear.'

'My *blouse?*' Freda thought that she must have misheard. He was *Management*, for heaven's sake.

'Yes, your blouse, your top. Off with it, dear. I need to see your assets.'

Freda faltered. The metropolis, she thought, and undid the top button. The water was reaching boiling point. She fingered the second button and then said, 'No, I'm sorry, I can't do that, Mr Varley.'

'Don't be a silly girl. Come along now.'

'No.'

He heaved his great bulk up from the chair and Freda gasped in horror at the sight of his unfastened trousers. Vanda's 'dangles' suddenly seemed a frivolously inappropriate term for what looked like uncooked giblets. What had he been *doing* behind that desk? She turned to leave, to jump from the pot, but he was astonishingly agile for a man of his size and before she could reach the door he had ambushed her, pressing her up against the wall, the whole enormous weight of his body squashing her so that she couldn't even breathe.

To her surprise, Freda's thoughts strayed unexpectedly to, and then landed and settled on, Margaret Clitherow, a Catholic martyr in York who had been pressed to death – she had been laid beneath a door and then large stones had been piled on top of the door. Freda only knew this story because the Ingrams were Catholic. In her experience, only Catholics tended to be interested in martyrs. The door was from Margaret Clitherow's own house, an odd detail that had always interested Freda. She would have preferred to have been smothered by a front door, any front door, than the elephantine bulk of Owen Varley.

'Come on, now,' he spluttered as he grappled with her clothes.

Freda could feel his fat, cold fingers fumbling all over her, places he shouldn't go. Mr Birdwhistle's assault on her defences seemed paltry compared to this. She was violated, Freda thought, a word that she hadn't previously known was in her vocabulary.

'Be a good girl,' Owen Varley grunted. He sounded as though he was choking.

One of them would die. He would either have a heart attack as he groaned and convulsed as if in pain, or Freda would suffocate from the lack of air. A martyr to fame and fortune.

Freda summoned every last shred of strength and snapped her teeth on to her offender's fleshy jowls, like a dog. And like a dog she hung on, even though she was gagging with disgust.

Owen Varley squealed – as well as a man can squeal when his jaw is clamped between a girl's teeth – and tried to pull away from her, but still Freda hung on. If she could have done, she would have torn his face off, but eventually she had to let go. Owen Varley crumpled heavily on to the floor and lay still. Had she killed him? Could you kill someone by biting them?

Run, Freda thought, run and don't look back. Run for your life. She had the presence of mind to grab Vanda's bag – her portfolio of photographs had been thrown to the floor, she didn't care about retrieving them, but she was not going to sacrifice their money or Mrs Ingram's jewels to Owen Varley.

No thread to guide her back out of the maze, Freda had no idea how she found her way out of the theatre, but she did. She sprinted past the stage doorman, past the surprised snake of fresh hopefuls on Maiden Lane. She was close to Corpus Christi church. Freda knew you could seek sanctuary in a church, but she preferred the safe haven of the Lyons on Coventry Street where Florence was waiting for her.

Freda regarded herself in the mirror of the Ladies' in the Lyons. She had rinsed her mouth out many times, but she was sure she could still taste Owen Varley's blood. She looked a fright. Her comb was in her handbag and the best she could do was splash her face with cold water and smooth her hair down with her hands.

'Are you all right, dear?' the elderly Ladies' attendant asked her solicitously.

'Yes, perfectly all right, thank you,' Freda said. The attendant's kindness made her want to cry all over again and she would have left a tip for the woman, but her money, thank goodness, was safely in her handbag, on a chair next to Florence. Imagine if she had left it in the Adelphi – she would never have been able to return for it. Florence would keep a guardian eye on it. Wouldn't she? Freda experienced a sudden sense of overwhelming dread and, gripped by an awful panic, she ran back into the body of the café, where a commotion was occurring. One of the nippies was shouting, 'Thief!' and many of the patrons were on their feet, as if they were at a spectator sport.

The excitement was already beginning to die down by the time Freda reached their table. People had resumed their seats, returned to their pots of tea. It was not their loss.

'They took your bag,' Florence said miserably when she saw her.

'They? They who?'

'Thieves. Women.'

'Why didn't you stop them?' Freda asked. She was cold, almost frozen with anger. How could Florence have been so careless as to take her eye off the bag? How could she have been so *stupid*?

Florence's lip started quivering. 'It wasn't my fault. It was you that ran off and left your bag, Freda. I knew you'd blame me.'

'Yes, I do!' Freda said. 'You are a stupid, ignorant donkey, Florence! I would be much better off without you!'

The Invisible Man

Frobisher loitered at the end of the street, coat collar up, hat brim down, aware that he must look rather furtive to anyone watching him. Frobisher, however, prided himself on being good at blending into the background, like H. G. Wells's Invisible Man. It would have surprised him to learn, therefore, that in fact he was himself being observed – by a man holding a small notebook that looked similar, nay identical, to the kind of police-issue notebooks that were doled out from the supplies cupboard that was in turn fiercely policed by a grey-haired shrew of a senior clerk in his own station at Bow Street. A new pencil was not granted until the stub of the old one was presented. Frobisher admired economy but disliked parsimony. He thought he might have a word with her, but she was low down on his list of priorities. Unless somehow she, too, was in the pay of the nightclub owners of Soho.

Frobisher had, in fact, been under this surveillance since the previous day, when the owner of the little notebook had been engaged to spy on him. The notebook already contained a plethora of jottings so banal that if Frobisher had been privy to them he would have been dismayed (although not surprised) at the mundanity of his life.

JOHN FROBISHER *left house in Ealing 6.20 (am), arrived Bow Street at 7.45 (am). 12.00 pm Frobisher left Bow Street at midday, walked around Soho/Covent Garden. Ate lunch (ham and chips) in Jonnie's in Floral Street.*

The notebook was snapped shut and pocketed.

Nearly every night since starting at Bow Street, Frobisher had come down here to monitor the many comings and goings at the Amethyst. A seemingly endless procession of people, intent on indulgence, made their way through the doors of the nightclub. The war had made people hedonistic, and yet you would have thought it would have had the opposite effect, that people would be relieved to embrace the calm sobriety of peace. Frobisher had never understood the pursuit of pleasure as an end in itself. A belief, he supposed, that made him stuffy in the eyes of others. He believed in a moderate life – he was not a Puritan, but he was pained by the extremes of behaviour he found himself witness to. There was enough of that in Ealing.

Now, of course, there was a new restlessness in the air. He supposed it was all this talk of a General Strike, as if London did not have enough to cope with as it was. Not that he was without sympathy for the workers. The war had undone them in many ways. They were living in a dystopia.

He was hoping to catch Maddox entering the Amethyst. There must be a second secret entrance somewhere. Frobisher had looked, of course, but so far had failed to find it. No one in Bow Street would admit to knowing its location, but he suspected that they all did.

A girl, more wraith than girl, stepped into the circle of weak light cast from a lamppost further down the street. Thirteen? Fourteen? Fifteen? It was impossible to say. She was doll-like with blonde ringlets, rickety legs. The spangles on her cheap dress caught the light of the street lamp. Restless, nervous even, she kept looking around as if expecting someone. Frobisher was about to break cover and approach her and tell her to run home and not to linger in places like this, but then a cab drew up, disgorging a group of noisy, excited Bacchants, and by the time they were inside the club the ethereal figure of the girl had melted back into the night.

He watched and waited. Finally Miss Kelling and Cobb arrived. Was Cobb the right man for this job? Frobisher had his doubts, but Cobb was keen and seemingly sensible – a word that had appeared to irk Miss Kelling for some reason.

Cobb – a skinny streak of a man – was even less prepossessing out of uniform. He was wearing an evening suit that was a size too large and the cost of its hire had come from Bow Street funds. Miss Kelling perhaps deserved better.

Reluctantly, Frobisher made his way to the Tube station. Perhaps, after all, he did understand why people stayed out carousing until the early hours. It meant they didn't have to go home.

Lottie had fallen asleep in her chair, her chest rising and falling gently with each breath. Beside her, the lid of her sewing-table was open. Inside, nestling amongst the skeins of vibrant wool needed for the parrots, was a needle and an empty syringe. She had started again, then. Frobisher felt dulled by the inevitability of it all. Who was supplying her with the morphine? As far as he knew she barely left the house, apart from visiting the small parade of shops two streets away. Even then it was Frobisher who picked up most of the groceries.

He removed the needle and syringe, closed the lid of the sewing-table and fetched a blanket to cover her with. It seemed she was determined on disintegration. He noticed that the tulips he had bought had already wilted – their soft stems had flopped over and their petals now gaped open voraciously. Served him right, he supposed, for buying them cheaply.

Carpe Noctem

'Everything all right at the Foxhole?' Nellie asked Betty when she and Shirley arrived at the Amethyst.

'Yes, Ma,' Betty said. 'Everything's fine.'

'And the Pixie? Nellie said, turning her attention to Shirley. 'No more fires?'

'No, Ma.'

'Who's in tonight?' Betty asked. It was a routine query rather than an interest in celebrity.

'Mixed bag,' Nellie said. 'Tallulah Bankhead, Frazzini, the King of Denmark.'

The King of Denmark? Shirley's curiosity was piqued, she never gave much thought to Denmark as a country or a king.

'He seems all right,' Nellie said, rather grudgingly. She had once had an encounter in her youth with Edward, the previous king, when he was still Prince of Wales. She refused to talk about it, but take a good look at Niven's nose, she once said when the New Year champagne had got the better of her.

'Give Mr Frazzini a box of chocolates, will you?' Nellie said to Betty.

Nellie sold the boxes for fifteen shillings each but bought them wholesale from somewhere in the north for a shilling a box, all prettied up with ribbons (a penny each) by soldiers disabled in the war. The dance hostesses made a great fuss of persuading their partners to buy the boxes for them and then, after a few chocolates had been eaten, the boxes made their way back to the storeroom they'd come from and were refilled, ribbons adjusted, and sent out to be sold again.

'You'll have to dance with the customers tonight,' Nellie said to them. 'We're a couple of girls down.'

'Which girls?' Shirley asked. The 'girls' were a collective noun to Nellie, she never seemed to know their names. It hardly mattered to her – one girl was easily replaced by another.

'Off you go now,' Nellie said. 'Don't dawdle.'

The flock of Cokers was gathering. Hard on her sisters' heels came Edith, considerably less lively. 'You've put on weight,' Nellie said without looking up from her ledgers.

'Good evening to you too, Mother.'

Nellie lifted her head from her bookkeeping and gave Edith a long look. 'You should do something about that,' she said.

'Kettle and pot,' Edith replied.

'Is it going to rain?' Nellie asked Ramsay when he rolled up.

'I don't think so.' Ramsay rarely paid attention to the weather. It was just one more thing that was beyond his control. 'Why?'

'The doormen say there are no carriage umbrellas, they've all been stolen again.'

'I don't think it's theft as such,' Ramsay said, 'I just think people forget to return them.'

'That's the very definition of theft. You can go to James Smith's on Monday and order new ones.'

'A porter can do that,' Ramsay said.

'So can you.'

Ramsay sighed his acquiescence. There was no point in protesting further. Nellie might walk away from a fight, but she never lost an argument.

'Your friend's in, by the way.'

Friend? Ramsay felt a little stab of alarm. Who was his friend?

'Now trot off downstairs and fetch me a sherry flip, will you? There's a good boy.'

Ramsay watched Freddie making the sherry flip, cracking an egg into a cocktail shaker before adding sherry and sugar to it. It made him feel even more nauseous. A rather wilted-looking Edith appeared at his elbow and said, 'The Swedish Match King's in.'

'Kreuger? Ma never said. Are you feeling better?'

'Not really.'

'You do look awful,' Ramsay commiserated.

'Thanks, that makes me feel so much better. Your friend's in. He was asking for you.'

Ramsay looked in the direction that Edith had indicated and spotted Vivian Quinn, sitting at a table with Michael Arlen and Tallulah Bankhead. Quinn was peacocking in this company, throwing his head back and laughing at everything that was being said, drawing attention to himself, of course. Bankhead – very dissolute, apparently – was in the play of Arlen's dratted book at the Adelphi. Naturally there was a play. There was even talk of a film – with Greta Garbo! Bankhead and Arlen were being orbited by the smart West Kensington set that comprised Arlen's acolytes. How Quinn must love being at that table, inside that charmed circle.

'Oh, when I was in Paris, of course,' he heard Quinn say, in that brash, loud way he had. He was always going on about Paris, but he'd only stayed there for two weeks last year on a trip round Europe. That didn't stop him talking about the Café de Flore and Shakespeare and Co. or name-dropping 'Zelda and Scott', 'Ernest', Pound and James Joyce. He was so pretentious he set Ramsay's teeth on edge. Distaste jostled with envy in Ramsay's breast. The green of envy triumphed. He consoled himself with an olive from a dish on the bar. He caught Quinn glancing in his direction and he moved swiftly behind the parapet of the bar and ducked down.

'Everything all right down there in the trenches, Mr Coker?' Freddie asked.

'Yes, perfectly all right, thank you, Freddie. It's rather hot in the room and it's nice and cool down here.'

'On the floor?'

'Yes, on the floor, Freddie.'

'Shall I tell you when the coast's clear, Mr Coker? When your friend's gone.'

'He's not my friend,' Ramsay said.

'Okey-dokey, Mr Coker, whatever you say,' Freddie said agreeably. 'If you make a dash for it now you should be all right.'

'Thank you, Freddie.'

'Mr Coker!'

'What, Freddie?'

'Don't forget Mrs Coker's sherry flip.'

'I'm going out to get some fresh air,' Ramsay said to Nellie.

'You've just had fresh air.'

'It isn't rationed, Ma.'

'Should be,' Nellie said.

Ramsay walked round to the alley at the back of the Amethyst. The club had a secret exit here, 'the escape hatch', Nellie called it, where those members of the Establishment who were particularly favoured by Nellie could make a hasty exit in the case of a police raid.

To reach the escape hatch you had to follow a tortuous route that took you into the courtyard at the back of the club where the outside toilets were and then through an unlocked door into the backyard of an adjoining shop, an ironmongery (the ironmonger was remunerated on a weekly basis), through the ironmonger's and thence through a door into the street. Many a Cabinet minister, peer of the realm and even the occasional bishop had escaped by this undignified means, like criminals on the run. It was not unknown for some to become confused and find themselves in the adjoining cellar of an Italian restaurant, stumbling around amongst the flagons of olive oil and Chianti.

Ramsey took out his cigarette case. It was chased gold with a ruby clasp, engraved inside with his name. From a shop in Bond Street, an unexpectedly generous twenty-first-birthday present from his mother. ('Cost a fortune,' Nellie said every time he took out a cigarette.) He plucked out a cigarette, lit it and inhaled, feeling his lungs inflate like a pair of leaky bellows. He smoked Balkan Sobranies, strong and tarry, bought on the basis that he was attracted to the exotic picture on the carton. They said smoking was good for you, but Ramsay wasn't so sure.

He wasn't allowed to enjoy his cigarette as Vivian Quinn rounded the corner and approached. 'There you are. I was wondering where you'd got to, you old camp. Are you avoiding me, Coker?'

'No, Quinn. Of course I'm not avoiding you.'

'Give us a fag, then, will you?' Quinn said.

Reluctantly, Ramsay offered the cigarette case.

'A light?' Quinn prompted. Ramsay sighed and produced a box of matches. Quinn cupped his hand around Ramsay's to shield the flame – the alley was always gusty. Ramsay wanted to shake him off, but he endured Quinn's touch stoically to avoid one of his scathing responses.

'The Match King's in,' Quinn said, prompted by the sight of the flame.

'Kreuger. I know.'

'The man's a fraud, you know,' Quinn said. 'Off-balance entities, gold debentures, derivative contracts. It'll come crashing down eventually, you'll see. House of cards.'

Ramsay had no idea what Quinn was talking about. Kreuger made *matches*, for heaven's sake. A lot of matches. Possibly *all* the matches. Why else would he be christened king of them?

Quinn dragged on the cigarette and spluttered and coughed.

'Christ, Coker, this is hellish stuff.'

'Turkish tobacco. It's an acquired taste,' Ramsay said. He couldn't restrain his curiosity. 'Is it true you're writing a novel, Quinn? What's it about?'

'About? Does a novel have to be *about* something?'

'Generally speaking.'

'How banal. Well, I suppose it's *about* "Bright Young People become tarnished" sort of stuff.'

'Does it have a title?'

'A rather good one – *Folderol*.'

Ridiculous title!

The thing was, no matter how much Ramsay denied it, he and Quinn *were* friends, albeit the kind of friends who didn't like each other much. They had chummed up out of necessity when Ramsay returned from Switzerland and Quinn, who had just been employed to write his column, was looking for someone to knock about London's nightlife with. Ramsay had been grateful to have a friend, even one who seemed only interested in his own advancement.

But then Quinn had made a clumsy pass at him in the cloakroom of the Sphinx, deep amongst the forest of furs and Crombies and men's evening cloaks, and Ramsay had been forced to wriggle like a weasel to try to get away from him. It was only the sudden appearance of Gerrit, yanking aside the coats and saying, 'Everything all right here, Ramsay?' that put an end to it.

'Oops,' Quinn had said, 'we don't want to make the Flying Dutchman jealous, do we?'

'I'm not like that,' a blushing Ramsay said to Gerrit when Quinn had gone, and Gerrit laughed and said, 'You don't know what you are, Ramsay.'

'Is it a *roman à clef*, Quinn?' Ramsay persisted. He couldn't bear to say that stupid title.

'*Folderol?* Worried you'll be in it?' Quinn said with a grin. 'A minor character, perhaps?'

Quinn feigned a vague aristocracy, but Ramsay knew he was actually the son of a county auctioneer, as much a fraud as he claimed Kreuger to be. Ramsay hoped Quinn was wrong about the Match King. His mother took financial advice from the man, alongside Alfred Loewenstein.

'The *Israelite*,' Quinn said distastefully.

'Well, Belgian,' Ramsay demurred.

'He's another crook.'

Was *everyone* crooked in some way, Ramsay wondered?

'Do you fancy coming with me to a spieler next week?' Quinn asked.

'A spieler?'

A 'spieler' was thieves' slang for a card game. Ramsay liked cards, he'd liked them ever since the Bolshevists in Great Percy Street had taught him to play Preferans. He had been to a few spielers with Quinn in the past – small, low-key affairs, peripatetic to avoid the law, cropping up in flats in districts like Bloomsbury and Marylebone. The occupants were paid a sum to move out for the night and then the rugs were rolled up, the furniture pushed back and spindly little card tables brought out for Gin Rummy or *Vingt-et-un*. Women were there too, so it stayed pretty civilized, it wasn't like a rugger crowd. A limit was put on bets, cheap wine and beer flowed and everyone had an increasingly amusing time before staggering home, a few pounds up or down. The stakes were low, Ramsay had never won or lost more than five pounds. It was hardly Biarritz or Monte Carlo. Nonetheless, Nellie would have been furious if she'd known.

Spielers were illegal, of course, but no one really cared. And anyway, one of the people who often joined them at the tables was a policeman, a jolly sort, not in uniform (that would have seemed like fancy dress), who said, 'What's wrong with a harmless bit of fun? Everyone likes a flutter.'

'This one's in Belgravia,' Quinn said.

'Belgravia?'

'Mm. Interesting people, quite a classy crowd, in fact. We're lucky to be asked, to be honest.'

'Sounds like high stakes.'

'No, I don't think so. They just play for fun. Well, think about it. I must be off. I'm going to the Gargoyle opening, I can get you in if you want to come with me.'

'No, thanks.'

'Suit yourself.'

It had begun to rain and Quinn unfurled the umbrella he was carrying. 'Well, ta-ta for now,' he said, sauntering away with a pretentiously casual air.

The umbrella, Ramsay noticed, was one of the ones purloined from the Amethyst.

When Ramsay returned to the Amethyst, not only were the doormen mysteriously absent from their post but his mother was no longer on her roost in the cashier's box, having been relieved of her position by Kitty. The glass containing Nellie's sherry flip had been drained and Kitty herself was looking particularly fresh.

'Where is she?' Ramsay asked.

'Dunno.'

She had, she admitted, inadvertently let in several members of the Hackney Huns who had capered past her, camouflaged in fancy dress as a Pierrot troupe. Some members of the Huns had lately adopted fancy dress to infiltrate the many costume and masquerade parties that seemed to happen every night in London. Ramsay thought of the Egyptian mummy and his friends last night. A gang of Pierrots might have seemed even more threatening somehow.

The Huns were clever, they tended to mingle anonymously amongst party guests, quietly relieving them of their valuables. The victims were so intent on enjoying themselves that they rarely noticed they had been robbed until it was too late.

'You'll be in for it if there's trouble,' Ramsay said to Kitty.

'I'm a child apparently, you'll be blamed.'

As if on cue, there came the sound of a tremendous uproar from downstairs. Ramsay hesitated. The front doormen were still absent. Linwood, on the other hand, was now flying up the stairs. 'Better come quick, Mr Coker,' he gasped, 'all hell's let

loose down there. The roughs are at each other's throats. Someone's going to get killed.'

As solemnly as if she were presenting a knight with a sacred
sword, Kitty handed Ramsay the policeman's truncheon that
was kept out of sight in the cashier's booth. Nellie had used it on
more than one occasion.

'Into the lion's den, Mr Coker,' Linwood said.

Ramsay advanced down the stairs, followed by a reluctant Linwood and an enthusiastic Kitty. Linwood pulled aside the
bombazine curtain and Ramsay, truncheon in hand, made an
effort to understand the pandemonium in front of him. Apart
from knocking a few heads together, there seemed little he could
do. Perhaps he should just let the brawl play itself out, burn
through the club like wildfire. Sometimes that was the best
strategy.

There were several factions at play that, when combined, had
produced a volatile set of circumstances, all related later to Ramsay by Betty, who had obtained a good view from the bandstand.
The Huns, drunk on both cheap whisky and their evening's
successes – their commodious pockets were full of loot from a
recent party in Berkeley Square – were ready to celebrate.

They had spent the evening taunting Frazzini, who was sitting
quietly at his table, refusing to be ruffled by them, much to their
annoyance. He even offered them chocolates from the box that
Nellie had earlier sent to his table, an act that enraged them further. Frazzini knew what the Huns didn't – that his own men,
having got wind of trouble, were even now making their way
through the secret entrance into the club, ready for the fray.

The tinderbox was sparked by one of the Huns, who had got
into a spat with someone over one of the girls when they both
claimed her for a dance. This girl, Ekaterina, a White Russian
emigrée, was much sought after by the regular clientele. She had
been lured from Paris, where Nellie had spent several months
trying to launch the ill-fated l'Angleterre. Ekaterina was reputed
to have danced at the Folies-Bergère, which naturally made

her very popular in the Amethyst as there was always an expectation that she might shed her clothes at a moment's notice. She never did.

The first Pierrot had thrown a punch, which acted as a signal for his fellow gang members to pile in, regardless of where their blows landed. The couples up from the suburbs cowered beneath their tables – this was taking their 'bit of fun' too far. The hardened habitués, however, readied themselves for a good show, especially as the Frazzini hooligans had now arrived and were joining in the skirmish. It wasn't long before half the dance floor was taken up with the melee, balloons and streamers hanging from the ceiling providing an incongruously carnival scene.

And then a Pierrot whipped out a revolver from one of the handily voluminous pockets in his white costume and proceeded to wave it around. Those nearest to him dived beneath the tables with admirable alacrity. A shot was fired, incredibly loud, even amongst the din in the club.

Ramsay did not know, of course, about the King of Denmark, who, as befitted a head of state, was accompanied by an armed retinue, primed to defend the Crown against all comers; they had now drawn their weapons and were aiming them in an alarmingly vague way at the centre of the crowd.

That first shot acted as a starter's pistol. After a brief, startled silence, it was followed by a fusillade as it seemed that anyone who had a gun began to fire at will. And many people did have guns, not just the roughs, for it was, after all, not so very long since a war. There were not only many 'souvenirs' left over, but also plenty of men who had been taught by the Army how to use them.

The band, unfazed by anything that ever occurred in the club, started up with 'Runnin' Wild' at an alarmingly frantic tempo that only served to intensify the fracas. It was possible that was their intention. Nellie paid them three hundred and fifty pounds a week, which she regarded as outrageous, but they had her over a barrel – the Amethyst was many things, but it was nothing without dancing. The band were a resolute bunch, the sort that would go down cheerfully with the ship. A bullet was later found to have driven a furrow through the piano on the bandstand, but the pianist had not deserted his post.

MASSACRE AT SOHO NIGHTCLUB – Ramsay could see the headline now. That would definitely be the end of the club, if not the entire family. Where were the police when you needed them? They were always around when you didn't. So much for Inspector Maddox and his 'protection'.

And then suddenly Nellie conjured herself out of thin air as if there were a *deus ex machina* hidden in the bandstand. Where had she been all this time, Ramsay wondered? She wielded her new stick like a lion tamer's whip. Several members of the band ducked out of the way. It was quite extraordinary, the power she had. She was so short she was barely visible and yet, within minutes, the club had quietened, the anarchic behaviour had dissipated, the guns had disappeared, and several abashed roughs hung their heads in shame. The band changed to something that sounded suspiciously like Mozart. Nellie would have something to say about that later. In her opinion, even the merest hint of classical music could be the death of a club.

One of the King of Denmark's retinue had a squealing Pierrot in a stranglehold. It could have been any one of the Hackney Huns as they were all in similar costume but it didn't matter, he represented them all – a trophy. With the slightest nod of her head towards the parties involved, Nellie signalled that the Pierrot should be handed over to Frazzini's roughs as a token sacrifice. Frazzini's gang members proceeded towards the club's secret exit with their condemned prisoner squawking his innocence as if he were being led away towards the noose and the long drop.

It was a miracle, but somehow the bullets seemed to have missed all of the club's guests, embedding themselves instead in the floor and the walls and the aforesaid piano, as well as popping most of the balloons, which now hung dejectedly limp from the ceiling. Lack of injuries aside, it still had the makings of a poor night for the club's reputation. ('A bit of an understatement,' Edith said.) It was fortunate that Vivian Quinn had already departed for the Gargoyle and the incident would only appear in his column third-hand at worst.

To mollify her guests, Nellie clapped her hands and said words that had never previously been heard in any of her clubs: 'Free drinks for everyone!' – an announcement that was greeted with a rousing cheer from the assembly. People emerged from beneath the tables and the dance floor filled once more with revellers. What a tale the couples from Pinner would have to tell on their return to their tidy mock-Tudors.

That was not quite the end of the night's drama, though, for a solitary guttural cry, like a fox on heat, now rose from the corner of the room nearest to Ramsay. Not loud enough to stop the dancers, but enough to send Ramsay pushing his way through the once again convivial mob to discover what new horror awaited.

He found one of Frazzini's men laid out on the floor, copious amounts of blood pumping from a wound in his chest.

Several people had gathered quickly round the fallen man, including both Nellie and Frazzini. Ramsay noticed the two of them exchange a look that was clearly significant but too subtle for him to interpret.

The rest of the Cokers gravitated rapidly towards the casualty. They were naturally drawn to trouble.

'We need a doctor,' Ramsay said, startled that no one else seemed to have voiced this imperative. Frazzini hissed something beneath his breath that sounded like *no police* and Ramsay saw that Nellie was biting her lip and gazing trance-like at the wounded man. This inaction on her part surprised Ramsay – was she just going to let the man die here, on the floor, without lifting a hand to help him?

Someone new pushed their way into the circle surrounding the injured man – a woman. She seemed to grasp the situation immediately and knelt down next to the victim's inert body,

207

placing a firm hand on the source of the spring of blood, careless of the gore. 'For heaven's sake,' she said to no one in particular. 'Don't just stand there, all of you. Go to the kitchen,' she ordered Shirley, 'and ask them for clean cloths. And hurry up!' Shirley scurried off obediently.

'What's his name?' the woman asked, and when Frazzini didn't reply she repeated impatiently, 'His name, please?' like a firm teacher compelling a recalcitrant schoolboy.

'Aldo,' Frazzini said reluctantly.

'Aldo,' the young woman said, addressing the injured man in a calm voice. 'Aldo, can you hear me? You've been shot, but don't worry, you're going to be all right.'

A slight murmur came from Aldo's bloodless lips.

Shirley came back from the kitchen with a pile of tea towels and the woman pressed one on to the man's breast. It was almost immediately soaked in blood and replaced by another. The woman, too, was soon covered in blood. She seemed indifferent to it.

'I need hot water and iodine, or, failing that, carbolic,' she said. 'Have you got a first-aid kit?' This addressed to Ramsay, who had no idea. Did they? They obviously should. 'Oh, for goodness' sake,' she said, finding him seriously wanting. 'Has anyone got scissors – or a knife?'

Betty silently, somewhat reluctantly, produced her penknife from her silver-mesh evening bag.

'You have to sterilize it in boiling water, can you do that?' the woman asked. She glanced up and noticed Kitty, who had now gone rather green. The colour *du jour*, Ramsay thought, unable to turn off his transcribing brain, even though he very much wanted to. His own nausea, not surprisingly, had returned.

'Are you going to be sick?' the woman said to Kitty. 'If so, can you please move away?' A startled Kitty complied. She had expected sympathy, not dismissal.

To Nellie, the woman said, 'We need to get him away from all this racket. Is there somewhere private?' Nellie, rather shocked to find herself being spoken to in a tone of authority that was not her own, gave a deferential nod, indicating one of the private rooms.

Niven appeared. He frowned at the drama in front of him. The club had been in jovial spirits when he left it earlier. What had happened?

Catching sight of him, the woman said, 'Can you help move him? We have to be careful, I think his artery's been nicked by a bullet.' Niven seemed momentarily dumbstruck and she said, more forcefully, 'Mr Niven? Will you help me?'

'Yes, Miss Kelling,' Niven said. 'Of course.'

Night in the Square Mile of Vice

To announce dinner at the Warrender, Mrs Bodley beat a bronze gong in reception, a vigorous feat on her part. It was the herald for a stampede of the Distressed, dressed in their finery – a motley of ancient, frayed evening wear that reeked of mothballs. Gwendolen decided to wear her old velvet at dinner, fearing that if she pitched up in her new finery it might invite unspoken criticism from Mrs Bodley and heart-stopping excitement on the part of the Distressed.

They dined on mulligatawny soup, followed by steak-and-kidney pie, topped off with jam sponge pudding and custard. Gwendolen wondered if she would be able to dance a step after such hefty fare or whether, indeed, she would even be able to get into one of her new dresses.

She had her instructions from Frobisher. She was to be picked up by a Constable Cobb at eight o'clock. Cobb was 'reliable', Frobisher said. 'A sensible sort.'

Do you have an evening gown, Miss Kelling? I do now, Gwendolen thought as she picked one out – a blue silk with silver filigree embroidery. It would do very nicely for her entrance on to the stage of duplicity and disguise. She was a snake sloughing off her old librarian tweed-and-wool skin and stepping out in a new silken one.

She camouflaged the bruises on her face with face powder – you could only see them if you knew they were there. *Maquillage*, she murmured to the mirror, such a lovely word for concealment.

Only her hair rebelled against renovation. Nonetheless, Mr Niven would be surprised if he could see her now, she thought, as she assessed her reflection.

Optimistically, she had hoped to avoid Mrs Bodley, but when she left for the Amethyst she was still on guard. 'There's a cab outside waiting for you,' she said.

'Is there a man waiting as well?' Gwendolen asked, just to ruffle the feathers.

'There is indeed. You seem to have a cohort of them, Miss Kelling.'

'Aren't I the lucky one?'

'Gwendolen,' she introduced herself, offering her hand to Constable Cobb, who shook it limply and echoed 'Gwendolen' hesitantly, as though simply pronouncing her name might put him in jeopardy of untoward intimacy. He has no sisters, she thought. She thought of Niven. She could tell that he knew women. She suspected there were sisters at home.

'And your name?' she prompted him. 'I can hardly call you Constable. I rather think that would reveal our cover. After all, we're supposed to be a couple.'

'It's William,' he conceded reluctantly. He seemed somewhat truculent, as though he had been press-ganged into this cloak-and-dagger escapade against his will.

At the entrance to the Amethyst, Gwendolen threaded her arm through Cobb's. 'Abandon hope all ye who enter here, William,' she murmured to him as they passed between the two brawny doormen.

'I'm sorry?'

'Dante.'

'Don't know him, I'm afraid.' He swallowed nervously, his Adam's apple bobbing up and down. It was too large for the thin stalk of his neck.

'He's not from around here,' Gwendolen reassured him.

Was he anxious about being in her company or about the task

ahead? Both, probably. 'Come, William,' she said firmly, 'best foot forward. *Carpe noctem!*'

It was not what Gwendolen had expected from the Amethyst. It was so much smarter than the 'den of iniquity' that Frobisher had denounced it as. Everyone was dressed up to the nines in jewels and silks, many of the men in full white tie. The cloakroom was stuffed with furs. Everywhere, she caught the cut-glass accents of the privileged classes as well a few American twangs and faces of many different hues. The Amethyst seemed to consist of little more than people enjoying themselves. Or perhaps that *was* Frobisher's idea of iniquity.

The evening began soberly enough. Once you were past the doormen you had to pass the cashier's kiosk, in which Nellie Coker was on sentry duty. Gwendolen was reminded of Mrs Bodley and her reception desk. They shared the same steely look of command. Gwendolen recognized Nellie Coker from yesterday morning, even though she was now dressed in an explosion of haberdashery.

She barely glanced at Gwendolen and her counterfeit swain, but Gwendolen felt under inspection nonetheless. ('She has eyes everywhere,' Frobisher had said.) The matriarch took Cobb's money and waved them towards a bamboo curtain, beyond which was a dark, deep staircase, at the bottom of which a smirking flunkey greeted them by pulling aside another curtain and saying, 'Welcome to the Amethyst.' He seemed to be expecting a tip but Cobb pushed past, rather rudely, it seemed to Gwendolen. Perhaps the budget that Frobisher had provided for the evening didn't cover gratuities. The ghost of the cornetist raised his mournful head and set in motion a train of thought that led first to her fall, then the theft and then her rescue. Niven. How would she feel if it was *his* arm she was on rather than that of the less than suave Constable Cobb?

'Miss Kelling?' Cobb said, derailing this particular train of thought.

*

They were shown to a table and a waiter duly approached. Gwendolen feared that Cobb might be teetotal – he certainly had an abstinent look about him. 'We should order a drink,' she murmured. 'An alcoholic one. Otherwise we'll look out of place.' Gwendolen thought that she might be better at this undercover malarkey than Cobb. But then, for her it was something of a diversion, for him it was a job. A test too, perhaps. Set by Frobisher.

'Yes, we should,' he said, to her relief. Gwendolen was no drinker but she felt an evening with William Cobb might require a certain amount of leavening.

A cocktail menu was presented to them. It was as vast as the Bible and neither of them had the faintest idea about any of the items on it. We are innocents abroad, Gwendolen thought. She started reading the menu out loud to Cobb. It was impossible to tell what the drinks contained from their names alone. The christening of cocktails must be a full-time job for someone.

'What do you think a Highwayman is?' she asked Cobb. 'Or, for that matter, a Sunbeam, a Mikado, a King of Britannia – what on earth might be in that, do you suppose?'

'Orange, cognac, Italian vermouth and quinine,' the hovering waiter reeled off without hesitation.

'Blimey. What about it, William – a Bloodhound? A Honeymoon? A Grand Desire?'

He blushed. He was easy to tease. 'Do stop,' he muttered, his patience wearing thin. 'What do you recommend?' he asked the waiter. 'Or we'll be here all night.'

Buster Browns were eventually proposed by the waiter, who disappeared to fetch them. Cobb lit a cigarette and then remembered Gwendolen. 'Do you?'

'No, thank you.'

Once baptized by the first Buster Brown, Cobb surprised Gwendolen by swiftly ordering another. Dutch courage, perhaps. Gwendolen had no idea what was in their drinks but they tasted as harmless as elderflower cordial. Primed by the cocktails, Cobb agreed to partner her in a two-step. Gwendolen's silver sandals were itching to join others on the dance floor. She had not danced since the war, and although she was rusty from lack of practice and Cobb seemed to have learnt to dance from a manual, after a few circulations of the room they started to fall into the swing of it. Cobb, once he had got over his reluctance to make physical contact with her (or any woman, she suspected), began to seem to enjoy himself a little.

The club was packed. Rather guiltily (she had all but forgotten), Gwendolen remembered the purpose of her visit here – to find the lost lambs. There was, unsurprisingly, no Freda or Florence, nor anything other than pretty, smiling girls doing what they were hired to do, which was dancing with anyone who paid the price. They were certainly, if not maids, then definitely merry.

The Buster Browns, it seemed, had not been as innocent as they had tasted, and feeling rather dizzy Gwendolen was about to suggest to Cobb that they return to their table when there was a tremendous hubbub, followed quickly by the unmistakeable sound of a gun being fired. The shot had the remarkable effect of shocking the boisterous room into complete silence.

Gwendolen could see several more men producing guns and, galvanized by this sight, she grasped a paralysed Cobb by the arm, pulled him to the side of the room and pushed him into a crouch. If shots were being fired, you did not want to go out of your way to make yourself a target. A volley of shots did indeed follow hard on the heels of the solitary gun. It was like suddenly finding yourself in the middle of a Zane Grey novel, Gwendolen thought. (Mr Pollock had lost the popular argument on him, too.) Or a war, of course.

The conflict was over so quickly that Gwendolen almost wondered if the cocktails had caused her to hallucinate. The band had not even stopped playing, no one seemed to have been injured, and within seconds people had emerged from their foxholes and started dancing again. Gwendolen turned around to look for Cobb. This might be a good time to leave. She had not found her stray lambs, but at least she would have a tale to tell Frobisher. She did not want to disappoint him by turning up empty-handed in Bow Street on Monday morning. To her surprise, she found that Cobb seemed to have come to the same conclusion – she had been abandoned! Before Gwendolen had time to digest this astonishing fact, she heard a howl of pain. It seemed that someone had been wounded after all. She supposed she should try to help. After all, if there was one thing she knew about, it was gunshot wounds.

'Is it always so lively in the Amethyst?' Gwendolen asked Niven when he drove her back to Knightsbridge in the early hours of Sunday morning.

He laughed. 'No, tonight was an anomaly.'

Well, that was an educated word, Gwendolen thought. Not that she had thought him uneducated, but he was a Coker, and Cokers seemed smeared with such blasphemy by all and sundry that she had expected their behaviour to be on a par with the Yahoos. She berated herself for her snobbery.

It was a good-tempered place usually, he said, people came to enjoy themselves, to spend money. 'To have fun,' he added, glancing at her, as if to assess what effect that word would have on her, as if she were the apocryphal maiden aunt.

'There's nothing wrong with having fun,' she said. She had, after all, briefly revelled in being in a roomful of people who were dancing themselves into a dervish-like delirium on a sea of alcohol. She had to admit, she had enjoyed the dancing, the cocktails, the tormenting of Constable Cobb. She had even, and it was perhaps something best kept to herself, taken satisfaction from dealing with a man on the cusp of death. She had felt more like herself than she had done for a long time.

What did Niven regard as fun, she wondered?

'Fun's overrated,' he said dismissively, as if she had voiced the question out loud. 'Although for those gangsters I suspect that was their idea of it. My mother doesn't tolerate violence in the club,' he added. 'It's bad for business, and business is everything for my mother.' It took Gwendolen a moment to remember that 'my mother' was Nellie Coker – she didn't seem like anyone's mother. And Niven didn't seem like anyone's son. Some people were complete in themselves, as if born from the earth or the ocean, like some of the gods. Which was not a compliment. The gods were ruthlessly indifferent to humanity.

It had been unexpected, to put it mildly, to discover that Niven was a Coker. Niven was his first name, not his second, that was what had misled her, of course. What a strange coincidence it was that the man who had scooped her up from the pavement in Regent Street the day before yesterday and the man who had been undaunted by trying to save a man's life tonight were one and the same.

Once Aldo had been stretchered away on an old trestle top that had been commandeered from somewhere, Niven had put his coat around her and said, 'I'll take you home.'

'Your coat will be spoilt by all this blood on me,' Gwendolen said, mindful of how expensive his coat appeared.

'Then I'll get another one,' he said.

'And will you get another car?' she asked as she slid gingerly on to the cream leather of his splendid car. He laughed and said, 'I'd rather not. He was a bleeder, wasn't he?' He added, 'Poor bastard.'

He made no excuse for his language, Gwendolen rather liked that. There had been camaraderie between them as they dealt with the wounded man. They had both seen worse.

They bowled along Piccadilly towards Hyde Park Corner. It was nearly three o'clock in the morning by now and the streets were deserted. Gwendolen supposed the Cokers were nocturnal creatures, quite used to seeing in the dawn. London felt fresh in the night air and she felt strangely elated. She glanced at Niven. In profile he was suspiciously handsome. 'You're staring at me,' he said, without looking round.

'No, I'm not.' She hastily changed the subject. 'How did it start? The catalyst for the fight? I didn't see.'

'Something and nothing. These gangs get worked up pretty quickly. Your partner seemed to abandon you at the first sign of trouble, not very gentlemanly of him. Who were you dancing with?'

'A man,' Gwendolen said. 'I was dancing with a man. I don't know his name.'

He was amused. 'So – you came to the Amethyst on your own? And danced with a stranger? Generally only women of ill-repute come to nightclubs on their own and dance with strangers. You don't strike me as being of ill-repute, I seem to recall you telling me the other day that you were a librarian.'

'I came to London for a friend,' she said. 'To look for her sister and her sister's friend.'

'On a mission, then?' he said.

Was he being sarcastic? It was hard to tell with him.

'And this man, the stranger you were dancing with, is he helping you on your mission?'

Gwendolen squirmed under this further catechism. How to explain Constable Cobb, both his appearance and disappearance? To her relief, they had reached the Warrender. They drew up outside the hotel and Niven turned the engine off. 'You'll be in trouble with the Mother Superior, coming in after curfew,' he said.

'You're determined for it to be a convent.'

'I could drop you at the Savoy instead, it's not far. They know me there. We'll pay the bill, of course. We've inconvenienced you.'

The Warrender did look rather uninviting. The building was completely dark, not even a light to illuminate the porch. 'This will do me just fine,' she said firmly.

He shrugged, as if he didn't care one way or the other. How irritating he was. He got out and opened the car door for her.

'Was it you who returned my handbag?' Gwendolen asked. 'It

217

must have been you,' she added, without waiting for confirmation. 'How did you find it?'

'Let's say I know people.'

'Thieves?'

'Isn't everyone a thief in some way?'

'No!'

'What a life of virtue you must have lived.'

'You make it sound like an insult.' She slipped his coat from her shoulders and handed it back to him, saying, 'Good night, then.'

'Good night.'

She had already mounted the steps of the Warrender when she realized that she had no key for the front door. And there was no night porter, Mrs Bodley had made a point of telling her. (Mrs Bodley had made a point of telling her many things.) She would have to raise her from her bed. Oh, my Lord, what a thought. What would Mrs Bodley make of her dishevelled, blood-spattered state? She must look as though she had murdered someone. She might not be let in, she might be left out on the street like a stray. She shrugged helplessly at Niven, still standing on the pavement. He laughed at her predicament and held open the car door for her. 'The Savoy, then, Miss Kelling?' he said.

And thank goodness, really, as in the Warrender the bathroom was at the end of the hall and she would have had to spend what was left of the night scrubbing the bath of the blood she had sluiced off herself, never mind what Mrs Bodley would have had to say about a guest drawing a bath in the middle of the night. The plumbing in the Warrender was alarmingly noisy and would probably have woken the Distressed, who, according to Mrs Bodley, were very light sleepers. The alternative would have been an unappealing cold-water sponge bath in her room from the ewer and basin.

Her room in the Savoy, on the other hand, had the luxury of

a warm en-suite bathroom with an endless supply of hot water, and if she did leave behind traces of a London gang member's blood the chambermaid probably wouldn't bat an eyelid. No doubt the large London hotels, unlike the Warrender, made allowances for indiscretions. After all, wasn't that what people paid for?

Gwendolen assessed herself in the cheval mirror in her hotel bedroom. What a sight! The Trojan women after the sacking of their city probably looked in better order. Her beautiful new dress, in her possession for only a handful of hours (but what hours!), was ruined beyond rescue. The delicate blue silk – previously the colour of a summer sky – was now little more than a damp scarlet rag; her petticoat, too, as she had been soaked to the skin with the blood of that poor man. The lovely silver sandals that had been fit for an Arcadian princess were now only fit for the dustbin. She peeled off her soiled clothes and put them in a wicker laundry basket in the bathroom. Perhaps she should leave an extra tip for the maid. The clothes were followed by the sandals she had danced in half the night, ruined now beyond repair. *Who were you dancing with?*

What *had* happened to Constable Cobb? *Your partner seemed to abandon you at the first sign of trouble.* Niven was right, it was not the conduct of a gentleman. Gwendolen could only presume that Cobb had been frightened out of his wits, or – a more generous explanation – that he had thought it best not to have his 'cover' lifted and had hurried to report back to Frobisher. Or perhaps he was just avoiding the bill at the end of the evening.

The man – Aldo – had, thank goodness, not died, at least not on her watch, but had been taken away in a car by his fellows. They were under the command of the short, well-dressed man who had seemed ambivalent about Aldo's fate. Luca, she had heard Nellie Coker call him. Frobisher had told her that the Amethyst was crawling with criminals and Frazzini and his men certainly did seem to fit into that category, although they had behaved in a decent fashion towards Gwendolen. She had made them promise to take their comrade-in-arms to a hospital, even if it was only to drop him at the door before driving away. Most of them seemed to have been in the war and one or two of them had obviously seen the inside of a field hospital. They recognized her for the nurse she had been, as she had recognized them for the soldiers they once were. Hopefully Aldo would not be left in a gutter somewhere. (*Sorry, Sister . . . Sorry, Sister . . . Sorry, Sister.*) Of course, one could never predict how a thing would end.

After the bath (glorious) she sank into the bed with its lovely thick sheets – so much nicer than those in the Warrender. She was sleeping naked for the first time in her life. It felt transgressive. What on earth was she going to wear in the morning? She supposed the Savoy was the kind of place where they would go and buy something for you. They must get many stranger requests. The alternative would be to walk naked from the Strand to Knightsbridge like Lady Godiva, although without the horse. Or the modest veil of hair, for that matter. Now *that* would be transgressive. And what's more would probably lead to her being arrested. Frobisher would have to come and free her. The thought of standing naked in front of Frobisher made her feel flustered and she was grateful that he wasn't capable of policing her thoughts.

She closed her eyes, worrying that it would take her a long time to get to sleep after the evening's excitement, but before the thought had even formed fully in her mind she fell into soothing oblivion.

Keeping the Sabbath

'I can't see anything about the fight,' Betty said. She was yawning her way through the Sunday papers, a great pile of which were delivered to Hanover Terrace every week. She was on the look-out for anything that might have been written in the gossip columns about Saturday night's skirmish in the Amethyst.

Sundays were languid in the Coker household, it being the day that they all dismounted from the mad, whirling carousel, for even nightclubs needed a day of rest. 'I don't see why,' Nellie grumbled. 'If the British Museum can be open on a Sunday, why can't we?'

'Not quite the same thing, Ma,' Shirley said.

'Open is open,' Nellie said, 'closed is closed.' A remark that made no sense at all.

'I can't believe it hasn't made the news,' Betty said. She put the papers to one side and started to hollow out a solitary egg with a small spoon. She had been obliged to boil the egg herself as the cook insisted on having Sundays off. They rarely bothered with the niceties of Sunday lunch like other families ('*le rosbif*,' Nellie called it dismissively). Roast beef was for the suburbs, for the couples from Pinner, not for the Cokers. If they wanted *rosbif*, Nellie said, then they could go to a restaurant. No Sunday church services either, of course. The Cokers were all heathens, although Nellie fully intended to be given extreme unction at the end in the hope that it would wipe the slate clean of her many sins.

'I thought Vivian Quinn was in the club last night,' Shirley said. 'Is there really nothing in his column?'

'No, it's all about the new Gargoyle, thank goodness.'

'Who was there?'

'Noël Coward, Virginia Woolf, Guinnesses, Rothschilds – everyone, basically. The novelty'll soon wear off, I expect. It always does. The dining room's based on the Alhambra, apparently. Ma won't like that, she's always hankering after something Arabian.'

'All the perfumes of Arabia,' Shirley said.

'Will not sweeten her little hand?'

'*Do* you think Ma has blood on her hands?' Shirley mused in much the manner she might have said, 'Do you think Ma's ever been to Broadstairs?'

'Murder, you mean?'

'*Murder?*' Kitty echoed, from her perch at the window-seat where she was keeping an eye on the man in the garden. He was back. She felt proprietorial. She wondered about running down and asking him what he wanted. Did he want *her*? It was more likely he wanted Shirley, she was beset with admirers.

'Wouldn't put it past her,' Betty said.

'Murder?' Kitty repeated.

'Wouldn't put anything past her.'

'Murder?' Kitty said again, and would have repeated the word indefinitely if Betty hadn't thrown her egg spoon at her and hit her squarely on the forehead.

There was no sign of Nellie or Edith, but they could hear Ramsay bashing the Remington's keys upstairs.

'Working at the typeface,' Shirley said.

'Clever,' Betty said. She had moved on to an apple, paring it with the little silver penknife. She ate a great deal of fruit, especially if she could use her knife on it. Grapes were of no interest.

'Did we find out anything more about that woman?' Shirley asked. 'The one that popped up out of nowhere and saved Frazzini's man? She must have been a nurse. It was funny how Niven

222

knew her – the way when he saw her he said "Miss Kelling" and came over all peculiar. She was covered in blood. I thought of Medea.'

'Did you?'

'Or any of the Greeks really. They always end up drenched in blood.'

Betty hadn't thought of the Greeks, she had thought about the tragedy of that lovely blue dress. It was from Liberty's. She recognized it. She had nearly purchased it herself. '*Was* he saved, though?' she mused.

'He was alive when they carted him off, I think.'

'She was called Gwendolen,' Kitty said.

'Dear God,' Betty said, 'Kitty's got a new idol.'

'How do you know she's called Gwendolen?' Shirley puzzled.

'I asked her,' Kitty shrugged. She had not found an idol, she had found a heroine. For, after all, she might need to be saved from kidnap again. Perhaps from the man outside in the co-respondent shoes. She was bored of him now and left her lookout post to butter more toast.

'Do you think,' Shirley asked Betty, 'that she was the woman you saw in Niven's car at the traffic lights, the one he took for a spin?'

'She didn't look the type. More spinster than spinner.'

'Clever.'

Betty's fears had been not for the wounded man but for the little knife, she had been worried that it would be used to dig out the bullet, and relieved when instead it had cut a tablecloth into bandages and the bullet had remained pocketed in the man's chest.

The long coil of apple peel spiralled in the air without breaking. Betty threw it over her shoulder and she and Shirley peered at it lying on the carpet as if they were haruspices from the Ancient world, trying to divine meaning from entrails.

'I think it's a C,' Shirley said.

'Could be a Q,' Betty said. 'Do I know anyone whose name begins with a Q? A Quentin?'

'No, several Cs though. Charles, the Brighouse heir, and Clement – that American in oil.'

They heard the front door open and close. Niven.

'What on earth are you doing?' he asked, kneeling on the floor to greet Keeper by rubbing his ears. The dog swooned.

'Looking for the initial of the man Betty's going to marry,' Shirley said.

'Such rational creatures,' Niven said. He fed the apple peel to Keeper before the prospective bridegroom could be pinned down conclusively.

'Where have you been?' Shirley asked.

'And where are you going?' Betty demanded as he clicked his fingers for Keeper to follow him out of the room. Niven ignored both questions.

'Should we do Edith an egg and take it up to her? Or toast? It's not like her to fester all this time.'

The house possessed an ornate electric toaster. They had all the latest gadgets in the Hanover Terrace kitchen, most of which were apparently intent on killing Nellie. Light bulbs were the limit of her beliefs where electricity was concerned.

Betty rose from the table and said heroically, 'I'll do it.'

'You are kind,' Shirley said.

'I am.'

Yes, I *am* a considerate sister, Betty thought, knocking on the invalid's door, plate in hand. And knocking. She opened the door cautiously – Edith could bite when cornered – but now she was reduced to a heap of miserable bedclothes.

'Go away,' she moaned when Betty offered the toast. 'Stuff your toast.'

'She's ill,' Betty reported back to Shirley. 'And I went to all that trouble with the toast.'

A Gentleman Caller

Niven strolled along the Embankment. It was the kind of balmy Sunday afternoon in spring which demanded that a man leave his car behind and walk with his dog.

In Niven, the rest of the family sensed backbone. It was strangely attractive to them, perhaps because of the novelty. Cokers had no backbone, only strength of will. Was 'backbone' another word for courage? During the war, Niven had run under heavy machine-gun fire to rescue a wounded man and had then run back to his trench with the man slung over his shoulders. And then he did the same thing again, though he was wounded himself by then, but he did it because they were boys, barely out of childhood, even though one was his commanding officer, and he didn't think they deserved to have their lives ended by the insanely stupid bastards in government who thought war was necessary and good. And furthermore he had said all of that to the Lieutenant Colonel who was trying to pin a medal on his chest, and thus found himself on a charge of insubordination. Perhaps that was foolishness, not courage.

And was it from foolishness or from courage that on this fine afternoon he was walking across town, thinking about a woman and wondering if it was better all round – for her and for him – if he never saw her again, unaware that even at this moment she was sharing a pot of tea with his mother in the dusty Sabbath stillness of the Crystal Cup?

Niven wondered if Gwendolen Kelling had enjoyed her brief

sojourn in the Savoy at his expense. He had paid for a fancy suite for her, with a view of the Thames and half of London, and had distributed enough largesse amongst the staff to ensure that she would be well cared for. He presumed that Yorkshire librarians didn't often stay in costly suites in the Savoy. He imagined her feeling indebted to him. He had never done a woman so many favours as he had Gwendolen Kelling in the last few days.

At first he had taken her for the timid, nervous sort, misled perhaps by the 'Ladies Only' accommodation, the attack in Regent Street, the mousy clothes – yet last night he had witnessed her in action under fire, rising to meet the moment. She had steel. He couldn't but admire it.

He had picked some wildflowers earlier, from the banks of the canal, thinking they sent a better message than the kind of hot-house blooms that his sisters were in continual receipt of. Niven was not in the habit of sending flowers, in fact he could not, offhand, recall ever having given flowers to a woman. Once perhaps, a long time ago, to his mother when he was still a boy. She had been indifferent to them, he seemed to remember. Nellie had brought her children up without sentiment. She said it was a gift.

'Yes? Can I help you?' Mrs Bodley said, meaning the opposite. Niven had previously made her acquaintance when he had returned Gwendolen's handbag. She seemed primed for hostilities then; now she seemed ready to repel all invaders. Men were clearly not welcome at the Warrender.

Niven doffed his hat. 'I'm looking for Miss Kelling.'

'I'm afraid Miss Kelling went out some half an hour ago.'

Of course she was out, Niven realized. Why would she be inside, in this stuffy place, in such pleasant weather? She had probably gone for a walk in one of the parks. Perhaps she had gone for a walk with the man who had deserted her in the club last night.

'I have no idea where she has gone, it is not my business,' Mrs

Bodley said. 'Miss Kelling is continually flitting in and out. Are those flowers for her?' she asked, grimacing at the sight of the straggly bunch in his hand. The flowers had seemed like a romantic gesture when he picked them, but now they just looked like half-dead weeds. 'Do you wish me to put them in a vase?'

'No. Thank you.'

'Whom shall I tell her called for her?'

'No one,' Niven said.

'You persist in your anonymity, I see. You know you are not even her first gentleman caller today.'

'Oh, really?' Niven said, feigning indifference. The deserter, presumably.

'Very popular young lady, Miss Kelling,' Mrs Bodley said.

She was clearly trying to needle him and she succeeded. 'Forget I was here,' Niven said, turning on his heel and running back down the steps. Sanctimonious old cow, he thought, flinging the humiliating flowers into the dank and mossy basement well of a neighbouring house. What on earth had he been thinking when he decided to come courting Gwendolen Kelling? Thank God she had not been in. He was saved from his own lunacy.

On his way back through town he thought he may as well stop off at the Savoy to check that everything had been taken care of. Perhaps, he thought, Gwendolen Kelling was still inside, lingering in the luxury of the suite he had paid for. He could invite her for a late luncheon in the Grill. (The lunacy had returned, apparently.) Perhaps they would talk about the war. More and more, as the conflict faded into the world's history books, Niven found himself not wanting to forget. Gwendolen Kelling seemed like someone who might understand the need to remember.

When the doorman at the entrance to the hotel spotted Niven advancing along Savoy Court towards him, he straightened to attention, saluted and deferentially murmured, 'Mr Coker,' as was the way of doormen.

A man had been indulging in idle Sunday chatter with the

doorman, but whipped his head round when he heard the Coker name. He was the brazen sort – scrawny, wearing a cheap suit and with a foreign look about him. Niven had known scrappers like that in the Army. He was wearing two-tone sports shoes as though he were on the golf course, although he was more caddy than player. Niven himself wore hand-made shoes – calf-leather brogues – and detested golf. Keeper, always a good judge of character, let out a quiet growl. The man tipped his hat at Niven and sauntered off into the Strand. Something about him made Niven's own hackles rise.

Yes, everything had been perfectly all right with Miss Kelling's bill, the member of staff on duty at the reception desk said when Niven enquired. In fact, Miss Kelling had insisted on paying it herself when she checked out. So, she was too proud to accept charity? If Niven had known she was going to reject his offer, he would have booked her into a more affordable room. More fool her. He felt cold towards her, where moments ago he had been ready to unburden his soul. Again, a lucky escape, the lunacy vanquished.

The doorman saluted him again on his way out. What was the name of the man who had been loitering around when he entered the hotel? Niven liked to have a name to put on a man. There were enough nameless men in the soil of Flanders.

The usual gavotte followed. The doorman set his features into a picture of blandness and said, 'What man would that be, sir?' and Niven withdrew the customary shilling from his pocket and with great theatricality the doorman suddenly remembered.

'Oh, you must mean Mr Landor, sir,' he said. 'A gentleman from Hungary, I believe.'

The transaction was paused as a police sergeant in uniform strolled past the top of the little street in that annoyingly slow way that a policeman on the beat adopts. He stared at Niven and then raised his forefinger to his helmet in a gesture of acknowledgement to the doorman. The doorman gave an almost imperceptible salute back and waited until the sergeant was well on his way down the Strand before resuming business with Niven. 'They call that bloke the Laughing Policeman,' the doorman said. 'After that song, you know?' Niven ignored this unrequested information.

Another shilling secured the answer to the question of why Landor had been scouting at the hotel.

'Enquiring about one of our guests,' the doorman said. 'Naturally, I gave him no information. The privacy of our guests is sacred.'

How sacred, Niven wondered? He grubbed up another coin. 'And what was it exactly that he was asking?'

'He wanted a name.'

Niven had run out of change. Reluctantly he produced a five-shilling note. 'And did you give it to him?'

The doorman was indignant with denial. Another note dampened his affront. Ten shillings secured the name of the guest. Niven would be bankrupt at this rate and the doorman would be able to retire.

'A Miss Kelling,' he finally admitted, replete with wealth. 'He was asking about a Miss Gwendolen Kelling.'

Niven caught a taxi, the charm of the day having worn off. He frowned all the way to Hanover Terrace. Why on earth was this man Landor spying on Gwendolen Kelling? Was 'Miss Kelling' not in fact a provincial librarian – which would be an excellent disguise – but someone employed to infiltrate the Cokers? By Azzopardi, perhaps? Or Maddox? In which case, she certainly appeared to have succeeded, duping even his astute mother. But then that still didn't answer the question of Landor's interest in her. Was Gwendolen Kelling in danger? Niven was surprised at how disturbed he was by this possibility.

Another Gentleman Caller

Sunday was turning out to be a particularly difficult day in Ealing, as it would have been the birthday of the child Lottie lost during the war. Frobisher had forgotten until reminded. He supposed it explained the morphine.

'*Elle aurait eu douze ans*,' Lottie kept saying, wandering from room to room as if she would eventually find the girl in the house. Lottie had nothing, not a lock of hair nor a photograph, not a scrap of christening gown or shawl. Sometimes Frobisher wondered if the child had really existed. The child, imaginary or otherwise, had been called Manon and had, Lottie said, been obliterated along with the village they lived in during the war.

He had been woken early this morning by the sound of a distracted Lottie roaming through the house calling Manon's name, convinced somehow that the child was hiding in a cupboard or behind a piece of furniture. 'Can't you hear her calling for me? *Maman, maman*. It's breaking my heart.' These hallucinations – this was not the first time – frightened him. What if one day they took over completely?

Eventually he persuaded her back into bed and fetched her Luminal and spoon-fed her the tincture. It would be easy when she was in this state to encourage her to drink the entire bottle. Better, surely, than the slow death she seemed intent on. Of the soul, if not the body. Both her soul and his. He replaced the stopper in the bottle and put it back on the high shelf in the kitchen where it lived, as if his wife were a child or a dog who wouldn't be able to reach it when all she had to do was stand on a chair to find oblivion.

She was soon drowsy and he left her to sleep, deciding that he may as well travel to Knightsbridge and find out how Miss Kelling had got on in the Amethyst, rather than wait until tomorrow for her 'report', as she called it. He had no expectation that she would have found the girls she was looking for, but perhaps she had managed to observe something untoward in the club, something that might be of some use to him. Going to the Warrender was legitimate police business, he argued with himself. It was a specious argument and he knew it. What he wanted was to see Miss Kelling, he wanted the respite of her company.

She was not at the Warrender, and he was shooed away by a termagant and then spent an hour in Hyde Park, thinking that somehow he would come across her amongst the weekend crowds, but the only person he saw whom he recognized was Niven Coker, ambling along with his dog as if he didn't have a care in the world. Frobisher couldn't imagine what it would be like to feel so unburdened by life.

Miss Kelling, however, was as fugitive as a wood nymph. Not a nymph, Frobisher reminded himself. He must not be fanciful. He must leave the sunshine and return to Lottie to suffer with her.

Necromancy

Gwendolen woke to a bright beam of sunlight slicing through a gap in the curtains. She had absolutely no idea where she was, but there was a handy clock by the bed – nearly ten!

She realized that she had been woken by someone knocking on the door, but before she could croak, 'Come in,' the door opened and a maid came in bearing a large tray, with a cheery 'Morning, miss. Did you sleep well?'

Hugging the bedsheet to her for modesty, Gwendolen struggled to sit up. 'I don't think I ordered any breakfast,' she said. The maid bobbed a curtsey, 'Compliments of the management, miss,' and scooted out of the door before Gwendolen could ask her anything else.

A silver pot of coffee, a jug of cream, warm rolls with pale butter, a dish of lime marmalade and, beneath an impressive silver dome, a perfect omelette, fluffy and flecked with Finnan haddock. A mere week ago she had been breakfasting on toast and jam made from blackberries foraged in York Cemetery, cultivated by the bonemeal of the dead. Her mother, so recently laid in that same ground, must already be feeding the soil. No doubt she would resent contributing.

Gwendolen wondered how long her money would last if she moved into a hotel and lived a sybaritic life. Not long, probably. Wasn't this how the devil caught you? You travelled in a cream Hispano-Suiza and shrank from the idea of returning to the omnibus. You tasted pheasant (or a perfect Arnold Bennett omelette) and your spirits drooped at the return to boiled mutton. Gwendolen could have added to this list indefinitely from her own experience of the last few years. She had boiled a good deal of mutton since the war.

She would never have thought of coming here if it hadn't been for Niven. What had Frobisher said? *It is very easy to be seduced by these people.*

It turned out that the Savoy was indeed the kind of place that would not only send someone to a shop on your behalf but could also persuade a shop to break the Sunday trading laws and open up just for you. Gwendolen gave her measurements to a very pleasant, uniformed housekeeper, much the same age as herself, who went to Swan and Edgar and bought a complete outfit, from hat down to shoes and all the layers in between. The housekeeper asked no questions and Gwendolen gave no explanation. The rich really do have different rules, she supposed. Gwendolen was beginning to realize that people in London didn't seem to care what you did, especially if you had money. 'In London,' Azzopardi had said, 'the law exists to be broken.'

'How much did that come to?' she asked the housekeeper when she delivered the new clothes.

'You can pay when you settle your bill, madam,' she said.

It was well after midday before Gwendolen – rather reluctantly – checked out, but when she came to pay, the man on reception said, 'The bill's been seen to, madam, it's on the gentleman's account.'

'And my Swan and Edgar bill?'

'That too, madam. All paid.'

Did she want to be beholden to Niven? Or any of the Cokers? On the one hand, it was, ultimately, the Cokers and their club who were responsible for the ruination of her clothes and for her being locked out of the Warrender, so perhaps it was only fair that they should have paid for her to stay here. Still, she had the odd feeling that she was being bought somehow.

'No,' she said pleasantly. 'Please void Mr Coker's cheque, I shall pay for myself.'

The doorman at the Savoy hailed a cab for Gwendolen to return her to the dull prospect of the Warrender. It may as well have been a pumpkin pulled by six white mice.

Had her absence been noticed by the eagle eye of Mrs Bodley? Or would the chambermaid have told Mrs Bodley that Gwendolen's bed had not been slept in last night? She had encountered the girl in the corridor once or twice, her arms laden with piles of folded sheets and towels, and they had exchanged smiles.

It helped, Gwendolen thought, as the cab disgorged her outside the Warrender, that she had no overnight bag with her and she was wearing her new Swan and Edgar outfit – a neat dress with a sailor collar and a kick-pleat skirt beneath a linen duster coat. A new hat, too, not a green one, she was celebrating spring with straw.

With any luck, she would look as though she had slipped out for a morning service at Holy Trinity, Brompton, rather than having lazily left a double bed in a hotel where she had slept naked between the sheets. *Quelle horreur!* Not to mention the blood and bullets of the previous evening's drama. The Distressed might be entertained by her adventures but Mrs Bodley would be appalled.

There was no avoiding Mrs Bodley at the reception desk. She greeted Gwendolen with 'Another parcel was delivered for you while you were out, Miss Kelling.'

Perhaps a parcel would appear every day, like some form of magic, or a fairy tale.

'By a good-looking man?'

'No. A delivery boy. On a Sunday,' Mrs Bodley added with a shudder, as if Christianity itself had been brought into question. 'I have never known such a thing.'

It seemed the Savoy was not the only power that could over-come the law, for Mrs Bodley took out a large Liberty's box from beneath the counter and said, 'Would you like it sent up to your room, Miss Kelling?'

'No, I'll take it myself.' It was an awkward shape, quite long and flat, and between them, Gwendolen and the box only just fitted into the cage of the elevator. It ascended slowly and she felt relieved when she was finally out of Mrs Bodley's disapprov-ing oversight.

Gwendolen untied the purple ribbon and took the lid off the box. And there it was in all its untarnished glory – the sky-blue silk dress with the silver filigree embroidery. For a wild second she thought it must be the original, cleansed of blood, but that, of course, would have been impossible (or a miracle). Niven, she thought. It was, like the paying of her hotel bill, a gallant (some might say grandiose) gesture, but he could just have given her money to cover the cost. And how did he know her size? She imagined him assessing her. It made her uncomfortable.

In the box, there was an envelope on which was written 'Miss Kelling'. So there was a note this time. Inside the envelope was a card, embossed with the words *Mrs Ellen Coker, Proprietor of the Amethyst Club* and a telephone number. Gwendolen turned the card over. On the back, in a very small, neat hand, was written: 'Dear Miss Kelling. Please find the enclosed in recompense for your trouble. Would you telephone me, please? I have something I would like to discuss with you.' It was signed 'Mrs Nellie Coker'.

So not Niven, then, but his mother. The infamous Nellie Coker wished to see her. To discuss something. What intrigue was this?

She delayed. Not so much from hesitation as not to seem to be at the Cokers' beck and call. There was a telephone in the hallway of the Warrender, in a wooden cabinet, although Gwen-dolen doubted the cabinet's walls were enough to protect her from Mrs Bodley's prying ears. After a decent interval and while Mrs Bodley was supervising the Sunday lunch, Gwendolen took a seat in the booth and dialled the operator and asked for 'Gerard 5875'. She was put through straight away as if Nellie Coker had been waiting for her call.

Nellie Coker was spreading fortune-telling cards out on one of the tables in the Crystal Cup. There was a pot of tea, too, one that Nellie had made herself as, it being Sunday, there was no one else here and club was closed and shuttered against the holiness of the day outside. 'Or would you prefer something stronger, Miss Kelling? I have some excellent plum brandy, a gift from the Polish ambassador.'

She was trying to impress, Gwendolen thought. It would take more than a diplomatic glass of brandy. 'I'm not much of a drinker, I'm afraid,' she said.

'Nor me,' Nellie said. 'You cannot profit from your own vices, only those of others.' Gwendolen thought Nellie Coker sounded like a street-corner evangelist.

'Your fortune awaits,' Nellie said. So perhaps more of a mountebank than a charlatan.

The cards were a mystery to Gwendolen. 'Is this the Tarot?' she puzzled.

'No, Lenormand, I prefer it. I'm presuming you think such things are stuff and nonsense, Miss Kelling.' She seemed indifferent to Gwendolen's opinion, her hands hovering over the cards as if absorbing their funny little pictures – a fox in the snow, a mountain, a snake, a little girl in a blue dress bowling a hoop along the road. A pair of mice. 'It doesn't matter what you think. You don't have to believe for the cards to tell the truth. Do you go to church, Miss Kelling?'

'Church? No, not any more.'

'No, nor me. It is a great freedom to lose your religion.'

The feather-and-glitter costume of last night in the Amethyst had been replaced today by a sober, loose-fitting dress revealed when Nellie Coker removed the fur she was wearing, despite the warmer weather. Last night she had been the ringmaster, today she was surprisingly matronly.

Gwendolen sipped her tea and was struck by a sudden uncomfortable thought. What if the tea was drugged? What if she was about to be slipped off somewhere, never to surface again, like the girls Frobisher was worried about? What if Nellie Coker – and here was an unpleasant thought – what if Nellie somehow knew that Gwendolen was in cahoots with Frobisher?

'PG Tips,' Nellie reassured, as if she could read Gwendolen's mind. (Could she? What a thought!)

'You summoned me,' Gwendolen reminded her.

'*Requested* your company. Spirits are summoned.'

'Why?'

'As I said, I have a proposition for you.'

'There, look at that,' Nellie said, moving her hands over the cards. 'Your fortune, your destiny, laid out before you.' Nellie gave Gwendolen a calculating look over her spectacles. 'You are going to love and be loved,' she said.

'A man?' Gwendolen said, as some response seemed to be expected of her, and yet she couldn't keep the cynicism out of her voice.

'More than one.'

Good Lord – how many more, Gwendolen wondered?

Nellie Coker frowned at the cards, no doubt for effect, Gwendolen thought. The woman was no different from any seaside charlatan. Or one of the many bogus spiritualists who had sprung up in the wake of the war, deluding the bereaved into thinking the dead were happy with their lot. Gwendolen's mother for one, of course. 'Harry says he likes it where he is,' she reported to Gwendolen after one of these seances, 'and doesn't want me to worry about him. Oh, and to watch out for scab on the apple trees.' Because, of course, the state of their orchard would have been on Harry's mind in the afterlife.

Nellie's brow furrowed, a genuine-looking frown this time. 'You are going to be an instrument of something.'

'Of what?'

Nellie turned suddenly pale. Her gaze had shifted from the cards to the wall behind Gwendolen. She was staring fixedly at it as if an image had been projected on to it, as if she had indeed summoned a spirit. Gwendolen turned to look, but there was nothing there.

'Mrs Coker?'

'Hm?' And then, with an abruptness that surprised Gwendolen, Nellie swept the cards into a pile. The clairvoyance was over, apparently. At that moment, the bells of St James's in Piccadilly began calling the faithful to Evensong.

'I must go,' Nellie said, heaving herself up from her chair with the help of her stick. 'One of my children is not herself.'

'Oh, Lord, I am sorry to hear that, Mrs Coker.' (Which child? Not Niven, surely? He had been very much himself last night.)

'One of my daughters.' (Again, the mind-reading.) 'My car's outside. If you'll walk me to the door, I'll pay for a cab for you.'

'That's very kind, Mrs Coker, but I prefer to walk back to the Warrender. It's such a nice sunny afternoon.'

'Is it nice?' Nellie said. She seemed to be questioning the character of the sun rather than its presence in the London skies. She lived a subterranean life, like a mole, and Gwendolen thought that the weather probably meant little to Nellie Coker.

Nellie struggled into the car with the help of her chauffeur – Hawker, she called him. She seemed rather weak – was she ill? But then she had just served a prison sentence, it was unlikely that incarceration was good for your health. A nurse Gwendolen had served with at the Front had been imprisoned in the cause of women's suffrage before the war. Despite the dreadful tales of prison life – she had been fed by tube and never really recovered – Gwendolen found herself envious of someone who had a passion strong enough to require sacrifice. Nellie Coker had offered herself up to imprisonment in the cause of a liquor licence. It hardly seemed worth it.

'Miss Kelling?' Nellie was leaning forward in her seat to speak to Gwendolen through the open car window.

'Yes, Mrs Coker?'

'Do think about my offer, Miss Kelling. I hope your answer will be yes. If you could let me know as soon as possible. You have my card.'

The chauffeur was back in the driving seat and Nellie knocked on the roof of the car with her stick as if she were in an old-fashioned hansom cab.

Gwendolen stood on the pavement and watched the car driving away, still flabbergasted by Nellie Coker's unexpected proposition. When she had agreed to meet her in the Crystal Cup, she had thought that, at best, Nellie wanted to thank her for her help after Aldo was shot or, at worst, wanted to try to secure her silence if he was dead. *Had* he died? Gwendolen reproached herself for not even enquiring about his welfare, but she had been so disconcerted by Nellie's overtures.

'You had two gentlemen callers while you were out, Miss Kelling,' Mrs Bodley announced when Gwendolen was barely through the door of the Warrender. Two? She was amused – were Nellie's prophecies already coming to pass? And who could the two gentlemen be? Was one of them Niven? Had she missed him calling on her? Gwendolen felt the hunger of disappointment. She sensed a fuse had been lit. How would it end – with a bang or a whimper? (She had acquired Eliot for the Library.) She was reluctant to give Mrs Bodley the satisfaction of asking.

'One of them was the gentleman – and I use the word loosely – who left a parcel for you the other day.' (Niven. Gwendolen's heart gave a little bump. Annoying!) 'Although neither of your callers gave their name. I think it very suspicious when a gentleman withholds his name.' Gwendolen burst out laughing. The woman was too much, she really was. A purse-lipped Mrs Bodley said, 'I'm thinking of your reputation, not mine, Miss Kelling.'

'You need fret no more about either of our reputations, Mrs Bodley. I shall be leaving the Warrender.'

'Leaving? You are going home early?'

'I'm not going home. I am going to stay in London. I have employment here.'

'In a library?'

Gwendolen had no intention of giving Mrs Bodley the satisfaction of a reply.

'Your last supper,' Mrs Bodley said as Gwendolen took her seat in the dining room on her final night in the Warrender. Dinner was kidney soup, followed by veal cutlets on a bed of mashed potato, and then a Sussex Pond pudding. Gwendolen would miss the Warrender's dinners. She would even miss the Distressed. (If she were to stay here any longer she feared she would become one of them herself.) She would not, however, miss Mrs Bodley. The Last Supper, she reflected, was followed by the crucifixion, a punishment not beyond Nellie Coker if she found out about Gwendolen's deception – according to Frobisher, anyway, who seemed extraordinarily prejudiced against Nellie Coker.

'I would like,' Nellie had said to Gwendolen over her fortune-telling cards in the Crystal Cup, 'for you to run this club for me.'

'But I know absolutely nothing about running a nightclub,' an astonished Gwendolen had said.

'You have an orderly mind and seem capable in a crisis,' Nellie had said. 'And you're rather good at making people do your bidding. That's all I need in a manageress, Miss Kelling. And it will be convenient for you, you can live "above the shop".'

The life waiting for her return in York had suddenly seemed appallingly empty. And, Gwendolen thought, she would be able to work covertly for Frobisher and continue the search for Freda and Florence, which was, after all, why she was here. And the fact that she would see Niven Coker again had nothing to do with it.

Sunday Best

And what of Freda, where was she on this day of rest? Unlikely though it seemed to Freda herself, she was attending the evening Mass in Corpus Christi church on Maiden Lane, mimicking the theatre of bowing and kneeling and miming the prayers and responses. Quick as ever to pick up a beat, she was barely a breath behind the rest of the congregation.

She had not intended to put on this performance of devotion, she had only gone into the church to see if by any chance Florence was there, unaware that there was a service in progress. A man had shooed her into a pew at the back, hissing, 'You're very late,' and she hadn't felt that she had a choice but to go along with the whole thing.

Hoping to slip away unnoticed when everyone started going up to the altar to take Communion, she was outfoxed by the same man, who almost frogmarched her to the front as if she were visibly in need of redemption. Again, she managed to imitate what other people were doing. As a reward, it would have been nice if the Communion wafer had been a bit more substantial as Freda had eaten hardly anything for two days and was fully expecting to drop dead of famine at any moment. Her growling stomach provided an embarrassing accompaniment to the liturgy. As it was Sunday, Covent Garden had been closed and she hadn't even been able to scavenge in the bins of leftover fruit and vegetables put out at the end of the day in the market. Not so much as a carrot. Her supper had consisted entirely of Florence's humbugs.

When the collection plate was passed around her fingers itched to remove a coin, but as her soul was probably already teetering on the edge of mortal danger she refrained from tipping it over. She took nothing from the plate but neither did she put anything on it, earning her a good deal of tut-tutting from the woman seated next to her in the pew.

She had no money to give. Worse – she had no Florence either.

After her encounter with Owen Varley it had not seemed possible to Freda that her life could get worse, but apparently it could. And it had.

Freda and Florence had reported the theft of the handbag in the Lyons to a desk sergeant in Great Marlborough Street police station straight after it had happened. Freda didn't know why they bothered as the police weren't in the least bit interested. Theft was so common in London that it made you wonder how anyone still had any possessions left.

'Now what?' Florence asked Freda as they left the police station. Freda sighed. Why was she the one who always had to make the decisions? Florence was such a lamb, always following, never leading. Perhaps lambs did lead, Freda didn't know, but no lamb could possibly be as useless as Florence.

The rent was due and if they didn't pay Freda knew that their landlady, Mrs Darling, would find no sympathy in her hard heart for their reduced circumstances. 'Unfortunately I am in reduced circumstances' was something that Duncan used to say in a funny voice that made both Freda and Vanda laugh. How she longed for Vanda to appear out of nowhere, like she said she used to do in her magic act. Vanda would have known what to do, and even if she didn't, she would wrap Freda in her soft fur and give her comfort. And Vanda would understand what had happened to Freda at the Adelphi. Vanda would find a way to heal her and make her feel better. (In retrospect, Vanda had grown unrealistically saintly in Freda's eyes.)

What *would* Vanda do, Freda wondered as they made their

weary way back to Covent Garden. She would be practical, she
didn't believe in worrying. 'You can always find something to
sell,' she used to say, 'even if it's only yourself.' ('No one would
want you,' Duncan had laughed.) A younger, more naive Freda
used to find it funny, imagining Vanda displayed on a counter in
a shop with a 'For Sale' sign on her forehead.

As they were making their way along Wardour Street, Florence came to a sudden halt in the middle of the pavement. Her
eyes and her mouth all made dramatic little 'o's of surprise and
she flung her arms open wide. Freda worried that she might be
having one of her visions.

'Can you see any angels just now?' she asked her.

'No,' Florence said. 'But I know they're all around us.'

Vision or not, she was creating quite a hazard for the other
pedestrians. Freda dragged her into a shop doorway and said,
'What?' quite abruptly, because obviously she was still furious
with Florence over the handbag.

Florence prodded Freda in the chest (rather hard). 'The
brooch! You're wearing the bluebird brooch.' Of course – Freda
had quite forgotten. All this while the little bluebird had nested
safely on her cherry-red cardigan, safe from the hands of thieves.

Freda reluctantly accepted that they would have to pawn the
brooch, but that didn't make her heart any less heavy at the
thought. She remembered with regret the tender look of affection on Mrs Ingram's face when she had unwrapped her gift
from Mr Ingram.

Pawnbrokers were not difficult to find in London and they soon
stumbled on one in Meard Street who scrutinized the brooch
through a little magnifying glass as if he were trying to find any
worth in it at all, and eventually only handed over a paltry amount
of money, a mite of what Mr Ingram must have paid for it. They
had a month, the pawnbroker said, handing them a ticket, before
he would sell the brooch. Freda couldn't imagine how they would
ever manage to redeem the pledge but they had to pay the rent,

and eat, as Florence had reminded her several times already. (It really wouldn't hurt her figure to starve for a bit.)

Freda crammed the ticket and money into her pocket and kept her hand on it the whole way back in case of pickpockets.

She had tried to explain to Florence what had happened to her in that awful room backstage at the Adelphi but had been met with a kind of dumb incomprehension on her friend's part. Florence still believed that babies were found beneath gooseberry bushes, so to try to explain to her the crude mechanics of what might lead to that gooseberry bush was beyond Freda.

'Kissing?' Florence hazarded. 'Mother always says I shouldn't let a boy kiss me.'

To tell the truth, Freda herself didn't entirely understand what had happened to her. She just knew she had been crushed by something brutal and that it was horribly unfair.

When they returned to Henrietta Street, Freda instructed Florence to go downstairs to Mrs Darling and pay the rent straight away, before there was any chance that she could fritter it away.

Freda lay down on the bed. She could have sworn that she could still taste Owen Varley's blood in her mouth. The day had been too long.

She had intended to rest for only a few minutes, but the next thing she knew she was being woken by the Sunday-morning bells of St Paul's church.

There was no sign of Florence. She was not lying in the bed next to her, where she was usually fast asleep when Freda woke, in fact her side of the bed looked unruffled. It was not like Florence to be up and about early, but might she have slipped out to buy breakfast for them both? Freda had sometimes gone out and brought egg rolls back to a sleepy Florence, but Florence had never reciprocated. ('First time for everything,' Vanda would say. 'Even for you, dear heart,' Duncan had sniggered. 'Back in the Stone Age.') But then, the church bells reminded her, it was Sunday and the cafés around the market would be closed.

Florence's coat, which usually hung on a hook on the back of the door, was gone, as was her crocheted beret. They were both unseasonably warm items, but Mrs Ingram was forever fretting that Florence would catch her death of cold and die of pneumonia in anything less than at least four layers of clothing.

Her clothes remained in the dilapidated wardrobe, her reading matter was still littering the room. Rooting around in the drawer in Florence's bedside cabinet, Freda found a paper bag of humbugs, the sweets stuck together in a clump, alongside several more packets of the 'Sights of London' postcards. What a ridiculous waste of money they represented. Freda wondered if she might be able to peddle them – stand outside the gates of the British Museum and hawk them like a street-seller.

One of the packets was open and missing its full complement of Sights. Freda thought she might use one to write to her mother, or perhaps Cissy. She could tell them that she was having a wonderful time, that her success was growing every day, or perhaps – a more sensible option – she could ask them to send her the money for her train fare home.

She slid Big Ben out of the greaseproof paper packet and a little flurry of white powder, like icing sugar or fine snow, drifted out on to the bed. There was more of the white stuff, Freda discovered, in the unopened packets – the snowy dust fell out when she opened them. Freda licked a finger and pressed it into the powder and then tasted it cautiously, not sure whether to expect the tongue-tingle of sherbet or the death-blow of strychnine. It had an odd taste, both sweet and metallic. Was it talcum powder? But why, Freda wondered, would you put talcum powder in the 'Sights of London'? It wasn't poison either, as she didn't drop to the floor in her death throes but instead felt slightly refreshed.

She replaced the postcards in the drawer. Detaching a humbug from the tenacious black-and-white cluster, she popped it in her mouth. Florence loved humbugs. Where was she? Perhaps the white powder was the breadcrumbs she had left as a clue. Might they lead to her, safe in a gingerbread house from which she could eat her way to freedom, one roof tile at a time? She would enjoy that. Gingerbread houses were few and far between in London, though. And, of course, Freda reminded herself, the gingerbread house was a prison, not a place of safety. It was where you were fattened up for the oven by the witch so you could be eaten, like a Christmas goose.

Freda was startled by someone banging loudly on the door. Opening it, she found Mrs Darling standing with her hand outstretched. 'Rent, please,' she said. 'But Florence paid the rent last night,' Freda protested. Mrs Darling was derisive. 'In your dreams, dear,' she said.

Mrs Darling, who knew the footfall of every tenant and who would have made an excellent spy, said that Florence had gone out 'about ten o'clock' yesterday evening, 'walked right past my door'. What's more, Mrs Darling had looked out of the window and seen her walking down the street in the direction of the Strand, 'all dolled up'.

Freda felt a little spasm in her heart. Had another Pied Piper, a more malevolent one than Freda, come along and enchanted Florence?

'And then,' Mrs Darling said, 'I saw her get in a car and drive off.'

Eventually, Freda escaped the sanctity of Corpus Christi, after much bowing and muttering. ('Mumbo-jumbo,' Duncan's words came back to her.) When she returned to Henrietta Street, she discovered that the front door was locked against her and her suitcase stood forlornly on the pavement. The satanic doorknocker seemed to grin at her with fiendish delight.

Never in the whole history of girls, Freda thought, had one of them felt as wretched as she did now.

Sacrifice

Frazzini had sent a message to Hanover Terrace 'requesting Nellie's presence' at an obscure address down by the docks. It was almost midnight by the time she set off. She had dropped off to sleep in the back of the Bentley during the course of the journey and when she woke with a start she was not entirely sure where she was. 'Somewhere in the docks,' Hawker said. They seemed to be in the hinterland of a railway line, Nellie could make out the sound of a goods train trundling its slow way through London. The smell of sugar was in the air, so she thought they might be in Silvertown, near the Tate and Lyle refinery.

There was hardly any street lighting and no houses, just the goods yard and some warehouses and lock-up sheds. It was the kind of place that was heaving during the day and dead as a graveyard at night.

Hawker was as confused as Nellie. In his hand he was holding a piece of paper on which was drawn a makeshift map with directions that Luca Frazzini had given to Nellie.

'Give it to me,' Nellie said impatiently. Hawker put the light on for her and she peered at the paper and said, 'I think you have to take a left up ahead.' She was holding the map upside down, but Hawker didn't point that out and the car continued its slow crawl through the cobbled streets.

'There,' he said eventually. They stopped beside a big barn-like wooden shed on the front of which was painted 'BA Holt – Removals'.

Nellie wondered if that was a euphemism.

'This won't take long,' she said to Hawker as he handed her out of the car. She rapped on the large door with her cane and was admitted by an unseen hand.

'Ah, Nellie, welcome,' Frazzini said when he saw her, as if she were arriving at an elegant soirée in Pall Mall rather than what at first sight was a Dadaist torture tableau. Not that Nellie had heard of Dada. For Nellie, art stopped at Frans Hals's *Laughing Cavalier*.

'Mr Frazzini,' she said, nodding her head in acknowledgement.

A lone chair sat in the middle of the vast packed-earth floor. A man in a bloodstained Pierrot costume was bound to the chair with rope, his now hatless head hanging low. He gave every indication of recent torture. Several of Frazzini's roughs stood around, as if interrupted halfway through their task. 'Squeezed him till the pips squeaked,' Frazzini said with some satisfaction. Another whine from the Pierrot.

The Pierrot had 'coughed up' Maddox, Frazzini said. 'Our guest here tells me that the Huns were paid to go to the Amethyst last night and cause trouble.' It was their bad luck, or plain ineptitude, that 'they ended up shooting one of my boys. I'm afraid my man Aldo is dead, but it could easily have been one of your guests.' The torturers crossed themselves reverently at the mention of Aldo's name.

It was Maddox, too, who had attempted to burn down the Pixie. In fact, it was himself, the Pierrot admitted (although not freely), who at Maddox's behest and for a reward of two pounds had bought a tin of Aladdin pink paraffin, soaked a rag in it and then lobbed it into the Pixie's kitchen.

'What are you going to do with him?' Nellie asked, contemplating the sorry figure of the Pierrot.

Frazzini ran his finger across his throat. 'Set an example,' he said.

'An eye for an eye,' Nellie said, unperturbed. A corpse for a corpse.

Hawker was snoozing when Nellie rapped sharply on his window with her cane, nearly causing him to have a heart attack.

'I think I'll ride up front,' she said, to Hawker's further alarm, clambering in beside him. 'See a bit of this part of London on the way back.'

'Not much to see,' Hawker said.

'There's always something to see,' Nellie said, 'even if it's nothing.' She chuckled to herself. It was the stuff of nightmares to Hawker's ears.

Den of Iniquity

London after the war was full of people who would sell you anything – drugs, guns, women. They would sell you back the goods they stole off you and offer their souls up for a square meal, but Niven was only in the market for information and in exchange for a small sum he was able to learn where Landor was to be found most evenings, drinking and gambling with his fellow lowlifes in a den of iniquity in Bayswater.

The building had a derelict air. Only a chink of light escaping from a shuttered basement window beneath a shop indicated occupation. It seemed Niven had arrived ahead of his target for as he approached the building he spotted Landor rollicking along the street, seemingly a man without a care in the world.

Niven stepped out in front of him as Landor was about to descend the steps to the basement and join his disreputable confrères.

'Evening, Mr Coker,' Landor said, quite unfazed by Niven's sudden appearance. Niven didn't bother with the niceties. He grabbed Landor by his lapels, picked him up and hung him by his jacket on the railings. 'My dog's ready to tear your face off, Landor,' he said. On cue, Keeper gave a throaty growl.

'What do you want?' Landor said, flippant in the face of threat. He was used to violence, on both the giving and receiving end.

'Why were you asking about Gwendolen Kelling?'

Landor didn't answer and Niven grasped him round the throat and shook him. 'Answer me. Why are you following her? Who are you working for – Azzopardi? What does he want with Gwendolen Kelling?'

'Azzopardi?' Landor seemed genuinely amused. 'You think I'm following that woman for *Azzopardi*?'

'For someone else?'

'You really don't know?' Landor laughed again. He laughed far too much for Niven's taste.

'No, I really don't know,' Niven said, increasingly annoyed by so much mirth. He drew his fist back, readying himself to smash it into Landor's grinning face. 'Who are you working for?'

'Your mother, Mr Coker,' Landor laughed. 'I'm working for your mother.'

Niven left him dangling on the railings and retrieved his car from where he'd parked it two streets away. He could swear he could still hear Landor laughing as he drove off.

'Well, what do you make of that?' he said to Keeper in the passenger seat as he sped along St John's Wood Road. His mother was using this man Landor to keep an eye on Gwendolen Kelling. It followed that Gwendolen must be working for one of Nellie's enemies. Azzopardi or Maddox. She could be in danger from either of them, but the greatest threat to her safety must surely come from his mother.

Niven's arrival back in Hanover Terrace coincided with the Bentley disgorging Nellie. Did she never sleep? It was three in the morning – where had she been? There was no point in asking her, she would never say. No point in asking her about Gwendolen Kelling either. She prided herself on her deviousness.

He had only just fallen off the cliff of sleep when he was being shaken quietly awake by Nellie. 'Get up quickly, she whispered. 'It's an emergency.'

The Pigeon

Freda woke on a bench in Drury Lane Gardens, where she had spent an uncomfortable night, her faithful little suitcase serving as a hard pillow. The gardens had once been a church burial ground and there were still gravestones near the wall. Spending the night in the company of the dead did not make for a sound sleep. Freda had scoffed at Florence when she had gone on about King Tut and his curse, but there had been moments during the night when she was prepared to believe in the supernatural world.

Freda had soon been harried off her bench and out of the gardens by a policeman, as if she were a tramp. The policeman had called her some dreadful names. *Impugning my virtue*, she thought, which was something Duncan used to say, putting on a lisp and a funny hand gesture. Freda couldn't have spelt 'impugn' correctly to save her life. ('From the Latin,' Duncan said. '*Pugnare*, "to fight".' He'd been to a 'good' school. 'Several lifetimes ago,' he said.) 'This is no place for tarts,' the policeman said, 'so get along or I'll have you up before the bench in Bow Street for vagrancy.' Freda wondered if he had a daughter of his own and if this was how he would like her to be treated, but she didn't ask. 'Meek, not cheek' when dealing with the Old Bill, Duncan used to caution.

She was an orphan of the storm, which was something that Vanda had once called her, even though she wasn't an orphan and the weather at the time had been quite pleasant, for once.

Freda was homeless and penniless, not to mention Florence-less. It was not a position that she had ever expected to find herself in. She had expected applause at the very least. *I am at a dead end*, she exclaimed to herself, melodrama being all that was left to her. She was also so hungry she felt as if all her insides had shrivelled back to her bones.

How long would it take for her to starve to death? Would any-one even notice if she did? Would she end up in the Thames, swept into the murky waters on the outgoing tide, along with the morning rubbish?

Freda's self-assurance had taken an awful battering. A lesser girl, in her opinion, might have given up by now. She was not a lesser girl. A lesser girl might consider selling themselves on the street, the choice of last resort. She was not that lesser girl either. Not yet.

By great good luck, on the way out of the gardens she spotted a sixpence glinting from a crack in the pavement. She could have cried with happiness. It was true that Vanda always used to say, 'Find a coin, pass it on or bad luck will follow,' but Freda didn't see how her luck could get much worse and so she pocketed the coin.

In a café in Neal Street that opened early for the market's por-ters, the sixpence bought the solace of a sausage sandwich and a cup of tea, and as sugar was free Freda stirred spoon after spoon of it into her tea. She ate the sausage sandwich as slowly as she could so it would last as long as possible, but eventually, as she knew she would be, she was kicked out of the café. 'Oi, miss,' the owner said, 'this isn't a library. You can't just sit there all day without spending money.'

Freda left reluctantly, hauling her suitcase along the Mall towards St James's Park, where she alighted on another bench. Wary of park-keepers, she tried to look as if she were merely enjoying watching the ducks. She had no bread with which to feed them. If she had, she would have eaten it herself.

A pelican waddled along the path towards her. What a peculiar bird. Freda was sure they had none of them in York. Was it even British?

As the pelican drew nearer, a horrified Freda could see that it had a pigeon in its mouth. It stopped in front of her and, as if putting on a performance, made a great show of gulping the bird into its pouchy beak, where Freda could see it still struggling to escape. To live. The pelican regarded Freda with a cold eye as if daring her to censure it. Hideous creature! Freda jumped off the bench and sped away, feeling an unfortunate kinship with the poor pigeon, for she, too, had been snared and devoured by a beast of prey.

Visiting Time

'You've had a small operation but you'll be as right as rain,' an artificially cheerful Nellie said to Edith. The unconscious Edith said nothing. Perhaps she knew, in the depths of anaesthesia, that the operation had not been so very little. ('Removed the lot,' the surgeon told Nellie with unwarranted satisfaction.)

Edith had been admitted to a small private hospital in the early hours, quietly but urgently, the Bentley stealing through the gates in the middle of the night. Nellie was furtive by nature, she didn't like anyone knowing of any weakness in the family.

Now they had all arrived to cheer on the invalid. All apart from Niven, who had already been discharged from duty. Edith was not in the clear, it was still touch and go, the crisis far from over, and the surgeon had intimated to Nellie that now might be the time for final farewells from her family, but Nellie had decided not to pass on this information to them. Edith, Nellie said, had 'women's trouble', a diagnosis that covered a multitude of possibilities, many of which could have been more metaphorical than medical in Nellie's opinion, although not in this case.

'A serious infection,' she added, leaving open the possibility of catastrophe but not inviting it.

'Is she dead?' Kitty whispered.

'No, she's had an anaesthetic,' Nellie said. 'She'll start to come around soon, I expect.'

'And will she be better?'

'Yes,' Nellie said stoutly.

Betty and Shirley looked doubtfully at the pale figure of Edith in the stark hospital bed. She didn't look like someone who was intending to improve. They had expected tubes and fluids and other unpleasant things, but Edith was unadorned by anything medical and looked as though she was awaiting the embalmer.

Kitty reached over and gently pawed the back of the hand that was lying lifelessly on the pale-green jacquard bedspread. She hadn't realized until now that she cared for Edith. The thought made her feel slightly sick.

They had been sitting around the bed for some time. Growing accustomed to the sight of the corpse-like Edith, they began to speak at a normal volume instead of the funereal murmurs they had been employing up until now. The novelty of hospital visiting was being slowly replaced by the fatigue of hospital visiting.

Edith would probably have been dead by now if maternal intuition had not led Nellie to the bathroom when she returned from the docks in the small hours. She had discovered Edith lying lifeless on the bathroom floor, her lips bloodless and the sheen of a cold fever on her skin. Nellie had woken Niven, whom she knew had the soldier's gift of moving instantly from the depths of sleep to the heights of readiness for combat.

Heroically, he had carried Edith downstairs – there was a strange awkwardness to her shape, it was like carrying a small camel or a giraffe. On Nellie's instructions he carried her through to the mews garage where the Bentley (and Hawker) lived. The bleary-eyed chauffeur was woken and helped to shuffle Edith into the back of the Bentley, Niven's car having been deemed unsuitable by Nellie, for which Niven was thankful as Edith began to vomit extravagantly. Nellie dismissed him and she alone accompanied Edith on her journey to the hospital in Kensington. It was a place where Nellie knew that, for a high price, medical skill was almost as important as discretion.

Shirley had brought a box of Turkish Delight for the invalid, but now, as Edith was clearly not going to be eating Turkish Delight for some time to come, if ever again, she placed the fancy box on the bedspread on top of Edith's immobile legs and they all helped themselves.

Nellie, more practical, had brought a cashmere shawl and a box of French lavender soaps.

'Should have brought some knitting,' Shirley said.

'You don't know how to knit.'

'Chance to learn.'

'So, Ma,' Betty said, 'that woman . . .'

'Gwendolen,' Kitty said.

'Yes,' Nellie said. 'Miss Gwendolen Kelling. She's going to be helping me out.'

'Helping you out?' a startled Betty asked. 'Helping you out how?'

'She's going to run the Crystal Cup for me.'

'*What?*'

Betty and Shirley spluttered their protests; even the torpid Edith seemed to moan a quiet objection.

'Well, I think it's a good idea,' Kitty said.

'Shut up,' Betty said fiercely. 'You know nothing.'

'We don't need anyone else,' Shirley said to Nellie. 'You have us. Betty and I can run the Cup.'

'She not *family*,' Betty added. 'In fact, she's a complete stranger to us. She might be a Trojan horse, for all we know.'

'What's that?' Kitty asked. She was intending to own a string of Arabian racehorses one day. Like the Aga Khan. She had met him when he came to the Amethyst. He had given her a liquorice chew and was thus in her good books for ever. You didn't expect someone like the Aga Khan to be carrying liquorice chews in his pocket.

'You're such an ignoramus, Kitty,' Betty said.

'Am not!' Kitty protested, under the misapprehension that an ignoramus and a hippopotamus were close relatives.

'It's deception,' Shirley said. 'It's getting inside the walls of the enemy under false pretences and then destroying everything within. For all we know, Gwendolen Kelling could be working for the police. A *spy*.'

'Frobisher,' Betty said and gave a little shiver. 'That man is as cold as a dead cod. She could be his minion, sent to destroy us all.'

'The Fall of the House of Coker,' Shirley said.

'What? Don't be so dramatic, all of you,' Nellie said brusquely. 'She's a librarian.'

'A *what?*'

Nellie stoutly ignored this chorus of dismay.

Out in the corridor someone began to walk up and down, ringing a handbell to signal the end of the visiting hour. 'Send not to know for whom the bell tolls,' Shirley said. Sometimes her education was glimpsed. Edith twitched in her sleep and murmured something indecipherable.

'Oh, look, Edith's back from the dead,' Kitty said.

Pastoral

Frobisher arrived early at Bow Street to take stock for the coming week. He was so early, in fact, that the night shift was still on duty, the amiable desk sergeant winding up the night's activities.

'Here's one for you, Chief Inspector,' he said, obviously highly amused.

'And what would that be, sergeant?'

'Part of the night's haul – a drowned Pierrot!'

'A what?' Frobisher thought he had said 'parrot' (the man had a slight speech impediment). It made him think of the unfinished parrots on Lottie's tapestry.

'Pierrot,' the sergeant said, enunciating more carefully. 'You know – end-of-the-pier performers.'

'Yes, I know what a Pierrot is, thank you, sergeant. Where is he? Here?'

'No, still in the Dead Man's Hole.' (Not again, Frobisher thought.) 'Didn't drown though, sir.'

'You just said that he did, sergeant.'

'Not drowned, pulled from the water sometime in the wee small hours. Slashed – here.' The desk sergeant paused to draw a finger across his neck. 'Big smile across his throat, sir.'

'A *Pierrot?*'

'I know, peculiar, eh? I reckon what happened was he goes to a party – in fancy dress, obviously – then he gets in a rumpus with someone, they stick the knife in and – *voilà!*' The desk sergeant had been at Verdun, he relished his few words of café French.

'Thanks for your analysis, sergeant. You should be a policeman.'

'Very funny, sir. There's another one of yours downstairs.'

'Mine? A Pierrot?' Frobisher didn't think he had ever used that word so often, in fact he was not sure that he had ever used it in his life.

The desk sergeant laughed. 'No, sir. A girl. Drowned.'

'Another little mermaid for your fleet,' the police doctor, Webb, said. 'Or should that be a school of mermaids?'

'I don't think there is a collective noun for mermaids, Webb, not to mention that they don't exist.' The man was truly dreadful. Was there a collective noun for Pierrots, part of his brain wondered? A concert party, perhaps.

'Flotsam,' Webb said.

'Jetsam, I rather think,' Frobisher corrected, although he was not in the mood to spar over vocabulary with Webb. He had worried that the girl might be the one he had seen on Saturday night outside the Amethyst. But here there were no blonde ringlets, no silvery dress, this girl was tall and on the plump side, she had been well looked after in her all-too-recent infancy. Too young to die. Webb had allowed her the decency of a sheet, he was glad to see.

'No clothes, only the crucifix she was wearing.' Webb had removed the cross and it was sitting now in a petri dish. 'She went with God,' he added cynically. He was a man of science, he didn't have religion. Neither did Frobisher, of course.

How helpful if this girl's parents had engraved her name. He would send the crucifix round the Catholic churches, perhaps someone would recognize it.

'And this one's not a virgin,' Webb said.

'"This one"?' Frobisher supposed that being callous went with the territory for Webb.

'Far from it, in fact,' Webb continued blithely. 'Signs of an abortion, I'm afraid. Very recent, very botched. The girl's a mess, massive blood loss. Water in her lungs, though, so I suppose someone thought it better to get rid of her. She would have died anyway.'

'But she was alive when she went in the water?'

'Maybe.'

'Christ,' Frobisher said. He was not usually given to blasphemy but he was struck with horror at what the girl must have suffered.

'Oh, and I almost forgot,' Webb said. He produced a pair of spectacles, the glass of one of the lenses crazed like a spiderweb, the other lens missing. 'She was still wearing these,' he said. 'It's a miracle they survived.'

The spectacles joined the crucifix and the locket from the previous week in Frobisher's pocket. It was a strange collection of mementos he was acquiring. He had been troubled by girls who disappeared into thin air. It seemed even more troubling now that they were reappearing out of it.

He returned to his office and summoned Cobb. His constable's account of his evening in the Amethyst seemed to contain some holes, in Frobisher's opinion. There had been a fight, gang members were involved, falling out with each other over something and nothing. Shots were fired but no one was injured, Cobb said. Miss Kelling disappeared in the chaos and he had presumed that she had run from the club. He could find no sign of her outside, but when he tried to return to the Amethyst to look for her there his way was barred by the doormen. 'I presumed she was safe,' he added lamely.

'Your *only* duty was to protect her,' Frobisher said sharply.

Cobb glowered at Frobisher's astringent tone and said sullenly, 'Well, if she had just stayed by my side she would have been quite safe.' He sounded churlish, something Frobisher didn't like in a policeman, or in anyone, for that matter. Frobisher was disappointed in Cobb, disappointed in himself for misreading the man.

'Have you heard from her?' Cobb asked.

'Miss Kelling?' He disliked Cobb's impolite 'she' and 'her', they were on a par with Webb's 'this one'. A diminishing of a girl, of a woman. 'No, I have not heard from her,' he said, 'but I am reliably informed that Miss Kelling returned to her hotel at the end of the night.' This was not entirely true. The virago who ran the Warrender hadn't been able to confirm to him what time Gwendolen Kelling had returned after her visit to the Amethyst, except that she wasn't in when she had locked up at ten thirty. Where had she gone? He winced at the memory of his visit to the Warrender the day before. He had behaved like any Sunday swain calling on a sweetheart when he had a wife – a grieving wife – at home.

'Sir?' Cobb said, shuffling restlessly from one foot to the other. 'Was there something else, sir?'

'No,' Frobisher snapped. But then, 'Yes, wait a minute, here . . .' He took the crucifix out of his pocket. 'Go round all the Catholic churches and see if anyone recognizes this.'

'All of them?' Cobb said sullenly.

'Yes, Cobb. All of them.'

'I would have thought one crucifix looked pretty much like another, sir.'

'You're not paid to think, Cobb. Just go and get on with it.'

Where was Miss Kelling? Frobisher was beginning to fret about her non-appearance in Bow Street. She should have been here by now and she gave every impression of being the punctual type. He couldn't deny the little leap his heart gave at the thought of her. Perhaps he could invite her for lunch somewhere. They could walk along to Simpson's, but then she might think him thriftless if they ate there. Somewhere less expensive was called for, perhaps one of the Italian restaurants – Isola Bella in Frith Street, where they served something he had enjoyed called *ravioli al sugo*, introduced to him by Lottie in the days when they ate out and went to the theatre or walked in the parks. The honeymoon period, he thought of it now. It had been short, but then honeymoons generally were, he supposed. They had stepped into marriage in a frail barque that had long ago entered the doldrums and floundered in the deep. Miss Kelling, on the other hand, looked like someone who would steer a steady course. He had entangled his mind horribly in sea-faring imagery, there seemed no way out of it except to abandon ship.

He wondered if her account of the evening would tally with Cobb's. And then there she suddenly was – conjured into being and framed perfectly in the doorway of his office.

'Reporting for duty, sir,' she said, smiling and snapping a neat salute.

Frobisher jumped up from his desk to greet her and tried to think of something droll to say in response, but nothing came, droll or otherwise, so he shook her hand, thinking how cool it was to the touch. It must have soothed many an invalid brow during the war. Despite (much) evidence to the contrary, Frobisher retained a romantic view of nursing.

'Inspector?' she said, regarding him solicitously. 'Are you feeling quite well? You look rather pale.'

'Quite well, thank you, Miss Kelling. Thank you for asking.'

The question of lunch reared its head again. Would she think he was trying to court her? (Was he?) And, of course, he supposed that where his heart leapt at the sight of her, hers might well sink at the sight of him. He must contain himself, and so instead of offering *ravioli* he said, 'Please have a seat, Miss Kelling. I am relieved that you have survived the Amethyst's excesses.'

She laughed. 'I survived them very successfully, Inspector. Now, shall we get straight down to the order of business – firstly, my report.'

'Please, go ahead.'

'My account, from memory, of my night "undercover" in the Amethyst nightclub. Constable Cobb and I shared cocktails – Buster Browns, to be exact – lethal things, and then we danced for a while – he's surprisingly light on his feet, for a policeman anyway. But I'm afraid when trouble broke out he proved use-less, in fact he deserted his post. I was cashiered!' She laughed again, apparently entertained by the idea.

Frobisher felt a fresh acrimony towards Cobb. 'He turned out to be rather slack, I'm afraid, Miss Kelling,' he admitted ruefully.

'There were rival gangs in the club, you see,' she continued blithely, 'and they got into a bit of a gunfight.'

'Gunfight?' Frobisher knew this from Cobb, of course, but he was surprised how easily the word sat on her lips. She was battle-hardened, perhaps not just by the war.

'I'm not entirely sure what happened, but Pierrots were involved.'

'Pierrots?' Frobisher echoed. Dear God, was there no end to the dratted creatures?

'Yes, there was a gang, in fancy dress, apparently they had been out a-robbing. The something Huns.'

'Hackney.' She seemed to have reduced him to single-word responses, but at least now he had an explanation for the Pierrot that had been trawled from the Thames this morning.

'Yes, that's it, Hackney Huns. One of them was shot—'

'Shot? A Pierrot? You're sure?' This morning's Pierrot had had his throat cut. How many murdered Pierrots were there, for heaven's sake?

'No, one of the other lot. The Frazziniellis – is that their name?'

'Frazzini.'

'A Pierrot started the whole thing though, I think. The injured Frazzini man – his name was Aldo – was in quite a bad way. I don't know if he survived. I helped them patch him up. One of the Pierrots was carted off, protesting very loudly – some kind of expiation, I think, gangs are quite keen on vengeance, appar-ently. Tit for tat, you know? Eye for an eye. I've no idea what happened to him but I didn't fancy his chances. *Anyway*, to cut a very long story short, Inspector' (Oh, dear Christ, call me John, Frobisher thought) 'the matriarch offered me the position of manager – I should say manageress – of one of her clubs – the Crystal Cup.'

He was startled. 'I'm sorry, Miss Kelling, could you repeat that?'

'*All* of it?'

'No, just the last bit.'

'I am to work for Nellie Coker. Isn't that perfect? I shall be able to report back to you from the inside. A secret agent!' Her eyes shone with excitement. He hadn't realized just how headstrong she was. Frobisher feared for her. What had he started? He sensed it would be unstoppable.

'Oh, good Lord, I almost forgot,' she said, as she got up to leave.

What now? Frobisher wondered with trepidation.

'This morning's post brought the requested photographs of both Freda and Florence. From my friend Cissy.'

'Yes, Freda's aunt.'

'Sister, actually, but it makes little difference.' She passed an envelope across the desk. 'I'm afraid Freda's photograph is one of her "professional" ones, in stage costume and make-up. They seem to be the only ones there are of her. They make her look much older than she is. To be honest, Inspector, I haven't seen her for a couple of years. I doubt very much I would be able to recognize her now.'

Frobisher slid the photographs out of the envelope and studied them. It was true, Freda seemed more woman than child, attired in some kind of insubstantial stage costume that looked rather risqué to his eyes.

Gwendolen laughed once more. 'An amateur production of *A Midsummer Night's Dream*, I believe. Freda was part of Titania's fairy retinue. I've never liked Titania – so imperious and capricious, to boot. Don't you think?'

Frobisher, who had never found himself needing an opinion about the character of Titania, gazed at Gwendolen rather stupidly before venturing, 'Well, I suppose she *is* a queen.'

'And queens are by their nature imperious. Yes, of course – you're right, Inspector.' (I am, he thought?)

She seemed to be completely ignoring his concerns over her extraordinary plan to work for the Cokers. How vexing she was. She was treating it like a 'lark', he admonished, when it was clearly a venture fraught with jeopardy. 'They're not what they seem, Miss Kelling. I don't think you know what you're getting yourself into.'

'Just a few days, then, Inspector,' she mollified him. 'Surely it's too good an opportunity to pass up. I shall find out as much as I can about the Coker enterprise and before you know it I'll be back on the train home to York.'

'York?' Frobisher echoed, trying to disguise the disappointment in his voice. 'To the Library?' he said. 'Of course you must.' She had a life elsewhere, he reminded himself, a life he knew nothing of beyond the Library. Perhaps she had a beau (or several) waiting for her, or a loving family. In truth, he knew nothing about her, only that she had a quiet magnificence that he both admired and feared and the idea of her leaving so soon gave him a hollow feeling in his chest. Was her working for Nellie Coker the price he had to pay for her not leaving London?

'Nellie Coker is an astute woman,' he said. 'She will see through the deception, and when she finds out that you are a viper in her nest then I don't like to think what she might do.'

'Rip my heart out, I expect, Inspector,' she said cheerfully.

He sighed his surrender and returned to the photographs. Unlike Freda, Florence still looked like a child. Hers was a school photograph – pinafore and plaits. Spectacles, too. Impossible to see if there was a crucifix beneath the blouse and tightly knotted tie. It was possible that she was the girl in the mortuary, but a drowned exsanguinated girl looked very different to a robust schoolgirl.

'Catholic?' he murmured, more to himself than to Gwendolen.

'You can tell simply by looking? What an extraordinary gift, Inspector! I imagine the Inquisition would have made wonderful use of you.'

He wished she wouldn't tease. 'I think you said she went to a convent school.'

'Did I? I don't remember.' She paused and then more soberly said, 'You sent me a note about a locket. It implies you have a body, Inspector.'

Frobisher flinched inwardly at her bluntness. She seemed lacking the usual boundaries. Again, the war, he supposed. He wished now that he had gone out and not been in a reserved occupation – he had tried to go but had been ordered to stay. He felt a lesser man for it. Alive, though. That was something, he supposed.

'A body?' he said. 'No, not at all. It's just one of the questions we ask.'

'Well, the good news is that the Ingrams say, no, Florence did not wear a locket. So that's something to be thankful for, isn't it?'

'Yes.'

'She wore a crucifix, apparently.'

After she had left, he sat at his desk and took some moments to gather his thoughts. He wished he smoked. Nothing to stop him starting, he supposed.

Lunch with Miss Kelling being off the menu now, he ate the *table d'hôte* menu at the Charing Cross hotel – a plate of liver and onions that sat heavily in his stomach so that yet again his thoughts drifted uninvited back to Shropshire, and, for some reason, the crumbly white cheese produced by the farm dairy. At fifteen he had been very keen on one of the dairymaids. She had the same clean, sour smell as the cheese that she made. Gwendolen Kelling reminded him a little of that dairymaid – not that she smelt of cheese, he had caught a hint of lily of the valley when she had bent over his desk to pass him the photographs of the two girls. But the dairymaid had had the same strength, the same . . . he searched for the word. Transparency, he eventually came up with. No – translucency. She was who she was, no dissembling. So few people were like that, in Frobisher's experience.

He couldn't remember the dairymaid's name. It was strange

how something that had once been so important could just slip away down the stream of memory, the waters muddied by time. He could have followed the metaphor further (drowning in nostalgia, and so on) but thankfully his thoughts were interrupted by the waiter from the Charing Cross hotel, who had chased him down halfway along the Strand. Frobisher had been so carried away by his reverie that he had forgotten to pay for his liver and onions. 'I was about to call the police,' the breathless waiter gasped when he caught up with him.

'Wouldn't have done you much good,' Frobisher said, tipping him a shilling for his athletic efforts. He had achieved drollery but with the wrong person.

On his return to Bow Street, he took the photographs of Freda and Florence down to the mortuary to make a comparison, but the girl had moved on.

'Southwark,' Webb said, lighting his pipe.

Frobisher sighed. There was to be no escape from this endless chase, was there?

He set off from Bow Street once more. Life was all just coming and going, wasn't it? And then eventually it was just going.

Oakes was out front, smoking a cigarette, pretending he wasn't. There was to be no smoking in uniform, Frobisher was insistent on the rule being followed and here was Oakes, a man he trusted, letting the side down.

There was a girl, skinny and young, talking to him – Oakes claimed that she was 'a tart' parading her wares. Frobisher gave the girl a half-crown and told her to get a hot meal. She reminded him a little of the missing girl, Freda. If you removed the heavy mask of stage make-up that Freda wore in her photograph they might have looked like sisters.

Eliza! he remembered as he reached Southwark. Eliza had been the dairymaid's name.

A Change of Scene

When Gwendolen arrived in Bow Street, she was informed by the desk sergeant that Detective Chief Inspector Frobisher was 'currently engaged' and would see her shortly. Did she have an appointment?

'Well, no, but I think he's expecting me.' And the nature of her business? 'I'd rather not say,' she said. This enigmatic statement, coming as it did from a woman, seemed to make her an object of curiosity. Presumably not many women had appointments with Frobisher.

She was directed to a seat opposite the desk – an uncomfortable wooden bench, its back to the wall. She felt unaccountably guilty.

Would she see Constable Cobb while she was here, she wondered? If she did, she might chastise him for his abrupt exit from the Amethyst on Saturday night. The morning was moving rapidly towards lunchtime, perhaps she could ask Frobisher if he would like to eat with her. You couldn't move in this part of London for restaurants.

A girl dropped heavily on to the bench next to Gwendolen and said, 'Gotta fag?'

'I'm sorry, I don't smoke,' Gwendolen said, trying not to sound pious. Bow Street didn't seem the place for piety. The girl crossed her legs, her foot jiggling nervously. One of her eyelids kept twitching.

'Where are you from?' she asked Gwendolen, her cockney

accent so strong that it took Gwendolen a second of delay before she could translate it. 'Not around here, by the sound of it.'

'No,' Gwendolen agreed, not from round here. Yorkshire.

'Christ,' the girl said with a little shudder. Gwendolen might as well have said the Mongolian steppes or the Arctic tundra as far as the girl was concerned. 'You're a long way from home.'

'I am,' Gwendolen agreed.

'Gertie,' the woman said, extending a hand in an unexpected display of manners. 'Gertie Bridges.'

'Gwendolen Kelling,' Gwendolen reciprocated, shaking the proffered hand. It was grimy but warm and Gwendolen felt a sudden affection for the girl. Beneath her tired, coarse make-up she was pretty and younger than Gwendolen had first thought. She bore a passing resemblance to Freda, or Freda as she might look nowadays. She was a curious little thing, a bright spark of interest on her features. She had dirty blonde curls, the kind of ringlets you got if you belaboured over tying your hair in rags at bedtime. Freda had the same.

'What are you here for?' Gertie asked.

Gwendolen considered her answer for a moment before saying, 'Deception.'

'Like fraud?'

'Something like that.' She was struck by a thought and said, 'I'm actually looking for someone – well, two people, two girls. Their names are Freda Murgatroyd and Florence Ingram.'

'Run away from home, have they?'

'Yes.'

'What are you, the ma of one of them?' She looked suddenly suspicious. 'It's not always good, being made to go home, you know.' A lot more nervous foot-tapping. 'I got taken back once. It was worse than before.'

'I'm sorry. They wanted to be on the stage.'

Gertie laughed. 'Don't we all, miss?'

'But where would you go, if you came to London?' Gwendolen persisted.

'London's a big place, you know. There's all sorts of places, isn't there? You can't keep track of girls in London. They pop up one minute and – poof! – they're gone the next.'

'Gone? Gone where?'

Gertie started to say something when she was suddenly yanked away by a police constable with an 'Ow!' worthy of Eliza Doolittle and propelled to the desk, where the police constable said to the sergeant on duty, 'Solicitation, dope, thieving.'

'Take her away and charge her.'

Gertie was led away. She looked over her shoulder at Gwendolen and said, 'Good luck,' and Gwendolen said, 'You too.'

Was this where Freda was heading, Gwendolen wondered? *Solicitation, dope, thieving*. How easy it was to fall in London. And how far it was possible to fall.

She glanced at the large clock on the wall. She suspected that she was being kept waiting on purpose, perhaps not by Frobisher but by the desk sergeant, as without consulting either Frobisher or the clock he looked up from whatever he was doing and said, 'The Detective Chief Inspector will see you now, miss.' Despite her irritation at the sergeant, Gwendolen's heart rose a little at the thought of seeing Frobisher. It took her by surprise.

Hopes of having lunch with him had been dashed and, regretfully, they had parted on rather frosty terms. He had been rather cantankerous with her and she had been increasingly cross with him. Gwendolen wasn't even entirely sure what the subject of the argument was. Her independence of him, perhaps.

Nellie sent her driver, Hawker, to pick Gwendolen up and take her to the Crystal Cup. He loaded her bags into the boot, overseen by a disapproving Mrs Bodley, for whom chauffeured cars seemed to indicate loose morals. Perhaps she was right.

When they arrived at the Crystal Cup, Hawker carried Gwendolen's bags up the stairs and handed over a set of keys for both flat and club.

'Will there be anything else, miss?' he asked when he deposited the bags in the hallway. She declined his offer of help and tried to give him a threepenny bit but he backed away from it, putting his hands up and grinning, saying, 'No, no, miss, Mrs Coker would have my guts for garters if she thought I was taking a tip off you. You're one of us now.' (What would Frobisher make of *that*, she wondered?)

There had been no welcome from Nellie in person but there had been a fruit basket on the table and a very pretty vase of dianthus. Pinks, Gwendolen thought – very fitting as the entire place was pink when she had been expecting the usual uninspiring greens and browns. A card had been propped up against the flower vase. It was a postcard, one of the ubiquitous 'Sights of London', in fact, which didn't seem like Nellie's style at all somehow. Gwendolen turned over the picture of Tower Bridge. *Welcome to your new home. Regards, Nellie Coker.* 'Await further instructions' was the order of the day, apparently.

The sight of the postcard had prompted her into being dutiful about her own correspondence. She dashed off the Houses of Parliament for Cissy and the Tower of London to the Misses Tate, Rogerson and Shaw. *London is very interesting. I think I shall stay a little longer to take in more of the sights.* Mr Jenkinson, her solicitor in York, received a picture of St Paul's and was informed of her change of address. *I am staying on a little longer, please send all correspondence to this address. Can you recommend a London bank?*

'Above the shop' at the Crystal Cup had turned out to be a surprisingly well-appointed apartment. It was entered through a nondescript door in a small street behind the nightclub. If you didn't know, you would not have discerned that the flat and the club were in the same building.

Beyond the door there rose a steep, gas-lit stair which took you to the flat itself. Gwendolen had harboured no great expectations of the place when she agreed to live there sight-unseen. 'Grace and favour,' Nellie coaxed, 'it will save you a considerable

amount of money, London rents being what they are.' Gwendolen, in the useful camouflage of a lowly librarian who had been
glamoured by the bright lights of the capital, expressed gratitude
to Nellie for this thriftiness.

Given the unremarkable exterior, the interior was a surprise –
a shock, even. No large muddy boot seemed to have ever
besmirched the pink carpet. No clumsy male hand to have drawn
the thick pink velvet of the curtains. There were deep sofas,
muted pink-shaded lamps, bevelled Venetian mirrors. There
were chrome fittings in the new bathroom and also in the spotless little kitchenette – clearly never used. The bedroom had
pleated pink chiffon shades on the bedside lamps and the bed
was already made up, the sheets and blankets topped with a
puffy, quilted satin eiderdown. Pink, of course.

There was a cocktail cabinet, too – a burr-walnut affair in the
corner that was masquerading as a wireless, something Gwendolen only discovered when she went looking for the Savoy
Orpheans' evening concert and on opening it discovered instead
the glass-and-mirrored insides, fully stocked with gleaming
decanters and bottles. What would Frobisher make of all this,
she wondered? (And why did she seem to spend so much time
speculating about his opinions?) She wondered if there was a
wireless pretending to be cocktail cabinet somewhere. If there
was, she couldn't find it.

The flat didn't feel as if it had ever been lived in. Had the
recently departed manager occupied it?

'That traitor?' Nellie said, who turned up unexpectedly in the
evening to see if Gwendolen had settled in. 'No, Miss Kelling,
no one has ever lived here. I like to come up here and just sit.'

'Sit?'

'Yes, sit. It's unspoilt. *Unsullied.* Nothing ever *happens* in here.
I find that a great relief.'

'Won't I sully it, Mrs Coker?'

'I don't think you will, Miss Kelling.' This said with the air of
someone bestowing an unusual compliment.

And then she was all business. 'My younger son, Ramsay, will pick you up tomorrow evening, Miss Kelling, and give you a tour of all the clubs – our little kingdom. And the Crystal Cup, of course – Ramsay will explain everything.'

Surely it would take more than an evening's tuition?

'Oh, there's nothing to it really,' Nellie said. (Very offhand!) 'Well, I must get going, Miss Kelling. Have a pleasant evening.' She left as swiftly and unexpectedly as she had arrived.

And so, Gwendolen thought, it begins.

An unexpected visit from Nellie had an alarming quality to it, and after she left, Gwendolen opened up the masquerading cocktail cabinet and poured herself a small medicinal brandy to revive her courage before settling on the pink velvet sofa. As a comforting antidote to her surroundings, she took out an old copy of *Cranford* that she had brought with her. She hadn't read it since she was at school and Mrs Gaskell seemed very out of place in the modernist flat. Michael Arlen's Iris Storm might have been more at home than poor old Miss Mattie.

Gwendolen woke with a start. She must have nodded off over *Cranford*. It had been a long day. If she had gone to the window and looked through the curtains she might have caught a glimpse of the man who was sheltering in the shadows of a shop doorway in the street down below. The way he was gazing up at her lighted window, he might have been mistaken for a lovelorn Romeo, one accompanied by an attentive Alsatian.

Niven was standing watch in case Gwendolen Kelling did something interesting. Initially, she had seemed the most straightforward of women; now she was a conundrum.

He was surprised to see the Bentley draw up on the other side of the street and he pressed himself further into the darkness. Nellie was helped out of the car by Hawker. She seemed infirm since prison, but perhaps it was an act, a feint intended to fool her enemies into a false sense of security. (Nothing was as it seemed with Nellie, who could have given Machiavelli a run for his money.) Perhaps that was her thinking behind employing Gwendolen Kelling, knowing all along that she worked for Azzopardi. Or Maddox. Niven had been unable to decide which of the two was more likely. What a dangerous game Gwendolen was playing.

Nellie went inside the flat and came out again half an hour later and was driven away. Niven watched as the rosy lamps in the flat were turned off, one by one, until only one remained, sending a sliver of light through the curtains.

He became aware of a rustling nearby – a rat, he thought, but then he saw the glowing end of a cigarette and Landor stepped out of the dark and grinned at Niven, tipping his hat as if they were brothers-in-arms on the same mission. Keeper growled at his retreating back.

The final lamp was turned off. Gwendolen Kelling had gone to bed. Niven imagined flannel and bed socks. He left abruptly, before his imagination went any further, Keeper close on his heels.

Pierrot

Frobisher unbound was walking the beat again, doing the rounds of the catchpenny jewellers of Soho. The longer the locket lingered in his pocket, the more he felt responsible for the dead girl who had worn it when alive.

The windows were full of cheap trumpery, Bond Street it was not. Most of them doubled as pawnbrokers. Many trebled as fences for the thieves of London. None of them recognized the locket. Would they have told him if they did? They grew coy even before he showed them his warrant. They knew the law when they saw it. It was a long shot, he knew, but it was something to tick off a list. Girls fished out of rivers brought up little evidence with them.

He entered another jeweller's shop, this one in Meard Street. There was a glass-topped counter near the front of the premises that displayed various trinkets. A christening bracelet that made Frobisher wonder what had happened to the child who had worn it. A man's signet ring bearing engraved initials. It would be of no use to anyone unless they shared the initials. (Frobisher didn't.) And a little brooch, a bird, made of gold and blue enamel. '*Bleu de France*,' the jeweller said. 'That's what they call that colour. It's French, *fin de siècle*. It's only just come in, sold to me a couple of days ago. I paid a good price.'

'Is it for sale?'

'This is a shop,' the jeweller said, giving Frobisher a pitying look, 'everything's for sale.'

Surely Lottie would like such a pretty thing? Lottie was French, she was not immune to beauty. There was something about the little brooch, perhaps it was its Gallic lineage or perhaps just its charm that made Frobisher think that she would appreciate it. Or perhaps it was guilt at his bachelor thoughts about Gwendolen Kelling. He borrowed the jeweller's loupe to check there was no engraving on the back.

'A lovely closed back on it,' the jeweller said. 'Sign of quality workmanship, that.'

There was an engraving, not another woman's name but in a tiny script was written, *To my Dearest*. It was all there was room for. It was a transferable sentiment, Frobisher supposed, and asked, 'How much?'

'Five pounds to you, sir.'

'*Five* pounds?'

'The eye's a real diamond.'

'A very small diamond.'

'It's a small bird. Three.'

'How about two?'

'You're killing me.'

'And a box.'

The man was a pawnbroker as well, of course, and only later, when Frobisher gave it to Lottie, did he realize that he had been far too ready to accept the jeweller's statement that the brooch's provenance was legitimate.

Next he did the round of opticians, but was not tempted to buy a pair of spectacles. Not a gift that Lottie would appreciate. She had excellent eyesight.

No one recognized the dead girl's spectacles, but then he had hardly expected them to.

He made it to the Austin showroom in Oxford Street just before they closed.

'Your chariot awaits you,' the salesman said.

Frobisher drove at a snail's pace, it wouldn't do to run down a pedestrian on his first outing, or indeed any outing. He had only driven a car once before – a police driver had shown him the ropes a couple of weeks ago.

The freedom of the open road awaited. He might ask Gwendolen Kelling to accompany him on a drive, take her for a spin. They could drive to the Eagle in Amersham and have lunch in the beer garden if the weather was good. Further afield, too – they could explore the southern coast together. Hastings, Broadstairs, Rye, or, further inland, Cookham or Reigate. He would need a motoring map and perhaps an almanac of some kind.

Frobisher suddenly realized that this preposterous daydreaming had left him in thrall to Piccadilly Circus. There was building work going on – enlarging the Underground station – and he had driven around several times, unable to find an exit. Eros had already fled the mayhem for the duration. Eros, of course (Frobisher was glad that he had no children to weary with unwanted facts), was not Eros at all but his brother Anteros, who represented a quite different kind of love, charitable and selfless rather than the rapture and lust of Eros. The thought of erotic love made Frobisher uncomfortable and he was relieved when he finally escaped the clutches of the Circus and was able to put his foot down on the accelerator pedal. (He had been assiduous in practising the naming of the parts in the preceding days.)

At the junction with Swallow Street he noticed a man on the pavement playing a barrel organ. He seemed to be an animal-monger of some kind as he was surrounded by boxes and cages. Frobisher could see canaries, budgerigars and a litter of tabby kittens. Would Lottie like a kitten? All women liked kittens, didn't they? He remembered the tulips. Perhaps he should stop making generalizations about the fairer sex. And anyway, Lottie was a woman apart.

He drew up at the kerb, which turned out to be a trickier manoeuvre than he had anticipated. The barrel organ was cranking out a tune from before the war, 'I Want a Girl, Just Like the Girl That Married Dear Old Dad'. Frobisher's own mother had been sweet-natured and endlessly forgiving of the failings of the world. How would he have fared with such a wife? Too late now.

On top of the organ, in place of the customary monkey, was a dog, some kind of small terrier, dressed incongruously in a Pierrot costume, complete with a little conical hat positioned at a jaunty angle and held in place on the dog's head by a strap of elastic. Frobisher got out of the car. The dog gazed impassively at him. It was impossible to read what was going on in its head – boredom mostly, Frobisher suspected. Dogs rarely had free will, constantly at the whim of someone else. Not so very different from people, if you thought about it.

He had begun the day with a Pierrot, it seemed he must end it with one, too. The Fates were laughing at his expense. 'How much for the dog?' he asked the organ-grinder.

'It's not for sale.'

'Everything's for sale,' Frobisher said.

When he eventually reached home, Lottie surprised him with a sunny mood and a *bouillabaisse* for his supper. Frobisher didn't like fish soup, not at all, but he cleared his plate and asked for seconds in gratitude for the change in the weather in Ealing. Lottie had already pinned the brooch to the neck of her blouse. '*Un oiseau bleu,*' she said, pressing her face against his neck. All thoughts of Gwendolen Kelling were thankfully banished for now.

Freesias

It was the scent of the flowers that pulled Edith from the deep, acting on her with the same unwelcome effect as smelling salts. Edith shared her mother's opinion of flowers, but felt forced to acknowledge the gesture by weakly raising an eyebrow. The freesias were lying on the pillow next to her head, which was a ridiculous place to have put them. Find a vase, for heaven's sake, she thought.

'Is that you?' she croaked. (Clearly it was.) He sat on the edge of her bed, squashing her leg. She tried to raise her head and failed. She felt horribly frail, as if all the sap had been drained out of her. Her lips were cracked and dry, her greasy hair, she knew, was plastered to her scalp. It was undignified to be on show like this. That was the thing about hospitals, anyone could wander into your room and gawp at you when you were at your very lowest, your most unflattering. She turned her head awkwardly, trying to get away from the sickly sweetness of the freesias, and gave a little cry of pain, feeling hot spikes hammering inside her belly.

'Are you all right, dear?' It was a long time since he had used any blandishments. She must have frightened him when she knocked on death's door. What would have happened if it had opened and she had stepped over the threshold to the other side? There would undoubtedly have been judgement of her sins. She would not have been able to put up a defence. 'I'm fine, thank you,' she murmured. 'You had no need to come, you know.'

'Of *course* I came. You are precious to me.' Precious? What an unlikely word for him to use. Ridiculous, really.

What time was it? There was none of the background murmur that accompanied visiting hour. What if her family found him here? They would draw conclusions. And they would be right. He held her hand lightly. She wished he wouldn't and she had to stop herself from pulling away, but he was rarely tender so she suffered it. She imagined Nellie walking in and seeing them. The thought made her deeply uneasy. She had confessed a great deal to Nellie in the back of the Bentley, but there were things her mother must never know. It was Edith, not Gwendolen Kelling, who had set in motion the fall of the house of Coker. The only thing that would redeem her now was if she could stop the collapse.

The lamps were lit and the unpleasant green curtains at the windows were drawn. The ones to the rest of the ward were open. Anyone could see in. Again the possibility of Nellie was troubling. What time *was* it? (What *day* was it?) 'Is it visiting time?' she asked him anxiously. Nellie had already visited, would she come again? Edith hoped not.

'No, I popped in on my way home from work.' He had a home and all that went with it, but he rarely mentioned it. She knew there was a new baby. It was a fecund household. Edith had seen his wife once, in the street, on his arm, going into a restaurant. She was more attractive and less downtrodden than Edith had led herself to think.

How did he get past the matron? You could have been the King himself, but if it wasn't between three and four in the afternoon you would be thrown out on your ear. Unless you were Nellie, of course.

He laughed. 'Said it was official business. They know me here anyway. You've been out of it for a while, they said you took the anaesthetic pretty heavily. Blood poisoning, they said. How on earth did that happen?'

Is that what the hospital had told him? Nellie must be spreading her largesse. 'Who knows?' Edith said. 'A rusty nail, perhaps.' She would never tell him what had happened to her.

He took a noticeable breath, she could see him gathering himself, it was a prelude to deception. She knew him. 'You didn't say anything, did you?' he said in an offhand way. 'When you were coming round? People can be unguarded after they've been out.'

She stared at him. *That* was why he was here? Not to be solicitous, but to make sure she hadn't accidentally blabbed. Edith felt cold, all of a sudden. The smell of the flowers was making her feel sick and she flapped her hand about until he grabbed an enamel bowl and helped her to sit up. Her insides heaved out.

'There, there,' he said, rubbing her back. He had children, she reminded herself.

What if she *had* blabbed? Or told him that she intended to? Told him that she'd had enough of his game and was going to turn him in? What would he have done then? Her brain felt febrile. She knew him to be ruthless, that was why she had liked him, but what if he turned that ruthlessness on her? She would have to stay on her toes. The thought gave her some energy and she said, 'You should go.'

'I'll see you soon, Edith.' He gave her a pecky kiss on her clammy forehead. She was relieved when he left. A nurse came in and said, 'What lovely flowers, Miss Coker, I'll put them in a vase.'

She could still see him, in the corridor. See him being ambushed by one of the night sisters, see him putting on the charm. He couldn't have got where he was without charm. She heard the nurse's silly trill of laughter as she said, 'What are *you* doing here? We're not all under arrest, are we, Inspector Maddox?'

Maddox! Nellie was so surprised – a rare occurrence – that she said, 'Oh,' out loud, prompting a passing ward nurse to ask her if everything was all right. 'Quite, thank you,' Nellie said. 'Are you looking for someone?' the nurse persisted.

'I've found them, thank you,' Nellie said, gazing at the end of the corridor, where Edith's room was situated. The curtains had been pulled aside (she must have a word with someone about that) and Nellie could see in quite clearly. The nurse lingered, it was long past visiting time and she was confused by Nellie's presence, but Maddox was not the only one who could circumvent the matron's regulations. A crisp, new one-pound note could get you in (and out) of almost anywhere, in Nellie's experience. She had a pocketful in her coat, a sable. Even her Chandos Place dressmaker could not tailor the coat to make Nellie look like anything other than a giant mammal. ('A beaver, or a very large otter,' Betty said to Shirley. 'When she dies, that sable is mine. *If* she dies,' Shirley said.)

Nellie made a gesture of dismissal towards the nurse. The nurse found herself obediently withdrawing, bewitched by Nellie's mysterious powers.

Edith had confessed to her mother when on her near-deathbed in the back of the Bentley. 'Back street?' a bewildered Nellie had said. 'Some woman with a knitting needle and a spoon?' When there were perfectly good clinics in Harley Street that she could have taken Edith to. What was she thinking?

Edith did not, however, admit to the identity of the father. 'Who is he?' Nellie persisted. 'Is he married?' But Edith had remained tight-lipped and then slipped into unconsciousness and Nellie had been left in the dark as well, which was not a place that she liked to be. Edith was never fawned over by men. She seemed an unlikely candidate for lust.

Now, Nellie was creeping around, spying on her own daughter in the hope that the mysterious lover might show his face. This was most certainly not a job for the spies she had in her pay. Far too private.

There he was, perched on the edge of her bed for all the world to see. Maddox – Maddox, of all people! – holding Edith's hand, like any common lover. He stood up as if to leave and Nellie slipped out of sight behind a screen, although not before she had seen Maddox lean over and kiss Edith goodbye.

All the time she had been in Holloway, Maddox had been seducing Edith. Edith was the key to the Coker empire – turn her and you had entrance. The books, the money, the connections, how it all worked. The pregnancy would have been the cherry on the top for him. Not only would he have possessed their secrets but her blood as well, although the two were interchangeable, really.

Edith had been corrupted by Maddox. Edith, her most trusted child. Edith must be brought back into the fold and protected from Maddox, who was undoubtedly using her for his own ends. He had already harmed Edith, how much more damage could he wreak? On Edith, on all of them.

If nothing else – God, patience, flowers, all lay by the wayside – Nellie still believed in loyalty. She had always known that Maddox would betray her one day, he didn't have a trustworthy bone in his body, but she was surprised at the method he had used to achieve his ends.

When she was sure that he had gone, Nellie made her way out to the Bentley, parked in a side street to avoid curious eyes.

'Home?' Hawker asked optimistically. He was hoping for an early night.

'No, drop me at the Amethyst,' Nellie said. She would have been a grandmother if the knitting needle had not intervened. The thought made her queasy.

Before she had left the hospital, Nellie had collared a young ward maid on night duty and told her to draw the curtains of Edith's room. 'And get rid of those freesias as well. Throw them out with the rubbish.' The ward maid did not do as instructed, instead she took the flowers home at the end of her shift and gave them to her mother. 'Freesias,' she said. 'How lovely.'

Though She Be But Little She Is Fierce

Tired and hungry, Freda trudged wearily on through the inhospitable streets, eventually finding asylum in, of all places, a public library, in Westminster. It must have been the owner of the Neal Street café who seeded the idea in her mind. ('Oi, miss, this isn't a library.')

Cissy, of course, had suggested to Freda that her friend Gwendolen might get her a job in York Library. Freda had recoiled at the idea, but now was a different matter. She would happily spend all day shelving books if it meant that at the end of it she had food to eat and a bed to lie in. It could not be worse than anything that had happened to her in the Adelphi.

The reference section seemed to afford the best refuge and so Freda chose a book at random from the shelves and took a seat at an empty table, tucking her suitcase beneath her feet in an effort to make it inconspicuous. So far she had managed to avoid the eagle-eye of any librarian. She imagined one saying, 'Oi, miss, this isn't a café,' although a librarian probably wouldn't say 'oi'. Gwendolen certainly wouldn't.

It wasn't long before an elderly gentleman approached her and Freda thought, uh-oh, here we go – she was either going to be thrown out or he was going to proposition her. But instead he bent down and in a gentle murmur said that he had noticed that she had no writing materials, could he lend her paper and pencil so that she could take notes from her book?

Thus it was that Freda spent a fair bit of the afternoon having to scribble nonsense from *Jane's Book of Fighting Ships* to maintain the charade. Who was Jane, she wondered? Women were not usually interested in ships, let alone 'fighting ships'. What on earth did people see in books? They were so *boring*, although not the Greek myths, she was willing to make an exception for them. If only books were edible, how much more use they would be!

Eventually, a grim-looking librarian advanced on Freda and Freda knew her time was up and she sighed and gathered her belongings. The kindly gentleman was still taking notes from his own weighty and dull-looking tome and Freda bobbed him a little curtsey of thanks as she passed him. He would probably have given her a shilling if she had asked, but that would have made her feel cheap. ('We're all cheap in the eyes of the gods,' Duncan said. 'He means the war,' Vanda said.)

The kindly gentleman smiled back at her and acknowledged her curtsey with a little dip of his head and then he reached a hand out towards her and she thought maybe this would be a shilling after all, but no, he was trying to fish beneath her skirt with his bony old hand. Not so kindly after all! Freda shook him off in disgust. If she hadn't already reshelved *Jane's Fighting Ships* she would have hit him over the head with it.

Sometimes Freda felt as though everyone in the world wanted to take a bite out of her.

Freda made her way back towards the familiarity of Covent Garden, hoping she might be able to beg an apple off one of the stallholders.

Without realizing, she found herself on Frith Street, the home of the Vanbrugh Academy of Dance. As she neared the dance school her legs began to wobble and her heart to pound. The idea of a chance encounter with Miss Sherbourne was too much. Miss Sherbourne had not had her best interests at heart. How many other girls had she sent to 'audition' at the Adelphi, or indeed any theatre? Freda turned and fled.

In Bow Street she passed the huge police station that took up half the street opposite the Royal Opera House. She should report Florence's disappearance. A policeman in uniform was loitering nearby, smoking a cigarette in a rather shifty way, as if he shouldn't be. It gave him a criminal air. Freda had never spoken to a member of the force before and wasn't sure how you addressed one. Eventually she approached, rather nervously, and said, 'Excuse me, sir?'

'Yes?' he snapped.

She persisted, despite his bad manners. 'A friend of mine has gone missing and I wondered if I should tell someone. In case something's happened to her.'

'Happened?' he said.

'Well, the day before yesterday I think she got into a car.'

'People get in cars all the time.'

'But she doesn't know anyone in London.'

'How do you know——?' But then his eye seemed to be caught by the sight of someone leaving the police station and he hastily cupped his cigarette in one hand and with the other gave a little salute and said, 'Sir,' to someone who was hurrying past.

'Oakes,' the man muttered in acknowledgement as he passed. He glanced back and, pausing in his stride, he looked at Freda. She felt inspected.

'Everything all right here, sergeant?' he asked, turning to the policeman, who said, 'Yes, sir, just a tart looking for business.'

'From a policeman in uniform outside Bow Street police station?'

Oakes laughed. 'They're brazen, Chief Inspector.'

The man, the Chief Inspector, set off again, and again he hesitated before returning and, after rummaging in his pocket, came up with a half-crown. Handing it to Freda he said, 'Get yourself a hot meal.' He marched off before she could even say thank you.

Freda's spirits had been lifted by the kind half-crown and she was already dreaming about a chop or a pie when the sergeant snatched the coin out of her fingers. 'You can forget that,' he

said. Without thinking, she lunged after the coin, but he produced a pair of handcuffs and, laughing again, said, 'Shall I arrest
you?' Freda shook her head (meek, not cheek, she reminded herself) and the policeman said, 'But if you want to earn money,
then I know a way. Do you? Want to earn money?'

Freda had always known that she had a price waiting to be put
on her own head, but she hadn't been expecting to have to pay it
quite so soon.

Florence! Freda was certain it was her! She had been traipsing
around Green Park with no goal other than finding a drinking
fountain – it was a toss-up to see if she would die of thirst or
hunger first – when she spotted Florence. Although she could only
see her from the back, she was sure it was her – the broad, rather
stooped shoulders, the plodding walk, the crocheted beret.
'Florence!' she bellowed. ('Project your voice!' she heard the
director of A Midsummer Night's Dream say in her head.)

Again, 'Florence!' And again. People were looking at Freda
but she didn't care. They would have heard her at the back of the
stalls, in the gods, too, but it was to no avail. The sturdy figure
plodded on. One more 'Florence!' at the top of her lungs just in
case. Her voice was hoarse, she had drunk nothing since the cup
of tea in the café in Neal Street this morning.

She broke into a run, the suitcase banging against her legs, but
it was no good. Freda thought she was making a little ground, but
then she came across some boys larking about and they started to
run alongside her, jostling her, making fun of her, and when she
wouldn't stop and talk, one of them put his foot out and sent her
flying. They ran off, laughing, leaving her to nurse a badly bruised
knee. She bit her lip to stop her tears. She would not cry.

As she clambered to her feet, another elderly gentleman
appeared by her side – London seemed to be full of them –
offering to assist her, but she shook him off. Who knew what his
intentions were?

There was no sign of Florence. Freda doubted now that it had ever been her. Hunger must have fed her imagination. Was there no bottom to the depths that despair could take her to?

After leaving Green Park, Freda had spent several more purposeless hours wandering around Soho, dodging unwanted attention. At last, thank goodness, a large clock hanging above a jeweller's told her that it was time.

She cast off her day clothes in a public convenience on Piccadilly, perching her suitcase on the toilet lid and taking out her dancing shoes and her favourite frock. It had grown small for her, even though she had lost a lot of weight recently due to her enforced diet of penury. It was not a frock as such but her Peaseblossom costume from *A Midsummer Night's Dream*. She had loved the spangled green dress so much that she had quietly slipped it in her bag after the last night of the production. Minus the wings. They wouldn't fit in the bag. She still missed them. Not theft, exactly – Mr Birdwhistle's wallet and the cherry-red cardigan from the Knits notwithstanding, Freda was not given to thieving. No, it had been the siren call of beauty and was therefore excused.

Hail, mortal! Freda had extemporized the exclamation mark and said her only line so resoundingly that you could hear it all the way at the back of the stalls in the Joseph Rowntree Theatre, or so Florence had reported. Freda had given her two tickets and she had brought her mother along. 'Very pleasant,' Mrs Ingram said afterwards, which was damning with faint praise – something Duncan used to say.

Where *was* Florence? She had disappeared as mysteriously as she had appeared on the doorstep of the convent as a baby. Absurd though it seemed, Freda couldn't shake the strange feeling that Florence had returned to wherever she had come from. She should have been bolder, she should have pushed her way into the police station in Bow Street and given them Florence's details. If she saw the nice policeman who had given her the half-crown (she still felt the pain of its loss), perhaps she could ask him to help.

When they first arrived in London, Freda and Florence had spent their evenings companionably wandering the exotic streets of Soho, marvelling at the variety of people and shops and restaurants. It was not just like being in a foreign country, it was like being in a hundred foreign countries at once. To their surprise, they had discovered that in the capital people seemed to do nothing but drink and dance as though they were possessed. It was as if one huge, mad party was cranked up after dark beneath the pavements of the capital, only to fade away with the dawn.

'Like fairyland,' Florence had said. Florence was very *au fait* with fairy lore, and she had a lovely illustrated book of Grimms' tales that Freda often used to leaf through for the pictures. Fanciful Florence had once claimed to have seen fairies in her garden, hiding in the laurels. Perhaps she should have her eyes tested, Freda suggested.

Florence had instructed Freda on the etiquette of fairyland, which seemed to be a very frightening place, not at all like *A Midsummer Night's Dream*. 'You must never eat or drink in fairyland' (as if she were planning a visit), Florence admonished. 'Always be polite and remember nothing is what it seems to be. They'll serve you wine in crystal cups and peaches on golden plates, but really the wine is pond scum and the peaches are snails. And all the gold and jewels are just rocks and ashes.' Florence could wax quite lyrical when it came to fairyland.

They spent quite a lot of time speculating about what went on inside the nightclubs of Soho. Florence had her vision of fairyland to fall back on, but Freda imagined it to be more like the pictures of Mount Olympus in her *Child's Guide to the Greek Myths* – people lying around on couches eating ambrosia and drinking nectar while someone played a harp.

Freda had to eat. To eat she needed money. *But if you want to earn money, then I know a way. Do you? Want to earn money?* the horrid police sergeant who had stolen her half-crown had asked. He had taken out his notebook and written something down in it and then he had torn off the page and folded it up very small and pressed it into her hand, as if they were playing a game of Consequences. 'It's an address,' he said. 'There's people there who'll find work for you.'

Freda stepped into her dancing shoes and applied lipstick, squinting at her reflection in the small, spotted mirror above the sink of the public lavatory. She sighed. She would have to do.

The warm day had cooled down rapidly now it was almost dark, but Freda decided against wearing her old coat, as it might give the wrong impression. Before folding the coat up and stuffing it into her long-suffering suitcase, she rooted in the pocket for the piece of paper the policeman had torn from his notebook. She unfolded it and read the address on it. Tisbury Court. 'Number 26,' he had written in a scratchy hand, 'two floors up, ask for Dame Wyburn.'

Tisbury Court was a dismal lane that ran between Wardour Street and Berwick Street, Freda had used it as a shortcut a few times. Dame, Freda pondered? She thought of Widow Twankey and Mother Goose. It seemed unlikely that anyone like that lived there. In the *Babes in the Wood* she had been in, the dame – Nanny Trott – was the children's nurse, 'completely invented', the director said, not in the original, 'but you have to cram a dame in there somewhere'. She – he, Freda was never sure how to address Nanny Trott – was played by a big, burly man who 'moonlighted' from acting as a boxer.

One last check in the mirror. She screwed up the piece of paper that the policeman had given her and flushed it down the toilet. She was no longer so naive that she didn't know what would happen to her in that house in Tisbury Court. Girls were currency in the capital and she would be bought and sold, traded again and again until she was worthless. Freda straightened her back and put up her chin. She was not that girl. She girded her loins.

Fairyland

Ramsay was following his well-worn path from the Sphinx to the Amethyst, having undergone the nightly ritual of being ministered to in the storeroom by Gerrit. He was walking slowly, holding himself carefully, in case he fell into pieces, as he ran the usual gauntlet of streetwalkers and drunks.

The streets were slipping around him, he must get a grip before he reached the Amethyst and found himself in front of the customary maternal inquisition. He was going to Quinn's Belgravia spieler later and he would need his wits about him.

There was a breeze blowing up the river from the sea and Ramsay thought he could smell the brine coming off the Essex marshes, possibly sewage as well. He spotted a pair of street-walkers advancing towards him like lionesses homing in on an antelope. He tried and failed to make a mental note of that image.

Neither of the women was in the first flush of youth. One had black hair that looked as if she'd coloured it with boot polish. The other was an equally unnatural redhead. 'Hello, sweetheart,' the first one squawked. 'What's a nice boy like you doing out at this time of night?'

The redhead was wearing a ratty fur that had once been white but was now yellowing and mangy. She laughed and put her hand on his arm. 'Would you like a nice time, pet?'

'A lovely time!' the other one cawed, grabbing his free arm. 'Both of us for five bob, if you like.'

The boot-polished woman was very close to him, even in the

dim streetlight he could see the grey skin beneath her eyes, her sloppy red lips moving like those of a cod, intent on ravishing him. The other one clung on tightly like a particularly determined clam until Ramsay finally managed to wrench himself away from the harpies and break free. He walked on quickly without looking back.

He had a horror of streetwalkers, they were such coarse creatures, or at any rate the London ones were. The Orient was a different matter, apparently, where it was all seductive *houris* and *odalisques*. A 'brother' of Nellie's (James) had turned up one day – a sea captain, apparently – just before they left Edinburgh for London ('I found you, then, Ellen') and spent an evening regaling Ramsay with dissolute tales of his time in Shanghai, while Nellie was occupied with the girls' bedtime.

She had returned from upstairs when he was in full flow, explaining in considerable detail the acrobatic skills of Chinese 'ladies of the night'. Nellie had thrown him out and told him not to come back.

'Well, someone has to teach him what it is to be a man,' he groused, as he made his way out of the front door.

'*I* can teach him that,' Nellie said.

'Well, then you're not doing a very good job,' he muttered.

They never saw him again. Edith said he wasn't really their uncle.

'Hello?'

Oh, God, not another one. You couldn't stand still for five minutes without one of them propositioning you. This one was young and wearing the oddest get-up, a gauzy green dress covered in spangles that wouldn't have looked out of place in a circus. A green fairy, he thought. *La fée verte.* It reminded him how much he liked absinthe. How much he wanted some now.

'Give us one, will you?' the green fairy asked, striking a very artificial pose and indicating the cigarette case in his hand. She was too young to be so world-weary, Ramsay thought. He suspected she was acting. She had a suitcase with her. Was she just off the train and already plying her trade?

'Please,' he said.

'Give us one, *please*.'

He offered a cigarette reluctantly and then lit it for her. She choked immediately.

'Turkish tobacco,' Ramsay said. 'Highly unsuitable for juveniles. You have to work your way up to them from something milder.'

She took another, less ambitious drag and, stifling a cough, said, 'I am not a juvenile.' Holding out a hand towards him, she said, 'Fay le Mont, how d'you do? It's my stage name,' she added defensively when she saw his sceptical expression.

Ramsay returned her handshake rather warily and said, 'Ramsay Coker. Not a stage name,' he added.

'Are you one of *the* Cokers?' she asked eagerly.

'Well . . .' he demurred. Must he always be tarred with notoriety? Never to have his own identity? But – a stage name! Why hadn't he thought of that? Not a stage name, a *nom de plume*. An identity far removed from his mother's business. The name Coker implied infamy, he would never be able to shake it off and acquire respect in the world of literature. What should he choose? Something manly, like John Buchan. Something more enigmatic. Ricard de Saint Pierre, Jean DeFlamme. That had been the name of his French teacher at school. They had—

'Still here,' the green fairy said, grinding out her barely smoked cigarette beneath the heel of one of her silver dance shoes. They looked identical to the one he had found in the storeroom of the Sphinx.

Ramsay sighed. 'What do you want?'

'A job.'

'A *job*?'

'Yes, a job. Dancing. In there,' she said, indicating the Amethyst. '*Please*.'

Nellie would never take her on. She was waif-thin, a half-starved stray. 'When did you last eat?' he asked, and without waiting for an answer he sighed again and, stubbing out his own cigarette, said, 'Follow me.'

In the office behind Nellie's booth Ramsay could see Kitty, sprawled on the sofa that was kept back there, leafing idly through a copy of *Picture Play*. Ramsay had to stifle the urge to join her, but he was under Nellie's whip now that he'd crossed the threshold of the club.

Their mother was wearing a strange concoction of feathers and fringing. Her dressmaker took the latest fashions and translated them for Nellie's figure. 'The Queen of Puddings,' Betty said. Both Betty and Shirley had evening dresses from all the best couturiers in Paris. Edith, too, for that matter, although she never wore them in the right spirit. The dresses were 'business expenses', according to Nellie, who said the girls had to 'look the part', as if they were characters on a stage.

'You are,' Nellie said.

Nellie raised an eyebrow at Ramsay. 'Who is this?'

'A girl,' Ramsay said.

'I can see that.'

'She wants a job as a dance hostess.'

'Does she now?'

Nellie peered at Freda over the top of her spectacles and said to Ramsay, 'How old is she?'

'Don't know.' He turned to Freda and said, 'How old are you?'

'Sixteen.'

'Sixteen,' he reported back to Nellie. Nellie laughed and went back to sticking bills on a spike. Freda glanced at Ramsay for clarification. He shrugged.

Eventually, Nellie looked up again and said to Freda, 'What's your name?'

'Fay. Fay le Mont.'

Nellie laughed scathingly now and said, 'And I'm the Queen of the Fairies. What's your real name, dear? Tell me the truth.'

Ramsay knew from a lifetime's experience (literally) that it was impossible to lie to Nellie when she turned the spotlight of her attention on you, and Freda crumbled like many before her and admitted, 'Freda. Freda Murgatroyd.'

'Take Miss *Murgatroyd* down to Betty, Ramsay. See what she makes of her.'

'Really?' Ramsay said, surprised. He had been expecting his mother to reject her. The girl would be a bagatelle down there, snapped up like one of the novelties that were sold in the club.

'Yes, really,' Nellie said. 'We're short of hostesses.'

'If you say so, Ma.'

'I do. Your friend's in, by the way.'

'He's not my friend.'

'Welcome to fairyland,' Ramsay said, propelling the girl towards the bamboo curtain and pulling it aside.

She hesitated for a moment but then said, 'Thank you,' and passed through the doorway and was swallowed by the Amethyst.

'Where are you going?' Nellie asked when Ramsay came back from depositing Freda in the club.

'Out,' he said.

'Out where?'

'Nowhere.'

'Nowhere?' Nellie said. 'Very popular place that. You're always going there.'

Ramsay sighed. Did he really have to answer to his mother for every movement he made? He was twenty-one, for heaven's sake. 'I'm seeing Pamela Berowne,' he lied. 'I'm taking her to dinner.'

'Where?'

'Kettner's.' He had eaten there last week and hoped he could remember the menu as Nellie would probably grill him on it later. She would make a better detective than Maddox.

'You'd better get a move on, then,' Nellie said.

Ramsay took a cab to Eaton Square at the appointed time. Quinn was already waiting for him on the steps outside the house, smoking furiously. 'Thought you weren't going to come,' he said.

'I'm not late,' Ramsay protested.

Quinn seemed oddly nervous as he yanked out the bell pull at the side of the front door. The brass door furniture was shined to a spotless finish, the black paint had been glossed so that it resembled a mirror. The usual impassive major-domo type answered the bell. Whether he was the butler of the house or whether he was hired for the night was hard to say. He took their names with very little in the way of greeting and then simply opened the door wider to admit them without announcing them, so they had to find their own way up the stairs to the drawing room.

The place was opulent. The rolled-up rugs were Persian this time, the lights hanging from the ceiling were lustrous chandeliers, and the 'card table' was a massive rosewood dining table. There was a buffet table off to one side which was lavishly laid out with oysters, devilled eggs, caviar and salmon mousse. It was bookended by several large silver ice-buckets of champagne.

Quinn remained jittery, perhaps because he didn't seem to be acquainted with any of the men in evening dress who were congregated around the buffet. At previous spielers Ramsay had attended there had been a scattering of women present, lending a pleasing animation to the proceedings, but here the company was exclusively male. Not that they weren't welcoming, indeed they were extremely well mannered, skilfully drawing Ramsay into a trivia of social exchanges. His champagne glass was constantly refilled by the man who might or might not have been a butler, so that by the time they actually sat down to play, Ramsay was decidedly squiffy.

A felt cloth had been thrown over the polished surface of the table and from nowhere a professional-seeming dealer appeared and took his seat. Ramsay was rather impressed. *Interesting people, quite a classy crowd, in fact* was how Quinn had lured him and Ramsay was hoping that the glamour of a spieler in Belgravia would be just the ticket for a chapter in his novel. He imagined Jones, his detective, righteously raiding just such a place, being rather disapproving in his Welsh way of the affluence on display. Ramsay could almost hear the satisfying snap as the handcuffs closed on the privileged wrists.

He took his own seat and looked around for Quinn, but could see no sign of him.

'We are playing Chemin de Fer, gentlemen,' the dealer announced.

Ramsay had never played 'Chemmy', as these people referred to it, but it seemed surprisingly easy to get the hang of and he won a good deal more than he lost. As the night wore on, however, the balance tilted and he began to lose more than he won, although he was so drunk by then that he couldn't always tell the difference. He'd been set up, of course, gulled into thinking he was as good, if not better, than the other players present. Afterwards he wondered if his drink had been laced with dope – spiked. He knew what it felt like to be drunk on champagne, but this had been different. It had been as if his free will had been removed, almost as if he were a puppet and someone else was inhabiting his brain, pulling his strings, forcing him to keep on playing.

The evening developed a sour undertone and he realized that he was in the company of a pack of hyenas masquerading in evening dress and preying exclusively on him. (Where *was* Quinn?) It was not long before the hyenas dropped their civilized masks and the atmosphere in the room turned increasingly savage as Ramsay's debts racked up – signed pledges and IOUs all over the place, even the engraved gold cigarette case that Nellie had given him for his birthday was forfeited.

And he just kept losing and losing, and the only thing he could do, the puppet-master in his brain said, was to plough on recklessly until the tables turned and he won it all back in one hand. The gambler's curse.

In the end he owed an enormous sum – nearly a thousand pounds in total, a king's ransom. He would never be able to find that kind of money. It was so much money it didn't even seem real.

He wondered if he could just get up from the rosewood table and walk away – would the hyenas bring him down in his tracks? But was he even capable of walking? The room was spinning intolerably, despite the fact that he was sitting down. And even if he left, the hyenas would hunt him down afterwards, wouldn't they?

Time jogged forward in a strange, jerky fashion and then all of a sudden the room was empty, the hyenas had left. Why hadn't they called in their debts before dispersing? The reason revealed itself. Not a hyena at all, but a snake, a sleek fat king cobra uncoiling itself from an armchair in a dark corner of the room. Had he been there along?

The snake spoke. 'Do you know who I am?' it said. It seemed amused by the fact that Ramsay had no idea. 'My name is Azzopardi,' the snake said, introducing himself with a flourish, rather like a conjuror.

He looked like a rather overweight Valentino. 'You are quite the reckless player, Ramsay,' he said. His accent was heavy but his English was good for a foreigner. 'You will be pleased to know,' he continued, 'that I have taken on your debts for you.'

Taken on his debts? What did that mean?

'It means,' Azzopardi said, 'that now you owe them all to me, and me alone. And I regret to say that interest will be added if the repayment isn't prompt. I will be in touch about it.' He took Ramsay's gold cigarette case out of his pocket and handed it back to him.

'You should be more careful with that,' he said. 'Your mother would be very disappointed if she knew that you had lost it by gambling.'

Ting! Ting!

Edith had spent a week in hospital before being returned to the fold yesterday and was currently in her bed upstairs in Hanover Terrace, where she was convalescing irritably, tucked in tightly by Nellie in an effort to imprison her in the bedsheets, in much the same way that Nellie had swaddled her like a small embalmed mummy when she was an infant. Edith had had a streak of restlessness from birth, as if nothing could ever satisfy. Now she had been given a bell so she could ring for assistance and the house had already grown weary of the sound of her summons. 'She should be called an *im*patient rather than a patient,' Betty grumbled.

'Clever,' Shirley said.

Against the odds (scarlet fever, measles, accordion lungs, the war, fishbones), Nellie had never lost a child and she was not about to start at this point in her life. Edith must be mended and made whole again, or at least as whole as she ever could be now. To this end, beef tea was endlessly ferried upstairs to her, along with warm milk sops and cold custards. It would have been cheaper to buy a cow, the cook said.

Nellie's first thought was that Edith's close call was due to Maud trying to exact her revenge. Now that Edith was on the mend Nellie worried what the dead girl would try next – for Maud manifested nearly every day now. Sometimes she seemed amused, sometimes she seemed angry, but generally she wore an enigmatic smile that was difficult to decipher but seemed to indicate a secret she wasn't yet ready to reveal. Nellie was considering exorcism. She imagined it would be exhausting on many levels.

'Going for a walk in the park,' she said to the cook, although it was none of her business. 'Never known her walk so much,' the cook said to Phyllis. 'Must be something up with her to be so restless.'

'Prison'll do that to you,' Phyllis said knowledgeably.

Ting, ting.

Would Edith ever stop with that dratted bell? Ramsay had been up and down too many times to count now, fetching and carrying things for her. Nellie had gone out and charged him with 'keeping an eye' on his sister, but there was a limit surely to being Edith's servant. Betty and Shirley were also out – shirking their duty towards Edith – and Kitty was the last person you would want looking after you. Ramsay suspected that Edith was asking for things for the sake of it. Out of all of them, it was Edith who was usually the first to get bored. And that was saying something as it was a highly competitive field in Ramsay's family.

The first time she summoned him it was to request a 'small cup of tea', which was duly delivered. Half an hour later she asked for another 'small cup of tea'. Why didn't she just ask for a large one the first time?

He was trying to write, but there was not much chance of doing that when he had to spend all his time fetching and carrying for a fractious Edith. In a fit of generosity, he offered to read to her, but she waved him away as if he were offering something reprehensible. Instead she was intent on badgering him into conveying an endless stream of food that even a restaurant would have had trouble keeping up with. Two crumpets *lightly* toasted and *thickly* buttered. A slice of ham. Is there any cold chicken? A pickled onion, a pickled egg. A book, a magazine, a copy of the *Radio Times*, a jigsaw puzzle. Bread and dripping! Their cook was becoming insubordinate. ('I can hand in my notice at any time, you know.')

Of course, anything other than slops and pobs was forbidden to Edith by Nellie, so Ramsay felt some sympathy for her for fancying something tasty. He remembered his time in the Swiss sanatorium, where the food had been excellent – endless mugs of cocoa and bowls of rich soup and plates of local cheese and ham. It had helped him get better, so how could it harm Edith? And the sooner she got better, the sooner she would stop needing to be waited on hand and foot.

Detective Chief Inspector Jones was patrolling the streets of Soho. Or prowling? Prowling had a criminal feel to it, though, didn't it? Perhaps he was a criminal as well as a policeman. Not impossible – look at Maddox.

Ting, ting.

Only ten days after starting his magnum opus he could feel his creativity dimming, coming in fits and starts with interminable longueurs in between. He felt overcome by ennui. Did people really do this for a living? Every day?

The typewriter keys glared balefully at him. Soldier on.

The Age of Glitter had rapidly become unwieldy. Yes, it was a crime novel, but it was also 'a razor-sharp dissection of the various strata of society in the wake of the destruction of war'. (Ramsay was not without ambition.) 'Hm,' Shirley said. Disappointingly, Shirley, usually his greatest champion, had reservations. 'Should you really be trying to portmanteau *everything* into it, darling Ramsay? Wouldn't it be easier just to stick with the idea of the body on the pavement? I rather liked that. And you haven't even written that bit yet.'

'And what about romance as well?' Kitty said, clutching her heart and pretending to swoon. 'You should have people who fall in love with each other.'

'No, I shouldn't,' Ramsay said. 'I can't think of anything worse.' But, on reflection, perhaps he *should* introduce a romantic element? It would open the novel up to a whole new readership (women). How would he go about it? He had no experience of either love or romance. The female sex seemed unattractive to him, but then living with his sisters, who could turn on a sixpence, was enough to put anyone off, let alone someone with 'the soul of an artist' as Shirley had pleasingly termed it.

Ting! Ting!

Great writers did not have to work under these conditions. Great writers had wives to keep the mundanities of life at bay. Perhaps that was what he needed, but who could he marry? Most of the girls Ramsay knew, like Pamela Berowne, were ghastly creatures who would hinder, not help.

Of course, there was an argument for marrying Pamela Berowne – she was filthy rich so it would solve his financial difficulties and he could repay Azzopardi the ludicrous sum of money he owed. The memory of the evening in Belgravia popped up unwanted and was promptly quashed. It had been a week now since the nightmarish spieler and Azzopardi still hadn't approached him for reimbursement. Ramsay was hoping that if he continued to ignore the problem it might just go away.

If (when) he became successful, people crowding into Hatchard's for his latest bestseller (*Do you have the new Ramsay Coker? I hear it's brilliant*), he would be independent, earning his own money, a proper income rather than the weekly alms doled out by Nellie from the profits of the clubs. Enough money to enable him to cut the ties of the apron strings. Not that he could remember ever seeing Nellie wearing an apron. ('In Holloway,' she said, 'every ruddy day.')

To his annoyance, Ramsay realized that he was on his last cigarette. He had consumed an entire packet since breakfast – smoking, he had discovered, really helped with writing.

In the dining room they kept a large alabaster box of cigarettes and when he returned from the kitchen for the umpteenth time with the invalid's latest demands ('a fried egg, yolk still runny') Ramsay stopped off to replenish supplies.

He couldn't help but notice the various papers that were

303

spread across the surface of the dining table. Nellie's solicitor had visited earlier and they had spent over an hour sequestered with each other. Solicitors were high on Ramsay's list of tedium (it was a long list), but he glanced idly at the table in passing. *The Last Will and Testament of Ellen Macdonald Coker.* Oh, there wasn't anything tedious about that at all.

They all knew that their mother made a new will almost every week, depending on how she was feeling at the time – adding codicils, removing beneficiaries, thinking of new bequests, settling old scores – but no one had ever actually had sight of any of these documents, in fact they sometimes wondered if they weren't invented by Nellie to keep them all on their toes. Kitty, for example, was told on a regular basis that she would be disinherited.

And now here was one of these mythical wills, on open view, unguarded. Was it a trap? Ramsay had heard Nellie go out earlier, but that didn't mean she hadn't left the will here to tempt him and the minute he looked at it she wouldn't jump out from a hiding place and catch him red-handed.

'Draft', it announced on the cover page, so presumably it had been brought to Hanover Terrace today for her final approval. Very cautiously, he lifted the page and turned it.

The clubs were to be divided between Niven and Edith, while Betty and Shirley were to receive a sum of ten thousand each and Ramsay and Kitty to have a meagre one thousand. (He was lumped together with Kitty? As if they were equal in his mother's eyes?) The injustice floored him. Was that really how she ranked her children? She demanded absolute fealty from them, yet gave none in return! He grabbed a handful of cigarettes from the alabaster box and stomped out of the room.

'This egg is cold,' Edith said.

Still seething, he returned to the Remington and took a large swig from the bottle of Dr Collis Browne's chlorodyne medicine that he kept next to it.

It was night and the gas lamps flickered. The menace of evil lay on the streets like a dark veil. (Actually, this was really rather good.) Suddenly

Ting, ting, ting!

Oh, dear God. He could strangle Edith, but although it would be interesting to find out what it was like to murder someone, Ramsay wasn't prepared to face Nellie's wrath, let alone the 'long drop' – as Jones would have called it – if he was convicted of it.

He shut the door to his room. Shut his ears as well. Let the invalid be damned.

Jones realized he must return to Taunton if he was to find out more. He checked the clock on the wall. If he hurried and the traffic was light he could make the quarter past four train. It would be

God, this was boring. Would it matter that he hadn't checked the train timetables? How many people would know whether or not there was a four-fifteen train to Taunton. Only people who lived in Taunton, and there surely weren't enough of them to trouble anyone? When *The Age of Glitter* was published, he might, he supposed, be deluged with letters from 'Concerned of Taunton' correcting him, but they could probably be safely ignored. His publisher, whoever he was going to be, would probably deal with any complaints.

He took out his cigarette case and filled it with the new cigarettes. The sight of the expensive gold case prompted the memory of the spieler again. It was causing a continuous low-grade hum of distress in Ramsay's brain.

Jones was on the hunt for one of Reggie Dunn's henchmen, a mongrel of dubious breed called Gresch. The way to find Dunn was through Gresch and the way to find Gresch, he reckoned, was through his paramour, a lady of somewhat easy virtue who went by the name of Lily Benson and was usually to be found at home in the flat she had above the Coach and Horses in Old Compton Street.

He had made Gresch a Maltese. He may as well make use of Azzopardi.

Kitty threw herself into the room and started dancing around, cackling like a malevolent spirit.

'Haven't you got anything better to do?'

'No.' She read over his shoulder, ' "Chief Inspector Evans was not averse to the charms of a good-looking woman." Not like you, Ramsay, you're averse—'

'Shut up, Kitty.' Ramsay threw a pencil at her. He missed of course and she danced out of the room.

Jones had to ring the doorbell several times before it was eventually opened by Lily. She pretended surprise. 'Cor blimey, if it ain't Mr Jones, haven't seen you in a while, not since this morning.' Lily was blonde, with an attractive baby face, marred by the hardness of her eyes. She was all curves and dressed in a way that emphasized every one of those curves. Her voice was coarse, however. (This was good!)

'What can I do for you, Inspector?'

'It's Detective Chief Inspector to you, Lily.'

'Then it's *Miss* Benson to you. What d'you want?'

'Seen your friend Gresch lately?'

'Not in an age, Inspector. We've not been getting on.'

'What about that club of yours, Lily? The one you're a "hostess" in?'

'Do you mean the Emerald? I thought that—'

'We've

The door to Ramsay's room was flung open. Jesus *Christ* – now what?

It was the little scullery maid, Phyllis, who flew into the room and said breathlessly, 'Come downstairs quick – it's Miss Edith!'

'What about her?'

'She's dead, Mr Coker.'

Frobisher Unbound

Frobisher had been in a dilemma ever since Gwendolen Kelling had moved into the flat above the Crystal Cup. 'Above the shop,' she called it, a phrase that seemed, liked so many things, to amuse her. How was he to meet up with her now that she was no longer at the Warrender? She could no longer call on him in Bow Street, of course, someone might easily spot her – the place was full of criminals, after all (on both sides of the desk). News of her visits would make its way to the Coker camp all too soon. Nor could he drop in on her in her new accommodation as he would undoubtedly be spotted by one of the Cokers or their aides.

They had arranged to meet via the written word, for although her flat above the Crystal Cup was furnished with a telephone, Frobisher was cautious about using it – what if it was a party line? Or who was to say that the Cokers didn't have the wire tapped? It was not unknown. The Refreshment Rooms in Paddington station had been Gwendolen's suggestion. 'We should be safe there,' she said. 'I don't think the Cokers ever travel by train, and they're quite territorial. Apart from their house, they hardly leave Soho. Their house is in Hanover Terrace – Regent's Park – did you know that?' He did. (Of course he did! Did she think him an incompetent?) 'I'm trying to wangle an invitation to go there,' she said carelessly.

'Please don't do that,' he said. Hanover Terrace was the very heart of the hive. 'It's too dangerous.'

'It's unlikely that Nellie would assassinate me over afternoon tea.'

'I wouldn't be so sure. Do you address her as Nellie?' he asked, surprised. It seemed very familiar for such a short acquaintance. Had she already been lured? It was not so much the Cokers themselves Frobisher feared on Gwendolen's behalf, it was that she might succumb to the temptations they offered. *Paradise Lost* came to mind, they had been forced to rote-learn great gobbets of it at school. Satan in the form of the serpent, looking for Adam and Eve, or perhaps just Eve – *his purpos'd prey, in bower and field he sought*. He disliked Milton as a poet, suspected he might have also disliked him as a man, but admired the tenacity with which he stuck to his grand design.

She laughed. 'Good Lord, no, only to myself. It is "Mrs Coker" always. She likes the formalities. Quite a stickler for them, in fact.'

He saw her glance at the copy of the *Mirror* that was on the table in front of him – he had been ridiculously early for their morning rendezvous and had been idly perusing the newspaper to pass the time. He had been interested, too, to see if there was anything about missing girls, but they rarely made the inside pages, let alone the headlines. He was embarrassed and said, 'I don't usually read this rag.'

'Of course not,' she teased. 'I'm sure you're a *Times* man, Inspector.'

Tea was ferried from the counter, along with an unprepossessing Chelsea bun that he had bought for her but which she insisted on cutting in two, then allotting him half. He was not used to sharing food, it seemed disturbingly intimate. Frobisher was an only child, he reckoned it accounted for much of his character.

The Refreshment Rooms were an extraordinarily noisy venue for an undercover tryst. Frobisher had imagined them having a quiet tête-à-tête, but they were conspired against by the clatter of cutlery and crockery, the hiss and squeal of the overworked tea urn and the arrival and departure of trains from the platform alongside, not to mention the occasional ear-splitting screech of an engine letting off steam. He had to raise his voice against this cacophony.

'Well, this is exciting,' she said, without apparent irony.

'Is it?' he said doubtfully. 'How?'

'An undercover tryst. Like spies. You know, *The Riddle of the Sands* or *The 39 Steps*.' She took a large bite out of her half of the bun. Everything was done with such enthusiasm, did she look for entertainment in everything? Frobisher wondered what it must feel like to tread so lightly in the world. Had she never been tempered by bereavement and hardship when so many had? He knew nothing about her, of course. The Library, that was all.

'Did you lose anyone in the war?' he found himself blurting out. This was what happened, he realized with regret, when you were badly schooled in the art of small talk.

She gave him a long, alarmingly direct look and for a moment he thought she wasn't going to answer, but then she said very matter-of-factly, 'I lost everyone, Inspector.' She returned her attention to the bun. When she had finished, she brushed the crumbs off her hands and said, 'You haven't asked me about my new accommodation.'

A safer topic for conversation than the war, he thought (or was it?), and obediently said, 'How is your new accommodation?'

'Pink!' she declared, laughing. 'Everything is pink, even the carpet.'

'A pink carpet?'

'I know. Fitted as well, such a novelty. Nellie designed the décor, she's very proud of it. I doubt it would be to your taste.'

'You presume to know my taste,' Frobisher said.

'I think I do,' she said merrily. 'And I very much doubt that it runs to pink.'

Gwendolen had said that she would work for Nellie Coker for just a week, but the week was already up and Frobisher was disturbed that she was showing no signs of returning home. But she had not fulfilled her quest, she protested. 'Freda and Florence,' she added, as if he needed reminding.

'I have not forgotten them,' he said stiffly, offended that she would think he had. She had persuaded him to investigate further a place in Henrietta Street, where she claimed Freda and Florence had been living before they disappeared. (She had been very pleased with her detective work. Overly pleased, in Frobisher's opinion.) He had duly asked Cobb to go to the boarding house and enquire about the girls.

Cobb reported a dead end. He had 'looked around a bit' but found nothing untoward at the Henrietta Street premises and the landlady – a Mrs Darling – had vehemently denied ever having had the girls beneath her roof.

'You haven't returned there, have you?' he asked.

'Of course not.'

'Because you can't go around interrogating innocent people.'

'I don't know about "innocent" and there is something wrong with that place,' Gwendolen insisted, replacing her teacup on its saucer with rather more force than necessary. 'You should go there yourself,' she urged him. 'You're bound to have a better nose for wrongdoing.'

'Are you trying to flatter me into action, Miss Kelling?'

'No! I never flatter if I can help it,' she said with a laugh, and, after a pause, 'You know, I wish you would call me Gwendolen.'

'And you would call me John then?'

'No,' she said firmly, shaking her head. 'It doesn't suit. I think I shall call you Frobisher. I do anyway, in my head.'

'Do you?' She thought about him when he wasn't present? In her head? It was a stirring idea.

'Although . . .'

'Although?'

'I rather like Inspector. Shall we have more tea, and shall I tell you what I have gleaned about Nellie's clubs?'

She had received a guided tour through the Cokers' underworld from Ramsay Coker, the younger son, she said. Virgil to my Dante. The Crystal, she said (again that irritating familiarity, he noted), seemed to be far and away the classiest of all of Nellie's clubs. Ticking them off on her fingers, she said she had encountered at least two judges, two Cabinet ministers, three members of Parliament, four members of the peerage and an Anglican archdeacon – all in one week!

'All men?' Frobisher asked.

'No, of course not, many of them were in the company of their wives.'

'But many weren't?'

'No different from any other London club, then,' she said. She was defensive, Frobisher thought. Or adversarial, he wasn't sure which.

'I'm sure it won't surprise you to learn that I am not the clubbable sort,' he said.

'Indeed it does not, Inspector.'

As to the other clubs – the Sphinx, she told Frobisher, was 'strange', the Pixie was 'rather nice – very good sandwiches' and the Foxhole 'energetic'. Ramsay, the second son, was 'a dreamer, young for his age'. She had met Betty and Shirley only briefly (they seemed to come as a pair) and had as yet been unable to form an opinion about them. The other sister, Edith, had been 'at death's door', according to Nellie, and was still confined to her sick bed. The youngest of all, Kitty, suffered abysmally from neglect.

'And the eldest son, Niven? What of him?'

'Oh, I've hardly met him,' she said casually. 'Gosh, it's hot in here, isn't it?' she said, fanning herself with her hand.

'Is it? I run rather cold myself, I'm afraid,' he said, without irony. 'And the Amethyst, the engine that drives the machinery of empire?'

The Amethyst defied description, she said, or at least it defied being summed up in one word. 'Exuberant', if she must find one, she said. Frobisher questioned the word, it seemed too

311

complimentary. The Amethyst was the only club she had experienced as a guest, she said ('at your behest, I should remind you'), and that had afforded her a quite different perspective. 'Fun – you know?' she said. (He didn't, in her view, clearly.)

'A man was shot,' Frobisher reminded her. 'Not much fun for him.'

'Fun up until that point, then,' she conceded. 'Have you asked around the hospitals? Did you find him? Aldo?'

'No, but these gangs often have a doctor on their payroll. One that's been struck off usually. And what of Nellie Coker? Have you had a hint of anything yet that might put her back in Holloway where she belongs?'

'Sorry, nothing. But I shall persist. You, in turn, of course, must continue to look for Freda and Florence.' That had been their agreement, she said. Frobisher objected that he had no memory of any such agreement, and she said, 'You must have a terrible memory, then.' So not flattery but coercion.

'You haven't eaten your half of the bun,' she said. 'May I have it?'

'And what about the girls?' he asked.

'The dance hostesses? They seem happy enough, certainly the ones who work in the Crystal Cup are. Nice girls, no funny business that I've seen. They're paid quite well, but really they're working for tips, which are substantial.'

'And what about you, Miss Kelling, are you working for tips?' Frobisher asked, watching her polish off the Chelsea bun.

'No,' she said. 'I'm working for you. Remember?'

'Again, my memory seems to be at fault. You give every impression of working for yourself.'

Frobisher couldn't help but compare Gwendolen's energy to Lottie's lassitude. As usual, his wife had remained in bed this morning when he got up. What did she do after he had left the house for work? Did she stay in bed all day, only getting up just before he returned home at night? Once or twice, she had still been in her nightclothes when he came in the door. He had not commented. He had searched the house looking for syringes and dope, but had found none. He knew that didn't mean there weren't any. Lottie, he had learnt over the years, was more than capable of subterfuge.

He sighed and Gwendolen said, 'Inspector? Is something wrong?'

'Not at all, Miss Kelling.'

'Gwendolen,' she reminded him.

'Gwendolen,' Frobisher echoed with some hesitation. Her name lingered awkwardly on his tongue, but she didn't seem to notice. He had equivocated long enough, he thought. What did Shakespeare say? *Screw your courage to the sticking place.* But it was Lady Macbeth who said that, wasn't it? And she was hardly a woman you should take advice from about the fairer sex.

He sighed again, took a deep breath and said, 'Gwendolen?'

'Yes, Inspector?'

He persisted with difficulty. 'I have something to ask you.'

'Ask away, Inspector. I am all ears.'

'I would like to extend an invitation to you.'

'Extend away,' she said.

He told her of his recent purchase of a motor car and asked if she would like to go on an outing with him.

'Absolutely,' she said.

'You will?'

'Of course. Were you expecting me to say no?'

'I suppose I was. When would be convenient?'

'Well, today's my day off, or perhaps I should say night off. I won't have another one for a week. But, of course, you can hardly play truant from your work at such short notice.'

He hesitated before saying, 'My truancy won't be a problem.' And then, '*Carpe diem*, Miss Kelling!'

'Gwendolen.'

'Gwendolen!'

He had sparkled. At last.

*

When they departed Paddington, he told her to go first and said he would follow separately.

'Cloak and dagger,' she said, a little too gleefully.

'Hardly,' he said. 'Just common sense.' Was he the dullest man in existence, he wondered? Possibly, he concluded.

From a safe distance, he watched her climb into a cab, chatting away to the driver as if they were old friends, and felt renewed envy at her ease.

He waited until the cab had pulled away from the kerb before leaving the station. He had not brought his car, feeling slightly nervous of the amount of traffic around Paddington. He needed the open road to come fully to grips with the Austin. And the open road he would have. He was elated – she had agreed to his invitation. He spotted a tram approaching on the other side of the road and set off in pursuit, spurred on by his success, too happy to notice that he was being observed.

In the Park

Nellie sat placidly on a bench by the boating lake in Regent's Park, a new, unfolded copy of the *Express* on her lap. She made no attempt to open it and read its contents, rather she sat quietly as if in contemplation, staring out at the lake. Anyone looking at her would have been unable to discern the inner workings of her brain. Not that anyone did look at her. A woman in her sixth decade, dressed in everyday drab, is more invisible than a librarian.

After a while, a man sat next to her on the bench, but her tranquil demeanour remained unchanged. This man, too, seemed to find nothing more interesting than following the progress of the little rowboats on the water. Nellie gave him the briefest of glances. Out of uniform he was insignificant, a bird stripped of its plumage. Nellie murmured to him like one skilled in the art of ventriloquism. 'Well, sergeant, do you have a report for me?'

What a piece of luck Sergeant Oakes was. When she had left Holloway he had dropped into her lap like a ripe plum from a tree, offering to be her informant. For a regular sum of money he would 'keep an eye' on his new Chief Inspector for her. Frobisher was a menace to Bow Street, he said, determined on upsetting the happy balance that existed between law-keepers and law-breakers. The nightclubs of Soho, he said, were not alone in feeling nervous about Frobisher, his fellow officers felt the same trepidation. Of course, Nellie knew exactly what he was up to. He had been sent by Maddox to spy *on* her, not *for* her. The pair of them must think she was in her dotage. The man was a

315

dolt and Nellie felt sure that she could use him to turn the tables on Maddox. And the added bonus was that he actually *was* reporting back on Frobisher's doings. What fools Maddox and his disciple were.

'You must make sure that no one knows of our little . . .' she sought for the right word.

'Arrangement?' Oakes supplied.

'Yes, our arrangement.' It was a surprisingly good word, Nellie thought. She was arranging.

The nannies made their rounds of the park. The small boys pushed their sailboats out on to the waters of the pond, the rowboats rowed and Nellie remained as serenely unmoved as the great statues of the Buddha in the eastern temples. (She had once considered them as a theme for a nightclub.)

'I've got a tip-off for you,' Oakes said. 'There's going to be a raid on the Foxhole tonight. You'll need to batten down the hatches early.'

'Thank you, Sergeant Oakes. I appreciate you telling me that,' Nellie said. 'You're certainly earning your keep.' He was easily flattered. Maddox must have organized the raid on purpose, Nellie realized, just so that Oakes could warn her about it and prove his credibility. Did he really think he could pull the wool over her eyes?

She placed her copy of the *Express* beside her on the bench.

They both remained there for a while, watching the water. Not a ruffle of wind disturbed it. Nellie knew that last century there had been a disaster here. Hundreds of skaters on the frozen lake in winter had gone through the ice when it cracked. Many had drowned. There was a lesson in that, wasn't there? About skating on thin ice. Nellie, beware!

She spotted Landor on the other side of the boating lake. The man popped up everywhere. She frowned at him. He was truly terrible at camouflage. She glanced at Oakes but he seemed oblivious.

Nellie employed her cane to lever herself up to standing. Time to get on, she had a lot to do. She left without saying goodbye to Oakes. On the other side of the boating lake Landor gave her a little nod of recognition. She ignored him, too.

She met regularly with Landor, usually in the little scrub of garden that separated Hanover Terrace from the mews behind, where the Bentley lived and where they were safe from prying eyes, apart from those of Hawker. Hawker was under instructions to ignore these encounters, despite the fact that he could witness them quite clearly from his window when he was washing his few pots and pans after supper.

Landor was another plum. The man was a mercenary, happy to follow the biggest paymaster. You could pick up a mercenary on any street corner in London, they were the dregs left behind by war, but Landor was special. He had no fear.

Nellie had made him her guard dog, charged with protection of the family, with oversight, with scurrying about the rat runs of Soho, truffling out any scraps of intelligence he could find. And perhaps, most of all, keeping her up to date with the comings and goings of Miss Gwendolen Kelling.

Nellie knew that Gwendolen had been engaged by Frobisher to insinuate herself into their lives. She had known it from the very beginning. Gwendolen had been spotted by one of the Forty Thieves in the back of a car with Frobisher outside Holloway on the morning of Nellie's release. The woman had told Agnes, Agnes had sent word to Nellie from Holloway via her niece, Phyllis, the little scullery maid.

Nellie presumed that it was Frobisher who had ordered Gwendolen Kelling to the Amethyst to snoop on them. What a piece of luck for Frobisher when Gwendolen had been able to help with Frazzini's injured man, Aldo. It had provided her with an excellent calling card. If the Pierrot hadn't given up Maddox's involvement under torture you might almost think that Frobisher had somehow manipulated the entire fracas in order to introduce Gwendolen into their sphere.

Landor knew which side his bread was buttered, unlike Oakes, who wanted it buttered on both sides and with jam on as well. Not that Nellie trusted Landor completely, but then Nellie trusted no one completely. Why would you?

Landor and Oakes were costing her a fortune – at this rate, if anyone succeeded in seizing power from her they wouldn't find much left in the coffers.

Setting off back to Hanover Terrace, Nellie found herself quite buoyed up by all this deception. It was toothsome stuff.

Azzopardi was mistaken to think that Nellie wasn't hungry enough. Nellie was planning to feast.

Edith was not dead, of course. It would have been unfortunate, Nellie thought, to have fought so hard to save her eldest daughter only to have her taken away on account of greed. Pickled onions – what did she expect would happen? Nellie fumed. Edith had hardly eaten a thing for weeks, thanks to her condition and then her operation, and now at the first opportunity she had gorged on everything she could get her hands on, facilitated by that idiot Ramsay.

It seemed that Edith had come down to the kitchen, looking for yet more food, at which point, the doctor reported, her blood pressure had dropped ('the stress on her stomach') and she had fainted at the foot of the kitchen stairs, giving every indication that she had fallen down the staircase and broken her neck. The diagnosis of gluttony was a relief. It was hardly something that Maud was likely to have engineered. Edith must be watched closely, and not just her diet. She was not safe as long as Maddox was around. His claws were still in her. Nellie would like to have locked her up. Instead, Edith was castigated and returned to her room with a box of Brand's meat lozenges to keep her quiet.

The words 'day trip' popped suddenly into Nellie's head. She could not remember when she had last been on a day trip. The thought gave her a sudden fancy for Brighton – the Pier, the Pavilion, afternoon tea at the Grand. She could go for a walk along the promenade, venture out along the Pier and push Maud off the end, return her to the water.

'I might go to Brighton,' Nellie said to Hawker as she clambered awkwardly into the Bentley.

'Really?' he said, unable to conceal his surprise.

'Yes, really.'

'Now?'

'No, not *now*. Are you getting in or not?'

'Sorry, Mrs Coker,' Hawker said, surprised by the unwarranted sharpness of her tone. He felt it necessary to point out that actually he was already *in* the car. 'She's been off her game since Holloway,' he reported to his daughter later, whose response was that he never took *her* to Brighton. She was a nag, but he was fond of her. When he retired, she said, he could move in with her in Clerkenwell.

'I wasn't talking to you,' Nellie said to Hawker. She watched as Maud gathered her dripping silks and climbed in next to her. She would ruin the Bentley's leather seats, Nellie thought.

'Got a plan, then, Nell?' Agnes asked.

'Maybe.'

'Surprised to see you back here so soon. Nice of you to visit.'

Nellie had not treated herself to the day trip to Brighton – quite the opposite, she had returned to Holloway. Brighton could wait when her entire existence was under threat.

'Well, you're a friend, aren't you? Of course I'll visit you.' It struck Nellie at that moment that her old cellmate was in fact the nearest thing she had to a friend. Where others might have felt despondent at this realization, Nellie felt relief. Children were obligation enough without the added burden of friendship. 'Brought you a box of Liquorice Allsorts,' she said. 'Handed it to a wardress, that one with the face of an ugly pug.'

'Edna. I'll never see it.'

'You will,' Nellie said with commendable certainty. A pound bribe and the knowledge of where Edna's mother lived were enough to ensure that the sweets would be handed over. Reward and punishment, the stones on which Nellie had built both business and family.

'Sweet-talking me, eh?' Agnes laughed. 'Thanks anyway, Nell. How's our Phyllis doing?'

'She's good,' Nellie said. 'A little gem.'

Phyllis, Agnes's niece, had declared a peculiar desire to live her life on the strait and narrow and Nellie had obliged by finding her employment in Hanover Terrace. Of course, Nellie might not have been everyone's definition of the strait and narrow, but everything is relative. Phyllis's own mother, Agnes's sister, was the nonpareil of shoplifters. The whole family were accomplished thieves.

'Well, you know we're grateful for you taking Phyllis in,' Agnes said. 'God knows what would have happened to her otherwise. Joined the police force, probably.'

'So,' Nellie said, now the niceties were out of the way, 'I was wondering what you might have heard on the grapevine.'

'You're double-dealing with Maddox and his sidekick.'

'Sergeant Oakes,' Nellie confirmed.

'The Laughing Policeman. Nasty piece of work.'

'He is that,' Nellie said. 'I'm hoping it'll give me a chance to thwart Maddox when he makes his move.' She shifted in her chair. 'Who's Azzopardi, Agnes?'

'Oh, yes, old Joe Spiteri, I heard he was back in town. Didn't realize it was him at first because he's changed his name – before your time, of course, Nell.'

'Yes, but who *is* he?'

'A thief, pure and simple, before the war anyway. A bit of a legend in his day, Spiteri was – used to shin up drainpipes, climb on rooves, that kind of thing – he was a cat burglar.'

'I don't think he'd get up a drainpipe these days.'

'Liked taking from the rich but not giving to the poor. Big houses in Mayfair, Belgravia. Hotels, too. The Ritz. Brown's was one, I think, the Goring was another.'

'The Goring?'

'That's where Spiteri – Azzopardi as he is now – was caught. He was trying to steal the jewellery of an American oil million- aire's wife. One of the millionaire's men had a gun, shot Azzopardi, only in the hand, but then hotel security got him. He was doing one last job before he retired. Never say you're doing "one last job", Nell. You'll curse yourself. Anyway, he was arrested, tried, sent to prison. It was a surprise to hear he'd popped up again. I'd forgotten all about him. Rumour has it that all the loot he'd stolen was stashed somewhere but he was never able to retrieve it. Jewellery, mostly, from a big job at the Ritz.'

'Jewellery?'

'Yeah, jewellery. Diamonds, rubies, emeralds.'

'Amethysts,' Nellie murmured faintly.

'Yeah, them too. What's he to you, Nell?'

Visiting time came to its usual abrupt end and Nellie heaved herself up from the unwelcoming chair provided for visitors. 'Well, good to see you, Agnes. You'll be out soon. Come to the Amethyst and celebrate. Champagne's on me.' She hesitated.

'Need something, Nell?'

'Looking for reinforcements.'

'Frazzini's lot not enough for you?' Agnes laughed. 'You need half of London on your side?'

'Need an army,' Nellie said.

'See what I can do,' Agnes said.

'The Amethyst?' Hawker asked, once Nellie was settled in the back of the Bentley.

'No, first go via the Foxhole. I have to warn them that there's going to be a raid tonight.'

'Rightio.'

Nellie brooded as they drove. She didn't like being taken by surprise. Azzopardi wasn't after her clubs, she understood now. He was after revenge.

321

Pork Pie

Once Nellie had gone, Sergeant Oakes picked up the newspaper from the bench where she had left it. He opened it and appeared to find the day's news fascinating. After a while, with rather good sleight of hand, he slipped a small envelope out of the newspaper and moved it into the pocket of his jacket. He didn't need to look to know that it contained two five-pound notes. Ten pounds. Every week, Nellie Coker had promised. He'd be able to buy a house soon. He'd be able to buy a street.

He was the servant of two masters now. He was feeling very pleased with himself. No one in Bow Street suspected him, that was the funny thing. Good old Sergeant Oakes, the Laughing Policeman, always willing to lend a hand, do the donkey work, yes, sir, no, sir, three bags full, sir. *Ho, ho, ho, hee, hee, hee.* They would see things differently when he and Maddox booted Nellie Coker out of her so-called kingdom.

He laughed and didn't stop laughing until he reached home. Even then, his good humour persisted through the four bottles of beer he drank, one after the other. He rounded off the afternoon by giving his wife a split lip when she asked him where he'd been. And she'd get another smacking if his tea wasn't on the table pronto.

After tea, Oakes went out again. He had another rendezvous, this time in a pub in Fitzrovia, where he joined the man who was standing at the bar, a pork pie and a pint of stout in front of him.

Maddox had enlisted Oakes in his scheme a few months ago. If he was to take over Nellie's clubs he would need a reliable aide-de-camp by his side. There was a limit to how much ambition a man could handle on his own.

Oakes wasn't the sharpest pin in the box. Although he had proved himself an enormous asset – there were no limits to the depths he was prepared to go to – unfortunately, Maddox was beginning to suspect that he might also be a huge liability. Still, Oakes was now in the perfect position to report to him on Nellie's comings and goings, and in return she could be fed harmless information designed to mislead her and keep her out of their hair while they set about unseating her. He bought Oakes a whisky.

'Ta very much, sir.'

'And you're quite sure,' Maddox said, 'that she has no inkling that she's being double-crossed?'

'The old bird's too obsessed with this mysterious Azzopardi bloke to be suspicious of anyone else.'

'You told Nellie about the raid we set up on the Foxhole tonight?'

'Yep. Very grateful for the warning, said I was "earning my keep".'

'Good. Anything else?'

'Frobisher sent Cobb to nose about in Henrietta Street. Said he was looking for two girls. Mrs D gave him short shrift. He "couldn't see anything suspicious", Cobb said. I asked him – casual, like. The boy's got farts for brains. And then—'

'What two girls?'

Oakes consulted his notebook again. 'Florence Ingram and Freda Murgatroyd. The Ingram girl's gone missing. It's not just Frobisher making enquiries, little Freda's been asking around about her too.'

'This Freda,' Maddox said thoughtfully, 'is she a problem?'

'Not one that can't be solved, sir.' He chuckled. 'Little Freda's easy to find. She's a dance hostess at the Sphinx. Oh, can I borrow your car again, sir?' Oakes kicked himself mentally for the repeated 'sir'. Outside of the station he preferred to think of Maddox and himself as equals, partners in the grand plan to take Nellie Coker to the cleaners. 'I've got a package needs delivering up west. I'll need to pick her up again later as well.'

'Time you got a car of your own, Oakes.'

'Well, I'll be able to afford a fleet of them soon, won't I, sir?' (Another kick.)

'Perhaps if you didn't gamble so much, Oakes, you would have one already.'

'Nothing wrong with a little flutter, sir.' (Kick, kick, kick.)

Maddox drained his pint.

'Home to the wife, sir?' Oakes asked. 'The old ball and chain.' Oakes was becoming over-familiar, in Maddox's opinion. He worried that the sergeant was starting to act on his own rather than following orders.

Maddox dropped a handful of coins on the bar and made a move to leave, but Oakes said, 'Hang on, before you go, sir. There's more. I got a juicy titbit off Mrs Darling. One of Nellie's daughters – the eldest—'

'Edith?'

'Yeah, that one. She paid a visit to our Mrs Darling as well.'

Maddox frowned. 'Paid a visit? What does that mean?'

'You know. Needed the old crow's services. The Coker bitch got rid of her whelp, as you might say. Nearly croaked afterwards, apparently. It even had Mrs D worried. You all right, sir? You've gone pale.'

Once Maddox had left, Oakes appropriated the pork pie. 'Waste not, want not,' he said cheerfully, winking at the barmaid as he took a huge bite out of it.

Pour le Sport

Gwendolen had adapted to her new role with surprising alacrity. And Nellie was right – to run a nightclub all you really needed was an orderly mind and to be capable in a crisis. The crises were small (No face powder in the Ladies'!) and frequent (Champagne stocks running low! The club's patrons drank an inordinate amount of champagne) and were as nothing compared to the challenge of trying to keep a dying man alive. It was true she had a string of questions for Ramsay – *Is this really the mark-up on beer?* (Yes) *Could I order better-quality soap for the Ladies' Powder Room?* (No, Nellie bought it wholesale) – and so on. It seemed to amuse him how intent Gwendolen was on running an efficient ship.

The only mishap so far was when one of the dance hostesses had suffered a sprained ankle, thanks to a clumsy partner. Gwendolen had bandaged her up and prescribed a stiff whisky. Otherwise, she was rather pleased with her new employment. She could only imagine what the Misses Tate, Rogerson and Shaw would make of it. And as for Mr Pollock, his head would probably explode if he saw her in her role as mistress of the nightly revels.

The dance hostesses were pleasant girls who handled the clientele with easy grace and at the end of the evening seemed eager to return to their own beds rather than those of the men who had paid to dance with them. Gwendolen suspected that it may be different in the other clubs, particularly the Sphinx, which had a Stygian aura. 'Not Greek, Egyptian,' Ramsay said when he had given her the tour. He talked a lot about the curse of Tutankhamun – surely he didn't believe that nonsense?

Gwendolen had received her first week's wages yesterday. Ramsay had brought her an envelope full of cash – ten times what she had been paid in the Library. ('You're surprised?' Ramsay said. 'Why else do you think people work for my mother?')

It seemed wrong somehow to keep these ill-gotten gains, she had no need of money, and so yesterday she had returned to Regent Street for the first time since the 'handbag incident', as she now thought of it, and had quietly handed the money to the blind cornetist. His repertoire had not grown any more joyful in the intervening time.

She had helped him secure the money in the inside pocket of his coat – to leave it in his instrument case would have been an open invitation to theft. He was horribly grateful, almost over-come. In the end she had helped him pack up his cornet and had retired with him to a nearby café, where they drank tea together and she learnt that his name was Herbert but that he liked to be called Bert and before the war he had played in dance bands on the great ocean-going liners, finishing up on the *Mauretania*. Gwendolen wondered if she could bring him on board her own ship, the *Crystal Cup*. She supposed decisions like that had to be referred back to Nellie. And perhaps his melancholy spirits would be unwelcome in the Crystal's dance band. They were a jolly lot, rightly disinclined to introspection.

Given the hours that she now worked (how different from Library hours!) she had had some time to pursue her lost lambs, but to no avail. Despite her assurances to Frobisher, she had returned to Henrietta Street, but her efforts to speak to the occu-pant came to nought. She had, somewhat against her will, gone to see *The Green Hat*. She had not asked Frobisher but had gone on her own, hoping that, against the odds, Freda might somehow appear on the stage. She did not.

The lambs remained stubbornly lost and, working on the

principle that no news is good news, Gwendolen did not report her lack of findings back to York.

After that first social call to the flat (or 'inspection', more accurately), Gwendolen had not seen Nellie again. Ramsay was the Coker who had been delegated to steer her passage through the protocol of the clubs, a subject on which he was remarkably apathetic. He was writing a novel, he said with some pride. He was green, almost naive, yet Gwendolen couldn't help but warm towards him, the elder sister in her rekindled.

All this had been duly reported to Frobisher in the Refreshment Rooms in Paddington.

She was back from Paddington by mid-morning and had time to consider what would be the most suitable outfit for the afternoon's excursion. She had been pleasantly surprised by Frobisher's invitation – it would be nice to get away from the grime of London's sooty streets, even nicer to get away from them with Frobisher. Although, of course, it would have been nicest of all – the superlative – to have gone away with Niven. She had seen neither hide nor hair of him since she had started work at the Crystal Cup. ('Comes and goes like a tomcat,' Nellie said.) Gwendolen was disappointed yet relieved. She had a core of iron, but he was a lodestone. There could be no sound outcome with a man like that. All would be ruined.

The sailor-collared dress, she decided, even though they were not going on the water. French blue with a crisp white trim. And her new straw hat.

'I hope you are not absent without leave, Inspector,' Gwendolen said as she climbed into the passenger seat of his car.

'Quite the opposite,' he said. 'I told the station that I would be out for the rest of the day on police business.'

'Is that what I am? Police business?'

'Exactly so. You're an informant, Miss Kelling.'

Gwendolen found herself shrinking from that word. It implied calumny. Treachery, even. And yet he was right, wasn't he?

'In the service of the greater good,' he mollified her, although rather pompously, in Gwendolen's opinion. It seemed to make him fret constantly that she would somehow be enticed into nothing short of sin by the Cokers. Was he religious? Did that account for it? Or a Robespierre, driven by the purity of a revolution?

Nellie Coker was Frobisher's *bête noire*, or perhaps the white whale that he had determined to pursue to the death. Was she really worth harpooning? She had corrupted Bow Street, he said. She corrupted everyone she came into contact with. 'Not me,' Gwendolen cheerfully assured him.

They had rendezvoused this time at King's Cross – perhaps they would eventually do the round of all the major London train stations. Frobisher pulled up at the taxi rank, engine idling, and she jumped in the passenger seat.

'Oh, my goodness, you have a dog, Inspector!' She hadn't seen the dog at first – it was sitting quietly on the back seat, waiting to be noticed. Now it sat up and regarded her with a hopeful expression. She leant over and scratched its head. 'He's such a sweet little thing. What is he? A fox terrier?'

Frobisher glanced over his shoulder and gave the dog a quizzical look. The dog seemed to return the look. 'I don't think he's a particular breed, more of a mongrel.'

Having a dog added a new dimension to Frobisher in Gwendolen's eyes. She had not taken him for a dog owner. She thought of the Alsatian that had been with Niven the first time she met him. It had seemed to reflect its master's character, as dogs often do. She wouldn't have taken Frobisher for a small, appealing terrier.

'What's he called?'

Frobisher took a moment to think. Surely he knew the name of his own dog? 'Pierrot,' he said eventually, sounding as if he were inventing it on the spot.

'Pierrot?' Gwendolen said. 'He doesn't look like a Pierrot. He's more of a Spike or a Smudge or a Pickle.'

'I didn't name him,' Frobisher said, and before she could ask who had, he said, 'We have to move. There is an angry cab driver bearing down on us. I think we've stolen his spot.'

Frobisher had drawn up a list of several possible destinations for their outing in his new car, but after she had climbed in Gwendolen said, 'I was wondering – is Oxford too far for you, Inspector?'

'Oxford?' He was surprised. 'Not at all. The city of dreaming spires. Oxford it is.' Still sparkling, she noted. (Keep it up, Frobisher!)

The drive west out of town was thrilling and terrifying in equal measure. Frobisher was a gung-ho driver who didn't seem to have had any tuition and with very little idea of how a motor car worked, and Gwendolen found herself holding on grimly to her seat in the little car for most of the journey through the Chilterns. ('Forty miles an hour top speed, Miss Kelling!') It was hard not to compare his motoring skills to those of Niven, who handled his beautiful, extravagant car with such casual competence. Niven had embraced the machine age in a way that Frobisher clearly had not.

Neither could Gwendolen help comparing her current feelings to what they would have been if she had been sitting next to Niven in the Hispano-Suiza, flying through the pretty rural villages, one after another. What would be at the end of that road? With Frobisher it would be tea and a tour of the colleges; with Niven she suspected their destination would be something different.

Frobisher had rather hesitantly put her in charge of directions, in the shape of an Automobile Association touring map of Great Britain (published, she noticed, by her old friend Bartholomew). 'I was once a Girl Guide,' she reassured him. 'I may have little sense of direction, but I can read a map.'

They stopped in Amersham for lunch – decent steak pies and half-pint mugs of cider in a pub garden. The dog sat at their feet and was rewarded with a sausage from the pub kitchen.

After lunch they went for a walk through the fields and admired the new-leafed trees and the fat lambs, the dog on a length of rope in case he worried the lambs. When the danger was past, he was set free and ran like a prisoner released, not just running but rolling over and over and over on the grass in a frenzy of excitement. 'He's a city dog,' Frobisher said. 'As am I nowadays.'

'I think I would make a very good rustic,' Gwendolen said. Perhaps, Gwendolen thought, her future life should not be in York or even London, but somewhere in the deep green of the countryside. A tumbledown thatch, chickens pecking on the verge. A bean pole with scarlet-flowering runners and heady-scented wallflowers in the beds. The rolling fields and the copses and shady woods, the tumbling sweet streams that ran through everything. She was quite carried away by this bucolic idyll. At a stretch, she could almost see Frobisher inside the tumbledown thatch, but she could not get Niven through the door. Or even the garden gate. She must stop comparing them, she chided herself. Frobisher never came out best, when really he should.

He surprised her by confiding that he was actually, himself, a countryman – the son of a Shropshire ploughman – and Gwendolen said, '*As the team's head-brass flashed out on the turn,*' and he said, 'Edward Thomas,' and she thought, oh, this is good, a man who knows Edward Thomas. Neither of them continued on to quote the next line, which was about lovers disappearing into the wood, and anyway the poem was not about the lovers but about the war and its losses, and so they talked about Thomas for a while and what a fine poet he was ('Elegiac,' Frobisher said, 'but no wonder') and what a finer one he might have become if he hadn't been killed at Arras.

They were both more sombre on their return to the car, but the mood was swept aside by the effort necessary to crank the Austin back into life after its siesta. It seemed to be an extraordinarily complicated process. 'I haven't yet learnt this by rote,' he apologized, passing her the car's handbook ('my Bible at the moment').

It will repay you to read these notes carefully, the handbook warned sternly. Frobisher had already fiddled with knobs and levers inside the car and now Gwendolen dictated to him. '*If the car has been standing for some time* – which it has, obviously – *starting should be assisted by using the hand priming lever on the fuel pump to give the carburettor a full supply of fuel.*'

'Yes, I'm doing that, Miss Kelling,' he shouted from somewhere beneath the bonnet. The dog sat on the verge next to him, as if willing help on him.

'And then – *make sure that the crankshaft is free, pushing the handle in to engage fully with the starting dog* – what on earth is that?' – the dog gave her an interested look – '*before turning it. The ignition key is turned to the right—*'

'Can you do that for me, Miss Kelling?'

'Rightio.'

Finally, they were back on the road once more, rattling along at a pace too noisy for conversation, and the melancholy mood soon dissipated.

'Why Oxford?' he asked when they arrived. 'Why choose it for our little run?'

'The elder of my two brothers was here. He didn't even finish his first term, but I had a fancy to see where he was. See what he saw.'

'He went out to the Front? And didn't come back? And you also had a younger brother?'

'Yes.'

'I'm so sorry.'

'Let's not dwell on lives not lived, it won't do any more. It's already half past four. I would imagine that Oxford is the kind of place where you can find a very good high tea.'

And so it proved to be.

Afterwards, they wandered around the college quads, and as the light was softening towards evening they came by chance upon a group of students putting on what seemed to be an extempore performance of *A Midsummer Night's Dream* on Christ Church Meadow. The costumes seemed to have been gleaned from a dressing-up box and many of the actors were reading from the text, but that did not dim the magic, indeed it seemed somehow to augment it. It would be exam time soon, wouldn't it? Perhaps this was a respite.

'How lovely,' Gwendolen whispered to Frobisher. 'It's my favourite play.' Frobisher said nothing. It was not a manly play and it was not midsummer so Gwendolen imagined he might object on both fronts, but then this, she reminded herself, was a man who found Edward Thomas 'elegiac' and possessed a dog called Pierrot, so perhaps was not the dry stick she kept taking him for.

He found a place for them to sit on the grass and put his jacket down for her. Lanterns had been lit around the lawn to denote the stage. The staging was very pretty and captured the essence of the play without fuss. Unfortunately, it was nearing its end, Hippolyta declaring that *Pyramus and Thisbe* was 'the silliest stuff that ever I heard', and Gwendolen thought how more than three hundred years later it was a judgement that could be applied to so many things.

The impromptu audience, spread out on the grass, seemed to be mostly composed of fellow students and friends. They were all of them full of strength and youth, just as their doomed predecessors had once been. War was a foul thing. It should be sent back to hell where it had come from and never let out again. She gave her head a little shake to rid it of unwanted thoughts.

'Miss Kelling?'

'A wasp, I think. It's gone now.' The dog settled down to sleep, its head against Gwendolen's knee.

The girls playing the fairies pranced and tripped prettily around on the grass and Gwendolen thought of Freda. She had played one of these fairies, hadn't she? Gwendolen would have liked to have seen her on stage. Perhaps she had done the girl a disservice, perhaps she had real talent. Where was she? Talented or not, I must keep looking for her, Gwendolen thought.

They had reached the restorative ending. 'Give me your hands, if we be friends,' Puck said – he wore a great deal of make-up and had little papier-mâché horns attached to his head – 'and Robin shall restore amends.' At which the actors took each other's hands and the members of the audience, on a whim, shuffled closer and did the same.

The girl nearest to Gwendolen, wearing a coronet woven from daisies, the kind a child would make, reached out a shy hand to her. Gwendolen was reminded somewhat incongruously of being in a Quaker meeting – she had attended them several times in York on her return from the war in an attempt to find solace or meaning, but had found neither. She looked to Frobisher on the other side of her. She expected him to be embarrassed, and perhaps he was, but nonetheless he held out his own hand and grasped hers in a brief but strong grip.

And then it was over. The dog woke up. Everyone dispersed into the gloaming and Frobisher helped her to her feet. 'Time to go home,' he said. He looked rather crestfallen at the idea.

Hail, Mortal!

It was over a week since Freda had been invited by Ramsay Coker to step over the threshold of the Amethyst and into 'fairy-land'. She had been very quickly disabused of her previous assumption that a nightclub would be an enchanted place.

Although, naturally, she had kept the information to herself, Freda had never actually danced with a man. At her dance school in York, they had kept up with all the latest dances on a Saturday afternoon after tap class, but they had practised with each other, taking it in turns to lead and follow. It was novel, and not particularly pleasant, to be partnered now by a member of the opposite sex.

The Amethyst was a raucous place, horribly hot and airless. Freda was surprised that people didn't die of suffocation. All trussed up in their evening suits, the men seemed to sweat from every pore, which only intensified the fug of tobacco and alcohol around them. And they all seemed so big compared to Freda – and very prone to standing on her poor toes. Still, she did seem to be quite a success, if success was measured in the volume of men who sought her out. 'She's a popular little thing,' Betty Coker told her mother. 'Quite the little bon-bon.'

'A novelty,' Shirley added.

I'm none of those things, Freda thought. I'm a girl.

She had garnered rather a lot of experience with older men now. Owen Varley was never far from her mind, but at least this time she was prepared for any onslaught, although the worst she had suffered by the end of the first night was a badly bruised big toe.

'Worse things happen at sea,' Mrs Coker said, which was a ridiculous thing to say, but Freda didn't mind because when the club was closing Mrs Coker raked ten shillings in coins out of a tin and handed them all to her. Ten shillings! Mrs Coker said it came from the goodness of her heart as she usually paid the girls at the end of the week, but she hadn't decided whether or not to take Freda on. She was 'on probation' apparently, which Freda thought was something that happened to criminals.

'Well, you can come back tomorrow,' Nellie Coker said, 'and we'll see how you get on.'

The amazing thing was that she had made even more in tips. She'd had no idea that you got tips for a dance until the first ungainly quickstepper pressed a shilling into her palm, leaving his moist paw in her hand just a little too long for comfort. And then another man tipped her, and another. Not quite riches beyond compare, but enough to stop starvation, although in fact she need never go hungry again if she worked at the Amethyst because there was a little side room where the dance hostesses went when it was quiet (which was never) or when they couldn't go on any longer without collapsing from exhaustion. A table was laid out with ham and cheese and cream crackers and jugs of water and a big pot of tea. 'Got to keep the horses watered,' Nelly said. (Not a horse either, a girl!) There were two kinds of jam as well. And biscuits. Florence would have loved it here, apart from the dancing, of course. Where was she? What if she was stuck somewhere with nothing to eat? Not even a humbug.

Freda had nowhere to sleep that first night, but by dint of some cunning hide-and-seek (she thought of Vanda, disappearing inside the magician's box) she managed to stay behind unnoticed when the club was locked up and make herself a little nest in a warm corner of the kitchen. It was much less troubling to be sleeping with the big pots and pans and the smells of stale fat than it had been spending the night with the old gravestones in Drury Lane Gardens.

The next morning, she slipped out before anyone appeared and had breakfast in a café in Dean Street, just around the corner from the Amethyst. The money she had earnt meant that she could feast on any number of sausages and she could barely get up from the table when she had finished.

The sensible thing to do then would have been to start a search for lodgings, but instead Freda was determined to return to the pawnbroker's in Meard Street, on a mission to redeem the little bluebird brooch. It seemed imperative somehow, almost as if it would be Florence herself who would be returned on production of the carefully treasured pawnbroker's ticket.

No Florence, of course, but also no bluebird brooch. Not just that, but the man behind the counter denied ever having taken the brooch into his guardianship. 'But I have the ticket,' Freda said, waving the little creased piece of paper at him. Despite this evidence, he claimed that she was mistaken. Freda wanted to scream with frustration, indeed she did exactly that, and the pawnbroker took out a cricket bat from behind the counter and threatened to 'knock her for six' if she didn't leave his premises. 'Go to the police, why don't you?' he said scathingly. No, thank you, Freda thought, remembering the horrid policeman who had robbed her of the half-crown and advised her to go to Tisbury Court.

The pawnbroker had sold the brooch, of course. He was supposed to keep it for a month and he must have sold it at the very first opportunity. What a wicked thing to do, and now some woman other than Mrs Ingram was sporting the little bird. Freda thought how sad Mrs Ingram would be at the loss. It was not as great as her loss of Florence, of course, but the two were all mixed up in Freda's head as she trudged miserably along Wardour Street.

And yet, for all she knew, Florence might have already returned home, simply caught a train and gone back to York, no longer interested in London or Freda. The thought cheered Freda. All would be forgiven by the Ingrams, even the loss of the pearls and the little bluebird, and Florence would take up her life where she had left off. Perhaps one day she would regale her own children with the tale of how she had once run away to London. Because, of course, Florence would go on to marry and have children (Freda imagined them adenoidal with large feet) and would never want for money or food or a roof over her head because someone else would always provide the necessities. The nearest that Florence would probably get to the stage in the future would be when she took those self-same children to the pantomime at York Theatre Royal at Christmas. Would she think of Freda when she watched the village children dancing and singing around Aladdin or Jack and his pocketful of beans?

Freda had quite convinced herself of this future for Florence and was already feeling annoyed with her for not having found a way to tell Freda that she was safely back in the bosom of her family. She could at least have dashed off one of her dratted 'Sights of London' postcards. But then it would have been delivered to Henrietta Street and Mrs Darling would probably have thrown it on the fire.

However, now that she had some money, Freda could telephone the Ingrams, couldn't she? Ask to talk to Florence and set her mind at rest. The more she imagined it, the more she was convinced that Florence was back home, sitting on the plush moquette of the Ingrams' sofa, raking her fingers through the little silver dish of sugared almonds. *Filigree*, Freda thought.

She made her way to Broad Street, to the new telephone kiosks that had been installed on the pavement there, and fed two pennies into the mouth of the box inside. She was startled by Mr Ingram answering straight away, as if he had been standing next to the telephone in his oak-panelled hallway. 'Who is this?' he shouted before Freda had a chance to say anything. 'Florrie, is that you?' Freda could hear the note of desperation in his voice. And then he startled her even further by saying, 'Is that you, Freda?' (He couldn't *see* her down the telephone wires, could he?) 'Do you know where Florrie is?' he asked. 'Freda? Freda?'

She didn't press 'button B' to talk to him, instead she fled. She didn't even bother retrieving her tuppence.

She felt too downcast to tramp around the streets looking for a room to rent and she spent most of the rest of the day in one Lyons or another, as they seemed the most likely places to spot the errant Florence, although in her heart she knew that, like the bluebird brooch, Florence had flown away.

In Piccadilly, trudging between Corner Houses, she passed a car showroom next to the Ritz. Like the hotel itself, it seemed to gleam with lacquered wealth. Freda was just idly wondering how it was possible to get a car behind the plate-glass windows when she gasped at the sight of one of them. It was the same car that Florence had got into on the Strand on the day of Freda's cursed audition.

The sight of it pulled her inside the showroom and she stood next to the car, staring at it as if hypnotized by it. It was impossible not to reach out a hand to stroke the shining bonnet of the machine and it was only when a snooty salesman hurried up to her and said, 'Excuse me, miss, can I help you in some way?' in a very sarcastic manner that she woke from the trance the car had sent her into.

At the appointed hour, she had pitched up at the Amethyst and was told by Betty to go to the Sphinx because they were short of a couple of hostesses. Freda had learnt that Nellie Coker owned five clubs and she wondered if she was going to be endlessly bundled about between them. 'Oh, and here, take this,' Nellie said, handing over a parcel wrapped in brown paper. 'A new dress, you can't keep wearing that ridiculous outfit.'

'New?' Freda said, excited by the idea.

'Not new,' Nellie said. 'New to you.'

Freda was still excited, thinking it might be one of Betty's or Shirley's cast-offs, but it turned out to be an old thing that had been worn to death by one of the hostesses and left behind when she 'moved on', although when and where to was not specified.

'She'll be feasted on in the Sphinx,' Betty said.

'Like a lamb in a pack of wolves,' Shirley said. (Not a lamb, a girl.)

It turned out that it was Ramsay Coker who was in charge over at the Sphinx. In Freda's opinion, Ramsay Coker was a first-class twit. His head was always in the clouds. 'I'm writing a novel,' he told her, as if that was something to crow about, as if there weren't enough novels in the world already. He was incapable of organizing a tombola, let alone a nightclub. The Sphinx would run just as well without him. Gerrit the barman and the Glaswegian manager were always scheming together about something or other in their incomprehensible accents. They were robbing the Cokers blind, skimming off the top, but Ramsay seemed oblivious to what was going on right beneath his nose.

Freda earnt only tips for her first night in the Sphinx because apparently she was no longer on probation and would get wages at the end of the week like everyone else, but that was fine as she still had most of the money she had earnt in the Amethyst. Some very odd types came to the Sphinx and kept her on her toes, in more ways than one. In the Ladies' powder room, she was always finding small cardboard pill boxes that had been abandoned. The traces of white powder in them were exactly the same as the stuff that she had found in Florence's packet of postcards. Tasted the same, too. 'It's dope,' one of the hostesses told her and then had to explain what dope was. A chill ran though Freda. She couldn't imagine Florence as a drug fiend. But then nor could she have imagined Florence disappearing into thin air.

Freda employed the same evasive tactics as she had at the Amethyst when it came to closing time and found a place to sleep in one of the storerooms. The Sphinx after hours felt very different to the Amethyst. There were strange creaks and taps and knocks all night long and she might as well have been walled up in an Egyptian tomb. There was a mummified cat – which was basically a dead cat – that sat on the bar and infected the air with its malevolence. She couldn't help but think of all the Ancient Egyptian mice it must have killed.

And then a miracle. An actual miracle. Not the resurrection of Florence, but something almost as wonderful.

The following day, Freda had been walking along Poland Street, where one of the hostesses at the Sphinx said there was a lodging house with decent rooms to be had. She was counting off the street numbers in her head when she heard a hoarse voice behind her cry, 'Freda! Freda!' and she turned to see a woman staring at her in amazement. The woman reached out a hand and touched Freda's cheek as if making sure that she was real. 'Freda, is that really you, pet?' she said. 'Of all the people in all the world, fancy running into you here,' and Freda found herself suddenly enveloped in ratty fur and the familiar scents of Habanita and Sarony cigarettes. It seemed Vanda was no longer in Grantham.

Vanda had a flat nearby in a dark alley that ran behind a row of restaurants. To get to it you had to weave your way past an obstacle course of galvanized dustbins giving off their scents of fish and offal and something darker and more offensive. 'They've been poisoning the rats,' Vanda said. The smell followed them into the building ('They've died in the walls') but had, thank goodness, mostly dissipated by the time they reached Vanda's front door on the third floor. 'It's quite a climb,' she said. 'I had one gentleman conk out on me on the second-floor landing. His heart. Dead as a dodo. Shame.

'Home sweet home,' she said, opening the door with a flourish.

And now Freda lived there, too. Somewhere to come home to every night and soak her aching feet in an enamel bowl of hot water, courtesy of a little gas water heater fixed to the wall next to the kitchen sink. There were two rooms – a kitchen and a bedroom. Freda slept in the kitchen, in a bed in an alcove, like a cupboard really but with a curtain on a string that she could pull across. To get to her little cubby-hole she had to negotiate a forest of Vanda's stockings and knickers ('trollies' she called them mysteriously) that were draped everywhere to dry.

Vanda and her friend Joan, who had the neighbouring flat, clacked up and down the stairs all night long, bringing 'gentleman friends' home with them, something Freda only discovered on her night off, because normally when she got back from the Sphinx the gentleman friends had gone and Joan and Vanda would be sitting in the damp, warm little kitchen, smoking cigarettes and sharing a bottle of gin. 'Mother's ruin,' Joan said cheerfully. She'd had a son in the Navy, she said. Freda didn't like to ask what had happened to Freda's Grantham baby.

Joan had a coarse face and strange hair, an unnatural black that she plastered down on her head to hide a bald patch, but she brought in Empire biscuits for Freda and made her cocoa. Joan had different gentleman friends to Vanda because she had what she referred to as 'specialities'.

'Like vanilla puffs and French fancies?' Freda asked, remembering Mr Birdwhistle and his cakes.

'Yes, pet, something like that,' Vanda said, still maintaining her role as the protector of Freda's innocence, not knowing that it had already been violated. Freda preferred to keep Owen Varley to herself, it seemed too late now for sympathy and understanding.

Sometimes the three of them played cards and Vanda reminisced about their time on the road with the Knits and what a card sharp Duncan had been. When Freda said that she had heard Duncan was in prison, Vanda said, 'You don't know, then?'

What didn't she know? 'Hung himself,' Vanda said, and Joan said, 'Christ,' even though she'd never known Duncan, and they toasted his memory in gin and cocoa and Empire biscuits.

The Sphinx had closed later than usual tonight. There was no sign of Ramsay, and the Dutch barman and the Glaswegian manager had stayed open to make some extra money for themselves.

Freda didn't like walking home in the dimly lit streets at this hour. There were always the unexpected she had to sidestep – people appearing out of nowhere like jack-in-the-boxes. Some wanted money or to sell something to her, but quite a few just wanted *her*. Tonight, she had the shivery feeling that someone was following her, but whenever she looked behind her she couldn't see anyone.

There was a cat yowling somewhere and she could hear the tail end of a drunken fight. A lot of singing and shouting as well, no doubt a consequence of alcohol, and she made her way through the side streets in an attempt to avoid whoever it was.

There *was* someone behind her – in a car that was creeping along slowly. The dance hostesses at the club were full of tales about girls being snatched off the street. Luckily, at that moment she ran into a group of drunken men and the car drove off. She wasn't much good with cars but she could have sworn it was the same one that she thought had taken Florence. A Wolseley Open Tourer, the man in the showroom had called it.

Not so lucky, it seemed, as one of the drunks caught her by the waist and lifted her up as if he were going to carry her off. The others just stood around laughing.

It never stopped, did it, Freda thought? Wherever she went, she was just some kind of trinket to be played with. First thing tomorrow she was going to arm herself with a knife.

She managed to twist out of the drunk's grip and run off. For a moment she worried that the pack was going to follow and hunt her down, but when she looked back they had disappeared.

'All right, pet?' Vanda asked when she came in. 'I stayed up for you. It's wild on the streets tonight. All kinds of strange folk out there. I'll make some tea, shall I?'

Folderol

Ramsay was hoping that at least the stupid Baby Party might give him some fresh material. The Bright Young Things were idiotic lotus eaters, but their inane excesses could provide a bitingly cynical chapter in *The Age of Glitter*. Not to mention the potential for piling up the corpses, because someone *ought* to murder those awful people, even if only between the pages of a book.

An effete-looking youth who had crammed himself awkwardly into a large perambulator was pushed past Ramsay by a hirsute nanny, who looked like a ship's stoker. The youth, in what appeared to be a bespoke romper-suit, was sucking on a baby's feeding bottle. Nearby, a girl whom Ramsay knew to be the daughter of a prominent member of the Cabinet was crawling on the grass with a comforter plugged in her mouth. She took it out occasionally in order to cry 'Waa-waa-waa!' as if in distress. Eventually, she was 'rescued' by another nanny, actually a member of the Brigade of Guards – Ramsay recognized him from the Sphinx – dressed in a nurse-like uniform apparently requisitioned from Norland College.

Whoever the uniform belonged to originally must have been awfully big, Ramsay thought. But then nannies often were. They had been in possession of one themselves for a while in their far-off Scottish childhood, long before Kitty was born. The woman – a giant – was later convicted of attempting to murder one of her charges. It could easily have been one of them. 'Lucky escape,' Nellie had said, unperturbed.

The Baby Party was being held in a garden square that fronted one of London's grandest houses in Lowndes Square. The square was brilliantly lit by strings of light bulbs, illuminating the antic parade of people still arriving – in perambulators or on scooters and trikes, dressed in baby clothes, waving rattles or sucking on comforters while clutching an assortment of dolls, teddy bears, toy boats and so on, so that it looked as though they had just come from raiding Hamley's. Once in the gardens, they rode wooden rocking-horses and scooters, bowled hoops or took it in turns to ride on a sorrowful troupe of seaside donkeys, all the while screaming with excitement.

Ramsay held himself aloof from this unabashed tomfoolery. Vivian Quinn's much-trumpeted (by himself) novel, *Folderol* (the title didn't get any less stupid), was about 'Bright Young People become tarnished sort of stuff', wasn't it? If Quinn could do it, then Ramsay could, too. And if he got his skates on, he could do it first and everyone would think that Quinn's novel was just a copy-cat – or an homage, which would be even better, really.

A donkey brayed loudly, or perhaps it was one of the party-goers, it was hard to distinguish the one from the other. These people were self-indulgent idiots. Edith had once encountered a posse of such women grubbing around on their knees on the dirty pavement at Seven Dials – they had a fad for scavenger hunts at the time. 'I say,' one of the girls had said to her, 'you haven't come across a stuffed wombat, have you?' Edith, with cunning presence of mind, told the girls that she believed they had one in the keep of the Tower of London, information that sent them yelping off towards the Embankment like the frenzied Thracian Maenads in pursuit of Orpheus.

'Is there really a stuffed wombat in the Tower of London?' Kitty asked. She had no idea what a wombat was. She had imagined a large bat – a female one, perhaps.

According to the papers next morning, a group of the Bright Young People had narrowly escaped arrest when trying to break into the Tower in an apparent attempt to steal the Crown Jewels as a prank. They were let off with an admonition.

'Should chop their heads off,' was Nellie's judgement.

When the scavenger hunts had grown stale, the hateful Bright Young Things had moved on to throwing parties, the more ludicrously exhibitionist the better, like this Baby Party with its dress code of romper-suits, matinée jackets and sun bonnets. Ramsay would rather have died than complied with it.

Of course, the Bright Young Things were not the only ones seemingly obsessed with ludic diversions. There were parties everywhere, all the time – 'snow' parties in Mayfair, opium parties ferried into Limehouse from the West End, orgies in Soho, cocktail parties in Knightsbridge, and bacchanalia of all kinds behind the closed doors of private houses, like the one in Piccadilly that Rollo had taken Shirley to the previous evening. The trick of this particular party, she said, was to stay in disguise as long as possible, and to that end people had brought several changes of costume with them.

Shirley, who thanks to her acquaintance with Rollo moved in more exalted circles than the rest of the Cokers, reported that she had been to another party last week in Piccadilly where the Prince of Wales had begun the evening as Bonnie Prince Charlie before donning the white robes of the Ku Klux Klan and then ending as a Chinese coolie. Three blind mice, a pair of white ostriches, Lord Blandford as a female Channel swimmer, Lord Berne as a 'monkey bride', complete with veil, Winston Churchill as Nero. 'Decadence piled upon decadence,' Shirley said gleefully. 'Oh, and, of course,' she added, 'your friend Vivian Quinn was there.'

'*Not* my friend,' Ramsay muttered.

Everyone at the Baby Party appeared to be already very drunk when Ramsay arrived. Liquor was being served in nursery mugs and the 'bar' was a baby's playpen. A cocktail had supposedly been designed especially for the occasion by the barman at the Ritz. It was called Mother's Milk – crème de cacao, gin, sugar and cream – and just the name of it made Ramsay feel squeamish, certainly when applied to his own mother – although, in fact, only Niven had gulped at Nellie's breast, the rest of them had had to survive as best they could on Cow and Gate and Nestlé's formula, Nellie having decided that she was hampered enough in life without having a child more or less permanently attached to her like an oyster to a rock.

Despite the name, the drink slid easily down Ramsay's throat without giving much of a clue as to its alcoholic content. The nursery mugs were small and he had already quaffed the contents of Little Miss Muffet and Old Mother Hubbard and was clinging on to Baa Baa Black Sheep as if it were a life raft. So far, he had – thank God – successfully managed to avoid encountering Pamela Berowne, the hostess of the party.

How his brother would abhor this lunacy, Ramsay thought, as a vigorous game of Catch started around him. Ramsay envied Niven his certainty – he had Passchendaele at his back to give credence to his simmering outrage, whereas Ramsay had only a Swiss sanatorium and a burning desire to be acknowledged on a wider stage. Or any stage at all.

He sought refuge in a reclusive corner of privet to make notes. He carried a notebook everywhere with him now, although he was currently far too drunk to write anything coherent and his jottings consisted mostly of repeatedly writing the word 'IDIOTS!' in capital letters. A passing waiter with a tray found him and, with an impassive face, asked, 'More Mother's Milk, sir?' Ramsay lifted a Jack and Jill mug off the tray. How would he engineer a murder here, he wondered? A fictional murder, but nonetheless you had to sort of act it out in your head, didn't you? A strangling in the shrubbery, a bomb that detonated on a hopscotch square? Poison in the Mother's Milk was the easiest one, he supposed.

Poison was easy to get hold of, you just went to the chemist or the ironmonger and said you had rats. There was an ironmongery next door to the Amethyst, part of the complex secret escape route, and he resolved to purchase some poison tomorrow. Strychnine, he imagined. Or arsenic. Cyanide, perhaps. They were all attractive words. He was intrigued to know what it would feel like to buy what was, to all intents and purposes, a murder weapon. Would he feel a twinge of guilt? But it would be quite legitimate – after all, they did have rats and they couldn't just expect Phyllis to keep on bludgeoning them to death all the time, although she had seemed to enjoy it in a way that had slightly unnerved Ramsay.

It dawned rather slowly on Ramsay how drunk he was, having by now imbibed almost the entire Mother Goose oeuvre as well as consuming the five-shilling packet of dope that he had armoured himself with before coming here. Nor was he any longer safe in the privet, as people with stupid names like Bunny, Bingo, Pingo and Pongo suddenly descended on him, mistaking him for a participant in their hide-and-seek game. They dragged him out into the open and it took a short yet vigorous bout of fisticuffs to escape them. Ramsay wasn't as good a scrapper as Niven, but he had spent time in the ring at Fettes, not always defeated, and, coached by Niven, was not afraid to face his enemies if there was no alternative.

As the evening dragged on, the place increasingly resembled Bedlam. It was when Ramsay found himself assisting the under-butler of the 'great house' with the task of ejecting a reluctant donkey from the library (no mean feat) that he decided he couldn't cope with the burlesque any more. He was about to call it a night when he caught sight of the enemy approaching – a two-pronged attack, with Pamela Berowne galloping towards him on his left flank and Vivian Quinn cruising towards him at a more leisurely pace on his right, the usual self-satisfied smirk on his face. Quinn, Ramsay noticed, was caparisoned in the costume of a Spanish matador.

Evasive action was called for. Ramsay sprinted away across the gardens, Pamela baying in pursuit. He had to negotiate a course of random obstacles – baby dolls that had been callously abandoned, the rocker off a rocking-horse, a pushchair broken when it had been used in a wheelbarrow race – and had just jumped over a series of box hedges like a nifty steeplechaser, almost making it to the iron railings at the boundary, when he was brought down at full tilt by a recumbent toy scooter and was sent sprawling on the grass.

'Mine, I think,' a triumphant Quinn said to Pamela Berowne, placing a foot on a spreadeagled Ramsay like a big-game hunter claiming his quarry. Or indeed, a bull-fighter who had conquered a bull. Pamela conceded before stomping off. She seemed to concede defeat rather easily, in Ramsay's opinion. Although relieved to have escaped being wooed by her, he liked to think that if he was keen on someone he would put up more of a fight.

'I belong to neither of you,' he said irritably as Quinn helped him to his feet.

'No, you're right, Coker, you don't,' Quinn said. 'You belong to Azzopardi.'

'Oh, what fools these mortals be, eh, Coker?' Quinn said as they lit cigarettes on the edge of the square.

'Why are you dressed as a matador, Quinn? The dress code was "Infant".'

'I'm going on somewhere grown-up afterwards.'

'Now you've mentioned grown-ups, Quinn, I'd like to know why you abandoned me at the spieler last week? I'm curious, all this go-between stuff with Azzopardi. Like a lackey. Or a lapdog. What was it – did the Maltese pay you to take me to Belgravia?'

Quinn remained unruffled. It was difficult to insult him, he seemed to take everything as a compliment. 'I think all that evil-criminal-underworld stuff's rather attractive, don't you? A frisson of danger.' He pretended to shiver, like a ham actor. 'Especially,' he continued, 'if you're using it in a novel.' He paused to make sure he would have an effect on Ramsay. 'As I have, you know.'

No, Ramsay howled silently. Quinn had no claim on the underworld, no understanding of it at all, whereas Ramsay lived amongst it every night. It belonged to him. He said nothing. He wouldn't satisfy Quinn with his outrage.

'Either that or an exposé,' Quinn carried on blithely. '*The Times* has commissioned a long article from me – I have contacts there. *The vicious individuals who rule the London underworld –* that sort of thing. Serious journalism.'

'You – a serious journalist?'

'We all have our ambitions, Coker. Some more attainable than others. Look at you, you're hoping to be a bestselling author. Good luck with that, old chum.' Quinn hooted with laughter and placed his arm around Ramsay's shoulders. Ramsay shook him off irritably.

'So, has it been accepted by a publisher? Your novel.' Ramsay refused to say its stupid title.

'No, no one's seen it, absolutely no one. I would hate to hand over something that wasn't perfect. It's sitting on my desk, waiting for a final polish. It won't be a problem, it's brilliant, though I say so myself. You haven't said whether you like my costume? It's called a *traje de luces* – a "suit of lights". Have you been to Spain, Coker? No, you haven't, have you? Actually, when I was in Paris I had a very interesting discussion about bullfighting with an American chap called Hemingway, a journalist, writes stories. He's got a novel coming out this year all about *los toros*, you should keep an eye out for it, he's going to be a real name—'

'Fuck off, Quinn!'

'Actually, I have a message for you from Azzopardi,' Quinn said, unfazed. 'He's looking for you.'

'I suppose he wants his money,' Ramsay said miserably.

'Nothing as common as that.'

'What, then?'

'I don't know. Some kind of forfeit.'

'Forfeit? What does that mean?'

'You, I expect, Coker. He probably wants you. You know – an old queen looking to press the flesh of a young prince. Probably just wants to spend a night with you as payment.'

Quinn's cynical mask slipped for a moment and he looked pained. Did Azzopardi have a hold on him as well? Quinn had a taste for some queer things – perhaps Azzopardi supplied them. Or blackmail. A man like Quinn invited blackmail.

'Anyway, must go,' Quinn said, the puckish mask back in place. 'I've a column to fill. *The Bright Young People surpassed themselves in their whimsical frolics tonight. Ramsay, younger son of famous nightclub owner Nellie Coker, was spotted enjoying the fun and games.* What do you think?'

'Don't you dare write anything about me!' Ramsay finally snapped and threw a punch, badly aimed as he was awash with Mother's Milk. The blow found only empty air as Quinn, surprisingly light on his feet, had already neatly sidestepped out of the way.

'You'd better be off before you do yourself an injury, Coker,' he laughed. 'Anyway, I'm going back to the party. Pingo's promised to play ball with me. Or was it Bingo? I don't suppose it matters. I'm sure it will be an *explosive* game. 'Night, Coker.'

He did a silly little skip as he returned in the direction of the gardens they had just left.

Ramsay thought he might kill Quinn. Stab him in the heart and watch him realize what a fool he was as his life ebbed away.

As soon as Ramsay parted company with Quinn it began to rain and, inevitably, there wasn't a cab to be found.

He turned a corner and noticed the car parked beneath a streetlight that illuminated its shiny yellow bodywork. He knew very well whose car it was. He panicked and spun round, ready to run, but, as in a nightmare, there was Azzopardi himself, blocking his way.

'Going somewhere, Mr Coker?' He grinned and waggled a finger at Ramsay, a gesture that managed to be both comic and horribly menacing at the same time. The reckoning was upon him, Ramsay thought, his stomach swooping high and then falling into the abyss. Azzopardi opened the car door and said, 'Shall we go for a little drive, Mr Coker? You'll be pleased to hear that I've thought of a way for you to repay me.'

Azzopardi dropped Ramsay off in the same place that he had picked him up and drove away. Ramsay felt so weak that he had to sit on the kerb to recover. He had promised Azzopardi the money he owed him, telling him that he would go to Nellie and ask her to give it to him. (Would she? Quite possibly not.) Or Niven, Niven had money, his brother would see him out of this hole. Surely? But no, it was too late for all that, Azzopardi had said.

Quinn was wrong – Azzopardi didn't want Ramsay as a for-feit. (Would he have agreed if it meant it would clear his debts? It was an unanswered question.) But Quinn had been right about one thing – Azzopardi didn't want money. He wanted something that he considered to be much more valuable. He wanted paper.

Ramsay lit a cigarette and as he looked up from the flame of the match his eye was caught by something on the other side of the street. It was that dratted Egyptian mummy from ten days ago again. Not lurching comically along like last time, but strid-ing quite purposefully in the direction of Lowndes Square as if it were late for something. The Baby Party, presumably, although the dress code had been ignored. Whoever was inside all those bandages must be particularly fond of their horrid costume.

The figure no longer struck supernatural dread in him – it was absurd to be frightened of such a stupid mannequin, he thought. But then, as if it had heard him, the mummy stopped in its tracks and turned to stare at him. Its eyes were almost entirely concealed by the bandages around its head but nonetheless Ramsay could feel the malice in its gaze. And then, horror, it stepped off the kerb and began to cross the road towards him. He didn't wait to find out its intentions but scrambled up from the pavement and ran.

Quinn walked slowly around Lowndes Square. He, too, was try-ing to clear his head. He'd ingested rather a lot of dope and was beginning to feel quite unwell. Someone had told him that some of the stuff doing the rounds wasn't good and he wondered if that was the problem.

Or maybe it was because he was feeling guilty – remorse was an unaccustomed emotion for him. He had delivered the head of John the Baptist.

He had taken Ramsay to that spieler in Belgravia at Azzopardi's request. Azzopardi had a hold on him, of course. Photographs, taken secretly, and so on. He would be finished for ever if they got into the hands of his fellow members of the press. He'd end his days in a grubby garret in Soho, living off the charity of some old queen, or, worse, back in Kettering, living off the charity of his ageing, appalled parents.

Someone in fancy dress approached. The Invisible Man. Or, more likely, an Egyptian mummy, as people were so obsessed by Egypticity. Quinn presumed it was a man as the figure was quite tall. 'Good costume,' he said politely as it drew near. Did it want something from him? An unlit cigarette dangled from its mouth, or rather from a hole in the bandages where he presumed its mouth was.

'Do you want a light?' Quinn asked. The mummy didn't respond but Quinn felt impelled to pursue a conversation with it.

'Are you going to the Baby Party?' he asked, indicating the gardens with a nod. 'They're all dressed like toddlers in there. Behaving like them as well. Biggest bunch of nincompoops in London.'

The mummy spoke, slightly muffled on account of the bandages.

'I'm sorry, I didn't quite catch that. Oh – am I Vivian Quinn? Yes, yes, indeed, the one and only.' He preened a little, he loved being recognized. 'Do I know you?' he asked. 'Are you the—?'

The question remained unfinished. Quinn looked down at the large knife sticking out of his stomach in disbelief. A *coup de grâce*. It was not the bull who had been gored, it was the matador.

Adieu, Adieu, Adieu

It was almost dark by the time they were back at the car.

By the light of a torch, Gwendolen read out instructions from the handbook while Frobisher wielded the starting handle, and then, of course, there was a whole new palaver over getting the headlights to work. By the time the road was moving beneath their wheels once again it was the deep dark that you only found in the countryside and they were totally reliant upon the weak beams. Gwendolen suspected her dreams would be haunted by the new vocabulary of 'strangler wire' and 'throttle' and 'double declutch', but it was exciting just now to be driving in the night-time, and they had been comfortably silent for a while when suddenly those same weak headlights were illuminating a road full of—

'Rabbits! Oh, Lord, rabbits everywhere, Inspector!' It was as if an entire warren had been tipped out on to the tarmacadam. Frobisher braked hard, jerking them both forward. Gwendolen wasn't sure if any had gone beneath their wheels, she imagined the crunch of tiny bones, but the rabbits seemed unconcerned about the juggernaut that had borne down on them. The dog, asleep again, had woken up with an excited start at the word 'rabbits'. Not such a city dog, perhaps.

The rabbits didn't move. Gwendolen supposed that they hadn't yet adjusted their lives to the terror of the modern combustion engine. Perhaps they never would. There were babies, too – adorable little things, frolicking innocently – although Frobisher seemed unmoved by their charms. He was a countryman, she reminded herself, he had grown up looking on rabbits as sport or food or both.

The rabbits remained unconcerned, claiming the road as their own, and eventually Gwendolen had to get out of the car and shoo them away, while Frobisher kept the engine running – God forbid they would have to start it up again. Eventually, the shooing being ineffective, she decided the best thing was to walk ahead of the car as someone would have had to do in the early days of motoring to warn horses and pedestrians, rather than rabbits, of the oncoming monster. There was a fairy tale she had once read about herding rabbits – or was it hares? Hares, more likely. It was considered one of those impossible tasks that the protagonist had to perform in order to be released from a spell.

She was laughing when she climbed back in the passenger seat and said, 'Well, that was silly.' She felt, suddenly, rather ridiculously fond of Frobisher and if he hadn't been gripping the steering wheel she might have reached over and touched his hand, or even his cheek. She would let him kiss her when they were back in London. Of course, he might not want to.

They proceeded cautiously, but there were no more rabbits. 'I shall expect to have you home by midnight,' he said.

'Before the car turns into a pumpkin?'

'Quite.'

She was prompted to ask, 'And where do you live, Inspector?'

'Ealing,' he replied, after a little beat. She had never met anyone so unwilling to divulge information about themselves.

'Ealing? In a house?' She had imagined him in a bachelor flat in Marylebone or Kentish Town.

'Yes, a house. Do you find that odd?'

She was thoughtful for a moment. 'With someone?'

'I'm sorry?'

'Do you share the house with someone, another person?'

There was a long silence. Perhaps he was hoping for more rabbits to appear or indeed any diversion to delay replying, but there was no wildlife to provide him with respite and eventually he said, 'Just my wife.'

'Your wife?' The spell was broken.

'Miss Kelling . . . Gwendolen . . .'

'Yes, Inspector?' she said coolly. They had exchanged barely a word since the revelation of the wife. What was there to say? She had been under the misapprehension that she was being courted (she who had had no wish to be courted!), that he was, indeed, in a position to court her, but this had turned out not to be the case at all. He had a wife! He was no better than a common Casanova.

'I'm sorry if I've misled you in some way,' he said. Do keep your eyes on the road, she thought. Was he pitying her? He'd better not be. He frowned as if in exquisite pain and said, 'A sin of omission, not commission.'

'Pah. Sophistry.'

'My wife,' he said, 'my marriage . . .' He stuttered to a halt.

'Inspector, I have no desire to know the details of your marital arrangements. There is nothing for you to explain as nothing has been said between us. As you said earlier, I am "police business". If there were implications that were misinterpreted, they are already forgotten. Let's not talk about it again.'

'Gwendolen—'

'No.' Her heart was closed against him. Was there a bigger fool on earth than herself?

After a painfully long silence he said, 'I presume you will be returning to York soon. The Library must miss you.'

'Oh, for heaven's sake,' she snapped, 'I'm not a librarian.'

'Not a librarian?' he puzzled. 'What are you, then?'

A woman, she thought crossly.

'I used to be a librarian until very recently,' she conceded. 'But I inherited money.'

He made to say something but she held up her hand and said, 'That's the end of the subject. And if you don't mind, I would rather you didn't say anything else to me for the rest of the journey.'

Frobisher did indeed get her home before midnight and for the sake of secrecy he dropped her off two streets away – the Crystal Cup was busy at this hour and it would be an unpleasant ending to an unpleasant drive if she was spotted in his company. 'Don't open the door for me,' she said, 'you may be seen by someone.'

She looked back after a few yards. The dog was peering wistfully at her out of the rear window of the car. It was his wife's dog, she thought.

She greeted the Crystal Club's doormen as she passed them on her way to the flat. 'Busy tonight?' she enquired, as if nothing was wrong. 'Very,' they assured. 'Did you have a nice day off, Miss Kelling?' one of them asked. He was a bit of a brute and seemed to be rather soft on her. She enjoyed imagining him in the ring with Frobisher. Frobisher did not come out of the bout well.

'Very nice, thank you,' she said.

As soon as she was through the door of her flat, Gwendolen flung off her hat and shoes and coat. She could feel the dirt of the road on her, she must have a bath. She was sullying the hitherto unsullied pink, not just with dirt but with the whole humiliating to-do with Frobisher. He was right, of course, which made her even more angry with herself – he had said nothing, done nothing that could be truly construed as courtship. They had misinterpreted each other.

She opened the cocktail cabinet, glad now that it wasn't a wireless, and poured herself a brandy, the usual remedy in the face of calamity.

There was a knock at the door. She was sure she had locked the street door, how had someone accessed her flat? And it was gone midnight, who on earth could it be at this hour? It must be Frobisher, who else? He had probably come to beg her forgiveness, to explain his behaviour. To explain his *wife*.

It wasn't that she didn't have sympathy for people – of both sexes – who were stuck in loveless marriages. Divorce was nigh impossible and adultery was inevitable sometimes and not always to be so frowned on. She had occasionally thought that she would herself be willing to be a man's mistress but not his wife, but one should be open and honest about such things, not sweep the poor wife under the carpet as if she didn't exist. Perhaps she was sick? Or mad. Like Rochester's wife in *Jane Eyre*. But that was still no excuse for erasing her. No, Gwendolen thought, she was not going to look to romantic novels for a solution. They dispensed the worst kind of advice (love). She poured another brandy, on the generous side, and took a big gulp.

The knock came again. Why couldn't he leave her alone, she fumed, and yanked open the door, ready for battle.

A surprised Niven stood there. He tipped his hat and laughed and said, 'You look fit to murder.'

'I believe I am.'

'Not me, I hope,' he said.

'No, not you. Why don't you come in?'

He removed his hat and followed her down the narrow hallway. It felt like letting in a tiger.

When they reached the living room he made a face and said, 'I see my mother wasn't exaggerating when she said everything was pink up here.'

'It's growing on me. I have had rather a long and trying day. I was having a drink and then I was about to have a hot bath. Will you join me?'

'In which? The drink or the hot bath?'

She poured a whisky and handed it to him and then poured one for herself. Niven seemed like someone who liked a good malt. Her father had. 'Both, if you wish,' she said.

'You are continually full of surprises, Miss Kelling.'

'But I must warn you – I am not a virgin.'

'As I said, full of surprises.'

'I'm not a librarian either.'

Surprise!

It took Gwendolen some moments to realize that it was the insistent ringing of the doorbell that had woken her. She opened her eyes to daylight and a splitting headache and a stale stomach. It appeared that she had drunk herself into oblivion the previous evening and must have retired, not very gracefully, to bed in a stupor. Before coming to London she drank so little she may as well have signed the pledge. She wondered what the Misses Tate, Rogerson and Shaw would make of such alcoholic debauchery. Their idea of giddy indulgence was the 'small sherry' that was drunk after closing time in the Library on Christmas Eve.

Debauchery! Her memory was unpleasantly revived by the prompt of the doorbell ringing again. Niven, dear God. Where was he? Not in the bed she leapt out of. No sign of him at all, in fact. No one else had slept in her bed, no one had stayed to make tea for her or bring in a tray of breakfast. No one had sullied the pink with their sex. Gwendolen herself seemed similarly untouched.

She reached for her dressing-gown, not her felted woollen one that had seen her through the war and its aftermath but a lovely silk peignoir, courtesy of Liberty's. It was a partner for the night-gown beneath it, silk garments fit for a bridal trousseau. Gwendolen had no intention of ever honeymooning but she didn't see why she shouldn't have the trousseau.

She paused on her way to answer the door and considered that nightgown. She had no memory of donning it last night.

Nor of removing the blue sailor dress she had been wearing for her outing with Frobisher. She glanced round the bedroom – the dress was hanging neatly over the back of a chair. She was fairly sure that in the extremis of inebriation she wouldn't have bothered to fold her clothes. What *had* occurred between her and Niven? What had she told him, *in vino veritas*? Nothing about Frobisher, she hoped.

The doorbell rang insistently.

She was expecting, at worst, Kitty, or, at best, Niven (although perhaps that should be the other way round), but it was neither, it was the mother of both.

'Did I wake you?' Nellie said. 'I'm so sorry, I didn't mean to surprise you. I just had some bits and pieces of business to do with the club to go over with you. Are you all right, Miss Kelling? You seem rather flustered.'

Nellie returned to the Bentley, parked outside the Crystal Club, and ruminated quietly in the back while Hawker waited patiently for instructions. Some days there was no point in rushing her.

Gwendolen Kelling, *en déshabillé*, a French term Nellie rather liked, although not one she had learnt in her convent school. It was thanks to Landor that she knew Niven had turned up at Gwendolen Kelling's flat at midnight and had not left until three in the morning. Nellie didn't need to guess what had gone on. But Niven, of all people, what was he playing at? First Maddox and Edith making an unlikely pairing and now Gwendolen Kelling and Niven. Were all her children betraying her, one by one?

Nellie liked to think that, thanks to Landor, she knew everything that Gwendolen Kelling did, everywhere she went. Yesterday, according to Landor, she had met with Frobisher in Paddington station. 'The café,' he had reported.

'The Refreshment Rooms?' Nellie had met a man there once herself. You expected to be anonymous in a railway station but there was always someone.

They were planning a little outing in his car, Landor had said.

'It was Miss Kelling's day off,' an imperturbable Nellie said. 'I expect she felt like some fresh air.'

'They were very friendly,' Landor said. 'Seemed close, seemed, you know . . .'

'I do,' Nellie said.

'Don't know where Kelling and Frobisher went on their little outing, of course,' Landor said. 'Would have to have a car of my own for that. Or borrow your Bentley.'

'In your dreams,' Nellie said.

'And then she comes back and spends the night with your boy.'

'Which boy?' Nellie puzzled.

'You've only got two,' Landor said, 'unless you've got a secret love child.'

'Well,' Nellie said.

'He beat me up, you know, your boy.'

'Someone should,' Nellie said.

Hawker glanced in his rear-view mirror at Nellie. You could almost see her brain working, he thought. It was terrifying.

He waited patiently until finally she said, 'Home,' and added, 'Hanover Terrace,' as if he might not know where she lived.

A Tryst

The benches surrounding the boating lake in Regent's Park were jostling for a supporting role in the Coker drama. Sitting on one now was a pale, still-frail Edith. 'Going out to get a bit of fresh air and exercise,' she told the cook, who had made a futile attempt to bar her exit from the house. Nellie was still insisting on bed rest for Edith, and in her absence this morning the cook had been charged with the impossible task of corralling Edith.

'She looks as if a puff of wind would blow her over,' the cook said to Phyllis. 'You'd better follow her. If anything happens to her we'll be blamed.'

You'll be blamed, Phyllis thought, but said, 'I'll get my coat.'

Phyllis wasn't the kind of girl you noticed. A wasted gift, her mother and aunt thought, given their trade. Phyllis didn't need to lurk behind trees or duck beneath hedges, she could simply stand in plain sight and yet not be seen. 'It's like looking at water,' her Auntie Agnes said.

Invisible Phyllis watched as a feeble Edith teetered along the path and dropped on to the first bench that she came to. 'Blood poisoning' was what had laid her low, apparently, and Phyllis's mother had said, 'Is *that* what they call it?' so Phyllis had a good idea what had gone on with Edith. Although Phyllis lodged in the rather spartan attic of the Hanover Terrace house, she still made regular visits home to Whitechapel. 'Like a little go-between,' her

361

mother said fondly. The family always welcomed news of Nellie. Who wouldn't?

It wasn't long before Edith was joined on the bench by a man. The man had a small dog on a lead that sat between them, looking from one to the other as they talked, as if following the conversation. And talk they did, for quite a long time, very serious. He frowned a lot, while Edith drooped, not even a smile between them, and then eventually he helped her to her feet and walked her to the park gates. He escorted her across the road, putting his hand up like a policeman to stop the traffic so that he had time to get the invalid Edith to the other side without them both being run over. They made their farewells to each other, very polite, and he watched her enter the house, as if he were worried something might happen to her in the last few yards between the front garden and the door. A proper gentleman, Phyllis thought. A policeman though, definitely. Given her ancestry she could spot one a mile off.

Phyllis lingered in the fresh air for a little longer. She had so much work in Hanover Terrace that she was beginning to wonder if the strait and narrow was all it was cracked up to be, when you could lift a wallet from a pocket and live off the contents for a week.

Despite the cook's objections, Phyllis was determined to tell Nellie about Edith's little escapade when she returned. She liked being in Nellie Coker's good books.

'By the way,' Phyllis said by way of greeting, 'you've got rats.'

'Tell me about it,' Nellie said.

'So who was it? Who did she meet?' Nellie asked when news of Edith's adventure in the park had been delivered. 'Maddox?'

'No,' Phyllis said. 'Not *him*. He's got the black heart of a Barbary pirate.' The girl read books. Nellie sighed.

'So, who was it if it wasn't Maddox?'

'You'll never guess.'

'No, clearly I won't. So, tell me.'

The Waste Land

Frobisher made his way on foot towards Tower Bridge. The outing to Oxford yesterday had made him averse to getting back behind the steering wheel, as if the Austin itself had somehow been responsible for the disastrous outcome of his day with Gwendolen Kelling. He cringed at the memory. A *wife?* The word reverberated in his brain. He was haunted, too, by the look of disbelief on her face. Distaste, as well, as if he were the worst of Lotharios. Well, perhaps he was. His actions may not have been those of a lover, but his intentions were.

For a moment she had provided him with a glimpse of a different life, an ease that was impossible in his present circumstances. He thought of Oxford, the dimming of the day, of holding her hand at the end of the play. A dream, and now the dream was over and he must concentrate on his real life, on his work, rather than trying to find a way to redeem himself in her eyes.

The dog bounced along beside him on the pavement as he followed the river. Pierrot, a silly name, but the dog had been without one until the moment Gwendolen had asked what it was called, and it was the first thing that had come to mind. It had simply been 'the dog' until then, which was how he still thought of it.

The dog had not received the welcome he had hoped for. Lottie had developed a tremendous antipathy to it since he brought it home just over a week ago, apparently under the impression that he was trying to replace Manon in her affections. He had been trying to give her something to love, so he supposed

363

she was right. The dog was now banned from Ealing when he was absent.

Frobisher couldn't think what else to do with it and there seemed to be no rule that prevented you from bringing your dog to work in Bow Street, presumably because it had never crossed anyone's mind that a rule was needed. 'A dog?' the desk sergeant had queried mildly when Frobisher came in this morning, the dog tucked beneath one arm to keep it from excitement at these novel surroundings.

'Yes, a dog, sergeant,' Frobisher said, without elaboration. In the docks in the north, the railway police trained Alsatians for protection. Frobisher was attracted by the idea of patrolling the streets of London with a dog by his side. Obviously not this dog. It had long since been stripped of its Pierrot costume but it was still a small dog, inclined to perform tricks without warning.

Another body had been harvested from the Thames, he was told, and awaited him in the Dead Man's Hole. There had been no other information and Frobisher, fearing another mermaid had been netted, had taken it upon himself to investigate.

When he arrived at Tower Bridge, the morgue attendant was on the small stone platform on which the drowned were landed. Frobisher began to descend the wet, slippery steps – there had been a particularly high tide and the swollen river was in flood. 'Only just managed to catch him,' the morgue attendant laughed, drawing on the cigarette that seemed to be permanently attached to his lower lip. 'He was going past like a clipper. Haven't moved him down into the morgue yet,' he added. His long grappling pole was still in his hand as if he were ready to grab the next unfortunate as they sailed past.

'Him? Not a girl, then?'

'A girl? No, some bloke in fancy dress.'

Oh, dear God, not another bloody Pierrot, Frobisher thought. 'A Pierrot?' he asked, still picking his way down the steps. The dog pricked up its ears. It surely hadn't learnt its name already?

'A Pierrot?' the attendant said as Frobisher reached him in the wake of the dog. 'No – see for yourself, guv.'

The dog sniffed the air, excited by the stench of river water and death. Frobisher held it back from investigating the body that was flopped, limp as a lifeless fish, on the stone.

Not a fish, nor a mermaid. Not a girl either. Not a Pierrot. A matador.

'Well, that's a first,' Frobisher said.

On his return to Bow Street, he was informed that there was a woman waiting for him. 'Put her in your office, sir,' the desk sergeant said. 'She was having a bit of a turn.'

'Does the woman have a name?'

'Mrs Taylor.'

Frobisher left the dog in the desk sergeant's willing custody. He liked dogs, he said. Frobisher wondered if the desk sergeant would be willing to take the dog on permanently and was surprised by the little pang in his heart at the thought of giving him up.

Opening the door to his office, Frobisher looked in cautiously – a woman 'having a bit of a turn' could be interpreted any number of ways. In this case it meant a weary-looking one who seemed wedded to the handkerchief with which she was dabbing quiet tears away.

He ducked back out and said to the desk sergeant, 'Make Mrs Taylor a cup of tea, will you, sergeant?' The sergeant sighed at being reduced to the role of tea-boy. 'Quick as you can,' Frobisher added, with no sympathy. 'Is Maddox in?'

'No, sir.'

A pot of tea was duly delivered, no cup provided for himself, Frobisher noticed.

Mrs Taylor was from Colchester, she said, and her daughter, Minnie – Wilhelmina – had run away from home three weeks ago. Mrs Taylor had remarried recently and 'my Harold' and

Minnie did not get along. Frobisher thought of Manon. Would he have got along with her if she had lived, he wondered? Mrs Taylor was sure that Minnie had been seduced by the bright lights of London. Minnie would be fifteen next month and wanted to be 'on the stage'.

Frobisher sighed inwardly. Why did these girls all want to be famous? It was almost impossible for them to achieve their ambitions. Why not set their sights on something more worthwhile (if equally difficult to attain) – becoming a doctor or a lawyer, for example? Frobisher was not at all averse to women taking on masculine roles, he suspected they would be rather good at them. They had managed well in the war, after all. He thought of Gwendolen. He could imagine her in the police, giving crisp orders to all and sundry. She would sort Bow Street out better than he appeared to be managing to at the moment. And look at Nellie Coker, she could probably run the country, although not necessarily for its own good.

He wrote down 'Wilhelmina Taylor, known as Minnie' but Mrs Taylor, monitoring his notetaking, corrected him. 'Taylor's my new name, my married name,' she said. 'Minnie has her dad's name – Carter, he died at Amiens. He was a good man. Harold is, too,' she added hastily, as if her second husband's failure to die in the war were a flaw in his character.

'I don't doubt it, Mrs Taylor,' Frobisher said, crossing out 'Taylor' and writing 'Carter' in its place.

'It's just that Minnie's got used to a bit too much freedom and Harold doesn't think it's right.'

'Of course,' Frobisher soothed. 'Tell me, Mrs Taylor, does Minnie wear any jewellery? A crucifix, for example, or a locket?' He was relieved that Mrs Taylor did not see the implication of the question.

'She has a locket, a silver one. Given to her by her godmother, my sister.'

'Anything in the locket?' Frobisher asked. He closed his eyes for a second. He didn't want to know. The woman's tears were noisier now. 'A photograph of me,' she said. 'We're close. Just because she's run away doesn't mean she doesn't love me, you know.'

'Of course not. And . . . just you, Mrs Taylor – no other photograph in the locket?'

She gave a little laugh that prompted more tears. 'Our old dog, Sammy. Died a few months ago. Minnie loved that dog.'

'A terrier?' Frobisher asked, his voice barely above a murmur. He was relieved he had left the dog with the desk sergeant. He realized that it bore a remarkable resemblance to the dog in the photograph in the locket.

'Yes, Sammy was a terrier,' Mrs Taylor said. 'Why do you ask?'

The locket, the crucifix, the spectacles and the solitary silver shoe now all lay in cardboard boxes in a cabinet in the evidence room. It was fast becoming a reliquary. Frobisher retrieved the box that contained the locket. He braced himself for maternal grief and opened it. 'Is this Minnie's locket?' he asked gently as he showed the contents of the box to Mrs Taylor.

She surprised him by snatching the locket eagerly from the box and cradling it in her hand. 'Oh, you've found her!' she said. 'Thank you, thank you. Where is she? Is she here? Oh, she'll be ever so glad to see me.'

Minnie had probably been sent to a cold pauper's grave by now, Frobisher thought, but he delayed telling her mother that; it would be too much to bear in one day. He would make enquiries, he told her. Frobisher wished the locket had been buried with the girl. Minnie. She had a name now. It made it worse, rather than better. It would have been preferable if she had remained missing for ever, stranded somewhere between two worlds, rather than being committed to the endless night without any hope of recall.

'What happened to her?' Mrs Taylor asked between retching tears.

Frobisher hesitated before eventually saying, 'The river took her.' It was not entirely untrue. He poured more tea in her cup. His own hand was trembling slightly, he noticed.

He saw Mrs Taylor out and into the street. He could think of no words of comfort to send her on her way. He came back inside feeling desolate. The world he traversed every day was a barren desert.

A woman was talking to the desk sergeant. Respectable, well dressed, out of place in this den.

'Who was that?' he asked after she'd left.

'A Mrs Ames, sir. She came in last week to report her daughter Cherry missing.'

'And you didn't *tell* me?' Dear God, what did he have to do to make them understand there was a problem that had to be tackled?

'You want to be told about *all* the missing persons?' The sergeant looked bewildered. 'There's quite a few, sir.'

'No, of course not all of them. Just the girls.'

'Well, not to worry then, sir. Mrs Ames came in to say she'd found her daughter.'

'Alive?'

The sergeant regarded him as if he were mad. 'Yes, sir, alive. She's in a thing at the Palace. It's a theatre,' he added, in case Frobisher misconstrued and concluded royalty. He wouldn't have been surprised.

He handed Frobisher an envelope and said, 'Message came for you, sir, while you were in your office with that woman.'

'"That woman" has a name,' Frobisher said irritably. He returned to his office to read the contents of the envelope. Even the smallest action felt as if it necessitated secrecy on his part in this place.

It was as well, he thought, that he hadn't read it in front of the desk sergeant as it was unlikely that he would have been able to keep the surprise off his face, although, of course, it wouldn't surprise him at all if the message had already been read and its contents disseminated around the station.

'Going out again, sir?' the desk sergeant said as Frobisher retrieved the dog.

'Yes,' Frobisher said.

'Like getting blood from a stone,' the desk sergeant said to Sergeant Oakes, who had just come down from the women's cells.

'Probably going off to see his fancy woman again, that Kelling woman,' Oakes said. He sauntered out of the station, leaving his chortling laugh behind like an echo. The Cheshire Cat came to the desk sergeant's mind. He had read *Alice in Wonderland* to his daughter, a long time ago. He had no idea why it was popular. It was complete nonsense.

'I prefer a cat, to tell you the truth,' Edith Coker said, eyeing the dog. It was sitting in front of her, one paw raised in supplication. It overestimated its winningness. 'Are you allowed?'

'To take it to work? Probably not.'

'Oh.'

Frobisher had thought he might be able to let the dog off the leash in Regent's Park, but there were ducks that made it flighty. The dog sat now quite placidly, gazing up at Edith Coker sitting on the park bench. 'He's very obedient,' Frobisher said. 'I think he might have come from a circus.' The dog turned its head to look at him. Frobisher didn't know why he said that, he had no evidence of a circus background for the dog. He supposed he was trying to make it more interesting in Edith Coker's indifferent eyes.

She had been ill, she said, 'at death's door', and she did seem worryingly brittle, her face leached of all colour and her voice tremulous. It was a shock to see her so weak, as Frobisher had heard that she had been cast from the same iron mould as her mother. He wondered what the illness had been, but it was hardly his place to ask. Instead he said, 'I hope you're feeling better?'

'Some,' she said plainly. She took a long, slow breath before adding, 'My eyes have been opened to many things. And now I'd like to open yours.'

Oh, Lord, he thought, a Coker who's caught religion. She's going to preach to me. An evangelical. She was, but not in the way that he feared.

'I have to tell you,' she said, 'about Inspector Arthur Maddox.'

'Go on, Miss Coker,' he said quietly, unwilling to put her off by betraying his eagerness. The dog was less inscrutable, wagging its tail, keen to hear the story that Edith's pale lips wished to tell.

Maddox had been her lover, she said. Frobisher blinked at the word, startled by her candidness. He had not been expecting the revelation of a secret paramour, he had been expecting ledgers, paperwork, accounts, all the ways in which Maddox was skimming money off the clubs and businesses that he 'protected'. No doubt, Frobisher had thought, the man also turned a blind eye to some dope-dealing and petty thieving. It seemed, however, that his venality was so much worse, so much more dreadful than Frobisher had ever suspected. (What a naive fool he had been.) At first, as Edith began to talk quietly, her voice hardly above a murmur, Frobisher felt cold disbelief for what she was telling him. Surely this tale had to be coming from a woman scorned, a jilted paramour seeking vengeance? Yet the more she talked in that steady, determined way, the more he knew in his heart that Edith was telling the truth.

She wove a tapestry for him, all the threads forming a pattern that he suddenly realized had been there all along, months ago when he was still in Scotland Yard, long before he came to Bow Street, but that he had been too blinded by his preoccupation with Nellie Coker to see. It was not the clubs that were taking the girls, it was Maddox and his sidekick, Sergeant Oakes.

'Oakes?' Frobisher felt more disappointment at Oakes's perfidy than that of Maddox. He had trusted Oakes. He had called him 'a safe pair of hands'.

Maddox was the gamekeeper-turned-poacher. He took girls 'who no one would miss, I suppose', Edith Coker said. 'Supply and demand, Chief Inspector, the oldest trade in the book.' Girls who had run away from home, girls from orphanages, girls from the street, girls from dance schools, girls lured with promises of a clean bed and a square meal or a transformation in their fortunes. Girls were sometimes transported by Oakes in Maddox's car to the better parts of town, Edith said.

'And brought home afterwards?' Frobisher asked. A feeling of dread descended on him.

'Not always.'

'And you knew?' She knew that the man she shared a bed with was running a prostitution racket all over London? She was a party to these vile schemes?

'I didn't *know*,' she said carefully. 'But I suppose I never asked. *Mea culpa*, Chief Inspector, I was a fool. A sin of omission,' she added, 'rather than commission.' It was what he had said to Gwendolen when he divulged the existence of Lottie to her. (*Pah. Sophistry.*) Gwendolen had been right, it was a weak defence at best, although really it was no defence at all. 'I was hoodwinked. I thought I loved him. Trust me, Chief Inspector, I have paid the price of my folly.'

'Those girls *were* missed,' Frobisher said. By the Mrs Taylors, the Mr and Mrs Ingrams. They hadn't forgotten their girls. They wanted them back.

And there was more, of course. Tisbury Court and Dame Wyburn – who sounded like a jolly character in a pantomime but was a bawd of the worst kind. And a Mrs Darling in Henrietta Street – he had sent the inept Cobb there to mollify Gwendolen. She had urged him to go there himself but he had laughingly dismissed her concerns. *Mea culpa, mea culpa, mea maxima culpa.*

Mrs Darling, according to Edith, was a procuress but also, worse, dear God, an abortionist. He thought of the damaged body of the owner of the crucifix, *alive when she went in the water.*

Did she have any proof against this woman? Edith laughed, a hollow, mirthless kind of laugh, and said, 'Only what you see standing before you, Inspector.' Oh, Frobisher thought, *that* was why she had been so ill.

He had thought that Edith would hand over hard evidence, perhaps even stand up in court and denounce Maddox and he would be put away for his malfeasance, but she shrank from the idea. She would not testify in court. 'Not in a million years.'

'Then why tell me?'

'So that you know everything, of course. You're the detective, it's up to you to find the evidence. Maddox is about to seize our clubs, Chief Inspector. More power, more money, more girls.'

Was that her motivation, Frobisher wondered? Not to atone, but to safeguard the family business?

'You can interpret it how you want, Chief Inspector.' She gave a helpless shrug. It might have been misinterpreted as callousness but Frobisher recognized the look in her eyes. She was past caring about life, he had seen the same thing in Lottie.

He escorted her out of the park, worried that she was too fragile to make her own way. The dog had long since tired of Edith's litany of depravity and had to be roused from sleep.

'No rest for the wicked,' the desk sergeant said merrily when Frobisher returned. 'Another body, sir. Someone phoned while you were out. Anonymously.' He had trouble pronouncing the word.

'At Tower Bridge?' Frobisher hazarded. It seemed to be his fate. He felt a kinship with Sisyphus.

'No. A murder. You'll never guess where. You're going to like this one, Inspector.'

I doubt it very much, Frobisher thought gloomily.

The Riddle of the Sphinx

Even though she was very late to her bed most nights, Freda still was up long before Vanda. On waking, the first thing she did was to fill the kettle before placing it on the single gas ring, a dangerous affair that perched precariously on the wooden draining-board of the sink. Then Freda cut a thick slice from a loaf of bread, buttered it and ate it while she was waiting for the kettle to boil. There was always bread and butter in Vanda's flat, but unfortunately that was all there ever was. Vanda didn't shop for food or cook it, something that had contributed to her hasty departure from Grantham apparently.

'What about the baby?' Freda had dared to ask eventually and Vanda said, 'Had to leave the little tickler behind. Believe me, it's the best thing for him, Freda. Walter's got an army of sisters and cousins that couldn't wait to get their hands on him. I did my best, but . . . no regrets,' she had added cheerfully.

Freda chewed vigorously on the bread; it was stale. She could hear Vanda snoring in the next room. She did seem surprisingly content with her new life.

Today, Freda decided, she was going to find a grocer and buy jam and a lump of cheese and maybe some ham, too, so that Vanda didn't waste her money by always eating in cafés. Tinned fish would be handy as well and perhaps corned beef. Vanda also brought plates of food in from restaurants and then never returned the plates. Cutlery, too, all cluttering up the place. Freda thought she might take them back if she had time today.

Once the tea was made, she took it through to Vanda, who always looked a fright first thing. Make-up all smeared and her eyes glued together, wayward tufts of hair everywhere. Clothes were draped all over the place and the room smelt ripe and salty and perfumed all at the same time. The occasional slight whiff of dead rat entombed in the wall added an unpleasant top note.

Vanda woke with a snort and, still half-conscious, murmured, 'You're an angel, pet,' when the cup and saucer were placed on her bedside table. She groped her way out of her shambled bed-sheets and reached for her cigarettes. Freda wasn't allowed to open the curtains. Vanda behaved as if a bit of fresh air and daylight at this time of the morning might kill her. She break-fasted and lunched on tea and cigarettes instead.

Joan, next door, followed the same slack routine as Vanda. If she ran out of tea or cigarettes she would wander in (she had a key) in her tatty housecoat and cadge off Vanda. Vanda recipro-cated. 'It's good to have a friend,' Vanda said. It was. Freda could attest to that. The trick was not to lose them.

After Freda had delivered the tea and drunk her own cup, she readied herself for the day, washing and dressing and setting about the satisfying job of cleaning and scrubbing and tidying the flat. The squalor seemed to spring up anew every day – plates and cups were piled up in the sink, cigarette butts everywhere, not to mention the trollies and big pink satin bras that festooned and garlanded the kitchen. Freda didn't remember Vanda being so haphazard when they did the Knits, but she supposed they had had Adele to keep them in order. 'What a bitch,' Vanda said with a nostalgic sigh.

Freda often came across some strange items in the flat – riding crops and rubber masks and washing-line rope. 'Joan's specials,' Vanda said. She didn't have enough room in her own flat for all the 'accessories' she needed. Freda had previously thought the word referred to articles like gloves and stockings. 'Mm, them too,' Vanda said vaguely.

Vanda and Joan chatted endlessly about renting somewhere

bigger together where they could have 'a waiting room'. 'Like in a railway station?' Freda asked and Vanda said, 'Exactly like that, pet.'

They certainly needed extra room. Freda had come back in the middle of the afternoon last week and found a man tied to a chair next to the sink, his mouth stuffed with a large handkerchief. She wondered if she should remove the handkerchief, but when she approached him he went bug-eyed with horror and shook his head vigorously. Vanda appeared at that moment and said, 'Put the kettle on for a brew, will you, pet?' as if it were perfectly normal to have to manoeuvre yourself awkwardly around a man who was bound and gagged in order to get at the tea caddy. Freda wondered if she should pour him a cup as well, but a stern Vanda said absolutely not, he didn't deserve anything except a good slap. He belonged to Joan, she said, one of her specials. 'Keeping any eye on him for her,' Vanda said.

No one was lurking in the flat this morning, thank goodness, and once she'd cleaned and tidied, Freda sang out, 'I'll be off now!' and Vanda shouted back in her gravelly morning voice, 'See you later, pet. Don't do anything I wouldn't!' which gave Freda a pretty broad canvas to work on.

'Cherry! Cherry!'

It was unmistakeably Cherry Ames. An eager Freda ran after her along St Martin's Lane, calling her name.

Cherry Ames seemed to have grown deaf since Freda last saw her, but she turned at last and stopped. 'Freda! Freda Murgatroyd,' she said (very cool, Freda noticed). 'Fancy bumping into you. How are you?'

Freda was not cool at all, in fact she felt mildly delirious at coming across a familiar face. 'I'm fine, thank you,' she said. (Or 'better' anyway, she thought.) 'How are *you*?' Cherry certainly looked well. She had always dressed with flair, but now she was very smart, in the kind of clothes that you only got in West End shops. Freda said, why didn't they go and get a cup of tea somewhere, there was a Lyons just around the corner, and Cherry sighed and drawled, 'There's always a Lyons just around the corner,' as if it were the most tiresome thing in the world. Oh, I get it, Freda thought, she's playing the part of the jaded, metropolitan girl. Well, we've all been there. She had played that part herself for Owen Varley, and for Ramsay Coker, too.

Reluctantly, Cherry agreed to the Lyons, although she hardly touched the tea in front of her, preferring to smoke. 'It keeps you thin, you know. Not that you need that.'

Hesitantly, Freda asked how things were at the Vanbrugh. 'Oh, that place,' Cherry said dismissively, 'I wouldn't know, I left *ages* ago.' Well, it wasn't that long, Freda thought, it's only a couple of weeks since I left myself. She was on the stage, Cherry said. She'd had an audition for *The Co-Optimists* at the Palace, 'And I got the part!'

'Well done,' Freda said. The word 'audition' made her flinch.

'It's a tiny part, of course, but I've had a review – *Ingenue sparkles* and so on. What about you?'

'Me? Dancing. In a nightclub.'

'Oh, poor you. Is it terribly frightful?'

Who *was* this person, Freda thought? Was the real Cherry Ames – sweet and kind and perfectly normal – trapped inside this brittle imposter? Freda was about to ask her if she had heard anything about Florence, but Cherry stood up abruptly and said, 'I'm awfully sorry, Freda, but I have to go,' stabbing her cigarette out in the ashtray. 'I'm frantically busy. We're rehearsing all day, they're always adding new stuff to the show. It's a crashing bore.'

'It must be.'

'I have to have dinner with one of the investors in the show afterwards at the Café Royal. I'm going to be *exhausted*.'

If you looked carefully, beneath the heavy make-up and the strained, tired eyes, the real Cherry was probably still in there trying to protect herself. Freda wondered what she'd had to do to get the part in *The Co-Optimists*. Although she didn't need to wonder, she knew. 'Well, lovely to catch up,' she said with a false cheerfulness.

They kissed goodbye, Cherry going in for a second cheek, continental-style – Freda had learnt that from the Sphinx. Sometimes people went in for three. Ridiculous. What was wrong with just shaking hands?

'Oh,' Cherry said, raking in her handbag, 'here . . .' She produced two tickets that she handed to Freda. 'Have these comps for the show. You can come to any performance. They're good seats,' she added. Suddenly she looked sad and, biting her lip, said, 'It really *was* nice to see you, Freda.' And then, turning back, 'I almost forgot, someone came to the Vanbrugh looking for you and Florence.'

'Looking for us? My mother?' Unlikely somehow.

'No, not your mother. I'm not sure who she was, I don't think she told me her name. How is Florence, by the way? Oh, golly,' she said, catching sight of a clock on the wall, 'I really have to run. Catch up another time. You know where I am.' And she was gone.

Who is looking for me, Freda wondered? Perhaps it was Mrs Ingram, although Mrs Ingram was surely too faint-hearted for London. Did Freda want to be found, by Mrs Ingram? What would she say to her? *I'm awfully sorry but Florence has vanished into thin air.* Freda had been found by Vanda. Would anyone find Florence?

'Oh, there you are,' Ramsay said when Freda arrived at the Sphinx. 'I've been waiting for ages.'

'Met a friend.'

'Let's get on with it, then,' he said. He'd asked her to come in early today to help with something. 'A plan.' He had lost an unimaginable sum (a thousand pounds!) at something called a 'spieler', which was a kind of card game, and he was terrified of the consequences. Why on earth did he play for such high stakes if he couldn't cover his bets? What a mug.

'I think I was doped,' he said, sounding very sorry for himself. 'They kept giving me champagne.'

'Did you eat anything?' Freda asked.

'I don't know – caviar, oysters? There was a buffet.'

'Hm,' Freda said. 'And then the next day had everything turned to rocks and ashes?'

'Well, metaphorically speaking.'

Freda had no idea what metaphorically was, but she got the gist.

Freda had initially thought that Ramsay had asked her to come in early so that she could show him how to play cards better, and if not better then how to cheat, giving him a chance to win the money back. (She had inadvertently confessed her skills to him one evening.) But a thousand pounds! That would be some slam for him to pull off and, let's face it, he was not the sharpest card in the pack.

Not cards, apparently. As she was hanging up her coat he asked, 'Are you any good at forgery?'

'Can't say I've ever tried it.'

'Always a first time for everything,' he said, which was something Duncan used to say, of course.

Ramsay explained his plan. It didn't seem exactly legal to Freda to forge a letter from his mother to her bank so that he could swindle her, but he said that she'd been perfectly happy to lie about her age and experience to get this job (it was completely different!) and anyway he had no intention of swindling Nellie, he wasn't taking her money out of the bank, he just needed to see some paperwork she kept there.

It still seemed like a swizz to Freda's ears, and she said, 'What's to stop me from going straight to Mrs Coker and letting the cat out of the bag?'

'Because you're my friend.'

'No, I'm not.' The idea made her uncomfortable. She only had one friend, and until she found her she wasn't interested in another. Ramsay was not her friend just because they spent quite a bit of time together. They were the same age really, even though he was several years older than her.

'Look, Freda,' he said awkwardly, 'it may sound melodramatic, but it's a matter of life and death.'

'Is that "metaphorically speaking"?'

'No, for real. This Azzopardi fellow says he's going to kill me if I don't do what he's asking.'

'Pay me, then,' she said. She had become very bold since working at the Sphinx. She was beginning to understand her worth.

'Five pounds?' Ramsay offered.

'Fifteen.'

'Ten.'

'All right, then,' Freda said. 'I'll put the kettle on.'

Freda went to the Sphinx's tiny kitchen and found that they were out of tea, so she shouted to Ramsay to get another packet from the storeroom. He didn't seem to hear her, so she went on the errand herself and found Ramsay standing as if frozen at the door of the storeroom. The red velvet curtain was pulled to one side and he was staring at something as if he'd been hypnotized.

'Something wrong?' she asked. He turned to look at her but didn't speak. His face was bleached of colour.

She had to shove him to one side to see what had transfixed him.

A girl lay on the floor, motionless amongst the mops and crates.

'Is she dead?' Ramsay whispered.

'I think she might be.' Freda knelt beside the girl and took her hand. She was small, the same size and build as Freda. Freda held the girl's hand and tenderly stroked her forehead. The girl didn't stir, not a breath. 'She's gone,' Freda said, her voice a whisper, although she supposed it didn't matter, you could shout at the top of your lungs and the dead wouldn't hear.

'I'll phone my mother,' Ramsay said. Nellie was always the first and last resort in an emergency for any Coker.

Freda wondered if she should cover the girl's face, that's what people did, wasn't it? When their elderly next-door neighbour in the Groves died everyone had trooped round to view him in his bed as if he were entertainment. Someone had placed copper pennies on his eyes. Freda didn't have any pennies, but she took off her cardigan and put it over the girl's face.

Freda nearly jumped out of her skin when the girl pushed the cardigan off and started coughing and spluttering. Ramsay, on the phone behind the bar, gave an unmanly wail of horror.

Holding her throat with one hand, the girl struggled to sit up. ''As 'e gone?' she croaked.

'Has who gone?' Freda glanced around in alarm.

'The bastard who tried to strangle me,' the girl said hoarsely. 'Gertie Bridges,' she said, offering her small, recently lifeless hand. 'Pleased to make your acquaintance. I could murder a cup of tea.'

Nellie arrived and the tale was reeled out over the tea, laced with brandy by Nellie. In the early hours of the morning, Gertie said, she had been nearby, 'working, if you get my drift', and a man had dragged her into the Sphinx. 'He had a key.'

There was a key at the back door, in a crack above the lintel. A lot of people knew where it was, Ramsay admitted. Nellie glared at him.

The man had tied her up, Gertie continued, and then gone away. 'And then he come back, not long ago, and throttled me.' She lifted her neck so they could see. 'Bruised, I expect?'

'Horribly.' Freda shuddered.

'And he thought he'd got away with it, 'cos I passed out, but then I came to and played dead – I've had to do that before – and he didn't realize because he's as thick as two short planks and a nasty bugger with it, and then . . .' She took a sip of tea and they all took the opportunity to breathe, which they'd been neglecting to do, so thrilling was Gertie's story.

'And then I heard him make a phone call, and he asked for the police and said he wanted to report a murder, and I thought that's a bit rum, blabbing against himself. He came back and I could feel him looking at me and I didn't even *breathe* – I should be on the stage. You only just missed him.'

'And do you know who he was?' Nellie asked.

'Don't know his name or nothing,' Gertie said, 'but I've seen him around. He's a copper, *that* don't surprise me. Do you know what the worst thing was?'

Freda couldn't imagine anything that could be much worse than what Gertie had already told them, but Gertie said, 'The worst thing was that he laughed all the time, as if it was the greatest joke in the world to try and choke a girl to death.'

'Bloody hell, this is like being a queen,' Gertie said, luxuriating in the leather of the back seat of the Bentley. Nellie had thought it best they leave the Sphinx before the police arrived. 'Too bloody right,' Gertie said.

'Where to, ladies?' the chauffeur asked them.

'Oh, just drive around, my man,' Gertie said loftily, putting on a silly posh accent. Freda and Gertie collapsed in giggles. They were bubbling with high spirits. Surviving a brush with death is a powerful tonic. Hawker smiled indulgently at them, remembering his own daughter at that age.

'Kingly Court, please,' Freda said when they had calmed down a bit. Gertie was already nodding off to sleep. Freda could have happily lived in this car. In the rear-view mirror she saw Hawker raise an eyebrow when he was told the address. 'You're sure?' he said.

Vanda was up when they arrived and said, 'Christ, Freda, I thought I was seeing double, you're like two peas in a pod.' Freda related an abbreviated account of the morning's events and Vanda said, 'Bugger me,' which was also something Duncan used to say, and Vanda used to laugh and say, 'Would if I could, pet.'

Gertie climbed into Freda's little bed in the cupboard and fell into such a profound sleep that Freda had to check that she hadn't died a second time.

*

A skulking Sergeant Oakes cursed as he watched the Bentley drive away. Freda Murgatroyd was a problem. Oakes had thought to make her Nellie Coker's problem instead. A dead body in the Sphinx should be enough to stop Nellie opening up again some-where else after they took over her clubs. He had been pleased with the initiative he had shown. Maddox would be too, surely? But now it seemed that rather than solving the problem of Freda he had made it worse.

He could have sworn that the girl had been dead when he left her in that storeroom, yet here she was, walking, talking and sitting in the back of Nellie Coker's Bentley. And not only that – there were now two of them, as if she'd multiplied in there. They were so alike that he didn't know which was the real Freda Murgatroyd. Now Oakes had two problems on his hands.

'Sit down and pull yourself together before the police arrive,' Nellie commanded Ramsay. 'Here, have more tea.' She added more brandy to his cup. 'When they ask, nothing happened, right?'

'Right.'

'Remember – there was no murder.'

'But there *was* no murder.'

'Exactly,' Nellie said.

Frobisher arrived at the Sphinx with a uniformed constable in tow. Not Cobb. For all Frobisher knew, Cobb was also Maddox's acolyte. Nellie's Bentley was parked outside but drove off as Frobisher approached. The criminal fleeing the scene, he thought.

The Sphinx was unlocked and they entered unhindered, pass-ing beneath a cheap reproduction of the mask of Tutankhamun and then down a steep corridor. It was unknown territory and unnerved Frobisher slightly. 'Use caution,' he said to the con-stable. 'If there is a killer, he may still be here.'

A nightclub was not designed for daytime. The unforgiving

electric lights illuminated every tawdry corner. A few orphan balloons bobbed around untethered and paper streamers littered the floor. The cleaner had clearly not been in yet. There were two people sitting at one of the little tables, Nellie Coker and her son Ramsay. Nellie was drinking tea, the picture of serenity. Ramsay, on the other hand, looked pale and agitated.

Frobisher frowned at this little tableau and said, 'I've had a report of a murder here.'

'A murder? Goodness me!' Nellie said, heaving herself up from her chair and advancing on him like a small tank, her hand outstretched. 'May I introduce myself?' she said, like a gracious society hostess. 'Mrs Nellie Coker. And you must be Detective Chief Inspector Frobisher. We've heard *so* much about you.'

Frobisher was not for charming. 'The caller said that a girl had been killed here,' he said gruffly.

'I'm afraid you were wrongly informed, Chief Inspector. I think perhaps you have been the victim of a malicious prank. As you can see, there are no girls here, only my son and I, and we are very much alive.' Ramsay nodded his agreement. 'But you are very welcome to search the place,' Nellie added, sweeping her arm around the club as if offering it as a gift.

Frobisher sent the constable off to search every nook and cranny of the Sphinx. He was convinced that some evidence of wrongdoing would turn up, if not an actual corpse. But the place was squeaky clean.

'Found this, sir,' the constable said, 'behind the bar. He was holding a silver shoe aloft. Frobisher took it off him.

'One of the dancing hostesses must have mislaid it,' Nellie said smoothly. 'The girls are always losing their shoes.'

There was the sound of someone coming into the club and they all turned to the entrance to see who it was.

'Oh, look,' Nellie said, 'it's Miss Kelling. Have you met Miss Kelling, Chief Inspector?'

*

Gertie woke in the late afternoon, and because the cupboard was still bare Freda made sugar sandwiches that a 'starving' Gertie wolfed down. Freda supposed that dying and coming back to life would give you an appetite. Jesus probably felt the same when he came out of his tomb. She was reminded of the big crucifix that hung over the altar in Florence's church. She had been going in regularly to light a candle. *You light them for someone else, not yourself*, Florence had said. Freda was lighting them for Florence.

'You all right?' Gertie asked.

'Yes.'

Vanda, on her way out, said, 'Well, you look a lot less peaky, pet,' to Gertie and gave her an old silk scarf to tie around her neck and hide her bruises. 'Keep it,' she said generously. 'It's not real silk.'

Gertie sighed and said, 'Well, I suppose I should get going.' She and Freda both felt rather deflated after so much adventure and Freda said, 'Tell you what – do you fancy going to a show? I've got free tickets for *The Co-Optimists* at the Palace.'

The Box

Ramsay had been relying on Freda, not only to help him forge the letter to the bank, but also to rehearse him for his 'performance' (after all, she was always telling him that she belonged on the stage). He had even hoped that she might come into the bank with him and lend him some of her fearlessness, but Freda had left with Gertie so he was going to have to go ahead without her support.

On the Amethyst's headed notepaper Ramsay had written, *Dear Sirs, To whom it may concern, I am afraid I am currently indisposed and am sending my son Ramsay in lieu of myself. Please give him access to my safe-deposit box. Yours faithfully, Mrs Ellen Coker.*

He had had to make several painstakingly slow practice runs at it before he produced something even half credible. It was like being back at school, writing out lines as a punishment. Ramsay had been deemed 'uneducable' at Fettes and beyond, his place at Oxford notwithstanding, and he enjoyed imagining the look on his old schoolmasters' faces when they happened to walk past Hatchard's and glimpsed *The Age of Glitter* prominently displayed in the window.

'Mr Coker? How can I help you today?'

He'd made a beeline for one of the tellers in the hope of bypassing the manager, Sneddon, whom Ramsay always found intimidating even when he was here to cash up the night's takings from the Sphinx. No such luck, for as soon as the teller read the letter he said, 'I'll just run this past Mr Sneddon, Mr Coker.'

'Must you?'

'Standard bank practice, I'm afraid,' he soothed.

It was an agonizingly long wait before Sneddon himself appeared and, frowning at Ramsay, said, 'Young Mr Coker, good morning – I believe you want access to your mother's private box?' Sneddon held the letter in his hand and perused it for what seemed like a lifetime, before handing it back to Ramsay, saying, 'Of course, Mr Coker, come this way. Oh, and you have the key, of course?'

Yes, actually he had the key, thank you very much. Taken from beneath Nellie's mattress yesterday afternoon while she was out and copied by a locksmith in Bridle Mews and returned to the mattress within the hour. If Nellie knew what he had done she would probably turn him into a goat or a lizard. If she knew what he was currently doing he would disappear in a puff of smoke, never to be seen again. He was about to betray her, at Azzopardi's behest, and yet he felt almost righteous. His mother didn't care a jot for him, she had proved it with her will, so why should he care for her?

Although the whole endeavour was terrifying, Ramsay was also finding it exhilarating. He wasn't just writing a crime novel – he was living one. Fiction had nothing on what it felt, after a lifetime of passivity, to be finally *doing* something.

Nellie had only one safe-deposit box but it was big and heavy and the teller who had accompanied him into the vault had struggled when taking it out and putting it on the table. Sneddon used his key, then Ramsay used his, and he was finally left alone to open the box.

He thought of Pandora.

He lifted the lid.

'What in God's name were you thinking?' Niven growled at him. He had Ramsay by the collar, as if he were a schoolboy, and was propelling him towards the Hispano-Suiza, which was parked outside the bank with its engine running. 'Get in,' Niven snapped, opening the passenger door and pushing Ramsay in the car and then roaring away down Aldwych as though it were a getaway. 'And don't whine.'

'I'm not whining!' Ramsay protested. 'How did you know I was in the bank?'

Sneddon had phoned him, Niven said. He knew Nellie would never send Ramsay to root around in her private box and anyway Sneddon had seen straight away that the letter Ramsay had written was a risible excuse for a forgery. The manager felt sorry for Ramsay, however, as he thought it must be some kind of stupid prank, 'the folly of youth', he said, rather than a criminal act, and not wanting to bring down the full wrath of Nellie on him, 'He phoned me instead,' Niven said. 'You should be grateful to Sneddon. And why did you need money so badly that you would engineer this farce? For dope? Gambling?'

'I didn't take *money*, it was just papers and stuff.'

'What does that mean? "Papers and stuff"?'

Sheepishly, Ramsay took a sheaf of papers from inside his coat. Niven turned into Tavistock Street and parked the car so he could study them.

'Title deeds, lease agreements for the clubs? The freeholds?' Niven puzzled. 'Why would you want these?'

Ramsay's lip trembled and tears pricked his eyes. Not from fear or shame or remorse, but from the relief of confession. He could stop being afraid now, Niven would sort everything out. He reeled out the whole sorry tale.

'Azzopardi? You've got yourself tied up with *Azzopardi?*' Niven was thunderous. 'You're an even bigger idiot than I thought. You understand what this means? With this "stuff", as you put it, he would own all of the clubs. Everything Nellie possesses.'

'But they're in her name.'

'He'll change her name to his. There are plenty of forgers in London a lot better than you. Or perhaps he'll blackmail her into signing them over. Threaten something she can't afford to lose.'

'Well, don't worry, it won't be me,' Ramsay said. 'Our mother would happily sacrifice me if it meant keeping her precious empire. I've seen her will, you know. You'll be all right, but she's more or less disinherited me.'

'I wouldn't blame her after this stunt.'

'Mrs Coker,' the teller greeted Nellie as she bobbed purposefully towards the counter. 'I hope you're feeling better?'

She ignored the question. 'I would like access to my safe-deposit box, please.' She raised an eyebrow that sent the teller scurrying to find Mr Sneddon.

Ten minutes later and she was back in the Bentley. Clamped to her knee was the box made of rusting metal that she had retrieved from her safe-deposit box. A war chest, Hawker thought.

'I think it's time we both laid our cards on the table, don't you think?' Niven said.

'Mine are laid out already,' Nellie said, nodding with some satisfaction at the Lenormand spread of cards that was in front of her. Niven looked at it with distaste. He often wondered if his mother really did believe in the occult or if she simply liked people to think she had some secret power she could use as a weapon if they crossed her. She was a showwoman through and through.

A rusty tin box was sitting on a chair next to her. Niven couldn't imagine what it contained, although it was just the right size for a large severed head. He wouldn't have been surprised. 'What's in the box?'

Nellie ignored the question. Niven had found her, after some searching, in the Crystal Cup. He should have known she'd be here, it was her place of safety. It was too early for Gwendolen to be in the club and he wondered if she was still upstairs in the flat and if she remembered anything about last night.

She had been fast asleep when he had left her in the early hours, knocked out by the brandies and malts that she had drunk recklessly, one after the other. He wasn't sure what had prompted this sudden bacchanal, but Oxford seemed to be involved some-where along the line.

In the course of this dissipation she had, unprompted, told him the story of her life, ending with her coming to London. 'And now,' she concluded cheerfully, 'I am a spy.'

'I suspected as much,' he said. The influence of alcohol had made interrogation easy. 'For Maddox?'

'No!'

'Azzopardi?'

'Who?'

'Who, then?'

'Frobisher, of course. He has me looking for evidence to bring your mother down. Bring all of you down, I suppose.'

Frobisher? Of course that made sense. Niven should have realized that she was in the sober employ of the law, she was hardly Mata Hari. 'Isn't secrecy the essence of spying?'

'I've given the game up,' she said. 'I am done with it, done with Frobisher.' She laughed and said, 'So – what are you going to do about it? Have me killed?'

'The same word but with two different letters in the middle.' She had drunk too much whisky to work it out so he said noth-ing and kissed her.

Just the one rather clumsy, whisky-flavoured kiss, but it dis-turbed him in a way he hadn't expected. Not so Gwendolen, who drained her glass and, putting on a temptress's voice, said, 'I'm going to bed. I hope you'll join me.' He had to stifle a laugh as he watched her weave her way across the room.

When he went to check on her after half an hour he found her sprawled on her bed, dead to the world. No flannel and bed socks, her nightclothes seemed designed for a new bride. Even if she hadn't been semi-conscious, Niven had no intention of bed-ding her. He pulled the covers over her and hung up her clothes which had been jettisoned on the floor. Then he turned off the light and left.

*

'Well,' Nellie sniffed. 'Did you enjoy your night with Miss Kelling? She is very wily, you have obviously been taken in by her charms. She's working for Frobisher, you know.'

'What's in the box?' Again she ignored the question and he sighed and said, 'Ramsay saw your will. It upset him.'

'He shouldn't be so nosy,' Nellie said. 'Is that why you're here? Or to talk about your "secret" meetings with Azzopardi. I thought maybe you were planning to usurp me.'

'*Me?*' Niven laughed. 'I'm the one looking out for your interests – I'm not sure anyone else is. Azzopardi tried to steal the title deeds for the clubs this morning.'

'No,' Nellie corrected. '*Ramsay* tried to steal them. He's a traitor,' she said, almost fondly, as if he had proved his Coker credentials somehow.

'The important thing,' Niven said, 'is that he didn't give them to Azzopardi.' (What was in the box?)

'Do you have them?'

'They're safe. Was Azzopardi going to make you sign them over by threatening you in some way?'

'He already has. Said he'd take Kitty and cut her into little pieces,' Nellie admitted. 'He'd probably eat her as well, given the man's gluttony. He had a dummy run at her the week before last, tried to take her off the street. Oh, it's all right,' she said when she saw the look on Niven's face. 'She's gone.'

'Gone?' Where had Kitty gone?

'Packed her off to a convent in St Albans. Know some nuns there who owe me a favour.' (Nuns owed Nellie a favour?) 'They'll keep her well hidden.'

'Apparently,' Niven said, 'you have something of his that Azzopardi wants back. Is it something to do with that box?'

Nellie sighed. 'It'll be Shirley or Betty that he goes after next. Can't keep 'em all safe for ever.'

'What's in the box?'

'I wondered when you would ask,' Nellie said.

*

It was like one of the pirates' treasure chests that populated his boyhood reading. Jewellery – diamonds, sapphires, rubies, and God knows what else. Even in the low light of the Crystal Cup they seemed to glow.

It was, Nellie confessed, how she had got started. Niven had been at the Front and had known nothing of Great Percy Street and the kindly old landlady. All Nellie had told him when he returned from the war was that she'd 'had some luck'. It seemed the old lady had been a fence and was holding the proceeds of several robberies for the man who had stolen them. 'His last one was the big one, he was planning to retire to the Riviera. Leave the life of crime behind for good.'

'Let me guess – Azzopardi.'

'Went by a different name then,' Nellie said. 'I didn't know anything about him. It was before we came to London.' The story, 'according to my friend Agnes' (his mother had a friend?), was that a man had come to the capital from Switzerland to hawk 'sparklers' to a Hatton Garden dealer. 'He was an agent, engaged by some Russian nobility – émigrés – don't know who. Every second person you met was claiming to be a Romanov in those days.' The nameless middleman had stayed at the Ritz and it was from there that Azzopardi – Spiteri was his real name – had pinched the lot.

'Let me get this straight,' Niven said, offering his mother a magnificently sceptical eyebrow. 'Azzopardi, or whatever he called himself, stole the Russian crown jewels and then you stole them off him?'

'Don't be silly,' Nellie said. 'The Soviets have flogged the crown jewels.'

'So that's where he was caught?'

'No, he decided to do one last job – at the Goring. Shot in the hand, arrested. Take that as a lesson.'

She had sold, Nellie said, one item only from the hoard – an amethyst necklace, a stake that had proved lucky. She closed the lid of the box and patted it affectionately. 'I was keeping the rest for my retirement,' she said. 'Give it back to him and he'll leave us alone.'

Niven didn't think he'd ever seen his mother concede defeat before. Perhaps Azzopardi had been right, it was time for her to leave the field of battle.

'We've got bigger problems than the Maltese,' she said. 'Maddox is about to make his move.'

'And have you got a plan?'

'Always,' Nellie said.

Niven made the delivery to Eaton Square himself. Azzopardi kept him on the doorstep and didn't check the contents of the box. He trusted Nellie to be honourable, he said. He must be the only one in London who does, Niven thought.

Where was Gwendolen Kelling? He went to the flat and pressed the buzzer on the street door for a long time, but there was no answer. He imagined she had gone shopping or was having lunch with someone. He liked her too much. He worried it was making him weak. But what if it was making him stronger?

The True Bride

'Oh, look, it's Miss Kelling. Have you met Miss Kelling, Chief Inspector?'

Frobisher shook her hand (barely touching it) while looking anywhere but at Gwendolen. He was not good at theatrics. Honest men rarely are.

Gwendolen was confused. Nellie had telephoned her, urging her to meet her at the Sphinx as quickly as possible. From what Gwendolen could discern from Nellie's caginess, she had had another 'casualty' (as she put it) that needed attending to. Had someone had an accident in the Sphinx? It couldn't be another gang fight surely, the club wouldn't be open yet. When she arrived there was no sign of anyone needing medical attention, just a rather exasperated-looking Frobisher, holding a silver dance shoe in his hand as if he had come to the unlikely venue of the Sphinx to find his Cinderella.

Gwendolen waited for a cue from Nellie, which was duly given. 'We resolved our little matter without you, after all, Miss Kelling,' Nellie said. 'I'm so sorry if I've wasted your time by dragging you here.'

'Not at all, Mrs Coker,' she said smoothly. 'I was nearby.'

'As Inspector Frobisher has finished here, perhaps he would escort you out,' Nellie said. Frobisher didn't look as if he thought he'd finished, but he said, 'Of course. Allow me, Miss Kelling.'

*

'Little matter, what little matter?' he asked quickly once they were in the street.

When Gwendolen ignored the question and marched ahead, he grabbed hold of her arm and pulled her back. She glared at his hand on her arm until he let her go. 'I'm not your dog on a leash, Inspector,' she bridled. The memory of Oxford hung between them.

'My apologies.'

He retrieved his actual dog from the lamppost that it was tied to. The dog greeted Gwendolen like an old friend, softening her mood, and she relented and told him how Nellie had phoned for help, and he told her of the murder that never was. 'Something happened in there,' he said, 'but I can't for the life of me figure out what.'

He flagged down a taxi and told her he needed to pick something up from Bow Street and then he had to go to Southwark mortuary.

'Dear God – not Freda or Florence?'

'No, no, I didn't mean to alarm you.' Much of their relationship so far seemed to have been built on them causing alarm to each other.

He soon returned from the police station, clutching another silver shoe, and held it up next to the first one, which he had left in her keeping. 'What do you think? Are they a pair?'

'Well, they *look* like they are, but it's hard to be completely certain. But look . . .' she said, turning over the shoe in her hand. 'You haven't examined it thoroughly. I make a better detective than you, Inspector.' The shoe had been branded with its ownership, initials burnt into the leather sole – 'with a charred stick, probably,' she said. 'My brother Dickie used to do that, not with his shoes but pretty much everything else. I expect the girls in the dance schools get mixed up all the time, they all look alike – the shoes, I mean, not the girls. An M and a C – does that mean anything to you, Inspector?'

He looked at the sole of the shoe he had brought from the

station. It was a match. The same initials. Yes, it did mean something to him. It meant a great deal. 'A girl called Minnie Carter,' he said.

'And she's dead?'

'Yes.'

'In the mortuary we're going to?'

'That *I'm* going to. I hope to find her there. I promised her mother. Minnie was wearing one of the shoes when she was pulled from the river.'

'And you found its partner in the Sphinx. What does that mean, do you suppose?'

'I think it means that someone killed her there,' Frobisher said. 'Isn't that obvious?'

'Not that someone wants you to *think* that she was killed there?'

Frobisher sighed heavily and said, 'Occam's razor, Miss Kelling. You have a tendency to overcomplicate.'

'And you have a tendency to oversimplify. There are people trying to ruin Nellie.'

'I am one of those, may I remind you.'

'And your Inspector Maddox is another.'

'So I have recently learnt.' Frobisher sighed again. 'We need to talk about "my" Inspector Maddox.'

On the journey to Southwark he related Edith's confession to her. Gwendolen had a strong stomach but nonetheless felt nauseated at what he told her. 'Can't you arrest Maddox?' she asked. 'Today, now, before he does more harm? Before he ensnares more girls?'

'I only have Edith's word,' Frobisher said. 'And to be honest, her motives are not entirely clear. I need incontrovertible evidence. Even if some of the girls came forward, I'm afraid they are not necessarily the kind that a jury will believe. I'm not one of those,' he added hastily. 'I will find a way.'

'I don't want you to accompany me inside,' he said when the cab drew up in Southwark.

'Yet I shall.'

The dog was more obedient and waited in the cab, guarding the silver shoes.

'The little lady was just about to move on,' the mortuary attendant said. 'You found her in the nick of time.'

It was, as expected, a bleak place. Several bodies lay on marble slabs, lining the walls. Some were still on the trolleys they had arrived on, all were covered by thin sheets. Cadavers. How Gwendolen hated that word. The cold air of the mortuary had a scent familiar to her from the war. Strong disinfectant fighting and failing to cover the scent of decomposition and, here, also the stink of formaldehyde from embalming fluid. She thought she might have to resort to the smelling salts that she always carried in her bag. For others usually, rather than herself. Miss Rogerson in particular had been prone to the vapours.

There were metal chambers at one end of the room. 'Refrigerated,' the mortuary assistant said proudly. 'They're the latest, we've only just installed them.' He seemed disappointed that they were not more impressed. Gwendolen was chilled by the idea of ending up in one of those icy chambers, shut away in the cold and dark.

One of the chambers was unlocked by the attendant and a large tray was pulled out. The body on the tray was covered by a sheet and the attendant pulled it back to reveal the face of a young girl. Oh, the pity of it, Gwendolen thought. She could understand men killing each other in battle, they were under orders, they might even believe in the cause they were fighting for, but purposefully to take a young life and snuff it out like a candle for some perverse gratification defied her understanding.

'All right, Miss Kelling?' Frobisher asked, an expression of grave concern on his face. He was a good person, she thought. A good man. With a wife.

'Yes, thank you,' she said and gave him the gift of a faint smile. Few smiled in this place, she thought.

'This the one, guv?'

'Yes,' Frobisher said, 'Her name is Wilhelmina Carter.' She had been claimed, he told the attendant – he was to make sure that he kept hold of her until her mother made arrangements for her burial. 'Do not send her on,' he said sternly, 'do you understand?'

'Yes, sir, keep her on ice for her ma.'

Gwendolen told the cabbie to drop her in the West End, feeling a compelling need to walk, to be amongst the crowds who knew nothing of the dank inside of a public mortuary or the evil of the netherworld beneath their feet.

Frobisher helped her out of the cab and she said, 'Let's be friends, not enemies, Inspector.'

'Of course, Miss Kelling. I wish for nothing less.'

They shook hands and she said, 'Keep me informed. About Maddox.' She felt an unexpected rush of affection towards him. She was merciful. He had given Minnie Carter back her name, so she gave him his. 'Goodbye, John.' An *au revoir* perhaps, rather than an *adieu*.

Death by Water

Gertie thought that *The Co-Optimists* was the best thing she had ever seen. As a veteran of the stage herself, Freda judged it to be on the thin side, but she didn't spoil Gertie's enthusiasm by saying as much. When Cherry Ames came on the stage she gave Gertie a little nudge and said, 'That's my friend,' which impressed Gertie no end. Freda thought that if she'd had a chance at Cherry's part she would have done a much better job of it, but when the cast took their curtain call she whooped and whistled generously as Cherry took her bow, so much so that Cherry looked rather alarmed and tried to peer into the audience to see who was making all the racket.

Gertie, rather star-struck, insisted that they go round to the stage door to see the cast leaving. They'd hadn't quite reached their goal when Freda spotted Cherry already rushing out, still in her stage make-up and wearing a pricey-looking fur stole. She made straight for a car that was parked outside and a man in evening dress who was holding the car door open for her. He was old enough to be her grandfather, except that he definitely didn't kiss her like a grandfather would, not that Freda had ever had a grandfather. This must be the 'investor' that she'd had to have dinner with, Freda guessed. She wondered how often Cherry was expected to have dinner with people. With men. She felt an unexpected rush of gratitude towards Nellie Coker. She had given her a job and hadn't demanded a payment for it.

'Looks like your friend's got herself a sugar-daddy,' Gertie said. Freda had never heard that term before but she could take a good guess at what it meant. 'You didn't say hello to her,' Gertie added.

'No, I don't suppose I did.'

'Well, anyway, I'm off,' Gertie said. She had a place of her own, she said, Freda must visit. 'I will,' Freda said, and wondered if she would. She walked with Gertie as far as Seven Dials, where they hugged goodbye and Freda said, 'Be careful,' and Gertie said, 'You too.'

It was so unexpected that Freda didn't have a second to reflect on it. One minute she was cutting through Tower Court, thinking about what she was going to have for her supper before going to the Sphinx (eggs and chips, she'd just decided), and the next minute she felt a tremendous punch to the side of her head and she crumpled on to the cobbles.

The blow had rendered her helpless, yet she was only too aware that she was being dragged along by someone. She couldn't speak, couldn't cry for help, and felt horribly sick. Her hearing was affected, too, but she caught a muffled female voice asking, 'Is the girl all right?' and the man who was dragging her picked her up in his arms and in the competent voice of authority said, 'She passed out in the street. A dope fiend, I'm afraid. I'll see she gets to a hospital.'

Freda tried to cry out, tried to wriggle out of his arms, but his grip on her tightened. Her face was pressed against the rough serge of his jacket and she mewled with distress, a small, helpless noise, until, very close to her ear, he snarled, 'Shut up, you little fucking whore.'

She had heard his voice before, but she couldn't think where, and before she could rake through her memory she was jabbed by something painfully sharp and a wave of darkness passed over her and washed her away. The last thing she heard was the sound of his laughter.

*

When Freda came to, she had the worst headache in the world history of headaches. It took her a moment to recall what had happened. It took her another moment to realize that she was trapped in the dark somewhere – was it a box? A *coffin*? Had she been buried alive? In a dreadful panic, she screamed for help until she was hoarse, all the while pummelling and kicking the sides of the coffin, until there was the abrupt sound of an engine starting up and her nostrils were suddenly filled with the heady smell of petrol. A car. She was in the boot of a car. Not the best place to be, but at least it wasn't a coffin.

The journey was mercifully short. When the boot was wrenched open she thought about jumping out and running, but she couldn't move her limbs. Before she could catch a glimpse of the face of her kidnapper, he punched her again and she fell back into the dark.

When Freda came to again, it was to find herself in the river. Her baptism in the freezing, dirty water of the Thames brought her back from the dead, only to find herself drowning. She had gone down so far that she thought she must have touched the river-bed. She thought of Duncan's pearl fishers. There was probably treasure to be found on the muddy bottom of the Thames – Roman coins and medieval rings lost carelessly over the years – but they were not Freda's concern. She came back up, choking on the river, and like Duncan's pearl fishers filled her lungs with air and then more air until she thought they might burst like balloons.

She tried to swim, but her legs still weren't working properly and the current was an unforgiving predator, holding her fast in its watery embrace until it suddenly lost interest in her and she went down to the bottom a second time. She was a good swim-mer, she reminded herself. She thought of the little trophies she had won in competitions in the Yearsley baths. She thought about Mr Birdwhistle, about the horrid milliner's in Coney Street. She remembered standing on the windy platform in York station waiting for the arrival of the train that would take them to London. The bluebird brooch. Owen Varley's leering face. The Corpus Christi church. And Florence. Dear good, stupid Florence.

It was what people said, wasn't it? That your life flashed before you when you died. It wasn't much of a life when it spooled out in front of you like this. Freda felt a surge of anger. She wasn't ready to go yet, she wanted more, much more, and better. She kicked and kicked and found air again.

Frobisher had been walking across Southwark Bridge, lost in contemplation about how he could bring Maddox and Oakes to justice and make sure they didn't wriggle out of its embrace.

The matador from this morning (how long ago that seemed) had been identified. He was a man called Vivian Quinn and he wrote one of those society columns that Frobisher avoided like the plague. Embarrassingly, he had not been identified by the police, but – annoyingly – by *John Bull* magazine. There had been a phone call when Frobisher returned to his desk after the visit to Southwark mortuary, from the editor of *John Bull*, asking him to write something for them about the murder. Was there any truth, the editor asked, in the rumour that one of the last people seen with Quinn was Ramsay Coker, son of 'the infamous Old Ma Coker'? 'I'm thinking something on the lines of "Vice Queen's son embroiled in shocking—" '

Frobisher had hung up on the man. Sufficient unto the day, he thought wearily.

On the bridge, his thoughts turned back to Gwendolen Kelling. She had called him by his first name. Should he read meaning into that? She was no longer the merry soul of a couple of weeks ago. He felt a stab of remorse. When he had first met her, he had been struck – captivated, even – by her sunny nature. Now he had somehow managed to obfuscate it, to eclipse her radiance with his shadows. He was pursuing the weather metaphors in his mind – dark clouds, befuddling fog and so on – when his attention was diverted by something in the water that was being swept along like more rubbish amidst the grubby flotsam of the Thames.

Not rubbish, a girl. Rolling and tumbling as if she were a canoe riding the rapids. The Thames was a river in spate, the ebbing tide running fast, yet the girl was trying to swim, trying to fight the river single-handedly. But she was too small and the water would be too cold (*we call it hypothermia*, he remembered Webb saying). Frobisher didn't hesitate or give any sane consideration to what he was about to do. Afterwards, he thought it was the act of a madman, not a hero. He shed his overcoat and pulled off his boots and dived into the murderous river.

He caught up with the girl at London Bridge and they were swept along on a parallel course. She shouted something to him but he couldn't tell what. He was growing weak, fighting to keep his head above the water – the girl was stronger than he was – but the river was surely too cold for either of them to last much longer. He made an effort to grab her, but they were moving too fast.

Tower Bridge was approaching at tremendous speed and if he couldn't get hold of her in the next few seconds she would be unstoppable, gone to the marshes, out to sea, lost for ever. He had a sudden clear view of her face and then the water closed over her head. With one last superhuman effort he got hold of her hair and then an arm, and then he rolled her over and got one of his arms around her neck from behind, and with the help now of the current steered them both towards the piers, to the steps, to the Dead Man's Hole.

They thudded into the jutting concrete. No sign, unfortunately, of the attendant and his grappler. Frobisher grabbed on to a big iron ring that was fixed into the wall and with his last iota of will somehow managed to push and pull them both up on to the platform. He had swallowed half the Thames and now he was coughing it up again. Likewise the girl, choking and hacking as if she had a bad case of the croup. Frobisher could feel his heart racing, about to go out of control. His engine, he thought. Not an ounce of strength left, they both limply lay on their backs. Like a couple of flounders, Frobisher thought.

They came back to life slowly, first the girl, then Frobisher. They had not been unnoticed and soon several people were making their way down the steps and crowding the small space. An ambulance was called for – Frobisher resisted for himself, but he rode with Freda when she was bundled in blankets and loaded into the vehicle. He leant across to speak to her as they rattled along to St Thomas's. 'How are you feeling now, Miss . . .?'

'Murgatroyd,' she murmured weakly, her eyes closed. 'Freda Murgatroyd.'

Frobisher laughed, a rare sound worth recording, like the nightingale's song, although Frobisher was no songbird. 'People have been looking all over for you, Freda.' She bore no resemblance to the photograph that Gwendolen had given him, but he was sure that he had seen her before. He had seen her everywhere. She was every missing girl in London who haunted his waking hours.

'Did you try to drown yourself, Miss Murgatroyd?' he asked gently as they approached the hospital.

Her eyes flew open. 'Kill myself?' A barrage of angry words followed, the gist of which was that a policeman had tried to murder her. Maddox, Frobisher thought, but then she added, 'In uniform. He laughed at me.'

Oakes, then. 'I will catch him and punish him,' he promised solemnly, but her fury had exhausted her. Her eyes were closed and she gave no sign of having heard him.

Freda was 'in surprisingly good shape', the doctor said, although exhausted. Sleep would cure her, he said. 'You too,' he added, taking Frobisher's pulse. 'Too fast,' he declared, and then something about 'a man of your age', at which point Frobisher stopped listening.

A night nurse gave him a change of clothes. 'We have a stock for emergencies,' she said. 'Second-hand – they come in very useful.' Frobisher wondered where the clothes came from and if the rough fustian trousers, collarless shirt and worn jacket he was wearing had come from the body of a dead man. He caught sight of himself in a mirror in the lavatories and was struck by how he looked like a completely different person. We're all dead men, he thought, from the moment we come into this world.

He kept watch by Freda's bed. The nurse told him that she had been given a sleeping draught and wouldn't wake for hours. His questions would have to wait until the morning. Where had she been? How had she come to be in the river? And, perhaps most importantly of all, where was her friend Florence?

He was ridiculously keen to tell Gwendolen, imagining her astonishment and delight when he presented the long-lost Freda, although he supposed her gratitude would be marred by his failure to produce Florence as well. Still, a bird in the hand.

'I had a dog with me,' he said to the night nurse when she was taking the sleeping Freda's pulse on one of her rounds.

'That's nice,' she said absently. There didn't seem much point in pursuing the fate of the poor dog. It must have either wandered off from Southwark Bridge or in an act of misplaced fidelity plunged into the Thames after him and been lost for ever beneath the waters. Perhaps in some greater arc of justice the dog had been the price to pay for saving Freda. His heart clenched with pity when he thought of such a very small dog in such a very big river.

'Are you feeling all right, Chief Inspector?' the nurse asked.

'Yes, yes, quite all right,' he said.

'You should go home.'

It was three in the morning when he reached Ealing in a ridiculously expensive taxi. Tomorrow he must face the Austin again.

Lottie was asleep, of course, and he didn't wake her. She was ignorant of his adventure and he doubted that he would tell her.

When he woke, she was not asleep by his side. He couldn't

remember her ever getting up first, but then he looked at the clock and saw it was well past midday. He had never slept so long in his whole life. It had done him good, he felt healed, almost whole, although slightly bilious, and his lungs were damp as if they'd sponged up the Thames.

Lottie was in a good mood, too. She made him coffee in the little French pot he had found for her in a shop in Soho. She cut bread and buttered it for him, even volunteered an egg, which he refused. He felt renewed guilt. It should have been Lottie he had taken on that outing in the Austin. His *wife*.

He shied away from the Austin at the last moment. Perhaps he wasn't meant to be a driver. He took a tram. Not to Bow Street but to St Thomas's, to see Freda.

'No Freda Murgatroyd here, I'm afraid, Chief Inspector,' the matron said. She had been summoned when none of the nurses on the day shift recognized the name.

'She came in last night,' Frobisher insisted. 'I pulled her from the Thames myself. She was asleep when I left.'

Well, a girl had been brought in, the matron said, her brow creased as she scrutinized the ward's records, 'but she discharged herself this morning.'

'Did she leave an address?'

'No, but her name wasn't Freda Murgatroyd. She was called Miss Fay le Mont.'

He set off to Bow Street in a renewed state of defeat. For a moment, he wondered if he had dreamt the whole episode.

The Age of Glitter

A raft of morning newspapers lay abandoned on the table in the empty dining room of Hanover Terrace. Ramsay had come down from his room in search of the coffee pot. Niven had told him yesterday evening that the spieler debt had been 'fixed', whatever that meant (he didn't need to know, Niven said), and that, as a bonus, he had persuaded their loving mother not to have Ramsay's dead body dragged around Regent's Park behind a chariot.

The coffee pot was cold and Ramsay wondered what the chances were that their recalcitrant cook would brew more for him. His eye was caught by the front page of one of the papers.

> Journalist murdered. The body of the society diarist Vivian Quinn was recovered from the Thames yesterday morning. He had been stabbed by a hand or hands unknown near Berkeley Square. A curious detail of the affair was that Mr Quinn was dressed in the costume of a Spanish matador.

Ramsay reached for the wastepaper basket and vomited into it.

Quinn? Murdered? It was the third item on the front page, not the headline – how Quinn would have resented that! He must have been killed minutes after Ramsay had spoken to him two nights ago. For a paranoid moment, Ramsay wondered if he had killed Vivian Quinn himself. He had certainly wanted to when Quinn was telling him about *Folderol*, and he had been in such a delirium of drugs and alcohol that he might have done anything and not remembered. Quinn's novel would never be published now.

The coffee forgotten, he returned to his room, where the floor – the only space that was big enough – was carpeted with a jigsaw of (badly) typed pages. They fluttered and resettled like birds in the draught when he opened the door.

The scales of vanity finally fell from his eyes as he regarded the pages with despair. He had become the victim of his own vaulting ambition. *The Age of Glitter* was going to destroy him, eat him alive from the inside out. He was not a good writer, in fact he was an awful writer! The sooner he faced that fact, the better. He would have burnt all the pages, but the fires in Hanover Terrace weren't lit until late afternoon at this time of year.

He resolved to start again. He owed it to art.

Quinn had lived in a small top-floor flat, a little bijou place, in Conduit Street. Ramsay had been there several times in the past. The landlady lived on the ground floor and acted as a kind of concierge, and she recognized Ramsay when he knocked on her door. 'Oh, Mr Coker,' she said, 'isn't it awful news about Mr Quinn?' Ramsay agreed that it was awful (it was) and said that Mr Quinn's mother had asked him to come and pick something up. 'A book of poetry, I believe, for a reading at the funeral.'

'So soon? He was only found dead yesterday.'

'She's thinking ahead.'

He was let into the flat. The landlady hovered, but he persuaded her that it might take him some time to find what he was looking for. In fact, the quest took hardly any time at all. The grail was sitting on Quinn's desk in plain sight. A big brick of a manuscript, the edges aligned meticulously. *Folderol*, it announced itself on the top page.

The fires were lit by the time Ramsay returned to Hanover Terrace, and he crushed the title page of Quinn's novel and threw it into the flames in the drawing-room hearth.

He took the stairs two at a time to his room – his malaise had lifted. Committing crimes seemed to give him energy. He sat in front of the typewriter and took a swig of Collis Browne. He flexed his fingers and cracked his knuckles and then took a new sheet of paper and rolled it into the Remington. For a few moments he gazed at the paper, as white as Alpine snow, in a kind of reverie. He typed a title – *The Age of Glitter*. The dedication followed on a second clean page. *For my friend, Vivian Quinn.* He placed the two sheets of paper on top of Quinn's manuscript.

Voilà!

The doorbell rang. It would not be for him. It never was.

Si Vis Pacem, Para Bellum

There was no one who saw it as their job to answer the door in Hanover Terrace and so the bell had been ringing for some time, clanging away in the hallway, refusing to admit defeat. The cook was making bread, an activity that always seemed to infuriate her. Even from upstairs Phyllis could hear her in the kitchen, thumping and thudding the dough on the big deal table.

Phyllis eventually surrendered and answered the summons. The determined bell-ringer was a small, filthy boy who looked as if he had just been up a chimney. She was about to box his ears and send him on his way when she realized it was one of her many cousins. 'Got a message for you,' he said, thrusting a piece of paper into her hand. 'Urgent,' he added, rather pleased with the drama that had sent him racing all the way from Whitechapel on a stolen bike. He lingered, hoping for a reward, and Phyllis said, 'Wait a minute,' and sneaked into the pantry while the cook was still intent on slamming the dough into submission and came out with a big wedge of sticky ginger cake.

'Tell 'em I got the message,' she said to the boy, giving him the cake. The boy couldn't answer because he had crammed the whole slice of cake in his mouth at once, but he gave her a thumbs-up and jumped back on his bicycle. 'And hurry!' she shouted after him.

'Who was that?' the cook asked. She was shaping the loaves now and had simmered down.

'Message for Mrs Coker. I'm to take it to her.'

The cook placed the loaf tins in the new refrigerator to prove until tomorrow. She liked her bread to have a long prove. The refrigerator was not unlike a mortuary cabinet. Peace reigned in the kitchen once again. The bread has been conquered.

'Off you go, then,' the cook said.

'It's tonight,' a breathless Phyllis told Nellie when she reached the Amethyst. 'Maddox is coming for you tonight.'

'Better get a move on, then, hadn't we?' Nellie said.

Maddox drank a cup of weak black tea at the breakfast table. He had an acid stomach and never ate before noon. Around him, his children were spooning up their porridge. All five of them, including the baby, had remarkable appetites. 'Eating me out of house and home,' he would laugh, but he wasn't really joking. If he didn't have to make endless provision for his children and his unsatisfied wife he wouldn't have to worry about money. His household didn't run on fresh air, unfortunately.

Eggs appeared next, boiled, two for each child, except the baby, who was still sucking at his wife's worn-out breasts. Maddox's children were as plump as piglets being fattened for the spit. He watched the skin stretching over their round pink cheeks as they chewed. Two of them were in school uniform, ready, if reluctant, for the walk to school. Maddox couldn't wait to be off himself. He loved his wife and children, but he couldn't stand being trapped in the house with them.

'Going to work again today, then, Arthur?' his wife asked, unable apparently to keep the sarcasm out of her voice. 'Your "bad back" still better, then?'

The doorbell rang.

'For goodness' sake, who's that at this time of the morning?' she said crossly. 'The postman's already been.'

She returned with an envelope in her hand. 'A chauffeur in a

flash car delivered it,' she said. 'What are you up to, Arthur?'
The children rushed to the door to look – a chauffeur-driven
flash car was not a common sight in Crouch End, but it had
already disappeared and they returned, defeated, to their eggs.

His initial plan had been simple – to put Nellie out of business by degree, orchestrating a series of misfortunes – the raid
on the Amethyst, the raid on the Sphinx, the fire at the Pixie, the
Huns running amok in the Amethyst – death by a thousand cuts,
lingchi, Brilliant Chang had once explained to him. They had
some business together occasionally. Dope and girls, the twin
pillars of crime in London. Chang was long gone now. Unfortunately, all Maddox's attempts so far had been dismal failures, in
fact the campaign was in danger of turning into a farce. Nellie
Coker had the luck of the Irish.

And now Oakes had gone rogue, 'used his initiative', he said,
and killed that girl in the Sphinx. An idiot with initiative, what a
recipe for disaster. And it wasn't even the right girl! Maddox
didn't kill girls – you didn't make money out of dead girls. He
had daughters himself, three of them, he was not inhuman. Had
he allied himself with a madman?

Just as well he was making his strike tonight. There was to be
one assault after another, starting with the most vulnerable club.
The Pixie was all women and would put up little resistance. Nor
would the Foxhole, and the elite members of the Crystal Cup
would disappear into the night at the first sign of trouble. The
Sphinx might be more of a challenge, there was the big Dutch
barman to contend with. And then, the culmination, he would
take the Amethyst. The citadel.

He recognized Edith's handwriting on the envelope his
wife handed to him and tucked it into his pocket to read in the
safe haven of the Wolseley. He left the house quickly, before his
wife could ask about the missive, kissing her fleetingly on the
cheek and saying, 'I'll be very late tonight.'

There was no Wolseley. Damn and blast. He had loaned it to

Oakes yesterday. He had been ferrying a girl uptown, a party favour for a group of male friends celebrating something or other. A sporting achievement or a successful investment, he really couldn't remember.

He paused at the corner of the street to read Edith's letter. The tone was melodramatic, which was not usually her style. *Dear Arthur*, he read, *it is imperative we meet. I fear we are undone. Come to the Sphinx before it opens tonight. Yours ever, Edith.*

She had taken him for a fool, first about the pregnancy and then about the abortion. What other betrayals was she planning? Since she had been shut away in Hanover Terrace, he hadn't been able to see her and he had no idea what her frame of mind might be. What had 'undone' them? Was it Nellie? Was it something that was going to scupper his plans for tonight? He sighed. He would have to see her.

He was not a bad man, he reflected. He went to Mass nearly every morning, twice on Sundays. He taught his children right from wrong, he believed in good manners and discipline. He believed a man made his own fortune. He was about to make his, he would not be derailed, by Edith or anyone.

Late last night Gwendolen had abandoned her post at the Crystal Cup and gone to the Amethyst, where she had asked Nellie if she could have a quiet word. They had sequestered themselves in one of the unused rooms at the top of the building. Nellie was fully aware that Gwendolen was betraying her at every turn and yet she felt a curious warmth towards her – a trust, almost. She had seen something in the cards that first Sunday, but she had been distracted by Maud gliding out of the wall of the Crystal Cup and had never reached a conclusion.

At the moment, Maud was daintily perched on a packing-case in the corner, examining her fingertips as though she were bored. She no longer had fingernails. She seemed to be disintegrating. Nellie would miss her if she disappeared entirely.

'Mrs Coker?'

'Sorry, yes, Miss Kelling?' Nellie said, giving her head a little shake.

'I have to confess,' Gwendolen said, 'I was sent to spy on you.'

'What a surprise,' Nellie said.

But, of course, this was just a prelude and Gwendolen proceeded to tell Nellie everything that Frobisher had told her about Maddox. She didn't mention Edith's part but it seemed Nellie already knew.

'Frobisher will bring Maddox to justice,' Gwendolen said. 'I'm sure of it.'

Due process, Nellie thought. The dry meal of affidavits and witness statements. The slow grind of the courts. And at the end of it, Maddox might be convicted, but equally he might not. Justice should be swift, not slow. It should be a knife in the heart. The black wings of retribution crushing Maddox in their righteous embrace. Nellie was feeling rather perky for a woman so under siege.

'Visitor for you, sir,' the desk sergeant said. 'I put him in your office. He was waiting on the doorstep first thing.'

The dog was sitting on his chair, its face just visible above the desk. For a moment Frobisher imagined it was going to give him orders, but then it jumped down and ran towards him, propelled by its whirring tail. Frobisher picked the dog up and buried his face in its fur and sent up a small prayer of thanks to a God he didn't believe in.

'Off out, sir?'

'Yes. I have good news to convey to someone,' Frobisher said.

'Well, *he*'s got a spring in his step today,' the desk sergeant said to Cobb when Frobisher had gone, the dog trotting happily in his wake. '*Cherchez la femme*, as we used to say in the war.'

'Share what?' Cobb puzzled.

'The women,' the sergeant explained. 'Share the women. And we did, believe me, son, we did. I caught the clap twice out at the Front.'

Cobb blushed. He hated that kind of talk.

Frobisher went first to Gwendolen's flat. There was no answer to his ring and the club below was closed and he was wondering where she might be when he saw her approaching along the street. 'I have good news,' he said, and she said, 'Walk with me.'

'We shouldn't be seen together. It will raise suspicions.'

'Too late, suspicions are already raised. I told Nellie about our deception. And I am still alive, as you can see. What is your good news?'

He skimmed over the river rescue – he didn't want her to think that he was boasting about his heroism to her. Skimmed, too, over how near to death he and Freda had both been, but nonetheless she stopped in her stride and touched his arm and said, 'How brave you were.'

It didn't surprise Gwendolen that Freda had styled herself as the mysterious Miss Fay le Mont, it was the kind of silly name that she would employ. 'I'm relieved she is alive, but where is Florence? And why would your Sergeant Oakes want Freda dead? Do you think she has evidence against Maddox? Could Freda *be* our evidence? If we found her?'

So many questions he had no answer to. (It was true, she would make an excellent detective.) And then at that moment an extraordinary coincidence, for he had spotted the man himself. Maddox on foot and in a hurry. 'That's him, that's Maddox,' Frobisher whispered to Gwendolen.

'Oh,' she whispered back. 'I imagined the devil, but he's quite good-looking.'

Frobisher frowned at her. Compared to himself, he wondered?

They followed him for several minutes – until, in fact, he reached the entrance of the Sphinx.

'Shall we pursue him inside?' Gwendolen said.

'No, we'll wait until he comes out and see where else he goes.'

But after ten minutes, when there was no sign of Maddox exiting the club, an impatient Frobisher said, 'I'm going in. I have an itch to arrest him today. Evidence can be found later.'

'You're acting on impulse, Inspector.'

'About time, probably.'

'I am coming in with you.'

'No.'

She did, of course.

The art of war, for Nellie, was simple. No attrition for her. You simply cut off the head and watched the body wither. Without Maddox leading them, his makeshift army would be as clueless as beetles and would quickly dissolve back into the dark places they had crawled out of.

She knew that Maddox would not expect her to surrender easily, he would be expecting a battle royal from her. He would be expecting the Coker defences to be up, for Nellie to have marshalled her troops – the Frazzini gang and any other roughs that she could tempt out of the East End to come to her aid. He would be expecting a wily Niven, and Gerrit with his fists, and an arsenal behind the bar of the Sphinx. He would be expecting at best a rout, at worst a fighting retreat. What he wouldn't be expecting was Edith.

'Hello? Is anyone here?' It was daylight outside, but the underworld of the Sphinx was illuminated only by a dim light emanating from somewhere near the bandstand. Maddox disliked the atmosphere in the Sphinx at the best of times, now it seemed ominous. He was not a superstitious man though and he raised his voice. 'Hello? Edith, are you here?'

'Arthur?'

'Edith. There you are.'

Even in the gloom of the Sphinx he could see how ill she looked. He made a move towards her and she shied away from his touch. 'Edith,' he coaxed, 'don't be like this.'

'I was at death's door,' she said.

Oh, God, Maddox sighed inwardly, here we go again.

'And I didn't like what I saw on the other side.'

'I'm sure none of us would,' he said, trying to strike a more jovial note. 'But you're better now, I can see that.'

'Repentance,' she murmured softly, too softly for him to hear, and then it was as if they had come out of the walls. Women darting towards him, surrounding him, a horde of them swarming, like wasps, pressing close as if they wanted to suffocate him. He recognized members of the Forty Thieves gang. Were they planning to rob him?

'Ladies, *please*,' he said, laughing. 'You'll crush me.'

Betty and Shirley stepped out of the swarm. Betty took the little silver knife from her pocket and handed it to Edith. 'You do the honours, Edith, dearest,' Shirley said.

'Go on, Miss Edith,' Phyllis encouraged. 'Stick it to 'im.'

Edith, however, needed no encouragement.

'This is a ghastly place,' Frobisher said to Gwendolen as they passed beneath the mask of Tutankhamun.

As they began to progress down the slope they heard the strangest noise. A great rasping, grating sound as though a heavy millstone was labouring to move. Or a fairground carousel was being wound into reluctant motion.

The noise had ceased by the time Frobisher and Gwendolen entered the club, leaving only a strange aura behind as if something of significance had just happened. There were people in the club, all women, and Frobisher recognized several members of the Forty Thieves. They gave the impression of taking part in a game of Statues. The older Coker daughters were there as well and Frobisher was taken aback to see Edith again. She had blood on her hands. And not a metaphor, although perhaps it was. Lady Macbeth came to mind.

Gwendolen was spurred into action. 'Are you all right?' she asked Edith. 'Let me have a look at your hands. Have you been injured?'

Edith smiled beatifically and said, 'Oh, no, don't worry, it's not my blood.' Frobisher wondered if she had gone mad. (Was everyone mad in some way?)

'Where is Maddox?' he asked sharply, not so much to Edith, too delicate for anger, but to the women gathered around her. A 'coven' was the word that came to mind. 'I watched him come in here, so don't lie to me. What has happened to him?'

'Detective Chief Inspector Frobisher,' Nellie said, appearing from nowhere. 'Another wild goose chase? I'm afraid Inspector Maddox has left. There is a door at the back of the club. It's not a magic trick, I assure you.'

There was a murmur of agreement from the women, wasps buzzing around a queen.

The staff began to arrive, heralded by a couple of dance hostesses clattering down the stairs.

'If you will excuse me, we must get on,' Nellie said. 'Our guests for the evening will be here soon.'

'I suspect we have been fooled again,' Frobisher said as they exited the Sphinx. He took a deep breath. Even the most noxious London air felt sweet compared to the Sphinx. 'What do you think?'

'To be honest, I no longer know what I think. About anything.'

They parted. Every time he saw her now, he wondered if he would ever see her again. 'Don't be silly,' she said. 'Of course, we'll see each other again. We're friends, aren't we? And there is still work to do. There is Florence to find, and Maddox and Sergeant Oakes to be brought to justice.' She stood on tiptoe and kissed him lightly on the cheek. A moth's wing.

*

417

Maddox's body turned up the following day, on, of all places, the doorstep of Bow Street police station. He must have been dumped there sometime in the night, unseen by anyone.

Webb recorded that Inspector Arthur Maddox had been stabbed with a sharp-bladed, small knife. Big enough, he heard Frobisher say, although of course Frobisher himself was not present. Frobisher would never be present again. Webb hadn't liked Frobisher very much, but he was sorry to hear about what had happened to him.

Mother's Milk

Niven parked his car in the mews behind Hanover Terrace. There was room for only one car in the garage. Through the dusty, cobwebbed window he could see that the Bentley was at home. Niven glanced up at Hawker's window above the garage to see if there was any sign of him. They usually saluted each other. He occasionally went up to Hawker's flat and drank a glass of beer with him. Inevitably, the talk would come round to the war. Hawker had been behind the wheel during the war, too, driving a four-star General. 'So never near the action,' he said wryly.

No sign of him now. No sign of the cook or the little scullery maid either.

He went into the house and heard a mumble of voices coming from the dining room upstairs. Through the open doorway he could see Nellie sitting at the table, calmly turning over her cards. She caught sight of Niven and gave an imperceptible shake of her head. He was put on guard and entered the room warily.

'Mr Coker,' Azzopardi said. He was holding a gun, the barrel casually resting on the table and pointing in the direction of Nellie. A Luger. A Parabellum. From the Latin, meaning 'always prepared for war'. Niven had seen enough of them in his time. The rusty box, he noticed, was also on the table.

'The mice and the ring,' Nellie said to Azzopardi, unfazed by the circumstances she found herself in. 'Dishonest promises.'

'How true,' Azzopardi said.

Niven nodded at the box and asked, 'Is something wrong?'

It seemed that Azzopardi had taken his precious box to a jeweller in Hatton Garden, intending to finally cash in his ill-gotten loot. He knew the jeweller from before the war, when he had dealt discreetly in the more valuable kind of goods, never questioning their source.

The contents of the box, the jeweller told him sadly, were nothing more than baubles – paste-and-glass replicas of the originals. 'Fakes.'

'Very good fakes,' Nellie murmured.

Niven stared at his mother in amazement. He had thought she might have lost her fire, but she was blazing. She'd had the brass neck to try to palm off counterfeit goods with no regard to the consequences. 'A thief,' Azzopardi said.

'Stealing from a thief,' Nellie countered. 'Seems fair to me.'

Where were the originals? 'I don't have them,' Nellie said stoutly. 'I sold them and invested the money. Stocks and shares. It would take weeks to get it back, even if I wanted to, which I don't.'

Why, Niven puzzled, had she replaced the jewellery with fakes?

'Good question,' Azzopardi said.

As insurance against this day, of course, she said. Nellie had always been good at playing the long game. 'I saw it in the cards,' she added, a piece of nonsense that was the final straw for Azzopardi. He raised the Luger, cocked it and aimed it at Nellie's head.

'Everything all right here, Mrs Coker?' Hawker asked loudly, appearing boldly in the doorway with the aim of disrupting this tableau.

Azzopardi's aim twitched towards Hawker. The shot was deafening, the noise ricocheting around the inside of Niven's skull. For a brief second he found himself back on the battlefield. Part of the ornamental plasterwork fell from the ceiling and plaster dust snowed down on Hawker, immobile now on the carpet.

Niven dived swiftly on Azzopardi and knocked his bulk to the floor and the Luger was sent skidding across the floor. Azzopardi was all blubber. Niven banged his opponent's head off the floor several times, as it seemed to be the simplest way of putting him out of action. Nonetheless, as soon as Niven was on his feet, Azzopardi was too, coming towards him like a lumbering bear intending to crush him in its arms. Niven took up a boxer's stance, ready for the fight, but then another deafening shot rang out and the bear dropped.

Nellie was holding the Luger. It looked ridiculously big in her hands. Plaster continued to shower down on their heads. When in God's name had his mother learnt to handle a gun? (Deer-stalking in the Highlands with her father, apparently.) Niven knelt beside Azzopardi and felt for his pulse, although his eyes were glassy and a great red stain was spreading on his white dress shirt.

Hawker, ghostly with plaster dust, struggled to sit up, sur-prised to find that he was alive and only winged by the shot. 'Christ,' he said with feeling.

'All right?' Nellie said to him.

He supposed that would be all the thanks he would get from her.

Landor was called for and he produced men who were easily bribed into hauling Azzopardi's carcase away. They drove it out to Canvey Island in a builder's van, where they launched him into the river on an outgoing tide, far beyond the reach of the Dead Man's Hole.

And For That Minute a Blackbird Sang

After he parted from Gwendolen, Frobisher's mind was so befuddled by the kiss she had bestowed on him outside the Sphinx that when he crossed Long Acre he failed to see the lorry bearing down on him. It had come from Spalding, bound for Covent Garden, and when it braked it shed some of its load – cabbages that rolled into the road like heads from the guillotine.

Gwendolen had taken the watch at many a deathbed vigil, but this one was perhaps the hardest of all to bear.

'He won't last much longer,' a nurse had whispered to Gwendolen as she lifted the marble hand and touched the marble brow. A massive injury to the brain. 'Why didn't you look where you were going?' she said crossly to him as tears rolled.

Frobisher was beyond rebuke.

He had been delighted to find himself suddenly transported from lying amongst the filth and ordure of a London street to strolling through a hay meadow in full midsummer fig. He murmured the names of the wildflowers to himself. *Yellow rattle and red clover, wood cranesbill, lady's mantle, meadow foxtail.* Such lovely words. He wished he could show them to Miss Kelling.

A lapwing was disturbed and took flight from its nest on the ground. A curlew cried. And – oh – the scent of the lilacs in the lane. His soul rose. He could put down his burden. He was home. At last.

A Long Prove

'So today I found an agent for *The Age of Glitter*,' Ramsay said happily. 'He says he'll have no problem finding a publisher.'

'You've finished it already?' Gerrit queried. 'I thought you'd only just started it.'

He was like an animal, Ramsay thought, limbs slack with sleep yet ready to move in an instant. They were lying naked in bed, one of Gerrit's great tattooed arms behind his head, the other around Ramsay's shoulders. Gerrit shifted and reached for his cigarettes, lit two and gave one to Ramsay. Ramsay sighed with pleasure. His life had finally begun.

Freda never went back to the Sphinx. She had recognized the man who rescued her from the Thames – he was the one who had kindly given her the half-crown, but he was also a policeman, and as soon as he had dragged her out of the water he told her that people were looking for her, and she wasn't about to hang about and find out who. But for the rest of her life she regretted that she had failed to thank him for risking his life to save hers. Nor did she ever go home to York. She never saw her mother again, or her sister, Cissy, never even sent them word of her new life.

Miss Fay le Mont attended her first spieler a week later, having persuaded Ramsay to take her and introduce her. It was a modest affair, just people enjoying losing their money, and Freda only cheated when she was in a corner, which wasn't often. The pair of them tried to spread themselves across as many different venues as they could, in case people grew wary of the little card sharp who had infiltrated their evenings. Freda was generous with Ramsay, sharing her winnings with him at the beginning, but eventually she started to go to games on her own.

Ramsay wasn't bothered, his book had been accepted by a London publisher and that was all he could talk about. *My novel* this, *my novel* that. It was called *The Age of Glitter* and had created a bit of interest amongst the 'literary crowd', as he referred to them to Freda, because it was supposed to be a 'romanaclay', which meant there were real people in it, disguised by different names – so, much like real life, then, as far as Freda was concerned. She read a few pages but it was hard going and she soon gave up. Other people did, too, and interest in the novel didn't last long and it didn't sell as many copies as expected. Ramsay wrote two more novels, but they failed to get a publisher. *The Age of Glitter* had gone 'out of print' within a couple of years, he told her indignantly. That was the last time she saw him – it was during the phoney war and she was running a little bar in Mayfair that she'd bought with the proceeds of her spieler winnings. It was quite a classy place and Vanda, it turned out, scrubbed up well to work behind the bar, where she was very popular. When the real war got going, though, despite her age, Vanda reverted to her old trade, too profitable to be ignored. Those boys in uniform needed mothering, she said. 'Well, that's one word for it,' Duncan would have said.

Freda lived a long life away from the stage and ended her days running a pub in Suffolk that she bought after the war. By then she was married and had a daughter, whom she had insisted on naming Florence after her lost friend, an old-fashioned name that the new Florence resented for the rest of her life. As the Sixties swung in, Florence became a fashion model and rechristened herself Jenny.

At the end of the war, when she was still living in London, Freda's eye had been caught by the name 'Ramsay Coker' in a newspaper. It was the report of an inquest, followed by a short obituary. Mr Ramsay Coker had been found on the pavement below his third-floor flat in Hans Crescent, and although there was some question of him having taken his own life, an open verdict was recorded after evidence was heard about his chronic alcoholism and drug addiction. The newspaper article failed to mention *The Age of Glitter*, only reporting that Ramsay was 'the son of the notorious nightclub owner Nellie Coker'.

After Frobisher's death, Lottie was institutionalized in a large house in the country. It was an expensive place, an asylum for the wealthy, blessed with extensive grounds, good food, plenty of pastimes to occupy the unbalanced minds within. Lottie's fees were paid for the rest of her surprisingly long life by a bene-factor, a Miss Kelling, who never visited.

Nellie lost nearly all of her money in the 1929 crash and died a few years later. According to her daughters, standing vigil at her deathbed, her last words were 'Oh, look, here's Maud,' words which made no sense to any of them. She had lived long enough to see both Betty and Shirley married to minor aristocrats. She treated herself to a new fur for each of their weddings. Luckily, she didn't live long enough to witness their divorces. Edith con-tinued to run the remnants of Nellie's clubs, less and less profitable as time went on. The Amethyst, along with Edith her-self, was destroyed by a direct hit during the Blitz. Kitty ended her days as a fixture at the bar in the Colony Room Club, where she slowly drank herself to death.

William Cobb retired in 1951 as a Superintendent in the Metro-politan Police, which just goes to show how far a dull man can rise if he simply turns up for work every day.

The spate of mysterious killings in London came to an equally mysterious end. The murder of Vivian Quinn was considered to be the final flourish of whatever 'deranged maniac' (the *Daily Mail*) had walked the streets of London choosing his victims at random. One of the many, many theories suggested over the subsequent years was that the killings were not in fact random, but misdirections to disguise the fact that Quinn was the intended target all along. No motive was proposed for Quinn's murder, although several rumours took life and then died. One was that he was writing an investigative piece about London criminals, who decided that he knew too much. Another suggested he had been involved in a 'homosexual liaison' with one of the more promiscuous members of the Royal Family. Eventually, Quinn's death faded to become no more than the occasional small footnote in the histories written about this period.

Arrangement

'You've got a dog?' Niven said, glancing at the little terrier that was standing in the hallway behind Gwendolen, regarding him expectantly.

'I do.'

'Are you going to let me in?'

'I suppose I should.'

They sat down at opposite ends of the pink velvet, rather formal. She had no memory of the kiss, although that didn't prevent her from imagining it now.

'Does he have a name?' Niven asked, making a fuss of the dog. Niven's own dog held himself aloof from sentiment.

'Pierrot,' she said.

'Pierrot?'

'He's Frobisher's dog.'

'Ah.'

'His wife's really, I suppose, but she didn't want him.'

'I didn't know he had a wife.'

'No, well, he kept her very quiet,' Gwendolen said. 'She's rather a sad case.'

'Poor Frobisher. I think you were close to him.'

'I was at his funeral this morning. I accompanied his wife.'

'Ah.'

'It was a fancy affair – dress uniform, sword salute, that kind of thing. He would have hated it. Did you want something? I'm rather tired, I'm afraid.'

'Yes. I came to ask you if you would come away with me.'

'Away? Where?' She imagined he meant Brighton or Eastbourne. Her last day trip hadn't ended well.

'Anywhere you like,' he said. 'France, Italy, America, even. We could buy a ranch. Ride horses.'

'Horses?' She laughed. 'I barely know you! I was thinking of returning to York. London's charms have rather faded for me.'

'Don't go. I don't want to live without you.'

'Goodness, how dramatic you are, all of a sudden!' Gwendolen said. 'We've barely exchanged a word and now you want to ride horses with me on a ranch in America. You sound like a romantic novelist.'

'I didn't say I *can't* live without you – I expect I can live without you very well, I've managed for thirty-odd years, after all. I said I don't *want* to live without you.'

'Is this really your idea of a proposal? To harangue me?'

'It's not a proposal. Not a marriage one, anyway,' he said.

'Well, thank goodness for that. Does love come into this arrangement?'

'Love?' The word startled both of them into silence.

Gwendolen surprised herself even more by saying, 'Can I think about it?'

'No,' Niven said. 'If you think about it you won't come with me.' He stood up abruptly and held out his hand to her. And there they must remain, suspended between coming and going for ever.

The Laughing Policeman

'Is it a hanging?' the boy asked his neighbour, standing in the crowd outside Pentonville prison. Yes, the very same newspaper delivery boy that we met outside Holloway many chapters ago. Always eager for an execution, his wishes were being fulfilled on a miserably wet morning in early December.

The jamboree crowd was particularly jolly, as the man having his neck stretched was an officer of the law. It was a shame, the crowd felt, that the execution was taking place inside the walls of the prison and was no longer a public show, although they were doing their best to make it into an occasion. A man was selling roasted chestnuts from a cart and another was hawking sixpenny broadsheets detailing the crime. There was an old-fashioned air to the event, it could have been Tower Hill or Tyburn three hundred years ago.

There were very few protests against the death penalty being carried out. The prisoner was getting what he deserved, was the general opinion of the crowd. In fact, the gallows was too good for him, several more bloodthirsty members of the congregation declared, to murmurs of agreement. Hung, drawn and quartered would have been their preferred punishment.

Inside Pentonville, the prisoner was still volubly protesting his innocence. He shoved away the priest who had come to give him succour in his final moments and the warder said, 'Oi, watch it, Oakes.'

*

It had been a complex operation to secure the conviction. Phyllis's mother and another of the Forty Thieves had quietly broken into Oakes's shabby little house during the day, while he was at work and his wife was visiting her sister. The bloody little knife that had done for Maddox and was now wiped clean of fingerprints was slipped into the pocket of Sergeant Oakes's coat, hanging on a hook in his narrow hallway. An anonymous tip-off as to the whereabouts of the knife was sent to Scotland Yard and several smartly dressed witnesses, all women, came forward to testify that they had seen Oakes and Maddox having an aggressive confrontation on the Embankment on the night that Maddox was murdered. 'A brawl, really,' one of the smartly dressed witnesses said. 'Looked like a fight to the death,' another one said.

When it came to the trial, the public benches were packed with more smartly dressed women who had come up from the East End. Some members of the court thought that their faces seemed familiar, but the jury was impressed by their composure and air of transparent honesty.

After the trial, Oakes's barrister, who had put up a woefully weak defence, paid for an expensive wedding for his daughter and then took his wife on a jaunt round Europe in a Wolseley Open Tourer that he had come home with one day, to his wife's surprise. Even the QC for the prosecution was spotted shopping with his wife for a new mink. He was a regular at the Crystal Cup and was compensating his wife for the many evenings he spent enjoying himself without her, courtesy of Nellie Coker.

The damning evidence was the little silver penknife. The initials 'BC' that were engraved on the handle remained a mystery and were considered irrelevant. Oakes was unfortunate enough to come up against Avory, the hanging judge. The gloriously thrilling moment when the Black Cap was placed on Avory's bewigged head and the verdict was pronounced was marred by neither cough nor whisper from the public benches. Only when Avory intoned, 'And may God have mercy on your soul' did the crowd send up a cheer, and Oakes himself broke into a choleric fury, roaring his innocence to the court. It made him seem even more guilty, the members of the public were agreed.

Theatre and music hall, they were also agreed, couldn't hold a candle to a good trial.

At a quarter past eight a warder came out of the prison and hammered a notice on to a wooden board by the side of the prison gate. It stated simply that the sentence of execution had been carried out on Leonard Percival Oakes for the murder of Arthur Edwin Maddox. The mood of the crowd turned from celebration to solemnity. The death of a man, any man, demanded a few moments of recognition. Then the convivial crowd came back to noisy life and dispersed quickly to get on with their day. 'Good show,' the newspaper delivery boy said to the man standing next to him.

By evening, Oakes's demise was forgotten.

The newspaper delivery boy's name was Norman. He joined the 4th Armoured Brigade in the next war and was killed during the invasion of Sicily in 1944.

And See You Not That Bonny Road?

Florence came home on a Saturday afternoon that midsummer, walking back into the Ingrams' house on Tadcaster Road without any fuss, as if she had simply been coming home from school or had been out on a bike ride with Freda. Mr Ingram was mowing the lawn and Mrs Ingram was in the kitchen washing their pots from lunch, so it took each of them several minutes to realize that a stranger was in their midst. A stranger who was their daughter.

A flabbergasted Mrs Ingram clutched her heart in shock at the sight of Florence and had to be helped to the sofa by Mr Ingram, who could hardly see for the tears of happiness that were pouring from his eyes. 'Florrie,' he choked, clutching Mrs Ingram's hand. 'Florrie's come home to us, Ruthie.'

Where had she *been* all these weeks? Mrs Ingram wailed, but all Florence said was, 'I'm starving. Is there anything to eat?'

Once she had recovered from her astonishment, Mrs Ingram couldn't stop touching Florence, as if she might not be real flesh and blood but a ghost conjured from her grief. 'It's a miracle,' she said. 'God answered our prayers and brought you home.' (How *had* she got home?) Florence seemed to remember nothing about the past few weeks, or if she did, she wasn't saying.

Was she the same Florence as before? She was thinner certainly, and a little taller, but she was healthy and showed no visible sign of harm. There would in time come a period when Mrs Ingram developed the belief that the new Florence was an imposter, a changeling who had taken her real daughter's place, but Mr Ingram gradually made her see reason. ('Poor Ruthie.')

Florence never did tell them where she had been, but, as Freda had predicted, she grew up and married and had two children (and yes, adenoidal and flat-footed), whom she did indeed take to the pantomime at York Theatre Royal every year, and there may well have been a moment during a production one year of *Babes in the Wood* when her memory was stirred by the sight of the villagers singing and dancing around a maypole, but the moment soon passed. Florence had no idea what had happened to her friend, in fact she seemed barely able to remember her.

Author's Note

As anyone familiar with this period of history will recognize, inspiration for this novel comes from the life and times of Kate Meyrick, who for many years was the queen of Soho's clubland. Her most famous club was the '43' at 43 Gerrard Street, now in the heart of Chinatown. She was imprisoned several times in her career for breaking the licensing laws.

Like Nellie Coker, Kate Meyrick also had a large brood that she was at pains to educate and 'elevate'. Two of her daughters did indeed marry into the aristocracy and one son, Gordon, became a published novelist, writing mystery thrillers, including *The Body on the Pavement* in 1941. (I may have stolen a line from him, in homage.) In a case of life imitating art, he died during the war in somewhat mysterious circumstances after falling from a window of his top-floor flat on to the pavement below.

Kate Meyrick's autobiography, *Secrets of the 43 Club* (John Long, 1933), perhaps not the most truthful account of a life, provided many small details for this novel – like Nellie, Kate knew the price of everything. *We Danced All Night*, Barbara Cartland's autobiography, was a cornucopia of little facts now largely lost. She is particularly good on the 'Bright Young People', and I owe my knowledge of 'Turk's Blood' to her, as well as a vivid description of the Baby Party. *Nights in London: Where Mayfair Makes Merry* by Horace Wyndham (The Bodley Head, 1926) was a rather horrifying insight into the waspish, highly prejudiced mind of a social commentator of the time, and *Dope Girls: The Birth of the British Drug Underground* by Marek Kohn (Granta, 1992) was informative. *London After Dark* by Fabian of the Yard (otherwise ex-Superintendent Robert Fabian), published by Panther in 1958, undoubtedly influenced Frobisher. From him I derived my knowledge of 'spielers'.

This is just a fraction of the background reading I did, but you can see that I largely eschewed traditional history books in favour of the gossipy, chattering kind. *Shrines of Gaiety* is fiction, not history.

And yes, I read *The Green Hat* by Michael Arlen (Heinemann, 1924), but it's difficult from this standpoint in time to see why it caused so much fuss.

As ever, there are real events in this novel and real people, but they are heavily outweighed by the fictional. The then Prince of Wales really did attend a fancy-dress party in the garb of the Ku Klux Klan, but I have no evidence that the Aga Khan went about with liquorice chews in his pocket. And so on. Some small details have been bent to my will – Niven, for example, races a dog at White City, but the track there wasn't opened until the following year.

The novel begins just before the General Strike in May 1926 – although no one except Ramsay is interested in the unrest happening in the country – so although that's a fixed foot, some things have shifted slightly. *The Murder of Roger Ackroyd* wasn't published until June 1926 so Ramsay would not have been able to read it in May. I could go on, but I won't, I'm just trying to pre-empt criticism!

The Bow Street police station was very real and is now a five-star hotel, although part of it has been preserved as a small but interesting museum. And I would commend to you W. Slagter's 1926 book entitled *Cocktails American- en Fancy Drinks IJsrecepten en -Dranken* (it's Dutch). You can find it online at https://euvs-vintage-cocktail-books.cld.bz/Vintage-Cocktail-Books-

Netherlands/1926-Cocktails-by-W-Slagter/IV. It's the most extensive list of 'historic' cocktails you'll ever find. Sadly, I have tasted
none of them.

DR. MEYRICK AT WIFE'S BURIAL

RECONCILED

BREAKS DOWN AT GRAVESIDE

The presence at Mrs. Meyrick's graveside, on Jan. 23, at Kensal Green, of her husband, from whom she had been separated so long, was the crowning touch of the half cynical, half sentimental Fate which wrote her life.

Ever since this remarkable little woman—her first instinct was to support her children—took the night side of London by storm, she seemed to live for publication in a sensational romance. The humanity and the bitterness of night life alike were emphasised by her solitude.

And, yesterday, at her funeral service, in St. Martin-in-the-Fields, she was mourned by hundreds.

Sufferers' Refuge.

Her husband, Dr. F. R. Meyrick, to whom she had been reconciled on her deathbed, saw about him representatives of all those who had worshipped at the shrines of gaiety set up by his wife.

He saw his wife's coffin borne across the pavement through a reverent crowd, and deposited in that church which typifies a refuge for so many sufferers. As the service went on its beautiful way—"I will lift up mine eyes unto the hills . . ." —he sensed grief and tears. At the graveside, later, he almost broke down.

With him were his two married daughters, Lady Kinnoull and Lady de Clifford, his four other daughters, Kathleen, Nancy, "Bobbie," and Irene, and his sons, Lyster and Gordon.

Lord Kinnoull came with his wife. There were Irish representatives of the family. The only stranger who left the house with the mourners was Mr. R. H. Carlish, who had been Mrs. Meyrick's manager for many years—at 43, Gerrard Street.

The clergyman who committed the body to the earth was Dr. Meyrick's brother.

The coffin bore a plate inscribed: "Mother Love Triumphant." That was from her children.

There were many wreaths.